Stephen Booth is the internationally bestselling, CWA Dagger-winning author of the acclaimed thrillers featuring Cooper and Fry. The series is in development as a TV programme. Booth lives in Nottingham.

ALREADY DEAD
STEPHEN BOOTH

sphere

SPHERE

First published in Great Britain in 2013 by Sphere
This paperback edition published in 2014

A CIP catalogue record for this book
is available from the British Library.

ISBN 978-0-7515-5172-3

Typeset in Plantin by Palimpsest Book Production Limited,
Falkirk, Stirlingshire
Printed and bound in Great Britain by Clays Ltd, St Ives plc

Papers used by Sphere are from well-managed forests
and other responsible sources.

MIX
Paper from
responsible sources
FSC
www.fsc.org
FSC® C104740

Sphere
An imprint of
Little, Brown Book Group
100 Victoria Embankment
London EC4Y 0DY

An Hachette UK Company
www.hachette.co.uk

www.littlebrown.co.uk

For Lesley

Acknowledgements

As usual, the fact that a book has made it to publication is due to the efforts of many people, to whom I'm grateful. But the one person who has been there from the very beginning of the Cooper and Fry series is my agent, Teresa Chris – and to her I owe my thanks many times over.

Before you embark on a journey of revenge, dig two graves.

Confucius

1

Tuesday

Glen Turner awoke to a drowned world. His brain felt waterlogged, his skin loose and wrinkled, his body as sodden as if he'd stayed too long in the bath. He was lying on his back, and shivering so uncontrollably that his hands twitched in helpless spasms. An icy chill had spread through his limbs and struck deep into his flesh, knotting his stomach with fear. Things had gone wrong. Very wrong. More badly wrong than they'd ever been in his life.

Turner's mind churned frantically, flailing for something to cling to, a solid fact that he could recognise as reality. For a while, there seemed to be nothing. Then, with a shock, he realised he was naked.

A flood of panic surged down his spine. Where were

his clothes? What had he been doing before he went to sleep? Had he been asleep at all, or was it something else? Had he had an accident? Had he been taken ill? A heart attack? A stroke? Could he be lying in hospital? His memory was totally blank.

Turner tried to force his eyelids open, but they refused to move. He sensed that he was surrounded by darkness and water. An unnatural silence was broken only by a faint pattering, like thousands of tiny feet. And it was *so* wet and dark, and cold. Wet, and dark, like – what? He didn't know. His mind couldn't focus enough to come up with any connections, let alone an explanation. The great blank space in his mind terrified him. Not knowing what had happened was more frightening than anything. It made him feel physically sick. His guts heaved, but his muscles cramped and seized rigid, forming a hard ball of pain in the centre of his abdomen.

He really was *so* cold. As cold as stone, and as stiff. He had to do something *now*, or he would die here.

With a great effort, Turner managed to move a hand. It seemed like a huge achievement, with each finger so inflexible that it was reluctant to peel away from the next. Slowly, he slid the hand across his body, finding that his wrist was too weak to lift it clear. He felt it crawl crab-like across his stomach, his muscles twitching as he recoiled from contact with his own skin. His limbs were completely numb. There was no blood circulating into his hand, and he had to push the entire forearm from the elbow, dragging it in a clammy trail across his hip until it dropped down and fell with a splash by his side.

Yes, that was a splash. He heard it clearly. So he really was lying in water. He could feel the liquid movement now, the water surging sluggishly against his shoulders and lapping around his ears, as if his numbed hand had been a fish disturbing the surface of a pond. He wanted to lift those fingers to his face, to feel his eyes and reassure himself they were still there. Why were his eyes still closed? Or were they actually open, and he'd gone blind?

For a few moments, Turner lost all self-control. His chest tightened, and his breath gasped in his throat. A sound came from him – a faint, whimpering croak that he would never have recognised as his own voice.

'God forgive me, whatever it is I've done.'

He said it again, over and over – but only inside his head, where no one but God would ever hear him. He was screaming in the darkness of his own soul, his terrors lashing out blindly inside in his brain.

Blindness was one of Glen Turner's greatest fears. The dread of being alone in the dark had haunted him since he was a child. He could still remember lying in his bed night after night, crying out for his mother, for light, or just for the sound of another person near him. He couldn't bear the thought of total darkness, even now. And blindness was surely his ultimate nightmare. It was being alone in the dark for ever.

He began to weep, his tears hot and slow as they slid across his face and dripped soundlessly into the water. They made no difference to his fate. Inch by inch, all around him in the darkness, the water continued to rise.

His paralysed body was trying to respond to the danger. It knew he was about to drown in the rising water, that in the next few minutes it would reach his mouth and cover his face, and that would be the end of him.

Yet Turner's mind was saying something different. It was sending him the message that he'd drowned hours ago. He could recall the pain in his airways, the gasping for breath, the pounding of his heart. In his memory, he relived the frantic, failing struggle to draw air into his lungs instead of water.

He knew it was impossible, but he remembered it clearly. And that was what bewildered him, the cause of his greatest fear. His brain kept insisting that he was already dead.

With a grunt of discomfort, Charlie Dean straightened his back and glared at his car. The night was as dark as he could wish for. As black as pitch. Night-time was his friend for so many reasons. And one of those reasons was pressing on his mind right now, as he stood by the side of a deserted back road in Derbyshire, with mud splattered on his trousers and the palms of his hands wet and sore from pushing.

Well, at least in the dark no one could see the colour of your car. The torrential rain falling on this part of the Peak District made his BMW gleam like a great, black fish. Charlie wanted to think of his car as a shark. Sleek and powerful, with a grille full of sharp teeth. But right now the shark was beached and helpless. The rear wheels of the vehicle churned uselessly in the mud at the side of the road.

He'd owned the BMW too long, of course. If he'd replaced it with a newer model, he could have had the all-wheel drive version. That would have got him out of the mud, for sure. Right now, though, he was stuck. The front wheels were on the edge of the tarmac, but there was no traction at the back, just his tyres hissing and screaming as they dug themselves deeper into the mire, spraying mud everywhere. Instead of creeping back on to the road, it was in danger of slipping further towards the shallow ditch.

'What if someone comes? We're sitting ducks here, Charlie. They'll see us in their headlights plain as day.'

Dean looked at the woman standing in the roadway.

He'd left only his sidelights on, to avoid flattening the battery. But they were good enough to pick out her skinny legs, a bright green skirt turning darker and darker in the rain, a pale face above thin shoulders hunched inside a totally inappropriate woollen jacket. When he'd picked her up earlier in the evening, her hair had been blonde and pushed into eye-catching waves. Now it was lank and sticking to her skull. The result wasn't very attractive. Not for the first time, he wondered what it was that he'd ever seen in her.

Headlights. Yes, she was right. Anyone could see the colour of his car in the beam of their headlights. And worse – they could make out the number on a licence plate too, unless it was obscured by mud.

Dean made sure the handbrake was on, then walked back to the rear of the car. It wasn't too bad. No shortage of mud there. He smeared a bit more across the plate, completely obliterating the numbers before the letters TKK. Those two numbers gave away the year the car was registered – narrowed it down to a six-month period, in fact. He didn't know much about these things, but he imagined having the numbers would make it much easier to trace a vehicle. How many models in the BMW 5 series were registered in the UK in those particular six months? Not many, he supposed. Especially this colour.

'Don't worry, Sheena, we'll be fine,' he said. 'There's

no one around at this time of night. We'll just give it another try.'

Up to now, he'd been doing the pushing, with Sheena at the wheel. But she did have a tendency to press the accelerator pedal too hard. She didn't seem able to exercise any restraint, no matter how often he shouted instructions at her.

'Too late, Charlie,' she said.

He looked up. 'What?'

'I said "too late".'

And she was right. Again.

Dean twisted round when he caught the flash of light in his wing mirror. He couldn't see the make of the other car as it turned the corner near the woods and came slowly down the road. Its lights were on full beam, and they dazzled him, so that he had to raise a hand to shield his eyes from the glare.

At first he thought the driver was intending to go straight past them, as most people would. Everybody was reluctant to stop and help strangers, especially late at night and in a remote spot like this. You just never knew what might happen, or who you were dealing with.

But the car braked and drew in to the side of the road. Dean found himself praying that the driver wouldn't be someone he knew. They weren't all that far from home, just a few miles outside Wirksworth.

And so far tonight his luck hadn't been good. He'd already missed the chance to push Sheena into the ditch and make her hide. They were picked out in those headlights like a pair of sitting ducks.

For a moment, the doors of the car remained closed. Who was sitting in there behind that glare? It wouldn't be a woman on her own, at least. No solitary female would have stopped in these circumstances. It was much too risky. It would have to be a man, perhaps two or more.

Dean began to get anxious now. He started to calculate what possessions he had on him that might be valuable to robbers – about two hundred pounds in cash, his credit cards, an iPhone, a decent watch. And of course there was the BMW itself. If they could get it out of the mud, they were welcome to it. There was nothing else of any value.

'Who is it, Charlie?' asked Sheena plaintively.

'I've no idea. Just keep quiet. Let me do the talking.'

He thought he heard her snort. She had an unappealing little derisive laugh that irritated him sometimes. But perhaps she was just catching a cold standing in the rain. He had a mental image of a sniffling Sheena with a red nose and watering eyes, her bag stuffed with tissues. That would be just great.

As he waited, Dean wiped the rain from his face and pulled up his collar. He was ready to run, if necessary. If there were two or three of them, it would be hopeless trying to resist. He pictured himself racing through the mud and hurling himself across the ditch into the trees, where he could disappear into the dark. They would never pursue him through the woods. He wasn't worth that much bother. Darkness was definitely his friend.

But just one man got out of the car. He stood behind the headlights, so that Dean couldn't see him at all, except for an impression of a large, bulky figure glistening with water, an outline that looked entirely the wrong shape for a human being.

'Hello?' said Dean tentatively. His voice sounded weak, and he decided to try again. 'Hello?'

When the man finally moved forward into the light, Dean saw that he was wearing a heavy rain jacket. It had a peaked hood and a double storm flap that fastened across the front of his face, obscuring his features, except for a pair of deep-set eyes faintly visible inside the hood. The expression in those eyes was one that Dean hardly dared to analyse. It made him look away uncomfortably, his skin tightening with unease.

'Trouble?' The voice that came from inside the hood was strangely hoarse. The man seemed to be breathing heavily, as if he'd been running or exerting himself for the last few minutes, rather than just having stepped out of a car.

'We're stuck in the mud,' said Dean, though he thought it ought to have been obvious to anyone, even with eyes like that.

'So I see.'

'Perhaps a bit of a push?'

'No problem.'

Dean got behind the wheel and the stranger positioned himself at the back of the car with his hands braced against the boot. A few seconds later, the BMW had finally churned and skidded its way back onto the road. It sat slightly askew on the carriageway, liquid mud dripping from its rear bumper, steam rising from the bonnet and mingling with the rain.

Dean slid down the driver's window and tried to locate the stranger in the darkness.

'Oh, that's great. Thanks,' he called. 'We can be on our way at last.'

'It's a bad night to get yourself stuck like that.'

'Yes, but— Well, we're fine now – thanks to you. So off we go, eh?'

He knew he was sounding too hasty and nervous, but he couldn't help it. He just wanted this man to go and leave them alone. He would have felt happier if he'd still been struggling with the car. Somebody else would have come along eventually. Somebody a bit more . . . normal.

Dean peered into the night, disorientated by the lights

and the drumming of the rain on the roof of the car. It was suddenly hurtling down, bouncing off the road and blurring the windscreen.

'I'm sorry? You were saying?'

The voice came from a direction he wasn't expecting. Dean realised that the stranger had moved closer to the side of the car without him noticing it, and he was now standing by the open window. Why did that feel so much like a threat?

'Thank you very much again for the help. But we really ought to be getting along now.'

'Are you in a hurry, then?'

Right up close, Dean saw that the rain jacket was red. He could see an expanse of fabric in front of his eyes, a deep, wet red that made him think only of one thing. Blood.

Though he was anxious to escape, he could hardly tear his gaze away from the glistening redness a few inches from his face. He began to think that he could actually smell blood on the air. His head swam, and he felt nauseous. In his wavering vision, the fabric of the jacket became a side of beef, the skin freshly peeled away to expose the red slabs of muscle underneath. When the man moved, leaning closer to the window, rain gathered and pooled in the folds of his jacket, dark splashes of water dripping on to the paintwork of the car.

'I . . . I . . .'

'Yes?'

'It's late,' said Dean. 'You're out late, too.'

The man grunted. Dean wanted to get a look at his eyes again, but his courage failed him. Instead, he tried a laugh, and nodded towards Sheena.

'She hates to be late for anything. Always blames me, of course. Says I'll be late for my own funeral. We're expected . . . somewhere, you see. But with all this rain and everything, and the mud. Well . . .'

Of course, Dean knew he was beginning to sound hysterical. He glared at Sheena, who still said nothing, clutching her coat up to her ears, her eyes wide. She looked as though she was frozen to the spot.

'Should you get in the car, dear?' said Dean loudly.

She stared at him stupidly, a rabbit in the headlights. Literally, almost. She was a scared animal, waiting for someone to tell her what to do next.

He tried to make his voice sound firmer: 'Get in, Sheena.'

But he was betrayed by a tremble on the last word, the final vowel sound cracking and pitching too high, like the voice of a pubescent schoolboy. It made him sound as though he was asking a question. Begging or pleading, even.

At last she moved. The passenger door opened and she squelched into the BMW, fumbled automatically with the seat belt. Dean winced when he thought of the damage to his leather seats from the water.

'Bye, then,' he said, and pressed the button to wind up the window. With that thin sheet of glass between him and the stranger, he instantly felt safer.

'Where did he come from?' said Sheena, when the windows were safely closed.

'I don't know.'

'Did he come out of the woods?'

'I couldn't see.'

'He scared me, Charlie.'

'We're okay, he's going back to his car.'

'Are you sure?'

'Absolutely. Fasten your seat belt and put the heater on.'

'Oh, I'm soaked.'

'Well, put the heater on, then.'

He squinted at the headlights still reflected in his rearview mirror and waited for the other car to pull out and pass him. A minute passed. Then two.

'What the hell is he doing? Is he waiting for me to go first?'

Dean felt uncomfortable about the idea of setting off with the other car behind him. What if this man followed his BMW into Wirksworth, maybe all the way back to his house? He didn't want anyone knowing where he lived. He certainly didn't want *him* knowing.

Finally, the headlights swung across his mirror. But instead of passing, they suddenly lit up the opposite side of the road. Dean looked over his shoulder, saw vertical sheets of rain illuminated into a glittering curtain, pools of water forming on the roadway, alive with light and fresh raindrops pouring in their surfaces. The stranger's full beam had turned the road into a stage set. What was the next act going to be?

'He's turning round,' said Sheena.

'So he is.'

The other vehicle twisted across the road and straightened up. Its tyres hissed on the wet tarmac as it accelerated away. Dean stared into his mirror, but the rear window was blurred by rain and he could see nothing of the car but two smudges of red light moving away. By the time he got the rear wiper working, the vehicle was too far away to make out clearly.

'Oh, well. That's it, then.'

He wondered why he didn't feel a lot better, now that the car had gone. The uneasy feeling had been just too strong. It would take time for it to pass. He'd need a few drinks, in fact. He had a hip flask tucked into the back of the glove compartment. Good quality brandy too. But maybe this wasn't the time to get stopped by the police and breathalysed for drink driving.

It turned out that Sheena was even jumpier than he

was. Before he could get the car into second gear, she cried out.

'Wait. What was that?' she said.

Dean slammed on the brakes. 'What was what?'

'By the side of the road. There was something . . . Oh, I don't know now.'

He shrugged. 'I didn't see it, whatever it was. A fox? A dead badger?'

She hesitated for a moment, then sagged back in her seat. 'It doesn't matter, I suppose.'

Dean released a long breath and put the BMW back into gear.

'Don't do that, Sheena. Just don't do it. You nearly frightened me to death.'

Glen Turner could sense that his mind was failing now. His body had already let him down. He'd been unable to move more than a hand, and now the water had risen until it was creeping over his face.

He was incapable of forming logical thoughts any more. Just one phrase kept running through his brain, over and over and over.

'Oh God, oh God, oh God.'

They said your whole life flashed in front of your eyes when you were dying. Yet his immediate past was a complete blank to him. His life was a desperate nightmare in which nothing had happened, and nothing ever would. When he looked into his own mind, he saw only a void. It was like standing in an echoing cave, a place as cold as rock and just as lifeless.

As the hours passed and the water rose, it stayed that way. Right up to the moment Glen Turner stopped breathing.

2

Wednesday

By Wednesday morning, the reality had become undeniable. In the CID room of Derbyshire E Division headquarters, Detective Sergeant Diane Fry felt herself tense with anger as she stared across the desk. She couldn't believe what she was looking at. It was like being trapped in a twisted dream. Fry felt as though she'd never be able to escape, that she would always end up back in the place she started from, no matter how hard she tried to flee, or in which direction she ran.

She chewed her lip until it hurt, tugged at her hair with clenched fingers, fought a physical urge to strike out at something, anything she could find, and smash it to pieces. How could such a disaster have happened to her? How long would the torment go on? There had to be an end to it, before she went completely mad.

Finally, she couldn't stand it any more. She had to break the awful silence.

'I'm not going to be here much longer, you know,' she said.

Her statement didn't seem to have any effect. From the other side of the desk, DC Gavin Murfin merely gazed back at her, chewing slowly. His face was pink and faintly damp, like an over-ripe pomegranate. His thinning hair showed tracks of pale scalp where he'd flattened it against his skull with the waterproof beanie hat he insisted on wearing when he had to go outdoors.

'Me neither,' he said.

Fry tried again. 'I mean, I'm only in E Division until everything is sorted out and back to normal. Then you won't see me for dust. I'll be out of here for good.'

'Me too,' said Murfin.

'No one could make me stay a second longer than I need to,' insisted Fry. 'Not a second. Do you have any idea of the caseload waiting for me back at St Ann's? There's a live murder inquiry in Mansfield, for a start. Two rapes, a series of armed robberies around Derby, and a suspected human trafficking operation under surveillance in Leicester right now. That one could blow up on us at any moment.'

'I've got some jobs to do around the house,' said Murfin.

Fry stared at him in outrage. 'You *what*?'

'Jean says the roof is leaking on the conservatory, and I've got some decking to lay when the weather clears up.'

'Decking?'

'You have no idea. My work is never done.'

'*Decking*, Gavin?'

Murfin sighed, and eased his backside into a more comfortable position in the office chair he'd been complaining for years wasn't big enough for him. 'I know, I just can't wait. If only I wasn't stuck here being a monitor.'

'Mentor,' said Fry, spelling it out in separate syllables like an elocution teacher with a slow student. 'You're a *men-tor*.'

But Murfin took no notice. She might as well have been talking to the desk. Fry had never been quite sure whether it was all a deliberate act with Murfin, or if he wound her up like this without even trying. Whichever it was, she had to admit it was the one thing he was really good at.

'I wasn't even allowed to be a milk monitor at primary school,' he said. 'Well, they only let me do it once. They complained there were fewer bottles of milk handed out to the kids than were delivered at the school. How was I supposed to know where they'd gone? The fact that I was collecting milk bottle tops for *Blue Peter* was a sheer coincidence.'

Fry looked around desperately for a more intelligent response. As usual, the younger DCs, Luke Irvine and Becky Hurst, had their heads down keeping out of trouble, though she thought she could see Irvine's shoulders shaking behind his computer screen. Even Carol Villiers would have provided a bit of relief. She was at least mature in her attitudes, had gained her experience in the RAF Police, where perhaps they didn't have the same tolerance for the Gavin Murfins of the world. But Villiers was out of the office on a temporary attachment to C Division, where they were short of staff for a major fraud inquiry. She was expected back in the next day or two. But right now, this was it. Fry shook her head in despair. God help her, and the law-abiding citizens of Derbyshire.

She swung her chair back, and banged her knee on the side of the desk.

'Oh, give me strength,' she said under her breath.

Out of the corner of her eye she saw Murfin stop chewing and smile. Perhaps it hadn't been all that under her breath after all. But she didn't care.

Biting her lip, Fry examined the paperwork in her in-tray. Brief as it had been so far, her time with the major crime team at the East Midlands Special

Operations Unit had spoiled her for this job in Divisional CID. It was endless volume crime – house burglaries, car thefts, run-of-the-mill assaults, and the odd street robbery to add a bit of excitement. The latest reports said that a teenager walking through Edendale town centre late last night had been robbed of his iPod by a trio of youths. What action should she take? Set up checkpoints on all the major roads? Close the airports? Call out armed response? Send in a SWAT team? It was a tricky one.

But this was only a short-term assignment. She'd been promised that. Absolutely promised. Her DCI on the major crime team, Alistair Mackenzie, had seemed genuinely sorry to lose her, even for a few months. But there was no one else to do the job, they said. It was funny how often there was no one else.

Fry surreptitiously rubbed her leg, and removed a small splinter of wood from the fabric of her trousers. It wasn't as if she had a good environment to work in. In Edendale, the old Divisional headquarters building on West Street was looking exactly that now – old. It had been built in the 1950s, and though it might have won an architectural award once, the past sixty years had left their mark. The Derbyshire Constabulary budget no longer stretched to structural maintenance, unless it was considered essential. Like Murfin's conservatory, there was a leak somewhere in the roof.

When it rained, the water ran through the walls, leaving damp stains in the plaster over the filing cabinets.

And it had rained a lot in Derbyshire recently. It was almost certainly raining now.

Well, she supposed she'd have to make the best of the situation. Some new blood in the division would have been ideal, of course, but Fry knew that was too much to hope for. There were fewer young officers applying for a transfer into CID. Why would they, when there was no extra pay, no promotion, no recognition of the extra responsibility? It just meant a lot more work to do, exams you could only study for in your spare time at the end of a long shift, a bigger and bigger caseload, a role as the muggins everyone turned to for help with their own investigations. You could be the entire CID representation on a night duty, called out to any incident the uniforms felt like passing the buck on. Not that there were many vacancies any more. But when they did get a recruit, they had to be pitched in at the deep end. Without a mentor, they would sink without trace, every one of them.

'In my day, they were called tutors,' said Murfin, as if reading her mind. 'When I was wet behind the ears in CID, I was sent to some fat old DC who basically just told me to watch my back and not volunteer for anything.'

'Not everything changes, then,' said Fry.

Of course, Gavin Murfin should be gone by now. His thirty years' service were up, and he could claim his full pension. His wife had been planning a Caribbean cruise for months. But Murfin had been pressed to stay on as a temporary measure in the current circumstances, and Fry had been presented with the fact as if management were doing her a favour by giving her someone with experience. He'd been bribed with more money, she knew. And probably with an endless supply of jelly babies, judging by the white powder on his fingers and the empty packets in his waste-paper bin. Yes, Murfin had experience. But it was mostly of the kind you wouldn't want passed on to posterity.

She wondered how much the changes in police pay had affected the service. In the 1980s, pay and conditions had been good, compared to similar professions. Police forces were finding it difficult to recruit the right people in those days, and they had to offer inducements to attract decent candidates. Now, though, it seemed they didn't want to be bothered by too many applicants at all.

Fry cast her eye over the room again. Becky Hurst was the most willing member of the team, never thought any job too routine for her to tackle. She was like a little terrier, kept at a task until she produced a result. Her hair was very short and its colour seemed to vary week by week, though right now it was a sort of coppery red.

23

'Becky,' said Fry.

'Yes, Sarge?'

Hurst came over clutching her notebook, her expression just a bit too alert and eager for Fry's liking. She was always suspicious of those who seemed a bit too good to be true.

'How are we doing with the cannabis farm?' she said.

It was the only interesting case they had on the books, a standout inquiry among the mass of run-of-the-mill volume crime.

'Those reports coming in from the public about a property in Matlock were out of date,' said Hurst. 'A Vietnamese cannabis gardener got scooped up when the premises were raided last year. He was given eighteen months inside – and he'll be deported when his sentence comes to an end. He's not our problem now, Diane.'

'He was just the gardener, though. What about his employers?'

'They were never located. The property was handled by a rental agent, and the actual tenant never lived there. They created a couple of steps to remove themselves from the gardener.'

'A dead end there, then?'

'Yes, we don't seem to be getting the breaks that C Division benefited from. Their operation was a gift from start to finish.'

Fry nodded. Like so many successful inquiries, the recent drugs case had started with a bit of luck. A nineteen-year-old Chesterfield man had been involved in a serious RTC, when his Renault van had skidded, gone off the road and crashed into a tree. While he was being taken to hospital with a broken leg and internal injuries, officers at the scene had examined the damaged Renault. They discovered that he'd been working as a delivery driver for a drugs gang, carrying small bags of cannabis in a cake tin under the dashboard. He had three mobile phones on the passenger seat of the van – one phone to take orders from customers, one to contact his employers, and a third to call his mum to tell her he'd be late home for his tea.

A full-scale operation had been launched after the trail led to a cannabis factory in a house in the eastern borders of Derbyshire, which turned out to have links to growers across the country. A search of the house found more than four hundred cannabis plants being tended by an eighteen-year-old Vietnamese man, who tried to hide in the attic when police arrived. Officers guarding the house on the night of the raid had noticed a suspicious car which drove past several times. They stopped the vehicle and found eight thousand pounds in cash, as well as more mobile phones and SIM cards. Phone records and text messages linked the people in the car to the cannabis gardener and other members of the gang. Warrants had been executed at two other addresses, in each of which a Vietnamese teenager was found hiding out with hundreds of cannabis plants he'd been responsible for.

As a result, a gang involved in growing hundreds of thousands of pounds' worth of cannabis across four counties had been jailed for a total of twenty-two years between them. They had more than a thousand plants under cultivation at addresses in Derbyshire, Nottinghamshire, and even down in the West Midlands. Their assets had later been confiscated under the Proceeds of Crime Act.

But the operation had left a few remnants of the drug trade still in existence. Somewhere in their area, at least one more Vietnamese was believed to be holed up in a house full of plants. The sad thing was, those cannabis gardeners were at the lowest end of the food chain in the illegal drugs trade, forced to live in squalid conditions and working practically as slaves for their masters. Fry couldn't imagine what it would be like for him now, with his contacts gone, his supplies dried up, just spending his time waiting for a knock on the door.

'So have we got any new leads?' she asked.

'No. But Special Operations Unit have got appropriate resources deployed in the Vietnamese community to gather information,' said Hurst, as if she was quoting from an emailed memo.

'Appropriate resources?'

'CHIS, I should imagine.'

'Of course.'

Covert Human Intelligence Sources. They used to be called informants, snouts, narks or grasses – at least until political correctness became the rule, rather than the exception. They were part of an age-old tactic. Get your information direct from the horse's mouth.

'So we're waiting for SOU?' said Fry.

'Unless you have any other suggestions?'

'Just keep on it.' She paused. 'Is there actually a Vietnamese community in Edendale?'

'Not that you'd notice.'

Murfin raised a hand like the clever child in class.

'I'm trained in multiculturalism,' he said. 'In fact, I was on duty at Mix It Up in June.'

'At what?'

'Mix It Up. The community festival, you know.'

'No.'

'It's all about the meeting of cultures, experiencing the differences. We were there on a community relations exercise. But you get the chance to try things out too.'

'So what did you try out, Gavin?' asked Hurst.

'Cossack dancing.'

'Really? So there's a thriving Cossack culture in the Eden Valley, is there?'

'You'd be surprised.'

'Yes, I would.'

Fry clenched her fist in her hair, wishing she'd kept it longer and had more of it to tear out.

'Luke,' she said.

Irvine's shoulders had stopped shaking by the time his head appeared from behind his computer screen. In one way, Fry had something in common with Irvine. He wasn't local. At least, he wasn't Derbyshire through and through, the way a lot of their colleagues in Edendale were. He came from a Yorkshire mining family, but had Scottish blood a generation or two back and liked to talk about his Celtic heritage. Maybe he was the one who ought to be a redhead, but he wasn't – he had a much darker look, as if one of those Spanish sailors who'd landed in Scotland from the doomed Armada was also in his bloodline.

'Yes?' said Irvine.

A less eager response. Fry suspected he might turn a bit bolshie, if he wasn't reined in soon enough. She'd overheard political arguments between him and Hurst, and Irvine was definitely out on the left wing.

'Luke, I want you to get out and interview this youth who had the iPod stolen,' said Fry. 'Poor little sod must be traumatised.'

Irvine sighed. 'Okay.'

'I'd lay ten to one he knew the lads who took it,' put

in Murfin. 'I reckon he probably swapped it for some E.'

Fry turned back to him, only now remembering that he was there.

'And why would you jump to that unfounded conclusion, Gavin?' she said.

'It's the way things go down on a Tuesday night in Edendale. You have no idea what it's like out there on the streets.'

3

As she creaked slowly towards her front door, Dorothy Shelley supported herself on a walking stick. She wasn't able to move very quickly these days. Well, she'd never exactly been an athlete. A walk with the dog to the end of Welbeck Street and back had been the limit of her exercise routine for more years than she cared to remember.

There was one time she'd tried horse riding during a holiday in the Scottish Highlands, persuaded into it by Gerald, who saw himself as some kind of John Wayne figure. Back then, her husband could be very persuasive when he set his mind on something. Persistent too. She'd always let him get his way in the end. It was such a relief when he died and she could do some of the things she'd always wanted to do on her own. And exercise wasn't one of them. It had taken her weeks to get over the bruising on her legs and backside from that horse. At least Gerald had been the one who fell off. Her life seemed to be made up of such small pleasures, scattered through the years of alternating tedium and irritation that had constituted her marriage.

Now, she was unsteady on her legs, and was frightened of moving too quickly in case the dog got under her feet and tripped her up. Jasper the Jack Russell was as elderly as his owner, or the equivalent in dog years. He wanted to stay close to her because he couldn't see very well now. Her wobbly legs and his bad eyes were a lethal combination. She knew she was going to come a cropper one day, and her family would lose no time getting her out of the house and into a nursing home.

When she opened the door, she saw that it was raining. Tutting quietly, she pulled on a coat that was hanging by the door and slipped a PVC hood over her hair. For a moment, she looked at the slippers on her feet, but decided it was too much trouble to change into shoes. She wasn't going far.

Mrs Shelley stepped out into Welbeck Street, taking her time negotiating the step. It was only a few paces to number eight, the house next door which Gerald had insisted on buying with the intention of knocking the two places together and forming a much larger property. A town house, he'd called it. A pipe dream, if ever there was one.

He'd never got round to finishing the project, of course. He never did, not once in his life. There had been a lot of dust and mess, then everything had stopped before a single wall came down. That was shortly before he died. His legacy was a house where all the plaster had been knocked off, the skirting boards ripped away, and the bathroom suite was sitting in a skip in the street.

At least the finished job had left her with a bit of income – a house converted in two flats, the rent coming in very handy to supplement her pension. It also provided her with a bit of company when she needed it, as well as someone younger to change a light bulb or put out the wheelie bins. She'd always made a point of getting the right sort of person when she was looking for a new tenant. Reliable and trustworthy professional people only.

Mrs Shelley was looking for her ground floor tenant now. She hadn't seen him for days. She hadn't even heard any of his music or noticed the smell of his coffee, which sometimes wafted out of the back door. She'd seen the cat in the back garden and tried to feed it a couple of times, but it had shied away from her, even when offered fresh chicken.

She knew she was getting a bit vague in her old age. Her son-in-law whispered that she was barmy, when he thought she couldn't hear him. He was desperate to take over her properties. Preventing him from achieving that ambition was the one thing that kept her going.

But things confused her sometimes. Names and details escaped her. The most obvious facts could slip out of her memory. She wondered whether her tenant had told her that he was going away on holiday. Usually she got him to write important things down. But she had a feeling that something had gone wrong, and he might not have had time, or not wanted her to know where he was.

She hesitated outside the door of the flat. There was no answer to her knock, and the curtains were closed. She had a key, of course. She was the owner of the property, wasn't she? Yes, she was quite sure she was. She hadn't sold it or anything. She was the landlady, and she had a right to enter in an emergency.

But she didn't want to do it. She was reluctant to intrude, didn't want to disturb anybody or make it seem as though she was prying. She had to admit that she was also little bit frightened of what she might find if she went in.

Mrs Shelley turned away and shuffled back to her own house, telling herself that she'd catch her tenant tomorrow. She'd forgotten that she had already spent the last three days looking for Ben Cooper.

★   ★   ★

33

DC Luke Irvine paused on his way out of the office, standing by Diane Fry's desk.

'Sarge,' he said hesitantly.

Fry looked up at him curiously, surprised that he hadn't left yet. Whatever faults Irvine had, being hesitant wasn't one of them. What was he nervous about asking her?

'What is it, Luke?'

'The talk is that the medical reports aren't good,' said Irvine. 'You know—'

She didn't need to ask what reports he was talking about.

'And how would anyone get to hear that?'

Irvine shrugged. 'You know how these things get around. People in this place gossip like a lot of housewives.'

'Whatever happened to the concept of confidentiality?'

She noticed that Becky Hurst had followed him to her desk, shadowing him like a watchful guard dog. Her hair was tied back in a businesslike way and she was dressed in a black trouser suit like a lawyer or company executive. Very professional looking.

'Housewife is an outdated term,' muttered Hurst. 'And women don't gossip any more than certain men do.'

Irvine ignored her as usual, and Hurst turned her attention to Fry.

'Is it true, then? About the medical reports?'

'How the hell would I know?' snapped Fry. 'I'm not his doctor. I'm not his nurse. And I'm certainly not his mother. You're asking the wrong person.'

'His mother died,' said Hurst quietly.

'I know,' said Fry. 'Look – yes, I know.'

She flapped her hands in despair and sat down at her desk, recognising a conversation that she wasn't going to come out of well. But Irvine decided to try again.

'We just thought—' he said. 'Well, we knew you worked together, and you were quite close for a while. So we thought you'd have been able to find something out. That you'd have a bit of information we don't. You could have asked somebody.'

'Close?' said Fry. 'Were we? *Close?*'

'You're more senior than us anyway,' Hurst was saying. 'The same rank as him. You could ask—'

'And that means nothing either,' said Fry. 'Rank and all that. Nothing. Or else why would I be back here?'

Irvine looked stubborn. 'I just felt I had to speak up.'

'Do me a favour,' said Fry. 'Next time you feel the need to speak up, do it with your mouth shut.'

Irvine and Hurst exchanged glances and reluctantly went back to work. Fry stared across the CID room thoughtfully, until Gavin Murfin caught her eye. He was chewing, slowly extracting the maximum satisfaction from whatever he was eating.

Murfin paused, and swallowed. Then, very deliberately, he gave Fry a long, slow wink.

Well, thanks a lot, Gavin. Always ready to give her just what she needed – a bit of support from the most experienced member of the team.

Fry left the room and walked up the corridor to the top of the stairs, where a large window looked out over the forecourt of the building towards the east stand of Edendale football ground. She watched Luke Irvine drive out through the barrier in the CID pool car and turn on to West Street. The rain was coming down heavily, and she saw him turn on the sidelights to be safe in poor visibility.

This rain had started suddenly after a long dry spell. For months, Fry remembered the water companies talking about a drought. Dry weather through the previous autumn, winter and spring had reduced the levels of their reservoirs dramatically, and the use of hosepipes had been banned. No amount of rain during the summer would make any difference, they said. It didn't soak into the ground, but evaporated in the warmer air. The drought would last until next winter at least.

Fry shook her head. In Derbyshire, nature had different ideas. The talk of droughts had lulled everyone into the idea that it would stay dry for ever. Had there been a warning on the weather forecasts? Possibly. But who took any notice of those? No one had since Michael Fish dismissed rumours of a hurricane, just before the Great Storm of 1987 killed eighteen people and ripped up thousands of trees across the south-east of England.

She'd seen it happen, all the predictable consequences. Right across the Peak District, car windscreens had become filmed over with dust and grease during the dry weather, encrusted with the debris of dead insects. When the heavens opened and the sky emptied its deluge on to the landscape, wipers had screeched into action, their rubber blades smearing thousands of windscreens into instant impenetrability. Tides of filth ran down the glass, and rain splattered into thick gobbets. Visibility fell to zero.

The emergency call centres had started to be deluged too, as drivers panicked, swerved, braked, and the roads were blocked by demolished walls, shattered glass, and dozens of rear-end shunts. There had been collisions on all the main cross-county routes – the Woodhead Pass, the Snake, the A623 and A6 – where streams of HGVs ploughed on through flash floods, their headlights blazing. Those were professional drivers, and their windscreens were clean, but their spray blinded motorists in their wake, preventing them from seeing the oceans of surface water before they found themselves aquaplaning straight into a stone wall.

Fry looked up at the sky, seeking a break in the cloud.

It wasn't getting any better. The news this morning had said that records for the amount of rain falling in a twenty-four hour period had been broken several times already. In one day, as much water had fallen on the Peak District as would normally be expected in a month.

Yet it showed no signs of stopping. The rain bucketed down every day. Fields had become mud, and roads turned into rivers. July and August had been washouts so far, the incessant rain keeping tourists away, closing caravan- and campsites, forcing the cancellation of outdoor events. Summer? This was more like a monsoon season.

Irvine had disappeared down West Street, heading into the centre of the rain-soaked town like Captain Oates walking into a snowstorm. He might be some time.

Two uniformed officers came up the stairs and gave Fry curious looks as they passed. A few yards along the corridor, one turned to say something to the other. She thought she heard a laugh as they went round the corner. She felt herself tense with anger again. She had no doubt she must be the object of their joke. She wondered what the station gossip was saying about her these days. Nothing good, she supposed. But at least they didn't chat about her medical condition.

When she was sent back to Edendale, Fry had known that she'd never be able to escape from the shadow of

Detective Sergeant Ben Cooper. Not while she was in E Division, where everyone knew him – even when she walked out on to the streets of the town, members of the public were likely to ask about him. And certainly not while she was running his old team. Those two young DCs had been taken under Cooper's wing like newborn chicks. She'd never get the loyalty from Irvine and Hurst that she might otherwise have expected. And Carol Villiers? She was an old friend of Cooper's since childhood. There was no way she could compete with that. As for Gavin Murfin, he was too old a dog to learn any new tricks. He'd always been inclined to make satirical comments from the sidelines, and he wasn't going to change.

And Fry didn't know what to do now, or what to think. Seriously? *Close?* The word had taken her completely by surprise. Had she and Cooper ever been close, really? What did that actually mean? Yes, she'd unwisely shared some personal information about herself with him, and he'd managed to infiltrate himself into her life in various ways. That was true. And there had been moments . . .

But no. That wasn't being close. You could do those things, and have those conversations, with a stranger you'd just met in the pub when you were both drunk. It meant nothing, didn't it?

It was true that the medical reports weren't good.

She'd heard those rumours herself. Of course she had. Police officers were worse for office gossip than any housewife had ever been. The word was that DS Cooper's extended leave would continue for a good while yet. Whether his ongoing problems were physical or psychological was less clear. No one seemed to know the details. Either that, or they just weren't saying.

Against her better instincts, Fry wondered where Ben Cooper was at this moment, and what he was doing. What would he be thinking right now? That, too, could be nothing good.

4

The garage door began to rise with a faint hum as Charlie Dean thumbed the remote. As he waited for Barbara, he stood on the drive for a few minutes under his folding umbrella, looking at the sky, wondering if it would stop raining today. A clear sky and a bit of sun made his job easier, encouraged his prospective buyers into a more cheerful and optimistic frame of mind, making them more likely to sign on the dotted line.

He was feeling a lot better this morning, more like his real self. In fact, he was back to the old confident Charlie who was such a talented property negotiator and so attractive to women. It felt good to be back to normal. The events of the night before had started to feel like an exciting little adventure that he might joke about with his mates in the pub for years to come.

Last night, he'd decided to go to the Old Horse for the last half-hour before closing time. He did it partly because he went there most nights, and a rare absence might be commented on by someone who knew his wife. But he went mostly because if he came home smelling of whisky, Barbara would never question where he'd been all evening. The word 'alibi' kept going through his mind, though he'd done nothing to feel guilty about. Perhaps he wasn't thinking logically when he turned into the pub car park, but seeking reassurance, the comfort of doing something. Or maybe it was just the drink he needed.

The Old Horse stood on a busy corner in the centre of Wirksworth. The old folk said this little Derbyshire market town once had a lot more pubs, but they'd been steadily dwindling in numbers. A couple more would close in the next few years, and the Old Horse would probably be one of them. It still relied largely on local custom, people who lived within walking distance in the town. It hadn't reached out to the tourists the way some of the other pubs had.

So Charlie had been in no doubt he'd see familiar faces in the bar, a few individuals who knew his name, would speak to him to say hello and would remember he was there. The landlord had a good memory for customers, and was always sober, even if none of his regulars were.

As soon as he got the first whisky in his hand, he'd begun to feel a bit more comfortable. The man in the red rain jacket had scared him, he had to admit. The thought that the stranger had come out of the woods made him go cold. He and Sheena had been in there only a few minutes before. He couldn't stand the idea that the man in the red jacket might have been a lurking presence, watching them all the time. What a bastard. He ought to be locked up.

But that wasn't going to happen, was it? It would involve talking to the police, and telling the story. The one thing that Charlie couldn't do.

He checked his phone for messages while he waited for the garage door to complete its arc. When it had stopped, he put the phone back in his pocket and looked up and down the road impatiently. He was supposed to be giving Barbara a lift this morning, dropping her off at the hairdresser's in the Market Place to get her roots done. She was scared to death of reverting to her natural colour. He couldn't even remember what it was now.

Sheena had been terrified on that roadside last night too. She'd told him many times that she was sensitive, that she could detect things about people by some sixth sense. It wasn't quite like reading auras, she said, but close to it. Dean didn't know what auras were, or how you'd read one, but he didn't say so. It was easier just to let Sheena talk when she got going. If she was interrupted, she got confused, and then tetchy. So he'd allowed her to tell him over and over again about this business of her sensitivity. She'd look at someone and say they were sad, or that she had a positive feeling about them. And Dean would nod and grunt, as if he understood. It was enough for her.

But when they'd stood by the side of the road that night and the stranger's car had pulled up behind them, he'd noticed an expression on her face that he'd never seen before. She looked like one of those young women in a horror film when they see the monster for the first time, or hear the deranged killer approaching. In the car headlights, he'd seen the pale oval of her face, her eyes wide and her mouth hanging open. Terror and dread. The frozen rabbit expression.

And for the first time, he'd believed that she might be sensitive about people. Because he'd felt it himself a few moments later, a sensation like a dark shadow falling across him, even though it was night-time. A chill that struck to his heart and made the tiny hairs stand up on the back of his neck. My God, he couldn't get away fast enough.

Charlie noticed Barbara standing in the lounge watching him through the window. She'd be wondering what he was up to, as usual. She was on the phone, of course, chatting to one of her friends, and no doubt complaining about him. But rather than concentrating on the conversation, she'd moved to a position where her eyes were fixed on his movements, staring with hawk-like intensity. She was gossiping about him and spying on him at the same time. And probably making an obscene gesture towards him with her other hand. He supposed she would call that multitasking.

He gave her a thin smile and rotated his finger in a 'hurry up' sign. But she stared straight through him and carried on talking. Charlie sighed. He and Barbara had been married for ten years and he'd been experiencing the seven-year itch for nine of them.

Last night in the pub, he'd taken a long gulp of Scotch and tried to think seriously about his relationship with Sheena. They'd met on a driving course at a hotel in Chesterfield. That was ironic. It was like a reversal of speed dating. They'd both moved a bit too fast once, driven over some artificial speed limit by a few miles an hour on an empty road, and got caught by one of those damn cameras. They'd had to sit in a classroom for four hours and be lectured about what naughty children they were. He liked to refer to it enigmatically as an SAS course. Let people interpret it in any way they wanted. He knew that SAS stood for Speed Awareness Scheme.

But four hours. And no driving involved.

'What?' he asked a mate who'd done the course before. 'So that's four hours doing . . . what? Sitting in a classroom being lectured?'

'You get to watch a video.'

'Oh, great.'

Four hours. It was enough to make you want to jump in your car and put your foot flat down on the pedal, just to prove that the rest of the world didn't move so slowly. Four hours. It felt more like a year off his life. He hadn't been kept in detention since his last year at school, and that wasn't for four sodding hours. He could have reported the school for breaching his human rights, if they'd tried it. But because his car registration number appeared on that camera, he was stuck in a room all afternoon to avoid getting three penalty points on his licence. It would have been terminally boring without Sheena to look at. Their speed had led to their meeting, but their first encounter had been *slow*.

Charlie made a deliberate pantomime of checking the refuse containers after yesterday's collection. They had no wheelie bins this far up The Dale, but there was a green kerbside food caddy, a blue box for glass and cans, and a blue bag for paper and cardboard. He checked that Barbara had removed the kitchen caddy and taken it back indoors, then locked the handle back down again. The smell of rotting food was unpleasant. He ought to clean that out one day.

He picked up a bit of rubbish from the drive, a scrap of paper dropped by a passing youth or a careless binman. Let Barbara find some reason to complain about that.

Yes, that driving course in Chesterfield had changed Charlie's life. At first, it had reminded him of the management seminars he'd been obliged to attend when he was a middle manager at the finance company, before he left to get a job selling property at Williamson Hart. You had to look interested at those things, and you were expected to participate. It had all the same buzz phrases and acronyms too. This one started with the Three Es for improvement of road safety – Education, Engineering and Enforcement.

Two-thirds of the class had been caught by speed cameras going over the limit in a thirty zone. The oldest attendee complained that he'd been driving for sixty-four years, always kept his insurance, tax and MOT paid up to date all that time, then got caught by a speed camera doing thirty-seven miles per hour, no doubt in his Fiat Uno or something. Another man said he'd volunteered for the course to get his insurance premiums down. One woman admitted she'd taken a re-test after being convicted of drink driving.

On the other hand, there were a couple of decent

blokes there who'd been a good laugh. One of them had arrived a few minutes late, looking flushed and sullen. He claimed to have done some advanced driver training in the military, and hinted at Special Forces. But throughout the session he shouted out the stupidest comments and answers he could think of, suggesting that from a pollution point of view it was better to flog a V8 Range Rover to death, then shoot a cow, because it produced just as many emissions as the car. As the afternoon wore on, he'd become more and more outrageous, until the presenter finally lost patience with him and threatened to throw him off the course, which would have resulted in three points on his licence. The other bloke had admitted he liked to drive fast, and blamed the government, speed cameras and the police for his presence on the course. It probably wasn't the attitude that was expected of them.

Well, they were the only people who'd made those four hours of his life even remotely worthwhile. At the end of the session, Charlie had got Sheena's phone number, and gone to the pub for a drink with the two blokes. It was one of them who'd made the joke about calling the session an SAS course. They were both full of it, really. But Charlie could see exactly where they were coming from.

Charlie had felt a bit sorry for that presenter, though. He looked professional, had his name badge on a yellow lanyard round his neck, and a Dell laptop running a PowerPoint presentation. He'd shown them an animated reconstruction of a multiple pile-up on the M4, in which fifty vehicles had collided in fog, causing ten fatalities as a truck loaded with gas canisters exploded and started a massive blaze. Then he handed out handsets to vote on test questions. What was the national speed limit on a dual carriageway? Half the group got it wrong. They discovered they could have been driving faster after all. Well, fast legally anyway.

The course was run by AA DriveTech. Didn't the AA used to stand up for motorists? He had a vague impression of his grandfather talking about driving his old car and being warned by an AA patrol of a speed trap ahead. Now they were part of the process of persecuting motorists, no doubt taking a decent share of the proceeds from the people in that classroom.

While the presenter was speaking, Charlie had done a quick calculation on his notepad. Twenty-six people here, who'd each paid more than ninety pounds to be on the course. The presenter said this was one of three sessions today. If the other sessions had the same number of people, that came to . . . over seven thousand pounds for the day. And that was just for the one venue. There were other places in the county he could have chosen. Nice work, if you could get it.

He pictured those two dozen people gathered in a

room at a hotel on the Chesterfield bypass, next to a Tesco supermarket. He bet that some of them didn't even drive often enough to get their cars dirty.

Charlie Dean stopped what he was doing. His eyes glazed over as he stared across the narrow street at the stone wall opposite. His umbrella sagged on to his shoulder and rain began to fall on his face. But he hardly noticed.

He'd just remembered the mud on his car. It must be all over the bodywork and the hubcaps, and coating the inside of the wheel arches. He'd forgotten about it last night, when he came back from the pub, but it would be obvious this morning in daylight. He recalled that he'd even plastered some over his number plate, in a misguided attempt at secrecy. If the number was still illegible he could get stopped by the police – not that many police officers were seen in Wirksworth these days. Just as bad, his bosses at Williamson Hart might start asking questions. He would be ruining his image. He couldn't do anything about it now, though. He'd have to find time to go through the car wash on the way to the office.

He looked at his watch. Damn, he was going to be late if Barbara didn't hurry up. He hated that. He wanted to be known as the perfect employee – the best salesman, the top negotiator, the guy who always arrived on time and stayed until the work was done. That made it much easier to get away with the rest of it.

So what was she up to? Surely she couldn't still be on the phone? He knew she must be doing this deliberately. For some reason, she had it in for him this morning. Well, what was new? She'd never needed a reason before.

Charlie looked down at the surface of the drive he was standing on. Lumps of wet mud lay on the concrete, either side of a set of dirty tyre tracks. Could he blame the binmen for that? Probably not. They came to The Dale too early in the day. Anyway, Barbara would notice the mud as soon as she set eyes on the car.

He took a deep breath, and knew he'd have to face the worst. He had a couple of minutes perhaps to come up with a credible story. A new property that was half built, a site where construction hadn't been finished and the access road was full of mud? It might work.

Last night, he'd driven in forwards and parked the BMW pointing towards the back of the garage. He normally reversed in, to give himself an easy exit. But last night he didn't want to be messing about turning in the road. There were always too many nosy people around, too many pairs of eyes peering from behind their curtains in The Dale.

He unlocked the doors of the car, and the lights flashed. He turned back from the road and looked at the BMW.

'Oh, shit.'

He froze, not knowing what to do. Or, at least, what to do first. He thought about panicking, kicking the walls, sitting in the car and turning on the engine to fill the garage with exhaust fumes and ending it all, right here and now. It would be preferable to going indoors to Barbara and telling her everything. He might as well kill himself now, rather than wait for her to do it. He could make it painless anyway. Barbara wouldn't consider that option.

Finally, he fumbled for the remote and closed the garage door, glancing over his shoulder again to see if anyone was outside the house, watching. He had a horribly vivid vision of the man in the red rain jacket, hood up against the downpour, watching him from the dark. But the road was empty. The coast was clear.

Dean let himself into the house, and poured warm water into a bucket with a trembling hand. He added a splash of washing up liquid, though he'd always told people it was too astringent and could damage your paintwork. He went back to the garage and found an old sponge on the shelf. He hesitated for only a moment before he began to remove the bloody hand print from the boot of his BMW.

5

That was the trouble with cars these days. One looked and sounded just like another. A lot were even the same colour. There was no telling whether it was the right one until it stopped and you could see who was driving.

Ingrid Turner stared out of the window as the latest car passed. She knew she fussed too much sometimes. Glen told her himself often enough. '*You're like an old mother hen,*' he'd say, though he always said it with a smile and she knew he loved her to fuss over him really. She loved her son. So, yes – she was fussy about him. Of course, she tried not to get in his way too much and be a nuisance.

But there was no denying it. He ought to have been home by now.

Ingrid sat down in her armchair, then stood up again nervously. It was funny, really. She had often thought it would be a good thing if Glen didn't come home one night. It would mean that he'd finally found himself a girlfriend. That would be such a relief. She'd worried about him for years, never been able to figure out why he hadn't formed any relationships with women, and too scared to ask him the obvious question. Well, she couldn't, could she? It was the sort of thing a mother shouldn't ask her son. If he wanted to tell her, that was different. But if she pried into his private life like that, he would never forgive her.

She heard the sound of another engine in the street, a vehicle slowing down. But it was just the postman, stopping outside the house next door to deliver the stuff they'd bought off eBay. They seemed to be forever buying and selling. Taking parcels to the post office in West End, having more delivered. She couldn't see the point of it herself.

Of course, she would have expected Glen to phone, if he'd met someone and wasn't coming home. He wouldn't have left his old mum wondering where he was. He'd know that she'd be worried and unable to sleep. She'd taken her pills last night, but still hadn't slept a wink. This morning, she felt weary and her head was buzzing. She had a feeling it was going to be important to think straight today. She didn't want to do anything hasty and mess it all up. On the other hand, she was terrified of hesitating too long.

She looked at her little patch of grass in front of the house. Somebody had walked across it during the night and left muddy prints from the bare flower beds. There was a beer can in the corner by the pavement. She'd go out and pick it up later, when it had stopped raining.

If he'd met someone and wasn't coming home. When she thought about it baldly like that, it sounded so unlikely. She couldn't imagine Glen picking up some woman in a club and staying the night at her place, getting up to goodness knew what. It just wouldn't happen. Not in a million years. He wouldn't have the confidence.

Now, all those scenarios that had run through her head during the night seemed like complete fantasies. They were so far fetched that she couldn't believe she'd entertained them, even for a moment. Perhaps she'd been asleep after all, and dreamed the whole thing. Somehow, she'd convinced herself there was a rational explanation for the fact that Glen hadn't come home. But there wasn't one. Not one she could believe in any longer.

The postman ran back down next door's drive and climbed into his van. Ingrid waited a moment, but he accelerated away. Nothing for her today. She was only putting off the moment.

She picked up the phone, and looked at the address

55

book. She had the number of Glen's office. She could phone his boss to see if he'd turned up for work or had called in with an excuse. But she was afraid of what they'd all say about her after she'd rung off. Afraid of what they would say about her Glen.

Ingrid put the phone down and looked at it, as if it might speak up for itself and give her the advice she needed. She dialled a '9', then stopped. Weren't you supposed to wait twenty-four hours before reporting someone missing? Especially if it was an adult, who might just be late home.

And was it really an emergency? She had no way of telling, but she didn't want to get in trouble. There might be penalties for people who made non-emergency 999 calls. She'd read about them in the paper, all kinds of silly people who phoned to say they couldn't find their glasses, or to ask for directions to Homebase. She didn't want to be considered a silly woman. But she couldn't do nothing either.

Instead, Ingrid began to dial a different set of figures. The non-emergency police number, 101. She heard a recorded message telling her that she was being put through to Derbyshire Police.

'Yes, thank you,' she said. 'I want to report a missing person. It's my son.'

★   ★   ★

56

Luke Irvine was glad to get out of the office. He was always unsettled by change. He hadn't been in Divisional CID long enough to get his feet firmly planted under a desk. Not the way Gavin Murfin had, and others like him.

Murfin had become the proverbial immovable object around E Division. He'd worked his roots so deeply into the carpet of the CID room that nothing had been able to shift him for years. The introduction of tenure had passed him by, performance reviews left him unscathed, the annual appraisal process had mysteriously found him doing exactly the same job each time round. None of it stirred him.

Well, not until his thirty years were up, anyway. Not even Gavin could resist that steamroller. Immovable object was meeting irresistible force. And suddenly the object wasn't so immovable after all. In fact, DC Murfin would roll aside like so much tumbleweed under the impact of Clause A19, if the force decided to follow neighbouring Staffordshire and invoke the regulation forcing retirement of police officers after thirty years' pensionable service. Most of those affected by A19 were senior officers, who'd worked their way up through the ranks over the past three decades and were at the top of their particular tree. Experience counted for nothing when it came time to cut costs.

And right now, E Division was down in numbers

across every department – not just CID, but uniformed response, civilian support staff, even forensics.

Irvine decided to dodge down the narrow back streets and wind his way across town past the parish church and Edendale Community School to reach the Buxton Road. It should mean that he would bypass the traffic that always snarled up on the main shopping streets like Clappergate. Even the Market Square got congested, though the businesses in that part of town were mostly banks and building societies, estate agents and pubs. Everything else had moved into the indoor shopping centre.

Edendale was a magnet for tourists, and they seemed to come in greater numbers every year, whatever the weather. The Eden Valley straddled the two distinct geological halves of the Peak District – the limestone hills and wooded dales of the White Peak, and the bleak expanses of peat moors in the Dark Peak. Its position made a perfect base for exploring the national park, and all the usual services had developed to cater for the tourists – hotels, bed and breakfasts, restaurants, outdoor clothing shops. Some of the old-fashioned businesses were still there, the butchers and bakers and antique shops. But to Irvine's eye, they looked more like antiques themselves, part of the picturesque scenery.

Gavin Murfin had been working in this area for so long that he knew a lot of useful things, and the best places to go. It had been Gavin who'd introduced him to May's Café, just off West Street, the place where everyone nipped off to now that there was no canteen. It was one of the most useful lessons he'd learned during his first week in CID.

But it wasn't the impending departure of Gavin Murfin that was bothering Irvine. He'd felt secure with Ben Cooper as his DS. You knew where you stood with Ben. He'd tell you the facts, give it to you straight, put you on the right path if you went astray. But you knew he'd always back you up. It was what you'd want from your supervising officer. It made you feel you were a valued member of his team.

Irvine had learned that being in the police was like being part of a big family. You didn't always agree with each other, or even get on very well. But you were still family. It was a crucial factor when it came down to the 'us and them', the moment when you faced a dangerous situation together.

Yes, the loss of Cooper was bad news, whichever way you looked at it – even if it was temporary, and nobody knew if that was the case or not. For Irvine, the reappearance of Diane Fry in E Division was like the tsunami after the earthquake. If you survived one, the other would definitely get you. The old one-two flattened you every time.

When he thought about it, Fry made a pretty good

tidal wave. She could knock you off your feet and leave you floundering.

He wondered how Becky Hurst truly felt about Diane Fry. It was difficult to tell with women. They were nice enough to each other face to face, but it was a different matter when their backs were turned. Becky was too smart to let it show if she felt strongly, though. She was an expert at keeping her head down and her nose clean. It was a skill he'd yet to learn for himself. Keeping his mouth shut was just too hard to do sometimes.

He'd known Hurst for a while – they'd applied for CID at the same time, done their detective training together, ended up being posted to E Division as a pair of new recruits. When he looked around now at other officers of his own age, Irvine was struck by how few of them showed any interest in CID. And why should they, when there was no extra pay, no promotion, not even any additional prestige?

There were specialist jobs in uniform which looked much more exciting – firearms, surveillance, air support unit. Some couldn't resist the continually shifting demands of being a response officer, the first on the scene to every incident, driving on blue lights all day long. But Irvine had found the continuous adrenalin rush too exhausting. The brain never seemed to catch up with the body when you were working constantly on instinct and training. Life in CID might be far more bogged down in paperwork and procedure than he'd imagined, but at least you were called on to think occasionally.

He'd thought of going into intelligence. Even a Senior Intelligence Analyst with Derbyshire Constabulary earned only about thirty thousand pounds a year. A successful professional criminal would laugh at that.

And life on the Senior Management Team didn't look enticing from this distance either. It seemed to him that the SMT tried to solve everything with spreadsheets and matrices. Common sense scared them. Extra resources meant more mobile data terminals, and more tasers. And for months now the chiefs had hardly been able to think of anything else but the new Police and Crime Commissioner and what priorities he'd decide on for Derbyshire.

Irvine laughed quietly to himself. If he spoke those thoughts out loud, people would think he was turning into Gavin Murfin. Except that Gavin had never understood what a spreadsheet was, or a matrix – and now he'd never have to. Lucky man.

He wished he was eligible to vote in the referendum on Scottish independence. But he was one of many thousands of Scots living in England who wouldn't get a say in the future of the union. Not unless he left Derbyshire and moved up to live there in the next twelve months. It didn't look likely to happen.

Irvine crossed the Hollowgate bridge in the centre of Edendale and found himself halted in traffic. He looked down at the river, and was shocked to see how high it was. The water was rushing over the rocks on the river bed and building up great white heads of foam. It had risen much further up its banks than usual, and broken tree branches were being pushed against the stonework. When he wound down his window he could hear the roaring of the water above the sound of the traffic.

The streets around this part of town looked safe from flooding. They were well above the level of the river. Downstream, it might be different. To the east of Edendale the valley widened out and the land became flatter, more prone to flooding when the Eden burst its banks.

Just across the river from here was Welbeck Street. Irvine knew nothing about that particular street. Except that it was where Ben Cooper lived.

6

Half an hour later, Detective Sergeant Ben Cooper stepped out of his front door on to Welbeck Street, and panicked.

He'd hardly set foot on the pavement when he found himself facing his landlady, Dorothy Shelley. He took a pace back, fighting a surge of anxiety. For weeks, it had felt like a shock every time he met someone, no matter how well he knew them. His throat constricted and the palms of his hands became suddenly sweaty.

Mrs Shelley stared at him from under her PVC rain hood. It had stopped raining now, but she seemed to have forgotten to take it off. A part of Cooper wanted to remind her, to tell her she didn't need to be wearing the hood this morning. That side of him hated the idea that people passing by in the street would think she was a batty old lady. She'd been good to him over the years. Mrs Shelley made him feel welcome in Edendale, and that meant a lot.

But another part of him found it was too much effort. The discomfort in his throat made it difficult for him even to get the words out. The conversation might get complicated, and that scared him too much. He felt anxious even thinking about it. So he said nothing. It seemed the safest option.

'Oh, Ben,' said the old lady brightly. 'There you are at last. Are you just going out?'

'Yes, Mrs Shelley.'

'Are you all right?'

'I'm fine,' he said. 'Just fine.'

Of course he didn't feel fine. He hadn't felt fine for a very long time. It seemed like years and years and years. He'd even forgotten what it felt like. But he nodded at Mrs Shelley and said he felt just fine. And when she eyed him dubiously, he nodded again and kept nodding, like an idiot. He could feel himself doing it, but couldn't stop.

Mrs Shelley scraped her stick on the pavement anxiously.

'And are you on your way—?' she said.

'Yes, the usual place,' he said. 'I'm going to visit Liz.'

He pulled his car keys out of his pocket and rattled them, as if to prove what he was saying. His Toyota was standing by the kerb a few yards away, waiting for him. He was free to go, wasn't he? There was nothing else he was supposed to do.

Cooper stopped rattling his keys and looked more closely at Mrs Shelley, wondering if there was something he'd forgotten. He felt almost certain there wasn't. He definitely didn't have to go to work. He was still on leave. Extended leave, they called it. That meant he didn't have to think about work for a while. He hadn't thought about it for . . . how long?

His airways spasmed and the pain began to spread into his lungs, making it difficult for him to breathe. The old burns on his arms itched, and his fingers clenched into fists. He recognised the signs, and his sight blurred for a few moments as he fought the attack. He gritted his teeth, determined not to let it show in front of Mrs Shelley.

When his vision cleared again, she'd moved a step or two closer and was holding out her free hand as if she was about to touch him. She looked almost as though she was expecting to have to catch him if he fell, as if he might faint and fall flat on the pavement at any moment. His landlady got such strange ideas. She was definitely going a bit batty.

'Would you like me to come with you?' she asked.

Cooper frowned. Why did she suggest that? In what universe would he ask Mrs Shelley to come with him to visit Liz? Didn't she understand?

'No, thank you,' he said. 'But—'

'Yes?'

'But it's kind of you to offer.'

That was right, wasn't it? That was the sort of thing you said to fob people off, when you just wanted them to leave you alone. He began to move towards the kerb, but Mrs Shelley was still holding out her hand. He was afraid she might be about to grab hold of his arm and keep him back.

'I could get you a taxi, perhaps?' she said.

'No, I'll be okay, really,' said Cooper. 'I can drive, I still have a car.'

Even as he said it, he felt his voice weakening. He looked towards the road again, to make sure the Toyota was still there. He did have a car. He was holding the keys to prove it.

'Of course. If you're sure you're well enough . . .'

Mrs Shelley's face was screwed up in concern. Cooper knew she must be referring to the burns on his arm. But they were healing slowly, and they weren't so painful now. The skin felt tight on his forearm when he flexed the muscle, but that was only a bit of discomfort. Why should Mrs Shelley think it would prevent him from driving safely?

'I'll see you later then, Ben,' she called as he walked away. 'Don't catch a chill.'

And the old lady stood on the pavement in her PVC rain hood and clutched her walking stick, as she watched him unlock the door and get into his car.

It was only when he was sitting in the driving seat of his Toyota and struggling to fit the key into the ignition that Cooper looked down at his hands and saw how badly they were shaking. They had a tremor so violent that it looked as though he was suffering from Parkinson's disease.

He took a deep, ragged breath, trying to steady the shaking.

'Okay, Liz. I got rid of her. I'm on my way now.'

He pulled out into Welbeck Street, his wheels splashing through a pool of rain water that was spreading across the road from a blocked gutter. Spray splashed on to the windscreen, creating a sudden glittering sheen like a shower of confetti as he turned the first corner.

He knew what he had to talk to Liz about today. It should have been their wedding next week. Liz had been planning her big day for the past year or more. Yes, probably for a lot longer, now he thought about it. She just hadn't told him until he'd needed to know. The reception had been booked, the order of service agreed, the honeymoon destination settled on. A cake had been ordered, the flowers chosen. It was all written

67

down in a special A4 notebook with a gold cover, which Liz had kept for the purpose.

A few minutes later, on the other side of Edendale, Cooper got out of the Toyota then saw that he'd parked it awkwardly, the rear end sticking out into the roadway. He used to be so good at parking, could fit the car neatly into any available space, and was careful never to cause an obstruction for other road users. But now he couldn't do it. He'd lost the necessary co-ordination. And it didn't seem to matter any more, either.

Last night, when he came home late, he'd been surprised to see that the boot of his car contained fencing spikes and a sledgehammer. Then he'd remembered that his brother Matt had left them there weeks ago, when he persuaded Ben to help him with repairs to a few fences at the farm. Matt kept reminding him about them, but he always forgot to take them back.

And that was the way he was now. Small details just slipped out of his mind as soon as he turned his back or lost sight of them. Cooper supposed the presence of the fence posts in his boot would surprise him every time he saw them. None of these things seemed important to him. Nothing mattered, really. Nothing.

He seemed to be experiencing sensory hallucinations too. When he got out of the car, he smelled fish and chips. Right there in the middle of nowhere, a powerful scent hit him, without a soul around, let alone a fish and chip shop nearer than half an hour's drive away. It wasn't the first time this had happened. Standing in his kitchen one night, he'd suddenly got the scent of horse manure. It was such a distinctive smell, very specific. Strange, then, that there should be no horses within a couple of miles of him. Not there in the centre of Edendale. Fish and chip shops, yes. Lots of them. But horses, no. His senses were having a joke.

He wondered if there was something wrong with him. He'd never heard of this happening to anyone before. But people did hear voices and see things that weren't there. Maybe hallucinatory smells were a symptom of some brain disease. It was a possibility he'd rather not think about just now.

Cooper walked a few yards to the entrance. Across the valley, he could see Edendale District General Hospital, a complex of white buildings on the far edge of town. It seemed an immense distance away. The hospital was too far away be any use to him now. And it always had been.

Cooper turned, recollecting what he'd come to do, and walked through the gates of the cemetery. The newer graves were at the far end of the site, and he had to walk a hundred yards or so on fine gravel that crunched like autumn leaves under his feet. Cooper knew the route well. He'd trodden this path every day for the last three months. Every day that he'd come to visit Liz.

And then the fire came again. Through the mask, he could smell the reek of petrol. He saw flames around the door, floorboards reduced to ashes, black smoke rolling across the ceiling, hanging like a curtain, sinking steadily downwards. Carbon monoxide. Two or three lungfuls would kill him.

He was in the passage again. A floor scorched where the carpet had singed through. Burning plastic and fibres. Blazing curtains falling on to furniture, glass shattering as picture cords snapped and frames crashed to the floor. When the flames reached the ceiling, they would cause flashover. It could reach five hundred degrees Fahrenheit in here. Boards over the windows were alight, reflecting the glow of the inferno inside. Fire mirrored itself, a vast furnace every way he turned.

And the smoke. He was peering through smoke. Pungent and choking, full of lethal particles. The heat was becoming too intense to bear. The exposed skin of his hands was roasting. Like a joint of meat in an oven.

And then came the moment. The moment he looked round to make sure she was still there. That she was still wearing her mask too.

But with an awful lurch in his heart, he saw that she was gone. He saw it again and again. He saw that she was gone.

7

With the Vietnamese connection still elusive, and the Edendale youth admitting that his iPod had been taken from him by his own brother, Diane Fry found herself winding down the day by wading through the volume crime reports. They were all finished and signed off by the time her shift came to an end. If she had to do this job, no one would be able to say that she didn't do it well.

Becky Hurst approached her as she was checking her latest emails. It was always wise to clear your inbox at the end of the day. Otherwise, it would just be twice as full in the morning, so you'd never catch up. And you never knew when you might have missed something that required a response yesterday.

'Yes, Becky?'

'Diane, we're meeting up in the pub after shift tonight. The Wheatsheaf. It's just off the Market Square, near the Town Hall.'

'I know where it is,' said Fry.

'So, obviously, if you want—'

'Yes, if I need you, I'll know where to find you.'

'Oh, yeah. But I didn't mean that. We were thinking you might . . . well, unless you've got something better to do, of course?'

'I probably have.'

'Right.' Hurst nodded curtly and turned away.

Fry began to relax again. The knots of tension had instantly begun to build up in her shoulders. She never quite knew how to deal with social situations. She'd never had any interest in drinking with the more junior ranks. It tended to make them think she was their friend, which was wrong. If she was going to drink, she'd rather do it on her own. At least she could relax then, instead of being constantly on edge and struggling to dredge up the right small talk without too many awkward silences. Although she was only in her thirties, the younger generation of officers like Hurst and Irvine made her feel like a dinosaur. Outside the job, she had no idea what they were talking about half the time.

She kept an eye on Hurst as Murfin joined her and they spoke quietly for a moment. Despite the difference in their sizes, Becky always looked as though she was the leader when she was with Murfin. She was like a diminutive sheepdog nipping at the heels of a lumbering bullock, steering him in the right direction.

But tonight, Fry had her suspicions about Murfin. He'd been plotting something against her all day, she was sure. He wasn't going to be content any longer with sniping from the sidelines. It was best to know where the stab in the back would come from.

A few minutes later, Fry climbed into her Audi, drove through the barrier and headed down West Street. She was remembering the first time she'd set eyes on Ben Cooper. She had only just arrived in Derbyshire following her transfer from the West Midlands and was already suffering a form of culture shock at the transition from working in the vibrant urban sprawl of Birmingham to the rural wastelands of the Peak District.

Cooper had been on leave during her first two weeks in Edendale. She'd heard plenty about him, though – everybody's favourite DC, the fount of all local knowledge. And when he finally appeared, walking into a room full of people, arriving late for a briefing at the start of a murder inquiry, she'd known straight away that he was no threat. Untidy, awkward, lacking in confidence, with a tendency to say and do all the wrong things. He was well meaning, but weak. She clearly remembered thinking that about him at the time, an instant assessment. She would have hated him otherwise.

Fry changed down gears at the bottom of the hill and slowed for the junction with Eyre Street. Cooper had changed since then, of course. The man she'd last seen, before the incident at the Light House pub, wasn't the same person at all. Promotion, responsibility, a fiancée, and a few more years under his belt – they'd all made a difference. He'd been almost unrecognisable as the awkward inconvenience she'd first met. Very different. And now he seemed more of a threat.

It was funny how that could happen to people. It made her wonder whether she'd changed too, in other people's eyes. Had she become a different person during these last few years, as a result of her time in Derbyshire and all the things that had happened here? She thought not. Oh, there might be a new scar, a few painful memories, and a lot more clutter in her life – not to mention a reunion with her missing sister, which seemed a century ago now.

But she was still the same person, wasn't she? She felt too much in control of her own nature to let any of those circumstances change her. There was no being swept along by the tide for her. Self-determination, that was what she believed in. She was in charge of her destiny, and it was important to remember it. Others should remember it more too. Yes, of course. Diane Fry was the same person she'd always been.

In Grosvenor Road, the little flat she'd lived in for years was starting to feel too small and too dismal now, the students and migrant workers upstairs too annoying. She didn't like the idea of sharing the house any more, got irritated every time she heard the front door slam. She'd got into an argument one day with a girl from Slovakia, and now no one spoke to her. They probably thought of her as a bad-tempered old witch. They certainly made her feel old anyway. She did have twelve or fifteen years on any one of them. And somehow, those years had aged her more than they should have done.

She looked in the fridge, and found nothing on the shelves that hadn't been there yesterday, and probably the day before. Half a two-litre bottle of milk, some limp lettuce, a few ounces of Cheddar. There was a small bottle of something dark at the back. Possibly soy sauce.

'Damn it,' she said, slamming the door. 'And nothing to drink anyway.'

Fry walked into the Wheatsheaf and paused in the doorway, surveying the bar. At a table in the far corner, under an enormous decorative mirror, she saw a huddled group, heads bent close together over a clutter of empty bottles and half-full glasses.

'Interesting,' she said to herself.

She saw DC Carol Villiers first. She was dressed off duty in jeans and a T-shirt, looking strong and fit, and full of vitality, like a woman who'd just come out of the gym – which she probably had. Luke Irvine was next to her, nursing a bottle of American beer. And Becky Hurst came into view across the table when Villiers leaned over to pick up a glass. An unholy trio, if ever she'd seen one. Up to no good, plotting in the pub behind her back. So where was—? Oh, yes – here he came. Gavin Murfin, lumbering back from the bar, a drink in each hand, four packets of McCoy's ridge-cut crisps dangling from his clenched fingers like trophies.

Fry watched as Murfin distributed the crisps – a red packet of plain salted for Hurst, orange Mexican chilli for Irvine. Villiers left hers untouched on the table as Murfin sat down and ripped open a green packet for himself. Cheddar and onion. She could almost smell it from here.

She wondered who'd organised this little gathering. She knew the youngsters were restless. It was unsettling to have so much disruption in the early part of your CID career. Hurst in particular was ambitious, and wanted to move up the ladder quickly. Fry recognised

76

it – she was the same herself at that age. Becky was careful to keep her nose clean, and tried to earn approval whenever she could. In fact, Ben Cooper really rated her – he'd often said that Hurst was the best of the new recruits to Edendale CID. But she'd be itching with impatience if she felt something was holding her back, if a lack of stability in the department was depriving her of opportunities.

Irvine was a different matter. To Fry's eye, he looked like a potential troublemaker. He adopted that sardonic style, made too many satirical comments, had too jaundiced an outlook for someone so young. Irvine was far more impulsive than Hurst, too. He was likely to act first and consider the correct procedure later.

But Fry's money was on DC Carol Villiers. She was older than Hurst or Irvine, and certainly no innocent. Villiers had been a corporal in the RAF Police before she left the forces and was recruited to Derbyshire Constabulary. She must have seen lots of servicemen go off the rails, heard plenty of mutinous barrack room talk in her time. She was capable of dealing with a developing situation like this, if she felt like it. But she could lead it too, if that was her inclination. She had the confidence, that elusive air of authority. And here she was in the pub with the rest of the team, when she was supposed to be on secondment assisting C Division until later in the week.

Fry's mind went back to a day not long after Villiers had arrived in Edendale. She'd wanted to talk about Ben Cooper, and Villiers knew more about him than anybody. Fry had made the effort, tried to be nice, smiled and done all the small talk. But Villiers hadn't been forthcoming. She'd been positively tight-lipped, in fact. Fry had felt vindicated in her belief that there was no point in trying to be friends with anyone. You could never rely on them.

Cooper would probably say she always saw the worst in people. And that might be true. But of course, she was usually right too.

Hurst was the first one to spot her across the bar. Not that Fry had been hiding or trying too hard to be inconspicuous. That would have been silly. She had just as much right to be here in the pub as anyone else. Let them react to her presence however they wanted. Let them all worry about her being there, and what she might have heard or suspected. It would make life interesting in the office tomorrow morning.

But Hurst was waving her over. Villiers was even calling her name. Fry shook her head, but automatically began to move towards the table. Some instinctive courtesy prevented her from just turning her back and walking away.

Irvine pulled over an extra chair for her, and the others shuffled aside to make room. But she remained standing, her shoulders stiff and awkward. She had never felt comfortable in unexpected social situations. She needed to be prepared for it. Well, if this *was* a social situation. Looking around the faces again, she realised they all seemed too solemn.

'Sit down, Diane,' said Villiers.

'It's okay. I'm just—'

But Murfin had been back to the bar, and now he thrust a glass into her hand. Fry looked at it and caught the aroma. Vodka. She didn't drink it often, only when she thought she was going to need it to get through the next hour. How had Murfin known? She'd never drunk with him, that she could recall, except when she was on soft drinks, and had always avoided any suggestion of a boozing session. If he'd asked her at any other time she would have chosen a J2O apple and mango flavour. But he hadn't asked.

With the glass in her hand, she couldn't help but take the chair. Irvine had placed it at the head of the table, making her feel as if she was the lady of the manor surveying her dinner guests. For a few minutes they all sat quietly, watching her out of the corners of their eyes. Eventually, Fry realised it was being left up to her to break the silence.

'So what were you all talking about when I came in?' she said, with an effort at lightness. 'It looked very serious.'

Glances were exchanged. Hurst fidgeted in her chair, Irvine began to tear a beer mat into pieces. Murfin developed a sudden interest in the barmaid.

'We were talking about Ben,' said Villiers.

'Ben Cooper.'

'Of course.'

'I suppose it's no surprise,' said Fry.

She could no longer get the lightness into her voice. She had never courted popularity, but deep in her heart she wanted respect, hoped that her team would at least be willing to continue working under her without becoming quite so desperate to get their old DS back.

In that moment, the disappointment struck her harder than she would ever have imagined it could. It felt like a betrayal. They'd been sitting here discussing how they could get rid of her and replace her with Ben Cooper again. And yet they'd invited her to join them and had sat her down at the table with a drink. What a nerve. With an overriding sense of relief, she began to feel angry again instead of hurt.

'So what have you decided?' she said. 'And is it a democratic decision, or have you elected a leader for the revolution?'

Fry glanced from one to the other. They looked puzzled, moody, uncomfortable. Gavin Murfin was calmly drinking a pint of Buxton Brewery's Black Rocks

IPA. She hoped someone else was driving him home tonight.

'It's not like that,' said Hurst. 'We're really worried about Ben. He's not answering his phone at home. He's not picking up calls on his mobile either. Luke and I went and called at his flat the other day, but we couldn't get any response. The curtains on the front window were closed, even during the day.'

'If it was anyone else, his friends would be asking questions by now,' said Irvine.

'So, what? Do you want to file a missing persons report? He's on extended leave, for heaven's sake. He may have taken a holiday, gone away for a while. He might be doing all the things he's never been able to do because of the job. In fact, he can do what the heck he likes. I should be so lucky.'

'That's just a load of old wazzer,' said Murfin.

'Gavin, you've known him longer than any of us,' said Irvine.

Murfin put down his glass and bit into an enormous crisp, licking a salty crumb off his lips.

'Actually no,' he said.

'But . . . ?'

Murfin glanced across at Villiers. She nodded slowly, a little reluctantly.

'Ben and I grew up in the same area. We were at school together. So I suppose you could say I've known him almost all his life. But that doesn't mean I know him best. Gavin has worked with him longest. I was away from Derbyshire for years while I was in the forces. Just the occasional visit home on leave. You lose touch, miss out on things happening in your friends' lives back home, no matter how close you once were.'

The others shifted uncomfortably when she said 'no matter how close'. Fry could understand why. It sounded strangely possessive, as if Villiers felt she had a prior claim on her childhood friend but had diplomatically stayed out of the way in view of his engagement to Liz Petty. It seemed particularly insensitive to be referring to it now.

But perhaps she hadn't meant it that way at all. People were awkward in these circumstances and said the wrong things all the time. Fry was deliberately keeping quiet. She knew she'd put her foot in it the same way herself. People would be shocked and look at her as if she was a heartless monster. It was best to know your own faults – in her case, it was difficult to deny them when so many others had pointed them out over the years.

The group around the table were looking at her now. Expectant expressions, a respectful silence. They were waiting for her to speak.

'No,' she said. 'No, no. You can't think that I know

him better than any of you. Ben Cooper is a mystery to me. I have about as much in common with him as with that pork pie Gavin has in his pocket for later. You were at school with him, Carol. Gavin, you worked in the same division with him a long time before I came to Derbyshire. You're both far better qualified than me.'

They said nothing, forcing her to keep on talking.

'In any case,' she said, 'it should be something his line manager deals with.'

That got a response at least.

'The DI? Paul Hitchens?' Irvine laughed. 'We're not talking about filling in a form and booking a counselling session. It needs a bit of action outside the HR process.'

'His family, then,' said Fry. 'He has an older brother. The one who runs Bridge End Farm. There's a sister too. One of them, surely . . .'

They still watched her, letting her run out of ideas. Well, she'd met Matt Cooper herself, and knew he was hardly the ideal person to handle an issue sensitively.

'The sister,' she said again. 'Does anyone know her?'

'She's called Claire,' said Villiers. 'She's a bit odd, in a New Agey sort of way. Doesn't really have her feet on the ground. I don't think Ben is all that close to her anyway. Not the way he is with Matt.'

Fry sighed, starting to feel trapped. Those eyes fixed

on her face were like the walls of the pub closing in around her.

'Friends, then,' she said. 'He's talked about a couple of mates he used to go on walking holidays with.'

'Yes. Rakki went back to Mombasa, where he grew up before his family came to the UK. Oscar got married last year and moved to Bristol.'

'All right. But . . . Ben must have been seeing a doctor.'

No one commented on the obvious fact that she was straying further and further away from practicalities. The people who could realistically do something about the situation were all sitting around a table in this grotty Edendale pub. The ability was here. But perhaps only some of them had the will.

'Anyway,' said Fry at last. 'You can count me out. I'm the wrong person for this.'

'But, Diane—' began Hurst.

'No,' she said firmly. 'It's a definite, definite "no".'

Diane Fry was driving as she and Becky Hurst turned the corner into Welbeck Street. She pulled the Audi in to the kerb and turned off the engine.

'It's number eight,' said Hurst. 'A bit further down the street. The blue door.'

'I know.'

'So why have we stopped?'

'We can walk the rest of the way.'

'We'll get wet,' pointed out Hurst. 'And there's space just outside the house. He has the ground-floor flat.'

'Yes, I can see.'

Fry found it difficult to explain to Hurst why she didn't want to park her car right outside Ben Cooper's flat. She had a vague idea about not wanting to scare him off, as if he was a wild stag and she was the stalker, or he was a suspect under observation, and she was a surveillance officer. It was probably just professional instinct, then. Not some silly superstition at all.

In fact, she would have difficulty explaining to anyone why she was in Welbeck Street in the first place. Hadn't she told them all plainly enough that she wouldn't do it? But instead of arguing with her, they'd sat gazing at her with their cow eyes, all four of them, and they'd let her think about it herself, without any hassle. That was a dirty trick.

With the ignition turned off, her wipers had stopped. The blue door at number eight was gradually disappearing in the streaks of rain running down the glass. Fry could have sat there all evening. She could have waited until it grew dark and the street lights came on, and then just gone home. But Becky Hurst was a woman on a mission.

'Okay, then,' she said, pulling up her collar. 'Let's do it.'

But there was no answer to the bell of Flat One, or to their banging on the door. Fry tried dialling the landline number, and they could hear the phone ringing inside the flat, until the answering machine cut in.

Like many of these houses whose windows looked directly on to the pavement, this one had net curtains and a couple of plants on the window ledge to discourage passers-by from peering inside. It didn't deter Hurst, who pushed her face close to the glass, shaded her eyes with a hand, and twisted herself into a position where she could squint into the sitting room.

She was quite still for a few moments, and Fry began to fidget impatiently, looking up and down the street anxiously, feeling like a potential burglar. Then Hurst started to tap on the window, as if trying to attract someone's attention.

'What is it?' said Fry at last. 'What can you see?'

Hurst straightened up. 'Pretty much what I expected,' she said. 'A cat.'

'That's it, then. A washout.'

'His landlady lives in the house next door.'

'Oh. I think you're right.'

Hurst strode boldly to the door of number six and rang the bell. They heard a dog barking inside. She rang again, and rapped the knocker.

'I remember Ben saying she's quite elderly. She's probably a bit deaf.'

Eventually, a chain rattled and the door creaked open a few inches. An anxious face appeared in the narrow gap.

'Can I help you?'

'Oh, you must be Mrs Shelley?'

'Yes, that's right.'

Fry wondered how Hurst had memorised the name of Ben Cooper's landlady. She couldn't recall him ever mentioning it to her. Though Hurst had been here once or twice in the past, so perhaps it had cropped up.

'We're police officers.' Hurst showed her warrant card. 'I'm Detective Constable Hurst. This is Detective Sergeant Fry.'

Mrs Shelley didn't even look at her ID. From the way she was squinting, she probably couldn't have read it anyway. But she responded with a big smile.

'Oh. You must be friends of Ben's,' she said, opening the door an inch or two more. She peered at Fry, as if she might actually remember her face.

'Yes,' said Hurst. 'We're his friends. Aren't we, Diane?'

'Of course. His colleagues.'

'Do you know where he is, Mrs Shelley?'

'No. Well, he went out a while ago. I couldn't tell you where. At least . . . no, I don't think he said where he was going. You could phone him.'

'We've tried. He doesn't answer,' said Fry.

'Do you want me to give him a message?'

'We were just wondering,' said Fry, speaking up clearly on the assumption that Mrs Shelley was also deaf. 'Well, do you have a key to his flat?'

'Of course I do.'

'We're a bit worried about him, you see.'

'So am I.'

'Could we perhaps . . . ?'

Mrs Shelley hardly hesitated. 'Oh, yes. I'll fetch it, shall I?'

Fry and Hurst exchanged glances while they waited for her to come back. Mrs Shelley had seemed far too eager to co-operate with the request. It was entirely contrary to the advice they were always giving to householders.

'This is wrong,' said Hurst.

'Yes, I know. But . . . ?'

Fry was shocked. Entering Ben Cooper's flat was like walking into the home of a psychopathic serial killer. Not that she'd ever done that – all the murderers she'd ever dealt with had been ordinary people who'd crossed a line. Everyone was capable of doing that, in the right circumstances. You didn't have to be a psychopath.

One wall of the kitchen was covered in cuttings, torn roughly from various newspapers. News reports of the arson at the Light House, and the shocking death of Derbyshire Constabulary civilian scenes of crime officer Elizabeth Petty. Coverage of the funeral, a tribute to the dead woman, a coffin carried by uniformed pall-bearers. *Killed in the line of duty*.

And photos. Lots of photos. Many of them were actually the same shot, but printed in different sizes and different resolutions, cropped to a variety of shapes. Then there were items about the arrest, the suspects being charged. It had been major news in this area. Every detail had been covered.

The media had managed to come up with mug shots of Eliot Wharton and Josh Lane too. Fry couldn't remember whether the press office had released those. It was quite unusual until after the trial, unless a suspect was on the run and the public was being appealed to for help. But in this case it had probably been judged that the public interest was overwhelming.

Towards the bottom of the collage was an obituary of Mad Maurice Wharton himself, the landlord of the Light House at the time it had been closed. The disappearance of the two tourists, David and Trisha Pearson, had been rehashed by the newspapers, of course. That was inevitable. In fact, the whole history of the events at the pub was here – the Whartons' disastrous financial commitments, the debts they couldn't pay back, Maurice's drinking. Then the arrival of the Pearsons in that snowstorm and the fatal consequences, the moorland fires intended to draw attention away from the abandoned pub and the evidence in the cellar. Fry remembered Nancy Wharton complaining that it never came to end, the cleaning and covering over. *The blood always seemed to be there.*

Free space had been left at the bottom of the collage. That would be for the eventual outcome. Verdict and sentence. The ultimate fate of the owners of those two faces, Eliot Wharton and Josh Lane, the men who had burned down the Light House and killed Liz Petty.

'As you can see, he's not here,' said Mrs Shelley.

Hurst turned to her. 'Just ask him to call, would you?' she said.

'Have you got a . . . ?'

Automatically, Fry began to produce her card. But she caught a glance from Hurst. She was probably right. Fry put her card back in its holder and let Becky hand over a card instead. Mrs Shelley tucked it into a pocket of her cashmere cardigan.

'Is he . . . ?' said Hurst tentatively.

'What?'

'Is he all right, do you think?'

The dog began barking again inside the house next door. Mrs Shelley began to edge towards the door.

'He told me he's fine,' she said. 'Just fine.'

Fry looked around at the cuttings again before she left the flat. No, you didn't have to be a psychopath to commit a murder. But it did help.

8

Ben Cooper's Toyota surged through pools of standing water, spray cascading over his bonnet, headlights probing through the rain at a darkened landscape.

For weeks now, he'd been driving around in the rain, with no idea where he was going, or where he'd been. He'd done this many times. Always driving at night, and always surprised when first light came that he was still so near home. It was as if he couldn't escape this area. He was drawn like a moth to a flame, a creature seeking warmth from the sun, but finding only lethal fire.

There was a film he saw once . . . well, there was always a film. In this one, people couldn't escape from a motel. They kept driving away through a tunnel and finding themselves back in the same place, going through the same actions, the same conversations, living the same day over and over. They had no escape.

Sometimes his life seemed to have been written a long time ago by a team of scriptwriters in the back room of a movie studio off Hollywood Boulevard. They'd recorded in advance all the incidents, triumphs and tragedies that would happen to him over the years and showed them on screen. Now and then, the script slipped into cliché. Tragedy, then disaster and another tragedy, until a character was pushed too close to the edge.

But perhaps he'd just watched too many films. There had been so many DVDs from Blockbuster, or late night B movies on TV, too many surreptitious downloads from his favourite torrent site. There would always be an echo of a parallel celluloid world where the same thing had happened to a stranger he didn't know and hadn't really cared about. Some odd, uncomfortable parallel, a shadow flickering behind him in a permanent flashback.

Now he could no longer watch films. There were enough horror stories playing out on the screen inside his head, so many screams reverberating in his memories. Too many real terrors were out there, stalking in the dark.

Some nights, he would drive up to Glossop and head

towards the Snake Pass. There was something cathartic about driving up and up further over the pass, swinging the car round the narrow bends, getting closer and closer to the steep drop off the southern edge, taking the inclines as fast as he could. He loved to watch the cat's eyes flicker past in front of his bonnet, the warning signs flash by on the edge of his vision, a narrow pool of light from his dipped headlights showing a few yards of road ahead, then a great ocean of blackness beyond. It was exhilarating not to know exactly what lay ahead of him in the darkness as he raced towards it. Stone walls flying by, glimpses of chevrons on the tightest bends the only indication of which way he should twist the wheel. He was overwhelmed by the sense of the hills out there watching him from the darkness.

At that time of night there was almost no other traffic on the Snake. He could put his foot down time and again as he reached a bend, letting the car slide across the centre line, heading further and further uphill until he was at the highest point of the pass and beginning to descend again, his wheels turning faster and faster as gravity took the weight of the car and the descent took him back down towards the valley. He would hurtle past the Snake Inn and the lights of a distant farm, slipping under the moors and racing down, down, down. Within a few minutes he'd be heading towards Ladybower, into the spreading arms of the great reservoir, seeing water stretching out dark and glittering to his right. And finally he'd coast towards the traffic lights marking the viaduct and the end of the Snake.

Each time, as he slowed and turned towards Bamford, all that he wanted was to go back and do it over again.

Tonight was different. Cooper had been driving on a straight stretch of road, with rain bouncing off the tarmac in front of him, windscreen wipers beating so hypnotically that he was driving on autopilot.

But he'd found himself on the wrong side of the moors. The realisation brought him to a juddering halt, his car swerving across the road as his foot hit the brake.

On the skyline stood the blackened remains of the Light House pub. Its lights were extinguished now – probably for good, unless the auctioneers, Pilkington and Son, found a buyer with more money than sense. Surely the only option would be to demolish the remaining walls and clear the site.

The old Light House had been a famous landmark, visible for miles, familiar to thousands of visitors to this part of Derbyshire. But any plan to erect a new building in such a prominent position in the middle of a national park? He wouldn't put much money on its chances. More likely, the site would gradually deteriorate and revert to the moorland. The outline of its foundations would disappear under a mass of heather and bracken until it was just one more enigmatic scattering of stones, like so many others in the Peak District.

He wondered if the cellar would be left intact when they demolished the walls. It had hardly been touched by the fire. Perhaps they would just seal it up to make it safe – a few truckloads of rubble tipped into the stairwell below the bar, a slab or two of concrete to cover the delivery hatch. Then it would become a cave, a grave, a dark hole in the ground where people had once lived and breathed. The cellar of the Light House would become indistinguishable from the abandoned mine workings scattered around it on Oxlow Moor.

He'd tried so hard to avoid reminders, to keep a firm control over the little things that could creep under his guard unexpectedly. But there he was, stumbling insensibly into a trap of his own making, acting without thought until he found himself plummeting into the darkness of memory.

He recalled pulling himself up to the delivery hatch in that cellar and peering outside, seeing the white Japanese pickup standing in the pub car park. As happened so often, it was a small detail that had let everyone down. That white pickup had been seen on the first day. It had been noticed by some of the firefighters tackling the moorland blaze that had left Oxlow Moor looking like a post-apocalyptic landscape. But the vehicle hadn't been identified, its owner never traced. If only he'd known that it belonged to Eliot Wharton. Things could have been so different. He ought to have put more effort into tracing the pickup. *Someone* ought to have. But they'd had other priorities.

And that was why Liz Petty had died. She'd only been doing her job, working as a scenes of crime officer, examining Room One at the Light House. It was known as the Bakewell Room, the place where a couple of tourists had died two years previously. Liz had been searching for bloodstains, sweeping for trace evidence. She'd died because he didn't get her out of the pub quickly enough when the fire started. If only he'd been upstairs with her, instead of in the cellar, or had made sure that someone was on watch outside.

That was the way fate swung between life and death. *If only, if only . . . .*

9

Thursday

On Thursday morning, a Derbyshire County Council gully-emptying crew had stopped on the roadside near the patch of woodland. They could see the stream of water running on to the road and forming deep puddles stretching right across the carriageway. They walked along the verge looking for blocked gullies, sucked out some mud and dead leaves, but found it didn't make any difference.

'Where is it all coming from?' one of the crew asked the other.

He shrugged. 'It must be a blocked watercourse somewhere in the woods.'

'I suppose so.'

'Not our problem anyway. Watercourses are the

landowner's responsibility. Them, or the Environment Agency.'

The driver was getting back into the cab, but his mate hesitated.

'It's making quite a mess of the road,' he said.

'So?'

'Well, maybe we ought to check what it is. So we can report it properly.'

'Are you serious?'

'You know what it's like these days – if a motorist has an accident on this stretch of road because of all the surface water, everybody will be looking for someone to blame. We have to make sure that's not us. So we cover our backs. Check it out, and report it to the appropriate people.'

'You're a real stickler, aren't you?'

'Just being realistic, that's all.'

The driver sighed and got back down from the cab. 'Come on, then. Which way do you reckon it's coming from?'

His mate pointed into the trees. 'Up above. Something's not quite right up there in the woods.'

In the CID room in Edendale, Gavin Murfin took a call. He looked at Diane Fry as he put the phone down. 'We've got a body,' he said.

Fry couldn't resist that old surge of excitement. It was what she'd gone to the Major Crimes Unit for. It was what made her life worth living most of the time.

'A body?' she said. 'What are we waiting for?'

'Well, it might only be—'

But Fry had already stacked her paperwork back in her in-tray and was putting on her jacket.

'Where is it, Gavin?'

'A place called Sparrow Wood. It's just off the B5056, west of Brassington.'

Fry hesitated and looked round the office. 'Okay, that's er . . . ?'

'South,' said Irvine. 'It'll take about half an hour.'

'We'd better get going, then.'

'Me?' said Irvine.

'Of course. Are you coming?'

'You bet.'

Grabbing his jacket, Irvine almost ran after Fry as she headed for the door. Hurst watched him go with a sour expression. Fry noticed it only for a second as she turned in the doorway.

'It's going to rain again, you know,' called Murfin. 'It's always bloody raining.'

The water running through the edge of this wood had been no more than a trickle three days ago, according to the local farmer who owned the fields above. It was only a narrow drainage channel, taking a bit of water off the hillside, not even worth the name of a stream or brook.

There was a bigger watercourse to the west where a torrent crashed over rocks and scoured away the roots of trees growing too close to its banks. But some of the flood water had diverted this way and found a route into the channel where the body lay. The past forty-eight hours had filled the channel and overflowed its side, so that the ground for yards around was a swamp, boots squelching six inches deep into sodden peat. The water had dredged soil and debris from both sides. Much of the detritus carried down from the woods up the hill had come to a stop here, clogged up by a blockage in the channel.

The blockage was a man, naked and sprawled out in two feet of muddy water. He was lying on stones with his head tilted slightly backwards, his eyes staring up into the trees, the white protrusion of a toe or a shoulder bizarrely incongruous. From Fry's vantage point on a rocky outcrop, the crime scene looked like a thick soup floating with pale, unidentified vegetables.

'This will be a long job,' said Wayne Abbott, the crime scene manager. 'We're trying to dam the water upstream and divert the flow. At the moment, the water is washing away our forensic evidence even as we watch.'

'What about the water he's lying in?' asked Fry.

'It'll have to be pumped into a temporary reservoir and then sifted through carefully. We can't see what might be in it otherwise. We're working on the practical details. But, like I say . . .'

'. . . it'll be a long job, yes. Did he drown?'

'The medical examiner thinks not.'

'You can drown in a couple of inches of water.'

'True. But only if you're lying face down, I think,' said Abbott. 'Our victim is on his back, and well jammed in between the banks. The water would need to be at least nine inches deep to cover his face, wouldn't it? Besides, the doctor says he's been dead too long. Between thirty and forty hours. The water has only built up since then. We'll know more when they can get him on the slab for a post-mortem.'

Fry nodded. 'Of course.'

Luke Irvine was beside her, looking down at the victim, jotting down details and first impressions in his notebook like an assiduous student.

'Wondering who he was?' asked Fry.

'Obviously. And I'm wondering who he met in these woods for this to happen to him.'

'Do you think it would have been a stranger?'

Irvine seemed to take her question as a test. Would he remember what he'd been taught in detective training?

'Well, an investigation begins with the assumption that there's no such as thing as a stranger murder,' he said. 'In almost all murders, the assailant is known to the victim.'

Fry hadn't really meant it as a test at all. But she could see that Irvine regarded her as some kind of strict schoolteacher who might put him in detention if he forgot his lines. There was no point in trying to explain what she'd really meant – it would take too much time and effort. So she might as well play up to his expectations.

'Well done, Luke. That's almost word perfect.'

Irvine looked at her. 'Yes, the "who" is sometimes easy, isn't it? But the "why" can be a lot more complicated.'

Fry blinked, taken by surprise. That was something that Ben Cooper would have said. She could almost hear him saying it now. Cooper was one who always wanted to look for the complications, to explore the tangled subtleties of people's relationships. He would certainly have wanted to know the 'why'. It was often the place he started from in an investigation, rather than the obvious 'who'.

In the past, she'd never worried too much about the differences in Cooper's approach. Sometimes he got there, but often he didn't. Sticking to the book, following the laid-down procedures – that always worked, eventually. So why was she thinking about what Cooper would say? If he'd been here in the woods alongside her she would have ignored what he said, treated his opinion with contempt, even. But it was another thing when he wasn't here. His absence was more powerful than his presence.

Fry turned to look at the landscape of the White Peak beyond the woods. An isolated farm, a derelict field barn, a couple of old cottages nestling in a narrow valley, trapped in a network of stone walls between wet hills scattered with sheep. It was Ben Cooper country. He should definitely be here.

'Do you think we have a murder, then?' she said.

'It's hard to tell,' admitted Irvine. 'So far, there's no evidence of a struggle, or even of a second person being present. And we'd need to know the cause of death.'

'Right.'

Fry shoved her hands in her pockets. Was it wrong for her to be standing in this damp wood hoping that an unidentified man had been the victim of a criminal act? Probably. This might well have been a suicide or an accidental death. There were certainly more of those around than murders. But her instincts were telling her something different. This man had ended up dead in the stream as a result of someone else's actions.

'Luke, call Becky Hurst and get her down here,' she

said. 'We're going to need another pair of hands before long.'

Although it was daytime, the overcast sky made the woods gloomy, and arc lights had been set up under the trees. Fry had found a remnant of stone wall that was just the right height to sit on while she waited.

When Becky Hurst arrived at the scene, she ducked through the cordon and looked down at the body.

'Look at the way his eyes are staring,' she said. 'Like a blind person.'

'That's probably right,' said Irvine. 'Imagine it was night-time, with a heavily overcast sky. And no source of light nearby. It would have been pitch black out here. I mean, *really* black.'

'Of course,' said Fry. 'So he wouldn't have been able to see a thing.'

'Yes, it's just like being blind,' said Irvine. 'I was visiting one of those show caves in Castleton once with Michelle, and the guide turned off the lights . . .'

'I know all about that,' she said. 'I know about darkness.'

Irvine glanced at her. 'I dare say you do.'

Fry shuddered. There was one thing for sure. Without the benefit of these arc lights, she wouldn't be out here in the woods at night, overcast sky or not. There were too many insects and tiny, crawling creatures waiting to drop on to her face from the trees when she couldn't see them coming. It wouldn't be her choice for a suitable place to commit suicide, or to have an accident. It wasn't her idea of a place to die at all.

She realised that Irvine had kept looking at her, as if he was expecting something. Fry sensed one of those moments when her people skills were about to fail her. She supposed someone other than her would know instinctively how to behave, and what to say. But it was impossible to figure out logically what was required of you: people had to tell you. While Irvine waited, she went back over what he'd been saying.

'Oh,' she said. 'Who's Michelle?'

'My new girlfriend.'

'Great.'

The face of the dead man continued to stare up at the trees, his eyes so close to the surface of the water that they reflected the glare of the arc lights. Strands of fair hair were matted with something dark. Blood? Perhaps.

Fry had felt quite comfortable on the wall until now, but suddenly the stones had started to feel harder, their edges sharper. She shifted uneasily, stood up and paced outside the cordon, until Abbott called her over.

'One of the search teams has found the victim's

clothes. All neatly piled up on a rock. It looks for all the world like he just decided to go for a shallow swim.'

By the time Diane Fry slithered a few yards through the woods, the clothes found by the search team had already been bagged, and markers were placed on the rock. Two SOCOs were struggling to erect a scene tent over the location.

Even in the best of circumstances, the loss of trace evidence from exposure to the weather was a major problem with an open scene like this. Any DNA in the vicinity would be degrading as they watched. And if the rain turned torrential again, the place would become a swamp.

'Do we know what the weather forecast is?' asked Fry.

Irvine pulled out his iPhone and tapped the weather app. 'An eighty per cent chance of rain by four o'clock,' he said.

'Is that thing accurate?'

'Spot on, usually,' said Irvine.

A SOCO handed her an evidence bag. 'There's your victim's ID, Sergeant.'

Fry turned it over to see a mobile phone and the contents of a leather wallet. Driving licence, credit cards, an AA membership card, a small stack of ten and twenty pound notes.

'Glen Turner.'

Hurst immediately made a call to check on the name. 'Yes, he's a misper,' she said. 'He was reported missing yesterday by his mother, Mrs Ingrid Turner. The description she gave fits, too. An address in Wirksworth.'

Fry still found her grasp of local geography was lacking, even after the years she'd spent in this area. 'Wirksworth? How near is that?'

'Pretty close,' said Irvine. 'Five or six miles to the east, I'd say, on the other side of Brassington. It's the nearest small town.'

'How long has Mr Turner been missing, do we know?'

'The mother says he didn't come home on Tuesday night. She waited a while before she reported it because she wasn't sure if it was an emergency or not.'

Fry nodded. It was a common belief that you had to wait twenty-four hours before reporting a missing person, but it wasn't true. You could make a report to the police as soon as you were convinced someone was missing. It sounded as though Mrs Turner had done that.

'We'd better get to the address straight away,' she said.

She called Luke Irvine over and instructed him to find out what car Glen Turner drove and get a search started for it.

'It must be somewhere,' she said. 'He didn't walk out here from Wirksworth. We need to find out as much as we can.'

'About the victim?' said Irvine.

'Of course, Luke. You know that's the starting point in victimology – working out what could have put two people in a particular location at that time. When we can answer that, we'll have a clue about what happened.'

10

Ben Cooper rolled his head over on the pillow and squeezed his eyes tighter shut. Promethazine hydrochloride had filled his head with glue. His limbs lay heavy and deadened, as if his body had been poured full of cement while he slept. His mind was too gummed up for logical thoughts to drag themselves free from the sticky embrace of the sedative.

For the past hour he'd been drifting in that state halfway between sleeping and waking, conscious of noises filtering in through the window, aware of the light flickering on the wall, but unable to dredge up the energy to stir himself. His mouth felt dry, and he longed for water. Deep memories swirled in the dehydrated depths of consciousness, and his body twitched with pain. They were memories filled with heat and flame, smells and sounds that churned and splintered in his mind but refused to coalesce.

A thump on the bed made him automatically stretch out a hand. Hope the cat purred loudly as she rubbed her head against his fingers. Cooper croaked a faint greeting through parched lips. The cat purred more loudly, and gave him a silent cry. He tried to push himself up into a sitting position. Apparently, it was feeding time.

There was no clock in his bedroom. He'd come to rely on his iPhone for the time, but he'd left it switched off for a while now. He wasn't even sure he'd charged the battery recently.

He shuffled towards the kitchen, put the kettle on for instant coffee and prised open a tin of cat food. When the cat was satisfied, he drank his coffee in silence. The taste was dull. But he didn't have the energy or interest to produce something better for himself.

His electric shaver had no charge left either. He'd forgotten it had stopped working yesterday, and he couldn't be bothered finding the charger. It didn't matter, though. Shaving was a nuisance, and there was no one to make the effort for. He wouldn't see anyone again today, except his brother. He tried to look out to see what the weather was doing, but the windows of the flat were filmed with water. He ought to get round to cleaning them some time. At least the rain might run off them, if they weren't so dirty.

The cat stopped eating, and gazed at him in sudden perplexity. Of course, she could sense the tension in the air. She had been restless for weeks, reluctant to stray too far from the back door of the conservatory into the garden, though it was surely a paradise for cats. Maybe it was just the rain she objected to. She'd always made it clear that she didn't like to get her paws wet.

Cooper looked at the clothes he'd been wearing yesterday. They were damp from the rain and streaked with mud, and he'd failed to put anything in the wash basket or leave it out to dry. What was it Dorothy Shelley had said to him? *'Don't catch a chill.'* He almost laughed at the absurdity. Catch a chill? As if a minor physical ailment could compare with the havoc wreaked on the inside.

At times his recollections had a clarity he associated only with the memories of the dying. They said your whole life flashed in front of your eyes in those last few moments. They never said that a few minutes of your life could pass before your eyes over and over, endlessly repeating. Would they never stop until you died?

After Liz's death in the fire at the Light House, the inquest had to be faced. Violent or unnatural deaths always required an inquest. But the coroner didn't perform the role that people often expected. The inquest was only meant to establish the identity of the deceased, the place and time of death, and how the person died. Not the cause, but how they came by their death. The legal difference could be too subtle for bereaved relatives to understand.

Cooper had seen it many times, been asked himself by families to explain it. He'd struggled to make sense of it for people already worn down by grief and now baffled by the system they'd been thrown into. Though witnesses were called, it wasn't a trial. The coroner went to a lot of trouble to make that clear. The verdict would not imply criminal liability. The purpose of an inquest wasn't to attribute blame. Well, of course not. No one wanted to do that. It wasn't politically correct. People weren't responsible for their own actions. It was all due to their upbringing, their genes, the abuse they'd suffered as a child, their disturbed mental state.

He'd heard all that said, and more. A chorus of angry voices, some of them shouting their objections during the hearing itself, but most waiting until afterwards to express their despair. It wasn't the British way, to make a fuss. But sometimes Cooper had been there, the person they could turn to with their feelings, the target for their anger, the man they hoped could put it all right.

Somehow he'd managed to get through his witness

statement. When he looked at his notebook, he thought another person must have written his notes. He couldn't tell. It seemed like a scrawl by some crazed fiction writer in the throes of producing a horror fantasy. It seemed to have nothing to do with him at all, this slow, careful prodding at the facts. The names, the times, the places, the extent and nature of the injuries. None of this was about Liz.

The outcome he feared most was a narrative verdict. It always seemed such a cop-out, an avoidance of judgment. Yes, it worked sometimes for families who didn't want to hear the word 'suicide', a ruling that their loved one had taken his own life while the balance of his mind was disturbed. It helped them to deal with the reality if they could walk away without that fact written down in black and white on an official form. But in terms of justice, it was no more than an evasion.

That hadn't happened. The jury returned a verdict of unlawful killing. Why did that feel such a relief?

And then there was the funeral. It had passed in a dark haze. Derbyshire Constabulary didn't go in for all the ceremony, the way some other forces did. Standing rules said that a serving member of police staff didn't get even a coffin shrouded in a flag, as a regular officer would, though uniformed pall-bearers were provided on a request from the family. Mr and Mrs Petty had been happy with that, though. Simple, dignified. It was all they'd wanted.

Throughout the service and burial, Cooper had felt as though he wasn't really there with the other mourners. He'd been floating above the proceedings, looking down at himself in his black suit and tie, standing in the wet grass at the graveside, indistinguishable from all the others in their funeral clothes, just a flock of black crows squawking dismally in the rain.

Liz's parents lived in Bakewell, and they'd found a corner of the cemetery on Yeld Road for her burial. Relatives from Dundee had arrived, gloomy and Presbyterian, yet first at the bar when the party retreated to a local pub afterwards for the sandwiches and sausage rolls.

Bakewell's cemetery had hit the headlines in the 1970s with the murder there of a thirty-two-year-old typist, Wendy Sewell – the so-called 'Bakewell Tart' case. The place had become notorious all over again in 2002, when the man convicted of the Sewell murder, cemetery worker Stephen Downing, had his conviction overturned after serving twenty-seven years in prison. There was even a TV film, starring Stephen Tompkinson as a local newspaper editor who'd campaigned to get Downing released. Cooper didn't remember the original case, but he was a serving police officer when the inquiry was reopened after Downing's release. This cemetery had a different significance for a lot of people.

Like so many parish churches, the churchyard at All Saints had been closed for burials many years ago. Bakewell's four thousand residents would end up in this cemetery, or in the incinerator at Chesterfield crematorium. There were two chapels at the cemetery, one for Anglicans and one for Nonconformists, neither of them used any longer.

The arrangements had been in the hands of the local funeral directors, Mettams. All very traditional. Handfuls of earth scattered on the coffin. *'We therefore commit the body of Elizabeth Anne Petty to the ground. Earth to earth, ashes to ashes, dust to dust, in the sure and certain hope of the resurrection to eternal life.'*

He supposed his family had been supportive. Well, of course they had. They were all there, Matt and Kate and their girls, and his sister Claire making an appearance. His Uncle John and Aunt Margaret had turned up, both of them well into retirement now and spending most of their time on cruises. The Eastern Mediterranean, Islands of the Caribbean. Their suntans looked out of place among the pale faces huddled in the rain.

When the crowd of mourners had dispersed, he still seemed to be there, a speck among the raindrops, gazing down on the freshly filled grave surrounded by a sea of mud. The ground had been churned by the feet of the mourners as they shuffled and stamped in the rain. Their departure had left a desolate quagmire where once there had been green blades of grass growing in the sun.

This wasn't his world any more. Something was wrong with it, the whole earth was askew. He found he would often turn suddenly, twisting on his toes, holding his breath – thinking that if he was quick enough he might see Liz standing there, or catch a glimpse of her shadow passing from one room to another.

And then there were the lists. Even now, he would sometimes put his hand in his pocket, open a drawer or turn over a cushion and find a list. She'd made a lot of them, one for every aspect of their wedding preparations. They weren't printed out, but written in her own neat hand, which made it worse. He didn't have to read the words, but could recognise her personality in the curl of a 'g' or an 's', the decisive ticks and crosses where firm decisions had been made. He could even identify the colour of the ink, her favourite electric blue ballpoint.

Table decorations, wedding breakfast menus, car hire companies. They were all listed somewhere. The options they'd once discussed were preserved on paper like the enigmatic remains of a distant civilisation, people long gone from the earth but for a few scraps of their hieroglyphics, perhaps significant at the time, but meaningless now, symbolic only of something lost. They were a glimpse into the past, a fragment of a world already dead.

He'd been trying to remember the last thing they'd said to each other. What had been their final words? He couldn't recall. He knew all the words were there, deep in his memory, but he couldn't dredge them up from the sludge. When he tried, all that he found were the more familiar images and sounds, the ones that recurred over and over in his nightmares, all the sensations from the minutes that had seemed like hours as the Light House burned around him. But Liz's voice was missing from his recollection of those last few moments.

Sometimes it seemed the whole universe was outside, trying to get in. So many people called with their expressions of grief and pity that it became one long, meaningless howl.

Emotional numbness had set in soon after the funeral, his feelings becoming anaesthetised even as physical injuries racked his body with agony. It was as if he could only take a single kind of pain at any one time. The bodily anguish he couldn't do anything to resist was pushing the psychological suffering out of his mind, and from his heart.

The human brain had functions that were still incomprehensible. One was its ability to filter out experiences and memories that it considered too traumatic, in order to protect sanity. The trouble was, he knew the physical damage would heal eventually. The sting of the burns would fade, the pain in his lungs would retreat into a background ache. And then his brain would turn off the filter and open the floodgates. When might that happen? Would he have any warning? Or would it poleaxe him in the middle of the street one day, or come crashing into his nightmares one night as he slept?

It was like having an anonymous stalker, a menacing shadow just waiting to pounce when he least expected it. No matter how often he looked over his shoulder, he would never see the darkness coming.

Cooper blinked and flinched, thinking a shadow had passed across his vision, flicking too close to his eyes. A fly, or a moth, or a speck of dirt thrown up by the rain. But there was nothing visible. Nothing real, anyway. Perhaps it was the first sign of that darkness.

11

It was an old cottage, with walls that bowed outwards to an alarming extent. Its roof seemed ready to collapse, its upper windows about to drop into the street if someone didn't push them back pretty quickly. In any other structure or object – a car, a bridge, an aircraft – this would be considered a dangerous level of deterioration and would call for immediate repairs, perhaps even demolition and replacement. But people loved that sort of thing in property. It was called having character.

Inside the house, Ingrid Turner was showing a bit of wear and tear too. She must have been in her sixties, which wasn't a great age. She would only recently have starting claiming her state pension. Many people were ridiculously fit and healthy well into their seventies these days – Fry saw them striding about the Peak District in their shorts and bush hats every weekend. But Mrs Turner had been worn down over the years, and looked an old woman. No doubt the worry about her missing son hadn't helped.

She was holding herself together, though. When she appeared at the door she was hugging her arms around her body as if afraid her disintegration could start at any moment and there would be no one around to pick up the pieces.

Mrs Turner invited Fry and Hurst in straight away, and sat them down in her little sitting room, around a small table covered in a white lace cloth. Place mats were already laid out as if she was expecting visitors at any minute.

Fry broke the news in the best way she could. There was never a right way, she'd found. People had so many different reactions to this kind of situation that you could never hope to anticipate every one. In Mrs Turner's case, there was stone cold denial. She'd turned a deaf ear to what she was being told. She was still waiting for someone to find her son and bring him home.

'Do you live here alone?' asked Fry, wary about what the next stage of her reaction might be. It was always best to keep people talking. A family liaison officer would be in Wirksworth shortly. But, like everyone else, the FLOs were busy, their services too much in demand for the staff available to cope with. For now, it was just her and DC Hurst trying to deal with it.

'There's just me and Glen,' said Mrs Turner. 'It's been that way for years, just the two of us. Why would he want to live anywhere else? I'm his mum, after all. I look after him well.'

'What was Glen's job?'

'He works for an insurance company in Edendale. Prospectus Assurance, they're called. He's been there about twelve years. He's very good at his job, Glen. Very good. Everybody appreciates his work.'

'I'm sure they do. What exactly did your son do?'

'He's a claims adjuster. It's a very responsible position.'

'We'll have to talk to his employers.'

'They're in the address book. I phoned them, but they haven't seen him today. I suppose he'll be in trouble when he gets into work tomorrow.'

It was so disorientating, this way of holding a conversation in two different tenses. Every time she mentioned Glen Turner in the past tense, his mother answered as if he was still alive and about to walk through the door at any moment. It was like being a time traveller, living in the past and present simultaneously.

Fry looked at the white tablecloth. There was an extra

place mat laid, an extra coaster, another cup and saucer, standing waiting for tea to be poured. None of them had taken sugar, but the bowl was there, filled and ready. She would take a bet that Glen had taken at least two spoonfuls in his tea.

'What about friends?' asked Fry.

Ingrid looked round, puzzled. 'There's Mrs Jones across the road. Or Pat Mercer. Pat and I go to the WI together. She's got a little car. All I have is my Mango card for the Sixes bus. I often use the 6.1 service to Derby via Belper.'

'No, I meant friends of your son's,' said Fry impatiently.

Hurst leaned forward to speak to Mrs Turner. 'It is something we ask, you know. I mean, when we have to give news of a death. We suggest contacting a friend to come and sit with the bereaved relative—'

Fry stared at her. 'Yes. Thank you, DC Hurst . . .'

Mrs Turner was looking from one to the other. 'He *is* dead, then? Is that what you're telling me?'

'Yes, Mrs Turner. I'm afraid so. That's what we told you.'

The last thing Fry wanted was to let Becky Hurst take over the interview. But Ingrid Turner seemed to respond to her. It was as if the woman hadn't heard anything that Fry had said to her when they arrived at the house. *Yes, your son is dead.* She must have imagined something like this when she decided to report him missing.

'I'm all right,' said Mrs Turner. 'I'll be all right.'

'Do you have any family, other than Glen?'

'He's my only child. We never had any more kids. And his father died a few years ago. Heart attack, you know. The usual.' She looked at Hurst brightly, as if she was trying her hardest to be helpful. 'I do have a sister in Manchester. She's got children.'

'Perhaps we should call your sister for you,' said Hurst. 'You shouldn't be on your own.'

'Or Pat Mercer,' said Fry.

Mrs Turner began to shake her head, looking thoughtful. 'No, Glen doesn't really have any friends,' she said. 'I don't know why, but he's turned out a bit of a loner. There's nothing wrong with that though, is there? A lot of people are happy with their own company. It doesn't mean anything.'

Fry could see that the initial shock was starting to wear off. The impact of what Mrs Turner had been told was about to hit her. She was running their conversation backwards in her mind until she reached the moment when she opened the door to two police officers and was told that her son was dead. But before she reached that point, it seemed that she'd finally heard Fry's question.

'He's single?' she asked. 'No girlfriends?'

'None that I know of. And I'm sure I'd know.'

'No girlfriends, then. So perhaps a boyfriend . . . . ?'

Mrs Turner began to shake her head emphatically.

'It's nothing to be ashamed of,' said Fry. 'Not these days. It's all fine.'

'No, you don't understand. His father wouldn't have liked it. Clive was dead set in his views on the subject.'

Fry sat back in frustration. Yes, some fathers still cast that shadow, no matter how absent they were. Even the dead fathers, it seemed. Clive Turner wouldn't have liked his son to be gay, so he wasn't. It was as simple as that for Ingrid.

But perhaps it wasn't at all simple for poor old Glen.

'Did Glen have any enemies, then? Had he fallen out with anyone recently? Got himself into trouble of some kind?'

But it was too late. Mrs Turner's mental rewind had reached the critical juncture. Her body sagged, the lines of her face began to crumple and blood suffused her cheeks as her veins swelled with an enormous pressure.

Just like her house, Ingrid Turner seemed about to collapse.

Charlie Dean thought he must be getting paranoid. Everywhere he looked, he seemed to see a hooded figure with staring eyes. He glimpsed it on every street corner in Wirksworth, lurking in every entrance in the area of narrow alleyways people called the Puzzle Gardens. He saw a dark shape at the bottom of the garden when he was showing a young couple round a semi-detached house in Brassington. He felt as though someone was standing waiting in every room of an empty property he'd been asked to value in Cromford.

It was ridiculous, of course. He'd never been the over-imaginative type. Down to earth and reliable, that was Charlie Dean. He left the flights of imagination to the women. Sheena was good at it. And Barbara, too – though the ideas that ran through her mind were always the worst things she could imagine about him. She loved to torment herself like that, creating entire fantasy scenarios in which her husband was always the villain, the cold-hearted monster. She probably pictured herself taking revenge on him for whatever she dreamed he'd done.

Because it had been like that at home since Barbara had convinced herself so firmly of his guilt, Charlie had decided a long time ago that they might as well enjoy some of the things he was considered guilty of. He might as well be hanged for a sheep as a goat. Or something like that.

But that Thursday morning, as he drove back from Cromford to his office at Williamson Hart, the unsettling anxiety that dogged his working day was undermining Charlie Dean's confidence. He wondered once or twice whether Barbara had hired someone to follow him, some thug who'd been given the job of scaring him. If that was the case, he was doing a really good job.

But it was probably a bit too subtle for Barbara. She was the sort of woman who was more likely to cut up his clothes and pour paint over his BMW. He'd promised her the new kitchen extension she'd been nagging him about, and the builders had started delivering materials this week. But no matter how much money he spent, he knew it would never be enough for Barbara.

Charlie pulled into a side road between Steeple Grange and Wirksworth, recognising three little terraces of stone cottages that had been cleaned up and sandblasted, and separated with wrought iron railings. When he'd parked, he dialled a number on his mobile. But when it was answered he found he didn't really know what to say.

'Hi, mate,' he said. 'It's Charlie Dean. How are you doing? Yeah, great. Well, you know . . . not that great, actually.'

Confused by his own indecision, Charlie stared out of his car window at the rows of cottages. Each door was painted a different colour, but all had the same brass knocker. He wondered how he would market one. He liked each of his properties to be unique, with its own special character. That was Charlie Dean's style. He felt it reflected his personality.

'I need you to help me with a little matter,' he said. 'It's a bit delicate, so . . . Oh yeah, funny. You're such a scream.'

He looked down the road towards Wirksworth. He pictured Green Hill and The Dale winding their way up the slopes to the right until they were stopped by the walls of the abandoned quarry. Barbara might be up there at the moment, in their house on The Dale. That is, unless she was out visiting one of her friends, gossiping about him in a sitting room or yakking over a cappuccino at PeliDeli in St John's Street.

'Meet me for a drink,' said Charlie. 'Then we can talk about it.'

12

That afternoon, Ben Cooper was standing on the wall of the Iron Age hill fort at Carl Wark, waiting for his brother. His lungs were sore, and a wheeze escaped from his burning airways with every breath. But his muscles tingled from the steep climb, and that felt good. The clean air on his face was like a refreshing shower.

The entire Hope Valley stretched out in front of him, closed in by the rocky ridge of Stanage Edge and a line of southern moors. He could see over the villages as far as Castleton, with Mam Tor blocking the head of the valley and the grey bulk of Kinder Scout lurking in the distance, its outline obscured by low-lying clouds.

Southwards over Millstone Edge and the hump of Eyam Moor was the town of Edendale. But right now

Cooper couldn't see it, and he didn't want to. From here, he could try to pretend it didn't exist, that the town and everything it contained was a figment of his imagination, a feature of some parallel universe where his life might have taken a different direction. The windows of E Division police headquarters on West Street might seem familiar in his memories, but at this moment they were part of a half-forgotten dream. The ground-floor flat in Welbeck Street was no more his home than was this hill fort.

In his heart, he didn't feel he belonged anywhere, except to the air over the valley and the rain that fell continually on the Peak District. This feeling of dislocation ought to be frightening or unsettling, since he'd valued a sense of belonging so highly all his years. He should be disturbed by the loss of connection with his previous life. Yet he'd never felt so free.

All the time he'd spent in hospital, this was what he'd longed for. There had been windows in the ward, but the view was over the town, grey stone and wet roofs and the occasional curl of smoke. The tiny hint of distant views, the shape of a hill glimpsed in a bank of cloud on the horizon – that only made it worse. It was the taunting detail that made his captivity intolerable.

His brother puffed up the hill behind him. Matt was carrying too much weight these days. He spent so many hours sitting in the cab of his John Deere, letting the tractor do the physical work. He didn't even walk around his fields at Bridge End Farm any more, but used his latest toy, a quad bike.

'My God, why would people have lived all the way up here?' said Matt when he'd got his breath back.

'I don't think they did,' said Ben.

'What? They put all the effort into building this thing, then didn't live in it?'

'As far as they can tell from the evidence. It's a question of interpretation what it was used for. There are theories.'

'I don't like theories. You can't eat them, or put them in your fuel tank.'

This hill fort was one of Ben's favourite places in the Peak District. The views from the top were as spectacular as you might expect, and well worth the slog up the steep slope among the debris of scattered stones. But wonderful views were everywhere in this area. Carl Wark was special because there was nowhere more steeped in history in the whole region. The fort might have been constructed between eight hundred and five hundred BC, but archaeologists said the use of the promontory dated back much earlier, to Neolithic times.

'This might have been a hill fort, or it could have been a ceremonial site of some kind,' he said. 'There are people who say it was a sort of court, a place that tribes could come to for the administration of justice.'

'Really?'

Ben shrugged. 'Like I say, it's another theory.'

'I prefer facts myself.'

'I know you do, Matt.'

'You make it sound as if that's a bad thing.'

Of course, one glance showed that Carl Wark was a natural defensive site, with steep cliffs on three sides and a stone rampart constructed on the fourth. They stood on the edge looking over the ramparts towards Hathersage Moor. It was amazing to think people had built this without tools, with only their time and sweat and determination, hauling materials up the hillside stone by stone until they'd built a wall to protect themselves against the world. Yet people hadn't lived at Carl Wark, but had used it as a refuge and perhaps for religious or ceremonial purposes. In other words, it was a sanctuary.

'Thanks for coming, Matt,' Ben said. 'I know it's difficult taking time away from the farm.'

'Oh, well. The weather's buggered everything up as usual,' his brother said grumpily.

'I know you can always find some jobs to do.'

'Which reminds me,' said Matt. 'Let me have those fencing spikes back. I'm going to need them.'

'I'm sorry, I keep forgetting.'

'Your memory is worse than mine.'

The landscape towards Eyam in the south was a

deep, damp green, washed by the constant rain. Ben had never seen such a vibrant green, nor such a range of shades. It was like looking into an emerald sea, with patches of mist hanging in the cloughs like smoke. They reminded him of the moorland fires, making the scorched skin on his hands sting, the back of his throat choke as if his lungs had suddenly filled again with smoke.

They'd parked on the back road leading into Hathersage Booths and crossed a stile to take the steep climb up Higger Tor. Within fifty yards of the road, it felt as though you'd stepped back in time. The dramatic view across to Carl Wark always made Ben pause for a while before scrambling over the rocks to find the path. Between the tor and Carl Wark, gigantic boulders were piled among the heather, as if a giant had started to build a castle but had got tired and given up. As they approached the fort, he'd been awed as ever by the wall rising above him, almost perfectly preserved as it had first been built all those centuries ago.

Carl Wark used steep natural cliffs as part of its defences. The wall of gritstone blocks at the western end of the fort was about ten feet high with an earth and rubble bank piled against its inside. Sheer cliffs rose to about eighty feet, surrounded by a steep bank. Across the neck of the plateau an L-shaped rampart had been constructed to form an entrance. This two-acre enclosure had been occupied by Roman troops during a Celtic uprising in the first century. And before the Celts? Even the name suggested that the origins of the fort were mysterious or unknown. Carl was a synonym for *T'owd Mon*, the Old Man. Otherwise known as the Devil.

'Are you okay, Ben?' asked Matt.

'Yes. Well – you know.'

Ben realised that the rock behind him felt cold. Far too cold. It was summer, after all. These stones should be warmed by the sun, the ground between them dry and dusty, not trampled with mud. There was definitely something wrong with the seasons. Nature had begun to feel out of order, the natural cycle disrupted by an unnatural event.

But then, there was something wrong with the rest of the world, too.

Next week should have been his wedding but his fiancée, Liz Petty, had died in a fire at the abandoned Light House pub. No, not just a fire, but arson. A deliberate attempt to harm, to kill, to destroy evidence of an earlier murder. That was what it should always be called. Just like the blazes which had destroyed large swathes of the Peak District National Park, the fire at the Light House had been no accident. Whether through recklessness or malice, there was always someone to blame.

If he couldn't see Edendale from here, he was

certainly in no danger of catching a glimpse of Oxlow Moor. The blackened remains of the pub still stood on a stretch of that moor, in the west beyond the Eden Valley. It was difficult now for him to drive that way out of town, except in the dark. The Light House itself had been extinguished, so it no longer lit up the skyline as it had done for so many years.

'Time,' said Matt. He hesitated, then stopped speaking, as if he'd lost track of his thoughts . . . Or, more likely, he'd realised the utter futility of completing the sentence.

'I hope you weren't going to say that time heals everything,' said Ben, 'that things might look bleak now, but everything will be marvellous again in a few months? That I just need some time to get over it?'

'Something like that, I suppose. I'll not bother, then?'

'We'll take it as read, shall we?'

Ben wished people would just stop saying these things. It made Liz's death sound so inevitable. As if it was part of some great pattern, a universal plan. Just time passing from one month to the next. The cycle of the seasons. The leaves on the trees growing, dying, falling.

But this wasn't inevitable. It was a person's death, and it should never have happened. It might not be the end of the world for everyone. But it could still feel like it for him.

'So what's the news on a trial?' asked Matt. 'You know – the son. The crazy youth.'

'Eliot Wharton. He's been remanded by the magistrates again. He'll appear in Crown court, but probably not until next year.'

'Oh God. Why does it seem to take forever?'

Ben shrugged. 'It's the way things work. The accused has to be given a chance to prepare his defence.'

'I think it's bollocks. What about the barman?'

'Josh Lane? You know about him.'

'He's still out, wandering around scot-free?'

Ben found he couldn't reply. His throat had constricted and the words were jammed in his larynx, immovable and painful, like a sharp splinter of bone from something indigestible.

During the past few weeks, Matt seemed to have grown used to getting no reply from his brother. They'd never spoken all that much before, had never really needed endless conversation to understand each other. But now Matt simply accepted a silence, without questioning whether it was the result of physical incapacity, or a more emotional form of pain.

'At least that bastard who ran the Light House didn't survive,' he said. 'Good riddance, I say.'

Ben nodded. The former landlord of the Light House, Maurice Wharton, had died not long after the fire at his empty pub. Known universally as 'Mad Maurice', he had been suffering from inoperable pancreatic cancer, and he'd passed away in St Luke's Hospice right there in Edendale. His signed confession was on file at West Street, but it was useless without forensic evidence or some corroboration from witnesses. Maurice had already been dying back then, with only a few weeks of pain-filled existence left to him. He would never have been dragged into court, even if he'd lived long enough.

Of course, there was his son. The crazy youth, as Matt called him. Though according to the psychiatric reports he wasn't really mad at all, any more than his father had been. Young Eliot Wharton was now on remand in Risley awaiting trial. He'd been granted an escorted visit to Edendale for his father's funeral a little while ago. The Coopers had stayed away from that. It had been too recent and too raw, the whole show too public.

But it had been impossible to escape completely. Ben had read in the papers that the church had been full. Many of the mourners had been former customers of the Light House, who wanted to remember the old Mad Maurice they'd known and treasured for his famous irascibility. Others in church were merely curious, or ghoulish. Some were anxious to get a glimpse of the widow, or of Eliot himself and his prison escort – hoping to see him in shackles perhaps, like a Death

Row inmate on the chain gang. A few just wanted to be present at an event they regarded as a piece of history – no different in essence from attending the London Olympics, or taking part in a Diamond Jubilee street party. It was in the papers and on the news. The TV cameras were outside. They might get interviewed by the BBC. And that was enough of a draw. Maurice Wharton had attracted attention, even in death.

The Crown Prosecution Service had yet to decide how many charges they would finally proceed with against Eliot Wharton. There might be two allegations of murder, and one of attempted murder. If a guilty plea was agreed with the defence, one of the charges might be reduced to manslaughter. That would suggest Liz's death had just been an unfortunate outcome, the unintended consequence of arson and criminal damage.

Well, at least the young Wharton would end up in prison, somewhere like Dovegate or Gartree. That much was pretty certain. Risley wasn't a pleasant place to spend your time on remand, but it was nothing compared to some of the Category B prisons that a lifer could be sent to. In the final reckoning, the system would have enacted its flawed version of justice.

'You don't still believe in the justice system, do you?' said Matt. 'You can't now, not after everything that's happened.'

He picked up a lump of rock and squeezed it tightly.

It filled his huge fist and Ben expected to see it shatter into fragments at any moment. Instead, his brother drew back an arm and hurled the rock as far as he could. It bounced off the top of the massive wall and flew out into space. Ben heard it a few seconds later, rattling down the slope, the sound getting fainter and fainter until it finally stopped.

'I mean,' said Matt. 'That barman. How can he not be locked up? It's a travesty.'

Yes, there was the barman. Josh Lane. That was a different case entirely. The CPS had concluded there wasn't enough evidence to make a charge of murder stand. No one involved in the incident at the Light House could be persuaded to testify that the barman had taken part in the fatal assault on two tourists, David and Trisha Pearson, who had died at the Light House more than two years ago.

He had certainly been present at some stage in Room One, the Bakcwell Room, where the Pearsons had been staying. But the tiny quantity of his blood recovered from the crime scene was too little to prove that he'd been involved in a fight. Lane had confessed to helping to deal with the aftermath. The DNA profile obtained from the blood trace by forensics put him at the scene, so he had little choice. But the blood was only from a scratch, he said.

After the amount of time that had passed, and as a

result of the clean-up carried out by the Whartons in Room One, nothing else could be proved. There were too many evidential weaknesses. No realistic prospect of a conviction. It was in the nature of the criminal justice system that the outcome of a case depended on the way a story was told. The prosecution presented a narrative which depicted the defendant as guilty. But the defence would tell a very different story, an alternative version of the same real-life events. They would dwell on the possibilities, highlight the ambiguities that the prosecution had tried to ignore. A change in emphasis was all that was needed to cast new light on a situation, to suggest a defendant's innocence, to put that all-important reasonable doubt into a juror's mind.

So the more serious charges had failed the Full Code Test at the evidential stage, and the CPS had no choice but to refuse to charge. A case which didn't pass that stage couldn't proceed, no matter how serious or sensitive it might be.

Instead, Lane had been charged with two counts of perverting the course of justice, once after the death of the Pearsons, and once for the assistance he'd given to Eliot Wharton in the arson case. And now he was out on bail. Cooper had details of the address specified in the bail conditions, and knew that Josh Lane was currently living in a park home near Cromford.

'Perhaps we should do something about it,' said Ben. 'Don't you think?'

Matt froze. After a moment, his chin sank and his shoulders hunched up towards his ears. Ben hardly dared to look at him. He knew the expression that he'd find on his brother's face. A pig-headed stubbornness. He'd been like that all his life, but became more and more stubborn when he knew he was in the wrong. If pushed, he'd dig himself in and become impossible to shift. He was like an old tree stump that needed explosives to root it out of a field to make way for the plough.

It was only what he'd expected. People had become so predictable, and there seemed to be no exceptions. He walked a few paces away, letting the wind blow in his face. He could see the clouds moving over the valley from Mam Tor, growing darker and darker as they came. It would rain again soon.

13

Fry had visited Prospectus Assurance before. She recognised the buildings rather than the name. Perhaps the company had changed hands or rebranded itself. That happened all the time, small outfits being swallowed up by bigger and bigger ones, almost always followed by a new name and a different image. All those changes made it difficult to keep track of a company's history – and perhaps that was the whole point of the exercise.

Nathan Baird was thin and angular, and dressed in a suit that hung all wrong for his shape. He had dark designer stubble and little wings of sideburn which seemed intended to enhance his already sharp cheekbones. Sharp was a good word for him. He was on the young side, too, to be Glen Turner's line manager and sitting in a separate office of his own, away from the cubicles and rows of computer terminals with operators mouthing their lines into head microphones, like a set of Britney Spears imitators. He clutched at the oak finish desk in front of him as if it was a form of protection or security. A symbol, perhaps, of his position in the hierarchy.

'Glen, Glen. I can't get over it,' Baird was saying. He shook his head, the empty shoulders of his suit jacket flapping like the sides of a tent in a stiff wind.

'Did anything unusual happen here on Tuesday?' asked Fry, when she and Irvine had been shown into his office.

'What? With Glen Turner, you mean? No, nothing unusual. Was that the day he died?'

'It seems so. He came into work as normal, then?'

'He came in as normal, left as normal at the end of the afternoon. I'm sure he did a normal day's work in between. That was Glen, really. Nothing out of the ordinary.'

'Was Mr Turner a good worker?' asked Fry. 'He'd been with you for quite a while, we understand.'

'With Prospectus, yes,' said Baird. 'I haven't been his line manager all that long. Personally, I'm a bit of a high-flyer, you might say. I had my talents spotted. So Prospectus poached me from—'

'Yes, sir. But Mr Turner?'

'Ah, well. Glen was never a high-flyer of any kind. But solid enough, I suppose.' He looked round the office. 'I can get someone to dig a bit of information out of his personnel file, if you want.'

'That would be useful, sir. But your personal impressions are more helpful at this stage.'

Baird steepled his bony fingers together and smiled as if she'd paid him a compliment. Did he think that *everything* was about him? Well, maybe it was. Fry found herself hoping that the inquiry would turn up some form of secret relationship between Glen Turner and his manager, which would allow her the chance to get Baird in an interview room without the security of his office and desk.

First, Baird signalled to someone through the glass partition, and a youth appeared at the door. He had red cheeks and wore a tie loosely knotted round an unfastened shirt collar, as if he was still at school and making a statement about his resistance to the uniform. Baird gave him instructions for the personnel file, and he scurried off. A blonde woman seated at the end of the row of desks watched him go, and cast a curious glance into the manager's office. Somehow, Baird seemed to be aware of her interest.

'You can't use one of the girls for that sort of job now,' he said. 'It would be considered sexist. We operate on very strict equality guidelines here at Prospectus Assurance.'

'I'm glad to hear it. I'll bear that in mind if I'm ever looking for a change of career,' said Fry.

Baird studied her as if she'd just come in for a job interview. 'Well, you'd probably bring some unique abilities to the job, Sergeant. Are you interested in insurance?'

Fry swallowed a response, aware of Luke Irvine hiding a smile. There was no point in explaining to someone like Baird that she'd been joking. If he didn't see it the first time, she was wasting her breath. He probably imagined she was so impressed with such a high-flying manager that she was desperate to work for him.

'I'm sure you're busy, sir,' said Fry. 'So perhaps we could concentrate on Glen Turner.'

'Indeed. My personal impressions.'

'I'm wondering in particular if Mr Turner seemed worried about anything recently. Did he have any problems at work? Any disciplinary issues?'

'No, no. We're a happy ship here in Claims. No problems. Or, if there are, I soon sort them out. My door is always open. The staff know that.'

Out of the corner of her eye, Fry could see the flushed youth hovering a few yards away on the other side of the partition. He was clutching a manila file, but he didn't seem to know what to do with it. Should he wait until he was summoned into the office? Or did the task of fetching the file give him permission to knock on the door and interrupt? She could see the conflict written all over his face and in his nervous body language.

'Your staff are happy to come and talk to you, sir?' asked Fry.

'Of course, any time. Look at my ID. My badge says "Nathan", not "Mr Baird" or "Team Leader" – even though that's what I am.'

'Very good.'

That was using symbolism as a substitute for people skills, as far Fry was concerned. A badge was an awful lot cheaper than employing someone who actually knew how to manage staff. But it was nothing new, and certainly not unique to Prospectus Assurance. Police forces used it all over the country. Everyone did, if it cut costs.

'So how much do you know about Mr Turner's personal life?'

'His personal . . . ?'

'His life outside the office. His home, family, his personal relationships, his interests?'

'Well. Er . . .'

'Did you ever speak to his mother, for example?'

'Why would I speak to his mother?'

'That's who Mr Turner lived with.'

Baird laughed. 'Is it? He was, what? Thirty-eight? And he lived with his mum?'

'Mrs Turner was advised by a police officer to phone here when she reported that her son hadn't come home. So who would she have spoken to, if it wasn't you, sir?'

He waved a hand vaguely in the direction of the cubicles. 'I don't know. Someone out there. The switchboard wouldn't have put a call like that through to me.'

Baird seemed to notice the hovering youth outside for the first time, and gestured to him irritably. The young man came in and handed him the file without a word.

'Thank you, Aaron,' he said.

He waited until the boy had gone, and grimaced at Fry. 'Aaron, I ask you. Why do so many parents give their kids these ridiculous biblical names?'

Fry hesitated. 'Perhaps they've never read the Bible and wouldn't know a biblical name when they heard one, Nathan.'

'You're probably right. Ignorance is everywhere.'

He thumbed casually through the personnel file as if he'd never set eyes on one before and wasn't really interested in seeing one now.

'Glen Turner, yes. Glen was a multi-line adjuster.'

'Meaning what?' asked Irvine.

'He handled different types of claim. Some adjusters

just deal with property claims, or liability cases like motor accidents or personal injuries. Turner had the experience to handle more than one type. He was multi-line.'

'I see. Does that mean he was particularly good at the job?'

Baird smiled at Irvine. 'Well, not necessarily. And certainly not in Glen's case. I'd say from his employment record that he was competent across the board, but not brilliant at anything in particular. You know the sort of employee I mean?'

'Yes,' said Fry. 'I believe we have that sort of employee in the police service too.'

'Of course you do. If he was outstanding in any specific area, it's likely he would have been promoted long before now.'

'Ah. Well, that's where our areas of business differ, then.'

He looked at her expectantly, with a faint smile. This time, he'd almost recognised the joke from her tone of voice, but seemed to be waiting for a punchline. When it didn't come, he continued as if she hadn't spoken at all.

'My personal impressions, that's what you asked for. Well, I think the word I'd use about Glen is "geeky". He was a hard worker, no doubt about it. He'd studied the business, gained his qualifications and all that. But

I never got the impression he had any wider awareness of the day-to-day issues that his policyholders had to deal with.'

'No personal experience of life, then. And no outside interests, perhaps.'

'Yes, you're right. I think that's what it was. Good insight.'

'All part of the job,' said Fry.

'Well, that meant Glen didn't have much conversation. It made him a bit boring, you know. And insurance isn't supposed to be boring.'

'Isn't it?'

Baird waved a hand, as if swatting a small fly. 'Absolutely not. It's a common misconception among the public. Here in Claims, we deal with claimants in all kinds of difficult circumstances. You'd be surprised, you really would. We have to learn how to deal with people sensitively.'

'I'm sure you do. None of us ever stop learning, do we?'

He clasped his fingers together in mock delight. 'I certainly hope not. I look forward to learning new things every day at Prospectus Assurance.'

Fry looked down at the file Baird had handed her. It was pretty thin. Its slimness suggested that Glen Turner's employers knew as little about him as his team leader claimed. She wondered what new things Turner had been learning during his time at Prospectus. Whatever they were, she suspected they weren't recorded in this file. Luke Irvine ought to have taken up the questioning when she paused, but Fry realised he wasn't going to.

'You have a lot of female employees here, Mr Baird,' she said.

'Certainly. They're good workers. They don't last very long, mind you. About eighteen months on average. We have quite a bit of churn in this department.'

'Churn?'

'Turnover. Old staff leaving, new employees arriving. It's like a revolving door sometimes.'

'They go on to do other things?'

'They take up all kinds of opportunities when they leave Prospectus Assurance. We give them a good grounding in essential work skills, and they go off to make use of them elsewhere.'

Fry nodded. Or more likely they couldn't stand the job for any longer than eighteen months. She wouldn't last anywhere near that long herself if she had Nathan Baird as a manager.

She looked at the row of call handlers. 'Did Glen Turner have any relationships with the female staff?'

'Certainly not.'

'It has been known.'

'It's against policy. We try very hard to discourage it.

During working hours, at least. That would be very inappropriate.'

'I wasn't suggesting they were going at it in the stationery cupboard all day long,' said Fry.

Baird looked shocked. 'I should hope not. What sort of company—?'

'But relationships are often formed in the workplace, aren't they? Everyone knows that. It's the most common way of meeting a future partner. So it's a perfectly reasonable question. One of these women working out there in the cubicles, perhaps? They must stop for a break occasionally, since they're not robots. What about the blonde one at this end, in the blue sweater? The woman who keeps looking this way, wondering what we're talking about?'

Baird's eyes flickered rapidly backwards and forwards in a desperate effort not to look at the woman Fry was referring to. Of course, he was afraid she would meet his eye, and that would be a complete giveaway. He began to go faintly pink with the strain.

'I—' he said. 'Well . . .'

Fry could have put him out of his misery and told him she'd guessed several minutes ago. His reaction to the hook she'd offered confirmed her supposition. But she let him stew for a while, and watched him shuffle uncomfortably on his chair. They were both aware that the blonde woman was staring unashamedly now, no doubt seeing Baird's discomfort and recognising that something was wrong. Fry turned slightly and gave her a smile. It wasn't her friendliest smile. The woman flushed, straightened her headset, and went back to her screen.

She looked back at Baird again.

'What's her name?'

He cleared his throat nervously. 'Dawn.'

'Married?'

'I . . . Well, it's not . . .'

Fry shook her head. 'It doesn't matter, sir. We're not investigating *your* affairs, are we?'

'Er, no.'

'But your friend Dawn might have mentioned something.'

'I never knew Glen Turner to show any interest in the female employees. And I've never heard it spoken about by . . . well, by any of the staff . . . that he made approaches of that kind. It's the sort of thing you do hear about in an office environment, if it happens.'

'Or you notice it,' said Fry. 'Those little glances.'

'Exactly.' He coughed. 'There was none of that with Glen. I'm quite sure he just wasn't interested.'

'Pity.'

'Pity?'

'It's often the first place we look, a relationship gone

152

wrong. You know, the two main motives for murder – money and sex.'

'I understand.'

Baird was relaxing now. He thought he'd got through the interview pretty well, all told. He gave her that expectant little smile again, though now there was a tiny tremor around his mouth that he couldn't control.

'So what's your next move, Sergeant?' he asked eventually.

'Well, we'll be following up any leads we can.' She tapped the file. 'Perhaps there'll be some information in here that will be helpful to us.'

'I hope so.'

'But I still need to ask you whether Mr Turner knew anybody well in the office. Perhaps not a sexual relationship, but was there someone he had lunch with, or talked to during a coffee break? Did he go to the pub after work?'

'To the pub? No, not Glen.' Baird looked thoughtful. 'Well, I suppose the person he knew best in the office would be Ralph Edge. He's a claims fraud analyst, works on the next floor up. I'd say they had a few things in common, Ralph and Glen. Being a bit geeky was one of them.'

'We need to see his work area,' said Fry.

'It's just down the corridor here. I'll show you.'

'Thank you, sir.'

Fry and Irvine followed him along a few yards of carpeted passage and into another room, where Baird gestured at a desk.

It might as well have been an unused space, for all the personal signs that Glen Turner had left. Most people who spent a lot of their time in office environments tacked up family photos on their partitions or stuck humorous slogans on the computer casing. *You don't have to be mad to work here, but it helps*. Fry had never gone in for the practice herself, but she understood that other people did. It was a kind of ownership ritual, she supposed – marking out your territory. Individuals wanted to feel that their colleagues and employers would remember something about them, even if they weren't actually present.

But Turner didn't seem to have had any worries about that. When Fry looked at his desk, she felt that he'd never been here. Even if he'd been present, the desk wouldn't have told her anything about him.

'May we take a look?' she asked Baird.

'I suppose so.'

She nodded at Irvine, who began to open a few drawers. They contained nothing but stationery supplies, fresh notebooks, a selection of pens, a copy of a book called *Birds' Modern Insurance Law*.

'No personal items,' said Irvine.

'He must have had a computer,' said Fry. 'Mr Baird?'

'Of course. He had a rugged laptop, with armoured casing. Standard issue for this job. They're vital on site.'

'But it's not here,' said Fry.

Baird shrugged. 'I suppose he must have had it with him. It might be in his car.'

By the time they returned to Nathan Baird's office, the cubicles were empty and the line of work stations deserted, a headset abandoned on each desk. No more claims would be handled at Prospectus Assurance tonight. Policyholders would have to wait until tomorrow to be dealt with sensitively.

'Ralph Edge?' asked Irvine as they walked down the corridor towards the exit.

Fry surveyed the empty rooms on either side. 'It looks as though everyone's gone home.'

'We could visit him at home.'

'It'll do tomorrow,' said Fry. 'We should have some initial post-mortem results in the morning. At least then we might have a better idea what sort of questions we should be asking.'

Their DI, Paul Hitchens, was waiting to hear from them when they returned to West Street. Fry brought Hitchens up to date, and he promised to keep the bosses in the loop. It was a makeshift briefing, though. No one wanted to believe they had a murder on their hands.

Without Hitchens having to say as much, Fry knew that he was far happier to believe they were looking at an incident of accidental death, or suicide.

Those incidents happened, of course. Some of the methods of suicide people worked out for themselves were bizarre enough. And when you thought about them, you realised they could only have been devised by someone whose mind was disturbed.

Charlie Dean heard about the discovery of a body on the local news that evening. As soon as he'd listened to the sparse details, he knew he needed to contact Sheena. They had emergency code to use, a signal by text message to indicate if one of them felt they need to speak urgently.

Barbara was on the phone to a friend again. She was grumbling about not having any new clothes and never going out anywhere. Nothing was ever right for her. But at least it meant she was totally absorbed in her own affairs, and wouldn't notice what he was doing.

When he got the return text from Sheena, he knew it was safe to call her. He stepped into the garage and closed the door. The sight of the BMW reminded him of what he'd found on the boot yesterday morning, and he turned his back to whisper into his phone, as if the car itself had ears.

'Sweetheart, have you heard the news? They've found a dead body. In those woods, you know—'

'Yes, I heard.'

'We can't say anything.'

'But, Charlie, there was that man—'

He cut her off. 'If we so much as mention it, we'll have to give statements to the police. They'd ask endless questions. Full details, Sheena. We'd have to explain what we were doing there at that time of night.'

'Oh, God. Jay would murder me.'

'Exactly.'

'We can't do that, Charlie.'

'That's what I'm saying.'

'I suppose I'd say something stupid, wouldn't I?'

'Well, we can't risk that, can we? Think of Jay.'

'And Barbara.'

Dean sighed. 'Yes, and Barbara.'

'I'll see you soon, won't I?'

'Yes, tomorrow. Just as we arranged.'

'That's great, Charlie.'

Irritably, Charlie ended the call and went back into the house. He hated it when Sheena talked about Barbara. It seemed wrong, hearing his mistress mention his wife. It was as if she'd called out the wrong name when they were having sex. It was just wrong.

Barbara had become really odd about sex in the last few years. So it was her own fault, really. She'd never recovered from the day she encountered a naked rambler on the roadside at Priestcliffe. He'd been dressed only in a rucksack and bush hat.

For many people, he wasn't just a naked rambler but *the* Naked Rambler, who had been on TV, but appeared far more often in magistrates courts charged with indecent exposure. He'd been rambling on a chilly November day too, so the shock factor ought to have been pretty small.

But an excuse was an excuse. Charlie supposed he ought to take it as a compliment that she even bothered to think a justification was necessary. He'd feel better about the whole thing when he'd sunk a few drinks tonight.

14

Ben Cooper peered into the distance to pick out the distinctive shape of Mam Tor. The mountain couldn't be seen from Carl Wark until you walked through the entrance and up on to the banks behind the walling. Then the dark, brooding silhouette suddenly appeared on the horizon. Mam Tor, the Mother Heights, the Shivering Mountain. And the destroyer of the old A625 too, the road which was swept away in the 1970s by tons of shale cascading from its fragile slopes.

Mam Tor was the site of another hill fort, and a Bronze Age settlement. It was strange to think of people looking out over this same valley two thousand years ago and perhaps seeing each other's fires in the distance.

What would they have been signalling? A friendly communication? Or a warning?

'I'm worried about you, Ben,' said Matt behind him.

Ben didn't turn round to look at him. He knew what expression he would see on his brother's face.

'There's no need,' he said.

'There is. I'm really bothered.'

'And there's really no need for you to be.'

'I'm concerned that you're still eaten up with guilt,' said Matt. 'There's no reason for you to feel guilty, Ben. None at all.'

'So you've said.'

'And I'll say it again and again, until you get the message.'

Ben didn't feel like arguing with his brother today, no matter how wrong Matt was. And Matt had definitely got it wrong. Wherever there was death, there was always guilt.

He recalled that although everything he could see from here was part of Derbyshire, Carl Wark itself had the distinction of being outside the county. It had been moved into South Yorkshire some time in the 1970s when local government boundaries were reorganised. The county border ran below him, past the remains of an old rain gauge and along the bottom of Millstone Edge to Surprise View. In a way, it felt even more like a refuge because of that. When he was on Carl Wark, he was outside his own territory, standing beyond the edge, existing for a while in the safer fringes of his world.

And safety was hard to find these days. Hard for anyone, it seemed. But perhaps he'd just been in the job too long. He'd seen all kinds of human cruelty.

'It's fine, Matt,' he said.

'No, it's *not* fine. None of this is fine at all!'

Ben looked up, startled by his brother's angry reaction. It took a lot to get an emotional response from Matt. He wondered what he'd done to provoke it. All he'd said was *'It's fine.'*

Right now, he was standing in the Dark Peak, looking south towards the more gentle hills of the White Peak. Those two distinct geological halves of the Peak District had always represented good and evil to him, one of those over-imaginative thoughts that he tried to keep to himself when he was among his colleagues. Dark and white, good and evil. It was obvious, really. Good and evil were right there in the landscape, laid out in front of him. He only had to make a decision. He had to decide which direction to head in from here. It was as simple as that.

'Will you help me, Matt?' he said. 'To put things right?'

'No. Not if you mean what I think you do.'

'But you're my brother.'

161

'No. I won't help you to destroy yourself, Ben.'

'Matt, please—'

'Find someone else.'

Matt stamped off towards the top of the path, and a few moments later Ben heard him clattering over the loose stones like a herd of clumsy cattle.

He didn't watch his brother leave, but remained gazing at the hills on the north side of the valley. The heather was coming into flower on the moors all across the Peak District. In late summer, many visitors came just to see the distinctive swathes of colour, the unending blanket of reddish-purple that had appeared on thousands of postcards and holiday snaps. But it needed sun to bring out the colour, and it looked doubtful whether Derbyshire would get any this year. The heather flowers would stay wet and dull under these overcast skies.

Ben found he was experiencing a sensation he sometimes had as a teenager – that he was the only real person in the world and everyone else was just playing a part, a bunch of extras acting out an elaborate pantomime around him. He couldn't imagine these people having separate lives once they went out of the door and disappeared from sight. It seemed as though they existed only to perform a function, to be mere props on his stage, accessories to his needs and desires. He was the centre of the universe, its reason and purpose.

All the thoughts and feelings in the world went on inside his head, and no one else could understand what it was like. How could they, when he was unique?

He supposed it was a failure of empathy. The part of his brain that made connections with other human beings was currently unavailable. He was unable to see the world from any point of view but his own.

Ben frowned, realising he was quoting to himself from a textbook on criminal psychology. That lack of empathy? It sounded like the classic definition of a psychopath.

Finally, he turned and looked down. He could make out his brother, hunched in a blue cagoule and a woollen hat as he stumbled down the slope and kicked angrily at a loose stone that went tumbling towards the road.

As he stood on the edge of Carl Wark, Ben seemed to hear a voice over his shoulder. It was probably just the trickle of water over rocks, the sigh of wind through the ancient ramparts, the muttering of a solitary ewe, damp and lost as it clattered on the scree slope. But for a moment he believed it was a ghostly communication, the echo of some tribal holy man whose spirit had been trapped for ever in these stones. He tilted his head and listened, trying to distinguish the words, or at least some recognisable sound that would reassure him it was just his imagination. But all the voice seemed to talk about was vengeance.

When people spoke about closure and moving on they hadn't a clue what they were saying. They didn't know what it was like to have this devil riding on your back, a fiend that you couldn't throw off. He was possessed by this idea, as much as by any demon.

But his voice was hoarse, and he burst into a spasm of painful coughing. In the bar, smoke travelling across the ceiling hit a wall and rolled down to floor level. His mouth was parched, his throat sore from the smoke penetrating his mask. His eyes streamed with tears so that he could barely see, even if the smoke hadn't plunged the pub into unfathomable darkness.

He fumbled blindly along the wall, found a steel bar under his fingers, and a door behind it. The fire exit. At first, the bar wouldn't move. Crying out in frustration, he banged at it with his fists, kicked out at it, thumped it again. Finally, he spun round and grabbed the empty fire extinguisher, swung it hard against the bar and felt it give way.

But he must have inhaled too much smoke. He was getting confused. He didn't know where right or left was, didn't know where the doors were, felt as though he couldn't breathe at all.

Irritants hit his eyes and the back of his throat. He could barely open his eyelids. He retched and took a deep breath, in involuntary reaction. The smoke he inhaled was disorientating, dizzying. He went down on his knees. He knew he was giving way to the carbon monoxide, but he was unable to fight.

Now he saw shadows in the smoke, flickering and shimmering, dancing and shuddering, fading in and out. Was that a figure outlined against the flames? The smoke was black and thick and choking. Boards over the windows were burning.

Glass shattered, and a blast of air exploded the flames into a great, roaring blaze, a wild beast devouring the furniture, ripping up the floor, stripping paper from the walls. A sheet of fire rolled across the ceiling and engulfed the room.

'Liz!'

His voice came as a feeble croak, and there was no answer.

Cooper thought he glimpsed a movement near him in the smoke. He reached out for an indistinct shape like a hand, but grasped at empty space and found himself falling forward into darkness, until his face hit the floor and his mind swam into swirling oblivion as he lost that last shred of consciousness.

All around him was shouting and screaming, a muffled roaring noise. The crash of falling stone. And the screaming.

Then silence.

15

At Sparrow Wood, a section of road had been sealed off, all the way from a point just past the nearest farm access to the turning for Brassington. Marked police vehicles had been positioned diagonally across the road at either end, and officers stood miserably in the rain in their yellow waterproofs to turn cars back and point drivers to the diversions set up through nearby villages.

From a traffic point of view, it was lucky this was such a quiet road. But from Fry's perspective, hoping to track down a few potential witnesses to the crime, it was bad news.

As she approached the scene, officers in boiler suits were conducting a search along the roadside verge, close to the strip of woodland. They were looking for recent tyre marks that would reveal the presence of a vehicle. They might find shoe prints in the mud, a piece of clothing, some item accidentally discarded in the grass. In fact, they were hoping for anything that might indicate why Glen Turner had ended up dead in the woods, and who else had been there at the time.

Most of the B5056 was bordered by dry-stone walls on both sides. Like so many roads in the Peak District, those walls left no room for a vehicle to stop or draw in without blocking the carriageway; there was only a thin strip of grass not even wide enough for someone to walk on. So the search team's efforts would be concentrated on a stretch of about three hundred yards where the line of trees skirted the road. There was a five-foot-wide boundary of muddy ground here, a few shallow pull-ins, and a stile where a wooden fingerpost pointed to the start of a public footpath through the woods. Some lengths of wall had collapsed on the uneven ground and the remnants were no more than two feet high, making it easy to step over from the road.

Where the small stream ran down the hillside, a culvert had been built to take it under the roadway. Since the stream had been dammed above the crime scene, the culvert was dry. An officer in wellington boots and long rubber gloves was patiently sifting through the accumulated silt in the channel.

Judging by the smell, the culvert hadn't been cleaned

out for decades. Fry couldn't bear to look inside. She imagined a sewer pipe sludged up with stinking litter, the bodies of dead rats, decomposing leaf mould – all the crap that built up over the countryside like a second, rotting skin.

She paused for a moment despite the smell. Though the flow into the culvert had been stopped, the weed-filled ditches on either side of it were filled to the brim with surplus water, which the concrete channel hadn't been able to cope with. The water was brown and filthy, swirling with torn foliage, broken branches and clods of earth, like an evil soup. There was no drainage capacity now to deal with more rainfall. Soon, these ditches would overflow on to the roadway.

Fry looked again at the officer in rubber gloves, now on his knees in the opening to the culvert. There might be a decision to make at some point in the search operation. If no useful evidence was found near the site of the body when the water level was lowered, and nothing turned up that might have been dragged a few yards downstream, then these ditches and the culvert would become the focus of examination. In the end, the road might have to be dug out to open up the culvert. She was glad she wouldn't be the one to make *that* call.

★ ★ ★

Wayne Abbott greeted her at the inner cordon. He'd just changed into a new scene suit, and his hood was pulled up over his head, though his mask was left dangling. He was disposing of the old suit in a plastic bag as Fry arrived, and she could see that it was heavily caked in mud. She wondered if she'd missed him slithering down the slope and falling on his arse in the stream bed. If so, she was sorry not to have been here at the right time. She'd have to ask one of the SOCOs later for details.

'How do you like this weather, then?' said Abbott when he saw her.

'It's lovely. It means I can see less of the scenery.'

He laughed, and gave her a twinkly sideways look from under his hood as if he was appreciating her joke.

'I'm not joking,' she said. 'I just thought I'd make that clear. The fewer times I have to set eyes on this place the better.'

'You mean this wood,' he said.

'No, I mean the whole damn Peak District.'

'You know people travel from all over the world—'

'More fool them. It's always been a wasteland. And now it's a wet wasteland. It's like being in the middle of the North Sea. We've got about the same chance of drowning.'

Abbott held up a hand. 'All right, all right. It takes all kinds.'

As the water level fell, a scattering of mud-covered detritus was being revealed around the body. Some of it was incongruous – a plastic two-litre Coke bottle, long strands of bright blue baling twine, the torn pages of a free local newspaper. No doubt most of these items were just rubbish, washed downhill by the water. But it would all have to be examined by someone. Fry felt glad that someone wasn't her.

Further down, there was more stuff – indistinguishable lumps and enigmatic shapes, all covered in a layer of mud.

'So what have you found?' asked Fry.

'Quite a selection. Take a look for yourself.'

There were evidence bags full of the stuff. Bags and bags of it. Most of it was just the general rubbish thrown out of cars or dropped by careless hikers. Crumpled cans, a Snickers wrapper, a supersize McDonald's carton.

Fry picked up the last bag. Who would come all the way out here to eat a portion of McDonald's fries? There were no golden arches in Wirksworth, and certainly none anywhere in the national park. The nearest place to get a Big Mac must be Belper or Ripley. But then, maybe someone had just brought an empty carton with them and thought these woods looked like a convenient place to dispose of it.

'We also found two towels,' said Abbott. 'They're just

small hand towels, a fairly cheap make. They probably came from a pound shop. One of them was caught in the roots of a tree further down, the other was in the ditch at the side of the road.'

'Any manufacturer's name on them?'

'Someone called Made in China.'

'Great.'

'If you're expecting to get any quick results out of this lot . . . I mean, what sort of connection are we going to make between a Coke bottle and a cheap towel?'

'I have no idea.'

'"Probably none" is the correct answer.'

'What hopes do we have of some quick results from the forensics?' she asked.

'Good for identification evidence, if we can find some. Anything else . . . well, you know what it's like now.'

Fry sighed. 'Yes, of course.'

She knew there was no point arguing. Trying to demand faster results would be a waste of her breath.

In Derbyshire, as in the rest of the country, the Forensic Science Service was badly missed. Since the dismantling of the FSS, the procurement of specialist forensic services had become a shopping trip. Senior police officers ordered tests by price from a menu, as if they were visiting a Chinese restaurant. Often there was no one to take an overview of a case and assess

171

what was actually needed and might produce useful results. It was all about what could be afforded in the budget, which evidence might convince the Crown Prosecution Service to take a case forward.

Fry stirred the toe of her shoe in the muddy water that streamed past her feet into the crime scene. Paramount among those forensic menu items was DNA. It was the chef's dish of the day, chosen by every customer who couldn't decide what else to order. Well, DNA persuaded juries, all right. Every juror on the bench had watched a series or two of *CSI: Miami* and knew you needed DNA analysis to prove a person's guilt beyond doubt. Without it, juries were reluctant to convict, believing the police and prosecution had fallen down on the job. They didn't understand how flawed DNA evidence could be, and how difficult to interpret accurately. And they didn't know it was impossible to obtain it from a waterlogged crime scene.

She noticed a civilian standing at the outer cordon. A small, wiry man in his sixties, wearing an old-fashioned oilskin, steel-toecapped boots and a tweed cap.

'Who is that?' she asked.

'The landowner,' said Abbott. 'A local farmer. He's keen to help, he says.'

'That makes a change.'

Fry went to introduce herself. 'I'm Detective Sergeant Fry, Edendale CID.'

He shook her hand. A firm, rough grip.

'Bill Maskrey.'

'Thank you for offering your co-operation, Mr Maskrey. It's appreciated.'

'We have to do our bit where we can. Your lot have helped me in the past.'

'They have? Well, good. And are these woods yours?'

'This part is. The bigger section over yonder is National Trust property, but on a long lease to the Forestry Commission.' Maskrey peered at the activity in the stream bed. 'I see your chaps are finding a lot of rubbish. That'll have washed down the stream, I suppose.'

'Do you get much litter left in the woods?'

'Oh yes, I find all kinds of things,' said Maskrey. 'I try to keep my livestock out of here, because you never know what they might pick up that would get stuck in their stomachs. Just a small plastic bag can be lethal.'

'So you must get people coming in. Hikers, perhaps?'

'A few. There's a public footpath from the road that goes up to the rocks.'

'Rocks?'

'Haven't you seen them? Eagle Rocks. Top of this hill. That's where people walk to. But the path skirts the edge of the wood. The hikers aren't a problem.'

Fry looked at him, wondering if she should revise her view of his co-operativeness. Would he turn out to be one more enigmatic local with a penchant for baffling hints and sudden silences?

'If not the hikers, then – someone else?' she asked.

'Of course, we have the big problem,' said Maskrey.

'Which is?'

'Off-roaders, of course. Don't you know about them?'

'Why should I?'

'We've reported them often enough. Trail bikes, but four-wheel drives as well sometimes. They've been churning the place up. Making a right mess.'

He gestured at the woods. Fry didn't see how they could be any more of a mess than they were now.

'I'll see what we have on record.'

'You should. They can turn nasty. That poor bugger down there might just have crossed them the wrong way.'

Fry's phone rang. It was Luke Irvine.

'Mr Turner's car has turned up,' he said. 'The blue Renault Mégane. It's in a car park at a pub in Brassington. The nearest village to your scene.'

Fry took a last look at the scene before she left. As the level of the water around the body dropped, the fingers of one hand had begun to protrude above the surface, along with a blue-veined foot. Streaks of dark blood made the white skin look like scoops of ice cream, drizzled with chocolate.

★　　★　　★

Available officers had been allocated to canvass any properties they could find in the area near Sparrow Wood, though Fry could see as she passed through that there weren't many of them. A couple of farms, the odd small cottage, a quarry company with a site access near the junction for the Brassington road.

The pub was only ten minutes' drive away. It stood a couple of hundred yards before the main street in Brassington, which seemed to be called Dragon Hill. According to a sign on a wall, the lane opposite was Maddock Lake. Fry realised it was going to be one of those villages where nothing was quite right.

Luke Irvine and a couple of uniformed officers were standing by a blue Renault Mégane a couple of years old, parked at the back of a small car park behind the pub. The car's doors had been opened, presumably without the benefit of Glen Turner's keys, since they were still in an evidence bag from the crime scene. Probably best not to ask.

'I've already checked at the pub,' said Irvine. 'They don't know Mr Turner, and they don't remember seeing anyone like him in the bar on Tuesday. But they say customers sometimes leave their cars here overnight if they've had a bit over the limit. They try to discourage drinking and driving, so they don't object.'

'Very responsible of them,' said Fry. 'But the Mégane

must have been here since Tuesday if Mr Turner left it himself.'

'Yes, that's right. They saw it here on Wednesday morning.'

'About the time Mrs Turner was reporting her son missing.'

Irvine nodded. 'I see what you mean, Diane. We might have organised a search for him on Wednesday if we'd known his car was abandoned here.'

'Yes, we might. But it's no use wishing for anything different now. Have you gone over the interior?'

'It didn't take long. There's not much to see. Mr Turner wasn't one for carrying his whole life around with him in his vehicle.'

'Is there a laptop?'

'Yes, a Dell Latitude. Looks a tough little bugger.'

Fry could see that the laptop casing was reinforced for hard use, as Nathan Baird had described. Glen Turner must have had some rough claims to deal with, or a few unruly customers.

'We need to get that into the lab so forensics can check it out. We might get something off it. Anything else?'

'A bit of equipment in the boot. A pair of wellies, a fluorescent jacket, a folding stepladder. Only what he might have needed for the job. Oh, and there was this on the passenger seat.'

Irvine unwrapped a paper package. Fry looked at the contents, but couldn't make head nor tail of what she was seeing. It looked like a lump of stone, but embedded in the centre of it was a curled shape like the shell of a sea creature.

'And that is . . . ?'

'According to the label, it's a fossil. An ammonite. There's a receipt in the bag. It was bought at the National Stone Centre on Monday.'

'The what?'

'The National Stone Centre. It's not far away, just outside Wirksworth.'

'I said "what"? not "where"?' said Fry.

'Oh. Well, it's a sort of visitor centre where you can go to look at, well, er . . .'

'Stones?'

'In a nutshell.'

'Why would Glen Turner have been there? Was he interested in geology? Mineralogy?'

'It's possible, I suppose.'

'We need to get Scenes of Crime here to go over the car. Fingerprints, trace evidence – any signs that someone was in the car with him, or anyone was near enough to touch the car. In fact, I want everything.'

Irvine clamped his phone to his ear. 'I'll arrange it.'

Fry looked at the fossil again, and sighed. 'My God,

this man lived a boring life. So far, the most fascinating thing about him is the way he died.'

When she received confirmation that a family liaison officer had finally arrived at the cottage in St John's Street, Diane Fry called and asked Mrs Turner's permission to examine her son's room. She didn't seem to care very much by then.

Fry took Becky Hurst with her, and they got to work after a few words with Mrs Turner and the FLO. It was difficult to make polite small talk in these circumstances, but equally it seemed rude simply to walk through someone's house and go upstairs, even when they'd given you permission. Members of the public got upset about things like that. And no one wanted complaints.

Upstairs, it was obvious that Glen Turner had used the biggest bedroom in the cottage as his own. It was remarkably tidy for a single man. Fry wondered if his mother did all the tidying and cleaning in here. In which case, he might not have left anything too interesting lying around to be found.

Apart from a king-sized bed and a wardrobe, the room was dominated by a computer work station with two monitors side by side. The screens were blank, and the computer was switched off. No doubt it would require a password to access it anyway. Fry sighed when she realised she was likely to need specialist forensic services if she hoped to get anything off the hard drive. She would have to arrange for the equipment to be removed from the house as soon as possible.

'Red striped curtains,' said Hurst.

'So?'

'They don't seem to fit.'

'He probably didn't choose them himself.'

'I suppose not.'

'Check some of those drawers. See what documents you can find. Letters, bills, bank statements.'

'I know. I've done it before.'

Fry examined the clothes in the wardrobe. Glen Turner didn't have much fashion sense, or even a wide-ranging taste in styles. A few dull suits, some casual jackets and trousers that were only slightly less dull. On a shelf, she found a small pile of sweaters and cardigans with bright Scandinavian designs. They didn't look as though they'd been worn, though. When she sniffed them, they still smelled new. Christmas gifts, perhaps. *Wrap up warm, son.*

There were a few personal items in the drawers of the dresser. An electric shaver, a small Kodak digital camera, an iPod, an Xbox 360. She wasn't surprised that Turner was the type to be playing on a games console well into adulthood. There were a surprising number of adults using Nintendos and Game Boys. Mostly men, of course. It was a sign of the failure to grow up properly.

She switched on the camera, hoping the battery was charged up. There had been a higher specification camera in his briefcase, which presumably he'd needed for his work. This must have been for personal use. When the display came up, she pressed REVIEW on the menu and scrolled through the images stored on the memory card. Fry sighed when she saw them. Glen Turner was becoming so predictable. All she saw were pictures of stately homes and show gardens – among them, she thought she recognised Chatsworth House and Haddon Hall, two of the best-known attractions in the Peak District. Some of the shots were general views of an elegant facade or a colourful flower bed. But many of them included Glen's mother, Ingrid Turner, smiling for his camera as she posed against a pictur-esque backdrop. So that was how the two of them had spent their weekends in the summer.

'There are a few statements and receipts in a box file here,' said Hurst. 'Nothing out of the ordinary. They're household bills, mostly – he seems to have kept about five years' worth. Very organised of him. And it looks as though the majority are printouts from the internet, Diane.'

180

Fry nodded. 'So he did most things online. We'll need to look at his emails.'

'What are we looking for?' asked Hurst.

'Any indication of who he's been in touch with recently, and why. He must have had some contacts, apart from work and domestic affairs. He had dealings with someone who met him in those woods. And if there's no obvious sign of them, Mr Turner must have had a reason for hiding the traces.'

16

Tonight, Ben Cooper was driving in the south of the area, in the district known as the Derbyshire Dales. And he was there for a good reason.

This was where Josh Lane lived. The former barman at the Light House had moved into a park home located a few hundred yards off the A6 near Cromford, just east of the river Derwent.

Lane's home had a small conservatory and an area of decking which reached into the surrounding woodland. From the months he'd spent looking at estate agents websites trying to find an affordable property, Cooper knew that some of these park homes sold for around ninety thousand pounds. From what he'd heard, there was one park nearby where the rules excluded children. That was probably a big attraction for some people. Though how anybody could object to children, he didn't understand. It was part of the life he and Liz had been planning for themselves.

For a moment, he thought he was going to faint. The sky whirled around him, and his feet stumbled on the tarmac. He stopped for a few minutes at the entrance to the park, taking deep breaths until his head stopped swimming. This happened sometimes. He wasn't sure whether it was his body letting him down, or his mind. No matter how often he told himself to think only about safe subjects, to steer his thoughts away from dangerous territory, it still happened. It struck him out of the blue, like lightning from a clear sky. This would go on for ever, he knew. He could never be entirely confident that the lightning wouldn't strike at any moment, when he was least expecting it. He could understand why people gave up the struggle, if they believed it would be like that every day of the rest of their lives.

He looked up at a St George's flag flying over the entrance to the park. Two rows of mobile homes and small bungalows curved away from him into a wooded dell formed from the site of a small disused quarry. He could hear traffic passing on the A6 between Cromford and Ripley, but he guessed it would be quieter once he entered the park, the trees and quarry walls providing insulation against the noise.

And there he was, stepping out of his door and looking up at the sky, smoking a cigarette. Lane looked the way he always had, since Cooper first met him at the Grand Hotel in Edendale. He was thirty-seven years old, a little overweight, with that discreet piercing in one ear, and his hair still gelled into short, blond spikes. From his appearance, you might think that nothing much had happened in his life during the last few months, except for a trip to the chemist's to buy a new tube of hair gel.

He was dressed in much the same way Cooper had last seen him too, denims and a sweatshirt. The casual gear had never suited him – he was a little too close to middle age to carry off the jeans. But his hair was still as neatly groomed, the discreet piercing in place, his smile permanently affable. He still looked like the member of staff he'd met at the hotel, ready to be of service, more than willing to help with Cooper's questions about his time at the Light House. The co-operative Josh Lane.

He no longer had the bar job at the Grand, though. Now he was living on benefits, and staying in this mobile home park, which looked much more downmarket than the one across the river that Cooper was familiar with, the park where they didn't even allow children. There were plenty of kids here, some of the younger ones running about between the pitches, jumping over fences where there were any, making the dogs bark in excitement.

It was no surprise that the hotel had dispensed with his services. Lane had a criminal record. A couple of convictions under the Misuse of Drugs Act, when he was fined for possession of Class B drugs. Cannabis and amphetamines. There were indications from intelligence that he'd also been involved in a small-scale Ecstasy trade at the Light House after it began to attract a younger clientele. He'd been investigated for supply, but never brought to court.

Lane had been lucky there. Courts could impose a maximum sentence of fourteen years for dealing, even Class B. If only someone had made a decision to put more resources into investigating those allegations more closely, Josh Lane might have been part-way through serving that fourteen-year prison sentence right now. At least the Whartons would have had to look elsewhere for assistance. Cooper knew it might not have saved Liz's life – but at least he wouldn't be looking at a situation where justice blatantly hadn't been done.

He shook his head quietly. There were far too many 'if onlys'. No matter how many of them you piled up in your imagination, they were never going to amount to anything useful.

Whenever there was a gap in the traffic on the A6, Cooper could hear the river. The Derwent was in spate, many thousands of gallons of water added to its flow by the rainfall running off the surrounding hillsides and crashing downstream from Matlock towards the mills in Cromford and Belper.

Today, news reports said that there were flood alerts in place right across the region, the last stage before a full-scale flood warning, when people were advised to take immediate action against the threat of flooding. Monitoring sensors located in the rivers at key points measured changes in the water levels. Data was recorded at fifteen-minute intervals, so the flood alerts were usually pretty accurate.

But high levels in the rivers weren't the only problem. Cooper knew how difficult it was to predict the exact location of flooding from groundwater, which was often related to local geology. No one could say for sure which properties were at risk of groundwater flooding. Add the complication of blocked culverts and drains, and thousands of acres of land already sodden from weeks of heavy rain, and flash floods could happen anywhere.

All of this stretch of the River Derwent was at risk. Just downstream was the Wigwell Viaduct carrying the Cromford Canal over the river, close to High Peak Junction. The low-lying fields on either side of the Derwent had flooded regularly in the past, and no doubt they would again. Millions of pounds had been spent on flood defences in the region, but only for the cities.

Cooper waited until it was dark, then turned the Toyota on the verge and spun his tyres deliberately in the mud as he accelerated away from Derwent Park. He crossed the river at Whatstandwell and let the car take its own direction through the network of roads around Wirksworth.

The rain began to come down harder, and cars became fewer and further apart. Very soon, he was driving too fast for the conditions. Water sluiced across his windscreen in torrents, the rain obscuring his view much faster than his wipers could clear it. The road was wet, with pools of standing water that appeared suddenly in the flash of his headlights and disappeared again a second before he hit them. Poor visibility and a dangerous road surface. It was a lethal combination that drivers were warned about constantly.

He had no idea where the figure came from. One second, he could see nothing but an empty road through the streaked glass, a bend a hundred yards ahead and overhanging trees cascading sheets of water on the muddy verges. In the next instant there was something moving in front of him, a shape slithering down the bank on his right and running into the roadway. It wasn't a dog or a fox, or even a deer. It was upright on two legs, arms thrashing wildly in the air as it ran, light reflecting off wet clothes, spray flying from the tarmac as its feet hit the surface.

'What the—!'

Cooper's foot hit the brake pedal and the car began to slide, the tyres pushing up a surge of water that hit the stone wall like a tidal wave. *Steer into a skid.* He swung the steering wheel, aware of his headlights swaying crazily from side to side, illuminating the trees, and then the road, and then a figure standing on the white line, a white face turned towards him in astonishment, not knowing which way to run. As he fought to get the car under control, he lost sight of the figure again. When he finally slithered to a halt, cursing loudly at the windscreen, the runner had gone.

Cooper sat for a long time, gripping the wheel tightly, staring out at the rain pouring down on his car out of the darkness. The engine had stalled, but the wipers were still thrashing backwards and forwards, their insistent rhythm the only sound in the night. His heart was thumping as fast as the wipers, and his eyes strained to see anything that might be lying in the road. He twisted in his seat to look behind the car, but there was nothing.

After a while, his heart began to slow, the adrenalin surge subsided, and he realised the Toyota was sitting diagonally across the narrow road, blocking both carriageways. Lucky that there was no traffic tonight.

Only a solitary person, who'd been running somewhere in the rain.

Cooper started the engine. His headlights flickered and brightened. The angle of the stationary car meant the lights on full beam were pointing at the woods on the far side of the road. They fell directly on a white painted sign, which leaped out of the night like a barn owl opening its wings for flight, the brightness startling and uncanny in the surrounding darkness. What did that sign say? He couldn't make out the words from here.

He put the car in gear and pulled it into the side of the road under the trees, where it was out of the way of traffic. Then he dug his Maglite out of the glove compartment, opened the door and walked across to the sign. Oblivious to the rain soaking his hair and clothes, Cooper pointed his torch at the board and read the words written carefully in black paint.

A.J. MORTON & SONS, NEXT TURNING ON THE RIGHT.

Where had he seen that before? *A.J. Morton & Sons*. It was strange how memories suddenly swam out of the darkness, appearing as half-seen shapes from a cloud of mist or smoke. It felt as though his mind was trying to suppress the memory of more recent events by tossing up random fragments of recollection to distract him, like the metallic chaff discharged by military aircraft to confuse a guided missile.

Cooper shook his head in bewilderment, scattering raindrops into the night. *A.J. Morton & Sons*. It came from way back.

He flinched in pain as something dripped on to his face. It was hot and scalding, like melted wax. He brushed the blob from his cheek and saw a smear of green, molten plastic on his fingers. Shielding his eyes, he looked up at the ceiling. The light fittings were melting. They had once been shaped like candles, but now they were drooping, slowly dissolving into liquid that spattered his scene suit and landed in his hair.

He pulled his jacket over his head, conscious as he did it how futile a gesture it was. His protection wouldn't last long once the flames touched him. He had to keep moving.

Cooper turned back towards the bar. Glowing embers faced him. Before he could move, a shelf bearing a line of optics tore away from the ceiling with a shriek and crashed to the floor. Glass flew in all directions, shattering into fragments, glittering in the flames like a shower of meteorites.

He pulled open the blackened door, keeping his body behind it in case of a back blast caused by a rush of air. The door handle was almost too hot to touch. Cooper looked at his hands, and saw that his fingers were red and blistering. The pain hadn't hit him yet, but it would.

He glimpsed something red on the wall by the door. A fire extinguisher. He grabbed it from its bracket, thumped the handle and sprayed foam towards the heart of the blaze. It subsided a little, and he kept spraying until the extinguisher was empty. Immediately, the fire flickered and sprang back to life.

'Liz! Where are you?'

17

Friday

The smell of disinfectant, the gleam of polished steel, an echo of footsteps off the cold tiles. Nothing spoke more clearly of death. The sensations of the mortuary had become so familiar to Diane Fry that she knew she'd experience them all over again one day, in her own dying moments. She was convinced she'd smell that odour on her deathbed, hear the echo of approaching footsteps as she breathed her last. The glint from a steel table, the flash of light on a scalpel – they were the last images she would see as her eyes closed in death.

Yes, and probably the person who'd be waiting for her on the other side would be the Edendale pathologist, Dr Juliana van Doon. The angel of death in a green apron and a medical mask. Then she would know whether she was in heaven or hell.

'Detective Sergeant Fry,' said the pathologist. 'Interesting to see you back here again.'

'Interesting in the sense of the Chinese curse?' asked Fry.

'Well, you can't deny we live in interesting times.'

'No.'

Fry thought the pathologist was looking older these days. Her face was harder, the creases around her eyes noticeably deeper. And she seemed very tired. It was the sort of tiredness that made her more spiky, more inclined to look for a target to take it out on. In other circumstances, Fry could have empathised with her. She suspected she might be like that herself sometimes.

But Mrs van Doon had long since taken a dislike to her for some reason, and they were well past the point where they might ever become friends.

'But if this is your latest career move, DS Fry, it has me mystified,' said the pathologist.

'I hate to be predictable,' murmured Fry.

'Oh, really?'

The body from the woods lay on the autopsy table. Like most victims of sudden death, the man's face had sagged into an empty mask, devoid of character or expression. Fry had seen relatives of murder victims have initial difficulties identifying a body in the mortuary. It was because the person they'd known in life was gone. Robbed of its animation and personality, the physical shell was blank and meaningless.

The victim's skin was pale and waxy, his lips shrivelled away to expose uneven teeth. He looked like a movie vampire sleeping in his coffin, waiting for a stake in the heart to destroy him, or a drop of fresh blood to bring him back to life. It wouldn't work here. No amount of freshly spilt blood would revive this victim.

'I suppose there's a sixty-four-thousand-dollar question, Sergeant?' said the pathologist. 'There usually is.'

Fry nodded. 'Yes. Did he drown?'

'Ah. Well, first of all, I'm afraid there are no universally accepted diagnostic laboratory tests for drowning.'

'That's unfortunate.'

'Indeed. How remiss of forensic science not to be perfect in every respect. We can perform so many magic tricks for you, yet we can't tell for certain whether someone drowned or was already dead when he went into the water.'

'I've never expected you to be perfect, Doctor.'

Mrs van Doon looked at her and pulled down her mask. Fry thought perhaps she'd scored a small victory, until the pathologist smiled in satisfaction. Then she realised she'd just been led into making the remark.

She'd proved herself to be shallow and predictable after all. Now she was at a disadvantage from the start.

'And you're right as usual, Sergeant Fry. So all is well with the world, after all.'

'Drowning?' said Fry stiffly.

'When a victim is dead at the time of submersion, water and contaminating debris can enter the pharynx, trachea and larger airways. Small quantities might enter the oesophagus and stomach. However, water will not reach the terminal bronchioles and alveoli to any significant extent. So if we find a substantial amount of foreign material in the alveoli, that provides evidence of immersion during life. Well – so long as the body is recovered within twenty-four hours, and from shallow water. The water was shallow in this case, I believe? Less than three metres deep?'

'Certainly. But twenty-four hours—?'

'Yes, that's our problem. Our victim was in the water a little too long before his body was recovered.'

'Any other way we can tell?'

'Well, if there was a large quantity of water and debris in the stomach, that might suggest immersion during life. But my examination shows very little in the stomach in this case.'

'So . . . ?'

'So what I can tell you is that I can't tell you for certain whether he drowned or not.'

'Great.'

'Basically, what we have here is a white male aged thirty-five to forty years, five feet ten inches in height, weighing around a hundred and ninety-five pounds. The subject was in good general health – though I would suspect a rather sedentary lifestyle. Cause of death unknown at this stage. We'll have to await test results. The blood alcohol level might be interesting. Accidental drowning in adults is usually associated with alcohol consumption or drug use. The literature says two-thirds of adult males found drowned have consumed alcohol.'

'But we don't know that he drowned.'

'And we don't know that he didn't.'

Fry bit her lip. 'Other injuries?'

'Well, these contusions are puzzling me,' said Mrs van Doon.

Reluctantly, Fry leaned forward to follow the pathologist's gesture.

'Yes, I see.'

Trust the woman to save the best detail for last. There were red welts on the body, each one a round mark surrounded by a halo of bruising. They looked almost like cigarette burns, but larger in diameter. And cigarette burns didn't cause bruises.

'Perhaps about four days old,' said Mrs van Doon. 'The colour of the bruising is starting to turn to yellow on the inner edge, look. Bilirubin.'

'Who?'

The pathologist restrained a smirk. 'Not "who", but "what". The yellow colour is a waste product called bilirubin. It's the same substance that turns your urine yellow.'

'I always learn something from you that I didn't want to know,' said Fry.

The pathologist took no notice. She rarely did.

'Bilirubin is the last bit of congealed blood to be broken down and dispersed by the white cells,' she said. 'First the dark purple – that's the colour of oxygen in the haemoglobin. Then the green of biliverdin. It's generally estimated to take about four days for only bilirubin to be left.'

'Unexplained contusions approximately two centimetres in diameter will appear on my report. Obviously not the cause of death.'

'The bruising is wider than two centimetres,' said Fry.

'Ah, yes. Well observed.'

A compliment was never what it seemed when it came from Mrs van Doon. Although it wasn't evident in the tone of her voice, she was certainly being sarcastic. The diameter of the bruising should be obvious to anyone.

'So?' said Fry.

'The bruising isn't actually at the site of the

contusion. With an injury like this, blood is forced away from the site by the impact and forms that circle around the contusion itself.'

'He was being hit with something.'

'Yes. But it was an odd choice of weapon, whatever it was,' said the pathologist. 'Minor bruising, that's all. It would have been quite painful at the time, I dare say.'

'Perhaps he was being tortured.'

The pathologist shrugged, without replying. It wasn't for her to say. It was speculation, and that was the job of the police. The shrug expressed a degree of professional disdain, her scorn for a lack of scientific rigour.

'Four days ago?' asked Fry.

'An approximation only. There's no way we can fix time of death from the temperature of the body when it was found. A body cools in water about twice as fast as in the air – about five degrees Celsius per hour. It reaches the temperature of the water usually within five to six hours. So all I can tell you is that he was dead in the water for at least that long. You'll have to rely on circumstantial evidence to establish the time more accurately.'

'Dead in the water?' repeated Fry.

'I always like to use that phrase. It has so many layers of meaning, don't you think?'

'I believe it refers to a ship when it loses power.'

'And metaphorically to someone's career,' said the pathologist.

'So he was tortured?' asked Luke Irvine when Fry reported on the post-mortem results.

'It looks like it.'

'It's more than just a simple robbery, then.'

'It never was a simple robbery,' said Fry. 'You don't dump your victim dead and naked in a stream if you're just robbing them for a few quid.'

'A robbery gone wrong,' said Hurst. 'It happens all the time.'

'Oh, yeah,' scoffed Irvine. 'On TV it does.'

'It happens,' insisted Hurst.

'It *is* possible. He could have been tortured to get the PIN for his credit card. Then he died. A weak heart perhaps, or something like that – the test results might tell us. And his robber panicked and dumped his body. That would explain why he was left naked. They took his clothes so that he wouldn't be identified. You can definitely learn that trick from watching TV.'

'What? And then they left the clothes piled up a few yards away for us to find? Complete with his driving licence to make it easy to ID him? And his credit cards were in there too. Not to mention the cash. Pretty slapdash robbers, Luke.'

'Could you two just call a truce for a bit while I'm out of the room?' said Fry. 'I want forensics chased up on Glen Turner's computer and laptop, so we can get a proper examination of his bank accounts. Then maybe we can pick it up when I get back.'

'It's such a pity we don't have Ben Cooper available,' said Detective Inspector Paul Hitchens when she'd brought him up to date. 'He's always been such a big asset to the team.'

'We can manage perfectly well,' said Fry. She didn't really feel she needed to answer to a Divisional DI. Especially not Paul Hitchens. She'd worked with him, and she knew him. Most importantly, she knew all his weaknesses.

'If you establish that it was murder, we'll have to call in the Major Crime Unit,' said Hitchens. 'But then, you know that.'

'If we need the MCU, we need them. What we don't need is DS Cooper. We'll manage fine without him.'

Hitchens chewed his lip. Fry could see the problem he was facing. No matter how he felt, how much misplaced faith he had in Ben Cooper, he couldn't display a lack of confidence in his own team.

But it turned out that wasn't what was on his mind. 'This won't come as a huge surprise to you, Diane,' he said. 'But I'm moving on. It's time for me to do something different. I don't fit in here any more. It was different when DCI Kessen was here, or Stewart Tailby before him. They were good to work for.'

'You used to take the piss out of them both,' said Fry. 'All the time.'

She had no idea what else to say. Hitchens was wrong – it *had* come as a surprise to her. But perhaps it shouldn't have done. She'd seen a leaflet on his desk one day, promoting a seminar for inspectors. *Meeting the challenges of the new performance landscape.* She'd thought it was just another Human Resources initiative. But he spoke as if she ought to have known. Perhaps she had missed all the gossip.

Hitchens coughed. 'Perhaps occasionally. But you understand. I did talk to you about it earlier in the year.'

'I don't believe you've ever mentioned it to me,' said Fry.

'Oh?' He looked confused. 'I suppose it must have been DS Cooper, then.'

'Yes, I suppose it must.'

'I've worked in E Division for a while, you know. I came to rely on Ben quite a lot. It was good having Cooper as DS.'

Fry said nothing. Presumably Hitchens had also forgotten that Cooper had replaced her as DS on his team. That was a convenient lapse of memory. It allowed him to speak the truth without worrying that she might take offence at the implications. *It was good having Cooper as DS. Much better than whoever it was doing the job before him.*

'We have reports coming in of vehicles sighted in the area the night of the murder,' reported Irvine when she got back. 'So far, we've got two white vans, a red car, and a BMW.'

'Are they reliable witnesses?' asked Fry.

'I don't know. The red car and the BMW were noticed by a passing motorist. There weren't many on that road at the time, so it's a bit of luck for us. And the two white vans were seen by an employee at the quarry company nearby. We've got good descriptions of the vans. A Mark 6 Ford Transit, and a Renault Trafic. One had a name printed on the side. Do you think either of those could be of interest to us?'

'Possibly,' said Fry. 'We'll need to talk to the witnesses to see how well they stand up.'

'Want me to run with that, Diane?'

'Fine.'

'*Two* white vans, though?' said Murfin. 'One is more than enough, if you ask me.'

'What are you talking about, Gavin?'

'I'm saying everyone is always looking for a white

van. Any inquiry I've ever been involved in, we were always trying to track down a white van. And when we found it, the driver never had anything to do with the crime we were investigating. He was always just passing or happened to be in the area at the time.'

'Maybe they've been sent as observers,' said Irvine cheerfully.

'What?'

'Observers. You know, like that American TV series – where these sort of bald aliens always turn up making notes in the background when anything significant happens. They're observers. It could be why there's always a white van man in the area when a serious crime is committed.'

Fry scowled at him. 'Now I have no idea what you're talking about, Luke.'

'When was that on?' asked Hurst. 'And what is the series called?'

'I can't remember,' said Irvine. 'It's American. A bit like *The X Files*, but more recent.'

'I think you just made it up.'

'No, I didn't.'

'Look, I don't care whether you made it up or not,' said Fry impatiently. 'Can we please get back to—?'

'*Fringe*.'

They all turned to stare at Gavin Murfin.

'It's called *Fringe*,' he said. 'The TV show that Luke

is talking about. There's this FBI agent and this mad scientist—'

Fry turned away from the conversation in frustration. How was she going to track down witnesses to the death of Glen Turner, or whatever went immediately before it? There were too many white vans, and too many dark nights. One vehicle looked much like any other in the black, rain-lashed depths of the Derbyshire countryside.

She looked out of the window as the thought came into her head.

'Oh God, look at it out there,' she said. 'What have we done to deserve this?'

Murfin turned and examined the water lashing against the panes. A thundering downpour filled the air, surging off the tarmac and overwhelming the surface drains in an instant to form swirling pools between vehicles in the parking compound. But for the sweep of headlights in the road outside, the world had been plunged into saturated gloom.

'Perhaps it's the kind of rain you can run through without getting wet,' said Murfin.

'Do you think so, Gavin?'

'Nope.'

Fry put on her coat and took an umbrella from the corner. It wasn't far across the compound to where her car was parked – just twenty-five yards or so. But it was far enough to get thoroughly soaked in this weather.

The umbrella was still wet from the last time she'd used it, and a patch of carpet underneath it was darkening with damp. They didn't provide umbrella stands for CID rooms. They weren't considered standard office furniture, she supposed, even in the Peak District. There was probably a crumbling patch of floorboard under this carpet by now, eaten away by wet rot. It was a fate she might be about to share.

A few minutes later, she was in the driving seat of her car, dripping on the carpet, with the wipers working, while she waited for the fan to clear the condensation from her windscreen. The noise of the rain drumming on the roof almost drowned out the radio, and she turned it off.

When her view was clear, she fastened her seat belt and drove out through the barrier, her tyres splashing through a stream of water running down the edge of the road. E Division headquarters had been built at the top of a hill, so all the rain was running down West Street and gathering at the bottom near the lights.

When she reached the foot of the hill, she could see that the junction might be closed completely later on. Drivers were already negotiating their way cautiously through a shallow lake, throwing up waves on to the pavement. Lights had come on in the shop windows, and passers-by were sheltering in doorways waiting for the downpour to stop, trusting that it was only a cloudburst. Without exception, they gazed upwards in awe, fascinated by the sight of gallons of water hurtling from the sky.

Fry had to admit there was something mesmerising about heavy rain. People could get quite obsessed with it. They dedicated their lives to recording rainfall and analysing weather patterns. They knew that Seathwaite in Cumbria was the wettest place in Britain. They could tell you that almost twelve and a half inches of rain had fallen there once in a twenty-four-hour period. Those self-appointed weather experts could reel off statistics all the way back to 1850, when official records began. Rain was one of the highlights of their week. They loved downpours, delighted in showers, positively purred over a torrential deluge like this one. They probably had forty different words for rain.

But for her, it was just wet. Ludicrously wet. It was starting to become unnatural.

As she drove through the town, taking care on the wet tarmac, it occurred to her that it would be quite different at the end of the journey. At her crime scene in Sparrow Wood, there was no tarmac, only mud. And then probably a lot more mud.

Back home in Birmingham, it had rained a lot too.

But at least in the city you could go indoors. And if you did have to venture outside, you weren't forced to wade through six inches of sludge to reach your car, or get your feet wet just crossing the road.

Fry knew this was a punishment. She'd done something wrong in a previous life. Whatever it was, she just hoped it was something she'd enjoyed.

Luke Irvine met her at Prospectus Assurance. 'Mr Edge is waiting for us,' he said.

When they entered his office, Ralph Edge spun in his chair and turned his shirt cuffs back, like a man preparing for a fight. He was older than Nathan Baird, and softer in outline, with smooth hands and a pudgy neck. His hair was receding to the point where he'd decided to shave the rest of his head, which gave him a strangely aggressive look that was at odds with the rest of his appearance.

'So how can I help?' he asked. 'What do you want to know about poor old Glen?'

'He was a claims adjuster here, is that right?'

'Yes. Their role is to determine the extent of the company's liability. They investigate claims. Interview claimants and witnesses, consult police and hospital records if necessary. Sometimes they have to inspect property damage. As an adjuster, you can work long hours, including nights and weekends. You have to be able to use a laptop, but a fifty-pound ladder as well.'

'Much personal contact with the public?'

'Well . . . you have to help the policyholder. You're the one familiar with all the technical terms. Depreciation, replacement costs, actual cash value. Most policyholders don't understand those things.'

'Would you say Mr Turner was happy with his work at Prospectus Assurance?'

Edge shrugged. 'I guess so. Everyone grumbles about money, of course. There used to be a bonus scheme. Up to ten per cent of your salary. That doesn't happen now. Austerity times, you know.'

'And how does your job fit in with the work he was doing?'

'We have to investigate claims to make sure they're genuine. Sadly, some people do lie.'

'Oh, I know,' said Fry.

'Of course you do.'

'How much did you know about Mr Turner's personal life?'

'Oh, I suppose someone has told you that I was his best friend or something, have they?'

'And were you?'

'I'd be a bit more upset, if I was,' said Edge.

'Yes, I'd noticed you weren't too distressed by his death, sir.'

Edge held out one hand in apology. 'Don't get me wrong. Glen was okay. We did talk a bit. But his personal life? No, not really.'

'Do you remember anything out of the ordinary about Mr Turner in the previous few days? Anything particularly unusual?'

'When do you mean exactly?'

'Say two days before his death.'

'That would be . . . ?'

'Sunday,' said Fry as he looked towards the wall planner for clarification. She followed his gaze and saw that the whole of the previous weekend was blocked out in bright red tape decorated with gold stars, as if it was a special occasion. A celebration, or some kind of anniversary. A wedding, maybe?

'Sunday?' said Edge. 'Oh, yes. I know what Glen was doing on Sunday, all right. He was getting himself killed. Over and over again.'

18

Josh Lane had been going out every day. He wasn't working, just taking a trip somewhere different each morning. If the rain had stopped, he went for a walk. Sometimes even when it was still raining too. Then he would stop for lunch in a pub somewhere.

As he followed Lane's silver grey Honda Civic from Derwent Park that Friday morning, Ben Cooper wondered what was going through Lane's mind when he did this. It was the sort of thing he imagined he would do himself, if he was facing the possibility of a spell in prison. Taking a look at the world around him before he lost it for a while. Getting the most out of that last taste of freedom.

But he couldn't bear the idea that he and Lane might

think the same way. That wasn't possible. He wanted this man to be eaten up by guilt. He needed to believe that Josh Lane was desperately seeking peace of mind that he might never get. And, if Cooper had his way, he'd make sure he never got it.

Peace was certainly available in many of these places, if your mind was in the right condition to see it. Today, Lane was driving the short distance up the A6 into Cromford, where he turned into the centre of the village at the traffic lights and headed up the long hill going south.

The road from Wirksworth ran steeply down into Cromford, carrying all telltale signs of nearby quarrying. The unnaturally white surface of the carriageway and the presence of crash barriers on every bend were the clues. Lorries loaded with asphalt and aggregates ground their way up and down this hill every day. No matter how well they were sheeted, or how often their wheels were washed, they left their traces on the roads as reminders of the quarry's existence. The barriers were there to protect residents living directly in the path of the lorries. If the brakes failed as one of them descended the hill, it would turn into an uncontrollable twelve-ton missile capable of demolishing a house.

As they passed the huge tarmac works at Dean Hollow, Cooper heard the siren go off – a long first blast, giving a two-minute warning of firing. The blasting engineer would be ready with his detonator and firing mechanism, sodium chloride fertiliser pellets packed into tubes to create almost instantaneous blasts. He knew from experience that the vibration would be felt down in the valley.

When they reached Steeple Grange, Cooper thought Lane was heading into Wirksworth. A wide arc of abandoned quarries curved west and north of the little town, forming a backdrop to many of the views over it. Several of those old quarries had been absorbed into the site of the National Stone Centre, which occupied fifty acres of land between the Middleton and Cromford roads.

During the Carboniferous period three hundred million years ago, Wirksworth had been under a tropical sea, which left it with vast quantities of limestone. Centuries of quarrying had left their scars on the area. But almost all of the quarries were disused and derelict now, forming Derbyshire's own lunar landscape. You could step off a track, or out of a meadow, and find yourself walking on a dead surface of dust and rock, your view blocked on every side by coarse limestone walls, as if you were standing in a crater on the moon.

The great upheaval for Wirksworth came in the 1920s with the reopening of Dale Quarry, known by local people as 'The Big Hole'. Mechanisation had arrived, and a vast stone crusher was installed. Dust, dirt and noise polluted the heart of the town. Anyone who could afford to leave abandoned Wirksworth, taking commerce with them. Jobs were lost, buildings fell into disrepair, fine old houses were left to decay. What had been one of Derbyshire's most important towns was blighted.

But in the 1970s the town had been chosen for regeneration. The Wirksworth Project had restored buildings that were falling down, and which now became part of the town's historic character. With regeneration came new businesses, and a different type of resident had moved in. It had become the sort of place that he and Liz might have wanted to live in.

Cooper was almost caught by surprise when Josh Lane's car slowed and indicated right near the Lime Kiln pub, well short of Wirksworth town centre.

'Damn. Where is he going?' Cooper said to himself, as the Honda waited for traffic to clear. It would be too obvious to pull up right on Lane's rear bumper for the turn, so Cooper drove on a few yards and stopped in front of a row of neat stone cottages, each with its front door painted a different colour – one green, one blue, the next black – but every one with the same brass urn-shaped knocker.

When Lane had completed his turn, Cooper reversed into an opening between the cottages and followed the grey Honda into Middleton Road. He found himself in front of the ornate gates of Stoney Wood, a park created from the remains of one of the quarries. Lane's car was in the pull-in by the gates, and Lane himself was already out of it. Cooper turned his head away as he drove past and parked on the grass verge near Middlepeak granite works.

He gave Lane a few minutes, then cautiously made his way through the entrance of Stoney Wood. The slopes of the old quarry had been planted with trees and filled with artworks. Lane was walking up the steepest part of the hill, past hundreds of stones laid out to form an infinity symbol. His head was down as he watched his footing on the slippery ground.

Cooper stayed just out of sight among the trees at the bottom of the slope, and waited. He remembered this place. Its conception had been part of Wirksworth's regeneration, yet here were all the signs of pagan folk memory that were inescapable in Derbyshire. In Stoney Wood, they were both formal and informal. Close by where he stood, someone had recently laid a pattern of holly and ivy wreaths on the stone seating. Near the top of the hill, he knew Lane would pass the Calendar Stones, modern monoliths placed to align with the sun at the time of the equinox and solstice.

He kept his eyes fixed on the figure picking its way gingerly over a patch of muddy grass. Lane circled the Calendar Stones and stopped. Then Cooper knew he was visiting the StarDisc.

This was just the sort of thing that his sister Claire

became enthusiastic about. She loved anything with the kind of New Age atmosphere she'd tried to create in her shop in Edendale. The StarDisc was on a different scale from her crystals and pendulums. It had been created here in Stoney Wood as a twenty-first-century stone circle. A celestial amphitheatre thirty-five feet wide, a temple without walls. Carved into black granite to evoke the darkness of deep space was a star chart mirroring the night sky, its surface inscribed with the constellations. Around the perimeter stood twelve seats denoting the months of the year. Scores of lights illuminating the StarDisc at night were powered by the nearest star – the Sun.

Claire had dragged him to the opening of the StarDisc a few years ago. She must have had no boyfriend in tow at the time, and of course she knew it was a waste of time trying to rope Matt in for something like this. It had been quite an extraordinary event, Ben had to admit. More than a thousand people had turned up to watch an outdoor screening of Steven Spielberg's *Close Encounters of the Third Kind* and listen to a specially recorded message from the astronomer Patrick Moore. The old lead miners and quarrymen could never have imagined that.

Josh Lane was moving around the StarDisc, walking over the constellations, crouching occasionally to read the name of a star system. He turned slowly to gaze over the scenery in all directions, and Cooper made sure he was standing completely still behind trees. Wearing his green waxed jacket, he wouldn't be noticeable as long as he didn't move.

Then Lane began to slither back down the hill to his car, and Cooper turned to make sure he could get to his Toyota in time before he pulled out on to Middleton Road.

Now they were definitely heading into Wirksworth. Down Hutchinson's Drive, past the Bailey Croft service station and the BP petrol forecourt, and under the arched footbridge that carried a pathway high over the road between Green Hill and Chapel Lane.

A maze of narrow streets and alleyways sprawled on both sides of the main street, some of them leading to an old church set in its own close like a cathedral. On Cooper's right, the limestone cottages of The Dale and Green Hill clung precariously to the hillside, as if Wirksworth was a Cornish fishing village with only the sea missing. In places it was possible to walk from the garden of one house on to the roof of another. Some residents had even erected greenhouses on their garage roofs in the absence of available space at ground level.

In the centre of town, Lane turned his Honda away from the tea rooms in Coldwell Street and squeezed his car through a narrow archway entrance into the car park of the Red Lion.

Cooper couldn't risk parking at the pub, but he found a space close by in the Barmote Croft car park, facing the old Temperance Hall. He didn't want to attract attention by getting a ticket on his windscreen, but the ticket machine wasn't working. And a passing Wirksworth resident said they never paid it anyway.

He walked a few yards to the Red Lion, wondering who Josh Lane might be meeting inside. And wondering even more what he himself was doing here. Why was he obsessing about Lane's movements? What could he hope to learn?

Cooper shook his head and tried to take in his surroundings. The old Wirksworth Town Hall stood directly across the street from the Red Lion. Golden stone, ornate pillars, an Italianate facade, even a clock tower. It was a Victorian creation for use by the local Freemasons. But now it housed the library and an Age UK charity shop. A whitewashed cast-iron milestone on the corner of the building told Cooper that London was a hundred and thirty-nine miles from the centre of Wirksworth. It felt an awful lot further away than that.

Charlie Dean cruised the BMW up Harrison Drive on the way out of Wirksworth, automatically glancing up at the footbridge over the road, checking for anyone watching him. There was no one on the bridge, of course. He was just getting paranoid.

And that was Sheena's fault. He was quite sure that she was wrong about Jay getting suspicious. They'd been much too careful up to now. They never phoned each other at home, only ever sent texts, and then deleted them at once. They had never risked being seen together too close to where they lived or worked. They'd made certain they had plausible reasons for all their absences.

But Dean had a sudden thought as he indicated to pull into the Bailey Croft service station. He knew that he'd always done those things himself. What about Sheena? He only had her word for it. What if she'd just been telling him what he wanted to hear? Had she been forgetting to delete his texts? Had she let drop some incriminating remark? Had she, God forbid, confided in one of her friends at the hairdressing salon? He knew she could lie. She'd been lying to Jay all this time, after all. Couldn't she just as easily be lying to him?

A worm of unease crawled in his stomach. Just when he'd been convincing himself that everything was fine and no one was going to ask them any questions, suddenly he wasn't so sure that everything was fine at all.

He turned in past the petrol station forecourt and the Spar shop, his foot on the accelerator pedal, ready to drive away again if something went wrong or he lost courage. They didn't know him here because he always filled up his car at a service station in Ashbourne, where the company had an account. But you never knew who you might bump into in Wirksworth. It was a small town.

Then he saw Sheena standing in the corner of the car park and the sight of her made him forget his worries. At least for a while. He opened the door and Sheena climbed into the BMW.

Half a mile further on, a Vauxhall Astra had skidded on the wet surface and gone off the road, ending up with its nose in a shallow ditch. Other motorists took no notice of its fate, hurtling on by to wherever they were heading so urgently.

Dean looked at the cars whizzing past, and the rear end of the Vauxhall in the ditch. 'I bet not one of them has been on a speed awareness course,' he said.

'What?'

'Never mind.'

His head still ached a bit from his session in the pub last night. It had been good to be able to relax, though.

Suddenly, Charlie Dean felt reckless. It was a tendency of his that Barbara had complained about often in the past. She said it was incredibly juvenile, this instinct to react to danger by confronting it head-on. Tempting fate, she called it. But he had better descriptions. Facing up to a risk. Showing the world he wasn't afraid. That was more like it. Charlie Dean wasn't a man to be cowed by threats.

'I've got a great idea,' he said. 'A bit of a treat for us today.'

'What are you on about, Charlie?' said Sheena, with that scornful little laugh of hers.

He pulled a bunch of keys from his pocket and jingled them in front of her eyes.

'There's a property I'm handling. We've just put it on the market this week. But the owners have moved out already and it's standing empty.'

'So?'

'Well, when I say "empty", I just mean no one's living there. The vendors have bought a villa in France and they're fitting it out locally. So they've left most of their furniture in place in the old house. It'll go into storage eventually of course, or get sold off. But it's easier for us to market a furnished property than an empty shell, you see.'

'Why are you talking about furniture?'

'Furniture. You know . . .' Dean winked. 'Beds, for example.'

'Oh. Where is it?'

'Right here in Wirksworth. Green Hill.'

'Isn't that a bit close, Charlie? You always told me we had to be careful.'

'It'll be fine,' he said.

Dean smiled as he pulled into the entrance to the Wirksworth Industrial Centre to do a U-turn. It was exhilarating, this living dangerously. It made him feel really alive, gave him a buzz that he never experienced in any other way. Certainly not in his job at Williamson Hart. These days he spent all his time dealing with frustrated vendors who couldn't find a buyer, and time-wasting buyers who wanted a property dirt cheap. Why not make use of the opportunities of the job when they came up? He'd heard of people doing this before with empty properties. He was pretty sure one of the senior partners, Gerry Hart, had done it in the past. So where was the harm?

'Is it a nice house?' asked Sheena. As if that mattered.

'Oh, you'll love it,' he said.

19

Diane Fry stared at Ralph Edge, wondering why he was laughing so hard at the idea of his friend Glen Turner getting killed. And what did he mean by 'over and over again'?

Edge just laughed even more when he saw her expression.

'Team building,' he said.

'What?'

'We were taking part in a team building exercise at the weekend. They took us to a place up in the north of the county. It's an enormous site, with all kinds of activities, and we stayed there the whole two days. Motivational talks, orienteering, lots of role playing. Even blind driving. You know the sort of thing.'

Fry did. Except for . . . 'Blind driving?'

'You don't know how that works? Well, they put two of you in a car, and the driver is blindfolded.'

'What's the point of that?'

'The idea is that if you're the one driving you've got to have complete trust in your navigator. If you're acting as navigator, you have to be able to communicate clearly. It's a metaphor for a good relationship in the workplace. Or something like that.'

Fry recognised the slightly jaded tone of someone who'd taken part in too many team building exercises, been sent on too many personal development courses. She'd heard the same tone in police locker rooms.

'Wait a minute,' said Irvine. 'I know that place. Did you go paintballing too?'

'Of course we did. They have a massive paintballing set-up. About a dozen different arenas. A paintballing session is always part of these things. You're working as a team under pressure, focusing your efforts on achieving a collective goal. And getting to splatter your boss with paint at the same time. It's brilliant.'

'And Glen Turner took part in this?'

'Everyone has to join in. In fact, we were on the same team. Green team, the claims adjusters. Glen was completely useless, of course. He got shot to bits by the red team. Some of those women in Sales are merciless. I bet he was sore for days afterwards.' Edge

223

began to laugh again, then coughed to a halt. 'Well, I mean . . .'

'Yes. He was only sore for a couple of days. And then he died.'

Diane Fry looked at Nathan Baird. He appeared to be shocked, even outraged – which pleased her more than it should have.

'We need a list of the claims that Glen Turner was working on,' she repeated.

'You're . . . you're suggesting one of our policyholders might have been responsible for Glen's death?' said Baird.

'I'm sure you get plenty of dissatisfied customers, don't you, sir?'

'Well, of course. It's in the nature of our business.'

'People who believe they've lost out on quite a large amount of money they were expecting to receive on an insurance policy?'

'We do have some large claims to deal with, of course.'

'Yes, large amounts of money that might make all the difference to someone's life, whether they can cope with their problems and carry on.'

'That's not our concern, though.'

'Exactly.'

'What do you mean?'

'I mean it probably becomes very clear to people

that you don't feel it's your concern, that you just don't care about them.'

'It's very unfair to portray our company like that.'

'Maybe. But I'm sure it must be a perception.'

'So much for the torture theory,' said Irvine a few minutes later when they were back in the car. 'Turner had multiple paintballing injuries on his body, that's all. He obviously wasn't wearing enough padding.'

'It sounds like a dangerous activity. Are we sure it's legal?'

'Properly organised venues are. They give you helmets and face masks. Padded gloves too. Most of the serious injuries have happened when someone gets a paintball in the face at close range. You can lose your sight that way. But if you're wearing the right gear, all you risk is a bit of bruising. And you have to be unlucky for a ball to hit you somewhere unprotected.'

'Turner was hit more than once. Mrs van Doon recorded fifteen injuries on his body.'

'True.'

Fry was on automatic pilot as she drove back through the centre of Edendale towards West Street. She found herself stopped at traffic lights on Buxton Road.

'I know it's all supposed to be about team building. But Mr Edge dropped in a comment about being able to splatter the boss with paint. So it's surely an opportunity to take out grievances on each other. And to create new ones too?'

Irvine nodded. 'Was Glen Turner very unpopular, do you think?'

'It's starting to look as though he was.'

As they drove on, Fry glanced at Irvine. He still looked too young for the job. He had a bit too much of the adolescent about him to give much confidence to the law-abiding public. He'd yet to gain the self-assurance that came from experience, though he must have dealt with a wide range of incidents during his time in uniform. But he had enthusiasm, didn't he? A sharp eye, a few new ideas to offer? A different interpretation to share?

'What did you think of Ralph Edge, then?' she asked.

'I didn't like him.'

Fry waited, but nothing else was offered. 'Is that it?'

Irvine blinked. 'I don't know what else you want me to say.'

'Great.'

She found herself wishing that Ben Cooper was in the car with her, instead of Luke Irvine. If she'd asked Cooper for his opinion, he would have given it without hesitation. In fact, he would have shared his views even if she didn't ask. Stopping him was the problem. And it would have been a thoughtful, considered opinion he'd formed of the man they'd just interviewed. He might have had an instinct about him . . . Instincts weren't always right, but sometimes they were. A balanced judgement, a useful insight. That was what she wanted. Fry was surprised how much she'd come to depend on it. Irvine couldn't hope to compete, or didn't want to. Perhaps he was too nervous to express an honest opinion when she gave him the chance. Was she so intimidating? Surely not.

Back in the office, Fry opened the personnel file that Nathan Baird had given her at Prospectus Assurance.

She could see from a glance at his CV that Glen Turner had been very serious about a career in insurance. Much more so than some of his colleagues, probably. It was the same in every profession. Some people just coasted along, doing the job and nothing more. But others were ambitious, always stepped forward to volunteer for new opportunities, and liked to get the appropriate training under their belt, just in case. Fry could sympathise with that.

But this was different. She wasn't sure why, but she got the impression in Turner's case that he might have been too obsessive, a man so focused on the job that he didn't have time for a social life, or any outside interests. That wasn't healthy. Lack of balance could lead an individual down the wrong path. It was possible to get things out of proportion, or out of perspective, and forget what was truly important in life. She'd seen it in so many case files, heard it in the story told by perfectly ordinary people who'd ended up in an interview room trying to explain their actions. She wondered if Glen Turner had been one of those people.

It wasn't clear at what point Turner had decided insurance was the ideal career. His father, Clive, had been a railway engineer. But it must have been quite early on in his education that he started to drift in that direction. Following an HND in Business and Management at the University of Derby's Kedleston Road campus, Turner had gained an MSc in Insurance and Risk Management from Glasgow Caledonian University, a three-year distance learning course, which had no doubt allowed him to remain living at home with his mother.

Then, while working at Prospectus Assurance, he'd received an Insurance Diploma from the Chartered Insurance Institute, and was studying for an Advanced Diploma when he died. He'd definitely been serious. He'd probably wanted to get on.

But qualifications weren't everything. That was certainly true in the police service and Fry had no doubt it was the same in the insurance industry. You needed to demonstrate a lot of personal qualities.

Drive, enthusiasm, initiative, an ability to work under pressure. And an aptitude for teamwork. You had to be the sort of person who got on well with your colleagues.

Was that the problem here? Turner hadn't exactly been the life and soul of the party, by all the accounts. He didn't chat to his colleagues much, and none of them knew anything about his life outside the office. He didn't go to the pub after work, or socialise in the evenings. He was everyone's target during the team building weekend. That wasn't a picture of Mr Popular. That was the geeky guy who didn't fit in and was laughed at behind his back. Turner really must have been good at his job to survive in that sort of environment, where it was obvious every day that he wasn't considered part of the team.

Of course, none of that was in the copy of his personnel file she'd been given. There must have been a regular appraisal or performance review. Didn't everybody do staff appraisals these days? Turner would have gone through one every twelve months probably. That would have been the task of Nathan Baird, or whoever had been his line manager before that. Appraisal reports were where this sort of issue would come up. *Working as part of a team? Room for improvement there, Glen. I'll have to rate you an E. Let's set some personal targets, shall we? Any concerns on your part?*

Bullying? Surely not. But appraisals were confidential, and they'd been removed from his personnel file before it was copied.

She turned another sheet, and discovered that Glen Turner had earned twenty-six thousand pounds a year. Less than a detective sergeant's pay. So all his hard-earned qualifications and his twelve years' experience in the insurance industry hadn't got him very far up the ladder.

There must be individuals in his company pulling in a much higher salary than that – even in Edendale, which wasn't known for its high pay levels. If she had to take a stab, she'd guess that the Chief Executive of Prospectus Assurance was getting a better remuneration package than Derbyshire's Chief Constable, who was said to be paid around £140,000. There would be perks too. A company car, private health insurance, a final salary pension scheme. And bonuses? Ralph Edge had mentioned that bonuses were no longer paid to the staff. But did that apply to senior executives?

In Fry's experience, there was a different rule for the bosses. The individuals with the highest salaries and the best benefits also got the biggest bonuses. That was always the way, wasn't it? She couldn't imagine a more effective recipe for creating resentment.

'Where's Becky Hurst?' she said, without looking up.

'I'm here, boss,' said Hurst.

'Check out this paintballing centre. Luke will give you the name.'

'The Eden Valley Adventure Centre,' said Irvine.

Hurst didn't look happy at the assignment, but she repeated the name.

'Yes, I know it,' she said.

'Find out what they remember about the team building weekend for Prospectus Assurance. And in particular the injuries sustained by Glen Turner.'

'Okay, no problem.'

Fry unclipped a photograph of Turner. It confirmed what she'd already observed at the crime scene, before his body was removed. He was a stone or two over-weight. He'd been carrying a layer of fat over most of his torso, marking him as flabby and unfit. Too much of Mum's cooking, she supposed. Mrs Turner had prob-ably stuffed her son with home-made cakes and cooked him pie and chips on a regular basis. Anything to keep him content, and less likely to strike out on his own, to hanker after living independently, when he might have to cater for himself.

All at once, she felt a pang of sympathy for Ingrid Turner. The loss of her son might have taken away her main purpose for living. Suddenly she would have no routine to follow, no structure to her day, no require-ment to see him off to work in the morning and watch for him to return in the evening to a meal ready and waiting for him in the oven. There must be a huge hole in her life – a void that no amount of WI meetings would be able to fill.

Fry put the photo back and closed the file. She might be reading the situation wrongly, of course. It was possible she was misjudging these people, making false assumptions based on her first impressions. At this stage, she would value a different opinion, a sceptical voice to question her judgement.

She looked around the CID room again, feeling that she was constantly searching for something that wasn't there. No questioning voice came to her. Just Gavin Murfin's tired rasp.

'What are you lot talking about?' he said as he ambled into the room and looked around at the assembled faces. 'You look a bit too flippin' serious for my liking. All those long faces are scaring me.'

'We're not talking about you, Gavin, anyway,' said Hurst.

'That's a relief. For a minute there, I thought I might be dead or something.'

'No such luck.'

'You've got yourself confused with Bruce Willis in *The Sixth Sense*,' said Irvine.

Murfin sat down and poked through his desk drawers. 'Well, it's an easy mistake to make.'

Fry was watching him impatiently. 'Have you got anything for me, Gavin?'

'Oh, yeah,' he said. 'I suppose you'll want to know. I've got a result on one of the cars seen by the motorist on Tuesday night. It was a BMW 5 series, with two people in it, a man and a woman. The registration number included the letters KK. The lady noticed that particularly because she's Irish.'

'Because she's Irish?'

'Apparently, in Ireland a number plate tells you which county a car was registered in. And KK stands for Kilkenny, which is where our witness is from.'

'Do we have any matching vehicles in this area?'

'Only one,' said Murfin. 'A red 5-series model with TKK in its reg. I've just got a name and address from the Vehicles database on the PNC.'

'Wasn't there a red car seen in the area at the time?' asked Fry.

'Yes, there was.'

'Well, get out there and bring the owner in, Gavin. And take DC Irvine with you.'

Forty minutes later, Luke Irvine was sitting in the CID pool car on The Dale in Wirksworth. Gavin Murfin was in the driving seat. And from the scuffed look of its interior, Murfin had driven this car before.

'So what do you say, Gavin?' asked Irvine.

Murfin scowled at him and gave a petulant yank at the wrapper of his Snickers bar, ripping the plastic away from the chocolate like a man who wanted to commit murder.

'I'm your mentor, not your minion,' he said.

'I'm just asking you. I'm appealing to your . . . well, your better nature.'

'You don't appeal to me at all. You're not my type.'

'Come on, Gavin. You're being a pillock.'

'That's more like it. Now I know you mean it.'

Irvine slumped back in his seat. Was he the only one to be concerned about Ben Cooper? That night in the pub, Diane Fry and Becky Hurst had been nominated for the job of checking him out but had returned without any information. Hurst had seemed more worried about whether the cat had been fed. And of course Fry was just relieved to have gone through the motions, as if that excused her from doing anything else. Now Murfin was proving a washout.

They were waiting for a red BMW to appear. They knew they had the right house for the owner of the vehicle, because they'd spoken to his wife, who'd told them he was expected back home any time. When they got back to the car, Irvine had suggested to Murfin that she might phone her husband on his mobile and warn him not to come home while the police were there.

'No,' Murfin had said. 'Didn't you notice the smile on her face? I bet she can't wait to see him in handcuffs in the back of a squad car. There won't be any tears from her as she waves him off to the cells.'

'What, her own husband?' protested Irvine.

Murfin had snorted derisively. 'You kids,' he'd said. 'You know nothing about marriage. Trust me, she'll be the last one to think of warning him.'

They'd been waiting almost a quarter of an hour since then, and Irvine was starting to get impatient. Murfin wasn't exactly fascinating company. In fact, Irvine wasn't entirely sure he was awake most of the time. He seemed to have developed an ability to sleep for a few minutes at a time, with his eyes wide open. At first glance it looked as if he was fully alert, until you tried to make conversation with him. Then it was obvious that his brain was switched off. Irvine supposed it was a trick he might learn after another ten or fifteen years doing this sort of job.

Murfin grunted and began to fish around in his pockets for something. Evidence that he was present in spirit as well as body.

'Do you know Wirksworth, Gavin?' asked Irvine.

'Nope.'

'I thought you knew everywhere and everything. You've been around long enough.'

'Oh, yeah. Since I landed off the Ark.'

'So why don't you know this place?'

Murfin glanced around the houses in The Dale. 'Probably because they don't have any crime.'

'There was the counterfeit currency case,' said Irvine.

'Forged notes? Not my speciality.'

Irvine remembered the case because the counterfeit banknotes had been Scottish. The inquiry had involved several businesses in Wirksworth after fake currency was used at shops all along St John's Street. It turned out to be a technique used in a number of towns up and down the country. A few months later, a counterfeiter in Glasgow had been arrested with fifty thousand pounds' worth of fake tenners in his car. He'd used digital images of genuine notes from his iPhone and reproduced them on an inkjet printer.

With a sigh, Irvine wiped condensation off the passenger window of the car. Now, shopkeepers in places like Wirksworth were suspicious of Scottish currency. Well, even more suspicious than they'd been before. If Scots voted in their referendum to become independent, those Bank of Scotland notes would probably cease to be legal tender in England anyway.

'Some of these houses are quite nice,' he said.

'Parking,' said Murfin.

'What?'

'There's no damn parking. Look where I've had to

stick the car. Every time something comes past it nearly takes the wing mirror off on your side.'

Irvine glanced automatically into the wing mirror.

'Heads up, Gavin,' he said. 'There's a red BMW coming.'

20

Carsington Water had a very low dam wall, nothing like the structures holding back the waters of the Upper Derwent further north. Reservoirs like Ladybower and Howden had been built in a different time and to a different scale, matching the size of the hills around them. Their history was dramatic too, the scene of training runs for the Second World War Dambusters squadron and their bouncing bombs.

But Carsington was a product of the 1990s, the last big reservoir built in Derbyshire. With its visitor centre, sailing club, water sports centre and nature reserve, the emphasis was firmly on leisure activities. That was surely a clear sign of changing times. It wasn't considered acceptable any more to flood vast tracts of land without any regard for the interests of local people. Villages were no longer destroyed to provide a water supply for the inhabitants of a distant city. Carsington was as much a symbol as a utility.

Ben Cooper slotted his Toyota into a space in the main car park for the visitor centre. The first thing he noticed as he walked towards the building was a display of drought-tolerant plants. Mimosa, calendula, juniper. He supposed it was part of the centre's overarching message about the pressure on available water supplies and the need for conservation. How to manage your garden during a hosepipe ban. Right now, it looked like a laughable irony. Flood tolerant plants would have been more appropriate.

He stopped to check his phone. Had he remembered to charge it up last night? The screen glowed when he touched the button at the bottom, and a series of icons appeared. Yes, he had. He felt unduly pleased with himself. Those little coloured squares on the screen labelled *Phone*, *Mail*, *Safari* were symbols of his reconnection with the world. He didn't intend to use them, but the fact that they were there signified an achievement.

He ran a hand across his face to see how it felt. Not brilliant, but a lot better since he'd found the charger for his shaver. He'd even found a set of clean clothes, since there was nothing he could do about the ones he'd taken off earlier in the week. He was wearing his old waxed coat with the poacher's pockets. It had seen a lot of muck in its life, and a bit of blood too. But he thought he would pass. As satisfied as he could be, Cooper walked round to the rear of the visitor centre to enter the courtyard.

Unlike most reservoirs, Carsington wasn't used as storage capacity for the supply system. Its function was to pump water in and out of the River Derwent, taking it out at times when the river was high and putting it back again when levels were low. There was an overflow in the dam wall, which had been planned to cope with the worst flood conditions that its designers could envisage occurring in a ten-thousand-year period. Looking at the weather forecast, those conditions could happen this week.

A time capsule was said to be buried in the reservoir floor near the value control tower. He supposed it would only be discovered when Carsington was emptied in the distant future. The area was certainly changing beyond recognition. Not more than a mile away from Carsington Water was an organic farm, where some friends of Claire's had once stayed in an EcoPod, with a solar powered shower and a compost toilet, and inquisitive goats wandering in and out from the surrounding fields.

Around the courtyard there were shops, an ice cream

240

parlour and an RSPB outlet. Cooper bought a filter coffee from the Watermark café and sat under a glass canopy in the courtyard, watched hopefully by a small flock of sparrows who perched on the tables and a magpie that eyed him from the safety of the edge of the roof.

For him, the highlight of this courtyard was the Kugel Stone. Three feet in diameter and weighing over a ton, it was a large black granite ball that floated almost magically on a thin film of water. Two pumps supplied jets of water at different speeds, causing the stone not only to float on the surface, but to rotate slowly. The lightest touch of a finger made the Kugel revolve in a different direction.

He looked up just as Carol Villiers entered the Watermark café. She was looking smart as always, that extra attention to detail making her stand out from the crowd, especially in CID. Her clothes always seemed to fit better, her shoes were less scuffed, she moved with a physical confidence that others lost when they spent so much time at a desk job. She even seemed to have reached the courtyard from the car park without getting wet or dishevelled, as if she'd simply materialised from a teleportation machine.

'Hello, Carol,' said Cooper.

'How are you doing?'

'I'm okay.'

She gave him that concerned look he'd come to expect. He'd seen it so often over the last few months. Cooper wondered if this was what disabled people sometimes complained about – the way people stared at them with an expression of mixed curiosity and pity. Each time he saw that look, it felt as if everyone was trying to fix him into a role of pitiable victim.

He ordered more coffee, and she sat down across the table. She hardly took her eyes off him, as though she was afraid that he would try to escape if she looked away even for a second.

'So what's happening at the moment?' asked Cooper. 'Anything exciting?'

Villiers didn't answer directly. 'You know we want you back, Ben. We need you at West Street.'

'Really? I don't think Diane Fry would want to see me back.'

'Yes, she would. You'd be surprised. She doesn't want to be there any more than we want to see her.'

Cooper shook his head. 'I just can't come into the office, Carol.'

Villiers sighed. 'So then,' she said, 'does it have to be unofficial?'

'I can be unofficial,' said Cooper.

Villiers regarded him steadily. 'You know, while you're on extended leave, you're just another member of the public.'

Cooper nodded. 'It has its advantages.'

When Villiers had returned to Derbyshire she'd been that much older and leaner than he remembered her, with an extra assurance in the way she held herself. When they were younger, they'd gone to school together, studied for their A levels at High Peak College at the same time. She'd been a good friend, a bit sports obsessed perhaps, really into swimming and running half marathons. She'd been Carol Parry then, the daughter of Stan and Vera Parry, who ran a bed and breakfast in Tideswell High Street.

But there had been another dimension behind her new self-confidence – a shadow in her eyes, a darkness behind the facade. Cooper had noticed it then, and he couldn't mistake it now. Part of that darkness might be explained by the loss of her husband, killed by a road-side bomb in Afghanistan. But perhaps there were other experiences too, episodes in her life that she would never talk about.

'Well, you know we have a murder case?' she said. 'It happened not very far from here, actually.'

'Yes, I did hear that.'

'You're not completely out of the loop, then.'

'It's the front page headline in this week's *Matlock Mercury*,' said Cooper. 'I noticed it when I was in the petrol station this morning.'

Villiers nodded. 'That's good.'

243

She made it sound like an achievement, as if he was a spinal injury patient attempting to move a finger for the first time, or a baby wobbling upright for a half a second before falling flat on its face again. Was he supposed to feel a warm glow that he'd pleased her with his powers of observation? Immediately he felt an unkind urge to puncture her expectations.

'But I didn't read the story,' he said. 'So, apart from that, I know nothing.'

'Oh. Well, I've been away in Chesterfield for a few days assisting C Division, so I'm only just catching up myself. But the victim's name is Glen Turner. There's nothing of any interest in his background. Not that we've found so far, anyway. He worked in insurance. A claims adjuster, employed by Prospectus Assurance. Unmarried, thirty-eight years old, lived with his mother in Wirksworth.'

Cooper felt a jolt of excitement so completely unexpected that he thought for a moment he'd been electrocuted. He put his cup down in its saucer with an unnecessary clatter. He'd suddenly seemed to have lost proper co-ordination.

'Prospectus Assurance?' he said.

Villiers brightened visibly at the tone of his response. 'Yes. Have you heard of it?'

'Oh . . . I think they have offices in Edendale.'

'Yes, they do.'

Villiers' coffee arrived, and Cooper took a moment to steady himself. His hand was shaking again, and he hid it under the table where he hoped she wouldn't see.

'So what happened to him?' he asked.

'Mr Turner was found dead in a shallow stream. Well, the stream wasn't quite so shallow as it normally would be . . .'

'Because of all the rain,' said Cooper.

'Yes.'

She gave him that look again.

'Don't say "good" again, Carol. I'm not a dog to be patted on the head every time I fetch a ball.'

Villiers had the grace to flush a little. Not that it didn't suit her. It took the edge off that hard exterior she'd come back to Derbyshire with, the tough shell of a woman who'd seen active service overseas and had gone through an unsuccessful marriage at the same time. It made her a bit more like the Carol Parry he remembered from their school days. It was a transition he'd been hoping to see signs of for months now. He wondered if she'd decide to revert to her maiden name at some point.

'I'm sorry, Ben,' she said. 'You're right, of course. It's just the way that everybody's been talking about you recently, it got into my head. I suppose it might have made me sound a bit, well . . .'

'Patronising,' said Cooper.

She smiled. 'Yes, patronising.'

'It's all right,' he said.

And it genuinely was all right. He didn't mind at all. The fact that she'd apologised straight away made Cooper feel warm towards her. He couldn't imagine Diane Fry sitting there and saying sorry to him without hesitation . . . Not in a million years.

'So. A flooded stream. And a dead victim called, let's see . . . Glen Turner?'

Villiers laughed. 'Are you taking notes?'

'No.' Cooper shook his head slowly. 'Just listening to you, Carol.'

She took a drink of her coffee, reluctant to meet his eye for a moment. 'He was lying dead on his back in the water. He'd been there for a number of hours before he was found by a council gully-emptying crew. His body was diverting the flow of water into the road.'

'He drowned?'

'Not sure. Cause of death so far unconfirmed.'

Cooper frowned. 'There are several questions springing to mind.'

'Well, I won't say "good" – but I'll admit that's definitely what I like to hear.'

Thoughtfully, Cooper looked down at his empty coffee cup. Outside the window, the Kugel stone slowly turned and turned, driven by its jets of water. It was a testament to the power of even a small amount of water that it could lift a ton of granite so easily.

'Was Mr Turner a big man?' he said.

'Yes. He formed a pretty good dam.'

'And his clothes were found, I hope?'

'Nearby in the woods. All present, including his wallet. Cash, credit cards, driving licence, mobile phone, the lot.'

He guessed from Villiers' expectant expression that she was waiting for him to say something about robbery being discounted as a motive. But that was obvious enough.

'Woods,' he said. 'Which woods?'

'Oh. Sparrow Wood. The other side of Wirksworth, near Brassington.'

'The Forestry Commission woodland?'

'No, a privately owned section next to it.'

'Car?' said Cooper.

'A Renault Mégane, but it was parked outside a pub about a mile away in Brassington.'

'His shoes . . . ?' said Cooper.

'Yes, mud on them.'

He nodded. 'And there were no witnesses.'

'Why do you say that, Ben?'

'It's a quiet road. Whatever happened took place at night, probably. And the weather has been bad. I suppose it was raining on the night he was killed. So there would be no one around to see anything. No witnesses.'

'Only a couple who saw an unidentified man in a four-wheel drive near the woods.'

'I see.'

Cooper gazed for a few moments at the expanse of water outside the window, where a boat was tacking across the little bay in the rain. Everything looked suddenly blurred and indistinct. Though he tried to concentrate on what had just been said, he found his mind drifting towards a nice pub that he knew, standing close to the western edge of the reservoir with views of the hills on the other side. The Knockerdown Inn. He was pretty sure it was open all day in the summer. There might be a log fire in the bar to dry out in front of. They served fish, chips and mushy peas with their own home-made batter.

Cooper's eyes had settled on the four wind turbines that had recently been erected to the north on Carsington Pasture. The wind farm was just outside the boundary of the national park, but very close to the High Peak Trail. He remembered the National Park Authority objecting to the scheme because of the impact on the landscape of turbines three hundred and fifty feet high overlooking the reservoir.

Close by the new wind farm was the Dream Cave, where the remains of a woolly rhino had been found and *Homo erectus* had visited during the warm inter-glacial period. By the time the Romans arrived more than two thousand years ago, they'd found a thriving lead mining industry in this area. Now, they would find tourists living in EcoPods.

Human memory seemed such a fleeting, fragmentary thing in this landscape. Ephemeral and transitory. It flickered into the mind and out again so quickly that it meant nothing. Nothing at all.

He became aware that Villiers was looking at him with concern, her coffee going cold in front of her. In fact she seemed to have been speaking his name, and perhaps had been doing so for a minute or two.

'Ben?' she said. 'Earth to Ben Cooper.'

'Sorry,' he said, shaking himself as if throwing off a heavy blanket.

'I have to say this, Ben, but you'd really lost it there for a while.'

'It's nothing.'

But he could see she wasn't convinced. He would have to work harder to pass muster, even with Carol Villiers.

'Focus,' she said. 'You need to focus on something useful, a practical objective.'

'You've told me that before.'

'Because it's the best advice I can give you.'

Cooper tried to smile. 'I'll remember.'

But Villiers was watching him closely. She didn't miss much. In fact, she never had.

'Well,' she said, picking up her phone and checking the screen, about to get up and leave. 'It's been great, Ben, but—'

'Don't go, Carol. Not yet.'

He'd blurted the words out. But as soon as they left his mouth he knew they made him sound desperate and needy. That wasn't the impression he'd been trying to give.

'Sorry, Ben, I have to.'

What was he going to do? Carol Villiers was the person he could rely on. He knew he could trust her.

'Where are you going now, Carol?' he asked.

'Into Wirksworth, then Carsington. I've got to see if this man in the four-wheel drive rings a bell for anyone connected to Glen Turner.'

'Mind if I tag along?'

Her mouth fell open. Then after a moment she smiled. 'It would be a pleasure.'

21

When they got Charlie Dean in an interview room at West Street, he spilled the whole story about his assignation with Sheena Sullivan in the woods, the car getting stuck in the mud, the mysterious stranger in the red rain jacket who'd appeared out of the night and made such an impression on them both.

'You can see why we didn't come forward,' said Dean.

He looked appealingly from Fry to Irvine, but found no understanding from either of them. Fry stared at him, seeing a man who thought far too much of himself, perhaps imagined he was the centre of the universe. Did Mr Dean really believe his actions had no consequences, except for himself? Yes, it was perfectly possible. He wouldn't be the first to sit in this interview room and look baffled that no one else thought he was important.

'You're a married man,' said Fry. 'And yet you took a woman into the woods in your car for sex. And you admit you've done this many times? What were you *thinking*?'

He stared at her as if she was an idiot. 'Well, obviously . . . I was thinking that I'd get away with it and never have to explain myself.'

'No excuses, no reasons? No rationalisation?'

'I always think rationalisation after the act is a bit futile,' said Dean. 'We all live in the moment, don't we? We don't feel we have to explain our actions to ourselves. So it's only other people who have those expectations of us. Excuses, reasons . . . ? Detective Sergeant, it's all so much bullshit.'

Fry supposed he might be considered attractive by a certain type of woman. He was dark and well built, with a boyish smirk and a mischievous gleam in his eye. Once he'd recovered from the stress of being picked up by the police and taken into the station, he'd collected himself well and told a good story. At the same time, he'd managed to exude an air of assurance and self-possession, a man who was in control and could handle any problem. It was his own image, she supposed, a role he'd created for himself.

She looked at the details Irvine had taken from him,

252

and remembered that Charlie Dean was an estate agent. It might be wrong to follow the stereotype, but it must be a job which gave him the opportunities to act out his role. If you were hesitant or unsure of yourself, you might be willing to let a man like Mr Dean steer you in whatever direction he wanted you to go. If he told you a house was perfect for you, it would be tempting to believe him.

'We need more details of this man you encountered,' said Fry. 'A description. What type of car he was driving.'

Dean shrugged. 'I'm sorry. It was so dark. And in the circumstances I just wanted to get my friend out of there.'

'Your friend. Whose name you told us earlier is Mrs Sheena Sullivan.'

'Yes.'

She could see that it had caused him some pain to reveal the name of the woman he'd been with. It was probably the sort of discomfort he felt when having to admit that the property he was selling you suffered from rising damp. There was no point in denying it once the survey had been done. In this case, he had no choice but to give up Sheena Sullivan's name.

'I wouldn't want her husband to find out,' said Dean. 'Obviously.'

He directed a roguish, bad boy smile at Fry, but the charm was lost on her.

'And your own wife, sir? You haven't mentioned her.'

'Oh, and Barbara too,' he said.

Fry had never met anyone she could imagine marrying and spending the rest of her life with. Encounters with the likes of Charlie Dean were enough to put her off the idea completely.

'You've made things a lot more difficult for us, sir,' she said. 'This sort of delay could have serious implications for our investigation, you know.'

Now Dean licked his lips nervously. 'You'll catch him, though, won't you? The man in the red rain jacket, I mean.'

'Let's hope so, sir. Let's hope so.'

Sheena Sullivan smoked a cigarette anxiously as she told her version of the story. They'd located her at the hairdressing salon in Wirksworth where she worked as a stylist, and she talked to Diane Fry in the back room of the salon. There was just room for two of them to sit among fresh supplies of gel sprays and boxes of Barbicide disinfectant, close to a tiny kitchen area.

Her statement was fractured and hesitant, though generally consistent with Dean's. She continually returned to the impression that the man in the red rain jacket had made on her.

'So what did you notice about him?' asked Fry.

'Anything would be helpful. Any small details that could help us identify him.'

'He seemed big,' she said. 'But he was standing against the headlights of his car, you know, so I didn't see much of him, apart from the coat. He frightened me, I can tell you that. He was already breathing heavily when he got out of his car. I don't want to imagine what he'd been doing. And there was something about his voice . . .'

Sheena shuddered visibly and took a drag on her cigarette. She'd opened a small window that looked out on to a backyard, but smoking in the workplace was still illegal. There were times to point these things out, but this wasn't one of them. Not when Fry wanted Mrs Sullivan to feel relaxed enough to talk.

'The coat?' said Fry. 'You mentioned the coat?'

'Yes, it had a logo on the chest. Red and blue, with a name next to it. I couldn't read the lettering.'

'But you saw the colours.'

'In the car headlights. The colours were reflected in the light. That's why I noticed the logo. It just sort of stood out.'

Sheena pushed her blonde hair back from her forehead and looked at Fry with a pleading expression. She looked frail and vulnerable, and a little lost. Fry really wanted to ask her what she saw in a man like Charlie Dean, and how she'd ended up in this situation.

But it wasn't the right time for that either. And she suspected that Sheena Sullivan wouldn't know the answer anyway.

'Berghaus,' said Luke Irvine when Fry described the logo. 'Everyone knows the Berghaus logo. You see BBC news reporters wearing it all the time.'

'I've never noticed,' said Fry.

Irvine looked at her. 'I bet you don't care about designer labels at all,' he said.

'What are you trying to say, DC Irvine? Are you making some comment about the way I dress? Do you think you're in a position to criticise my fashion sense?'

Irvine began to backtrack. 'No, no. I mean – I suppose you don't recognise it because you just don't watch much telly.'

Fry still wasn't mollified. 'Maybe.'

It was true that she didn't watch TV very often. The news, a few films. There seemed to be very little else of interest for her to watch. Not really to *watch*. The TV set was often switched on in the flat, but only for the sound of voices in the background, which made the place feel less empty. So she had been vaguely aware of programmes that everyone talked about in the office. There had been *Big Brother*, then *I'm a Celebrity*. *The X Factor* and *Strictly Come Dancing*. When their names were mentioned she could nod and feel some satisfaction that she at least knew whether it was reality TV or a talent show. But why she should have noticed what BBC reporters were wearing on the news she couldn't imagine.

'All right then, Luke. Get yourself a list of local suppliers and see if you can identify that style of coat. With a bit of luck it might be an unusual type.'

Irvine blinked. 'Have you any idea how many outdoor clothing shops there are in this area? Every village has at least one. I can think of six in Edendale alone.'

'That will keep you busy, then. You'd better get started.'

Like every other senior police officer, Detective Superintendent Hazel Branagh had a thankless job. She was tasked with managing crime in the sprawling territory of Derbyshire E Division, and she was having to do it with diminishing resources.

She'd sent a message summoning Diane Fry to her office, and first she asked for an update on the murder inquiry, though she had copies of the reports on her desk.

'These two people you've interviewed,' she said, after she'd listened to an outline.

'Charles Dean and Sheena Sullivan.'

'Are they potential suspects?'

'We can put them in the area, but we can't place them at the crime scene. Besides, what would be their motive? There's no connection with the victim that we can see.'

'Just witnesses, then.'

'And unreliable ones,' said Fry.

'Really?'

'They would never have come forward of their own volition. They've both got their own concerns, a need to keep their activities secret for obvious reasons. And I'm still not convinced they're telling us everything they did or saw.'

'There must be more that forensics can come up with?'

Fry shrugged. 'So far they've offered us a heap of garbage. Literally.'

'I've seen the list of items,' said Branagh. 'Evidential value?'

'Well, as evidence, it's all practically worthless. But some of it does give us another lead.'

'Does it?'

'Those woods are used by off-roaders, and there have been some conflicts in the past. Local officers say they feared a violent confrontation would result eventually. Nothing like this perhaps, but—'

'It's a bit of a stretch.'

'Everything is a bit of a stretch at the moment, ma'am. We can't even find anything in our victim's background that looks relevant.'

'So what do we have on him? Did he have any links with the location? This Sparrow Wood place. Was he in the habit of visiting the area?'

'Apparently not.'

Branagh stood up and turned away thoughtfully. Her broad shoulders blocked out most of the light from the window. Fry had heard some of the male officers say that she would make a good prop forward for the divisional rugby team. It was unkind. But, at this moment, she could see what they meant. With her bulky outline, she looked as though she could bear any weight that was thrust on her.

'Are you aware that Detective Inspector Hitchens is moving on from E Division?' asked Branagh finally.

'I . . . had heard some talk,' admitted Fry.

'He hasn't mentioned it to you himself?'

'No. Well, I don't suppose he would have thought it necessary. Not since I transferred to the Special Operations Unit. I haven't been a part of Divisional CID for some months now.'

'Of course. But you must have thought about it, Diane.'

'About what, ma'am?'

'The vacancy.' Branagh glanced at Fry over her shoulder and raised a sceptical eyebrow. 'Oh, surely? When I ranked as a DS, I had my eye out for any inspector's job that was coming vacant, no matter what the speciality. And some jobs that weren't vacant, probably.'

'I hadn't considered it. I mean, the SCU—'

'I know, I know. But there won't be any promotions available there, you know. Every chief officer in the region has the odd DI to spare. Here in E Division, if we don't find a suitable candidate locally, we'll have no trouble recruiting from outside. In fact, they'll be lining up at the door. And I don't want that. Personally, I always think the devil you know is preferable to the devil you don't.'

'I'm flattered, ma'am,' said Fry. 'I think.'

Branagh nodded, and gave an uncharacteristic sigh. 'You're aware, I'm sure, that there has always been a bit of competition between yourself and DS Cooper. Two good officers, but very different in style. I can see from the personnel records that it was already happening before I arrived in E Division.'

'Yes, I suppose it's true,' said Fry.

Well, of course it was true. Fry remembered it well, that first sergeant's job coming up after she'd transferred to Edendale from the West Midlands, and the glaring obviousness of Ben Cooper's desire for the promotion.

260

No, not a desire. That was the wrong word. It had been an expectation.

And that was the difference between them, she thought. Cooper had assumed the job would come his way by right, as a sort of inheritance, the proverbial dead man's shoes. Fry, on the other hand, had always been forced to work for these things, and she'd hungered for it. Someone like Superintendent Branagh would be able to recognise that. She was no fool.

Branagh was watching her now.

'You will think about it, won't you?' she said.

'Yes, ma'am.'

'Where are you headed now?'

'Back to Wirksworth. There's got to be something I can dig out about our victim, Glen Turner.'

Glen Turner's financial affairs had been examined, and his bank accounts looked unremarkable, as far as Diane Fry could see. The only regular incoming transactions were his monthly salary deposits. The largest payments were direct debits to Derbyshire Dales for council tax, E.ON for a quarterly electricity bill, BT for broadband services. In fact, it seemed he'd paid all the bills for his mother's house in Wirksworth.

A Visa card showed a service on his Renault Mégane at a local garage, an order for books from Amazon, a new suit from Marks & Spencers. There was nothing apparent in his bank or credit card statements that could have been a motive for murder.

But what else could she gather about Glen Turner's life? Fry had decided to pay another visit to Mrs Turner in her precariously leaning cottage in St John's Street. Now that a family liaison officer had been allocated to her and appropriate support systems were in place, Mrs Turner seemed much more willing, and able, to talk about her son.

'Glen? Yes, he was such a good son,' she said. 'Nobody ever had a bad word to say against him.'

'Really?' said Fry.

She'd heard that said about people before, but it had never been true. How could it be? Yet in Glen Turner's case it seemed to come close. Nothing bad, and yet nothing particularly good either.

According to his mother, Glen had actually left home for a while in his twenties. He'd rented a two-bedroom town house further up St John's Street for six hundred pounds a month, with a brick outbuilding for storage. But when his father died, he'd given up the lease and moved back to the cottage. In Fry's view, that was hardly leaving home. Even when he was paying his own rent, Glen had never been more than a few hundred yards away from his mother's apron strings.

Ingrid Turner had proudly reported her son's organic

credentials. He was a member of the Wirksworth Community Growers, and had always bought bread from the Old Bake House in St Mary's Gate. He was also a volunteer with the Ecclesbourne Valley Railway, which ran the restored line and railway museum at Wirksworth station, though the older blokes didn't let him do much except issue tickets. Sometimes, Glen went to the quiz nights on Sundays at the Red Lion on Coldwell Street, and liked to drink the odd pint of a Cornish beer called Doom Bar, sitting out on the beer terrace during the summer. Occasionally, on a special occasion, he ate at the Digler's Den restaurant. With his mother, of course.

It was an unexceptional existence. Surely no one could have objected to anything that Glen Turner did in his private life, though they might have made fun of him for the lack of excitement, the absence of any meaningful relationships but one. So why did Fry feel so uneasy about it?

'There's a place just outside Wirksworth called the National Stone Centre,' she said. 'Did your son visit it, that you know of?'

'Yes. He was quite interested in that sort of thing. History, geology.'

'We found an item in his car. A fossil. It seems to have been bought at the National Stone Centre on Monday.'

263

'Yes, they have a shop,' said Mrs Turner. 'Glen did take me there once. It wasn't my sort of place, though. Oh, I suppose it's all very fascinating in its way, being able to see the earth's crust and all that. But it all looked so dead to me. Just rock and dust. Even the animals they talked about there had all been dead for millions of years. Like that fossil Glen bought, I suppose. Me, I prefer gardens. Living, growing things.'

Fry nodded. 'It's odd that he should have gone there on Monday, isn't it? Shouldn't he have been at work?'

'Oh, he said he wasn't feeling well enough on Monday. He took a day off.'

'That would have been because of the injuries he received at the paintballing over the weekend.'

Clearly Mrs Turner was surprised by the turn of the conversation. 'Oh, you know about that? I didn't think—'

'What?'

But Mrs Turner had stopped. Her eyes glazed over for a moment. 'Yes, poor Glen. He was a bit sore after his experience. Like I say, he decided not to go into the office on Monday.'

'But he was well enough on Tuesday?'

'Yes. Well, he went back to work. But then he never came home in the evening.'

'I see.'

So what had happened on Tuesday? It was remaining

264

a blank day in a remarkably empty life. According to Nathan Baird, nothing out of the ordinary had taken place at the office that day, and Glen Turner had left at the usual time. But surely there must have been some banter about the team building weekend. A bit of sniggering behind Glen's back, a few subtle cracks about his humiliation. Perhaps some not so subtle hilarity. And after work? Why had he gone to Brassington, and who had he met up with?

Fry turned to Mrs Turner again and told her the scanty information about the stranger in the red rain jacket. She didn't expect much. The description was so vague that no one would have recognised it. So she wasn't surprised when Mrs Turner shook her head.

'It means nothing to me, I'm afraid. Is it somebody Glen met?'

'We don't know. It's possible. Did your son drink at a pub in Brassington?'

'He didn't drink much at all.'

'Of course he didn't,' said Fry.

'Well, the odd pint of beer. And he was always careful never to drink and drive. That's why we went to the Red Lion, or the Hope and Anchor. They're within walking distance of here.'

Fry noticed that 'we', and felt uneasy again. When Glen Turner did go to the pub, he went with his mother? There was something wrong with that picture. She was more than ever convinced that Glen had a secret he'd been hiding, even if it was only a tendency to slope off to the pub on his own occasionally. And perhaps a friend or two that his mother wouldn't have approved of?

'I don't suppose your son kept a diary?' said Fry.

'I don't think so. At the office perhaps . . . ?'

'He kept a record of appointments on his phone.'

She had been sitting on Ingrid Turner's sofa as they talked. Now Fry stood, and found herself looking out of the back window. There was a surprisingly large garden. She would never have expected it from the front of the property. There didn't seem to be any access to the rear of the cottage from St John's Street, so there must be a back lane.

A few minutes ago Mrs Turner had listed her son's membership of Wirksworth Community Growers as one of his plus points. Fry had assumed there must be an allotment somewhere, perhaps shared with some old geezer who actually did all the work. But here was a burgeoning plot filled with vegetables, and a line of canes supporting fruit bushes. One side of the garden was taken up by an expanse of glass and gleaming aluminium.

'You do have a nice garden,' said Fry.

'Thank you.'

'Is that greenhouse new?'

'Yes, Glen bought it for me. I'm the real enthusiast about gardening, I suppose. But Glen always took an interest. He was good that way.'

Fry thought back to her examination of Turner's bank and credit card statements. She couldn't remember every detail, of course. But this was a large structure, surely twenty feet long. A couple of thousand pounds, perhaps?

'It's wonderful. Where did Glen get it?'

'I couldn't say. Two young men arrived one day and put it up.'

'Do you have a receipt, by any chance?'

'Not me. Glen dealt with all that sort of thing.'

'There was no paperwork in his room. Hardly anything. Did he keep receipts and bills somewhere else?'

'I don't know,' said Mrs Turner. 'He never bothered me about bills. I just passed everything on to Glen. I suppose they must be somewhere. At the office, perhaps? In his briefcase?'

Fry shook her head. 'No, we found nothing like that.'

'I can't tell you, then. He did use the computer a lot. There was the one upstairs, and he had a laptop for work.'

'We've got people examining those,' said Fry. 'But it takes time.'

'I don't know why it should be important, though.'

'It probably isn't. But we have to look at everything if we're going to find out who caused your son's death.'

'I don't know how it helps.'

'Nor do I, Mrs Turner,' admitted Fry. 'Nor do I.'

22

The western part of Wirksworth was where the old lead miners and quarrymen used to live, a jumble of small cottages built mostly of random stone from the nearby quarries. In the area between the abandoned Dale and Middle Peak quarries, the cottages were linked by a maze of alleys and ginnels. There was no room for vehicle access, and the numbering of the houses seemed haphazard. It must be a nightmare for a new postman.

Ben Cooper knew a bit about this town, thanks to Liz. When they were property hunting, they'd come here to look at a Grade II listed cottage on St John's Street. It had gas central heating and a wonderful vaulted cellar that he could think of all kinds of uses for. As they passed through the town now, he saw from the estate agent's sign that the cottage was still for sale.

Liz had liked the idea of living right in the centre of Wirksworth. She'd loved the range of shops and businesses on St John's Street. There was an old-fashioned chemist and druggist with bow-fronted windows and a double entrance door. Founded in 1756, according to the sign over the doorway. A veterinary surgery, a couple of antiques shops. The Blacks Head pub, tucked away in a corner near the market. There were glimpses of the surrounding hills from every street and alley in the town.

After viewing the cottage, they'd stopped for lunch at a little bistro, Le Mistral. They'd eaten vegetarian soup, salmon fishcakes, Provençale vegetable and goat's cheese salad, an olive and houmous platter. Every dish was imprinted on his memory. He could taste the fishcakes now.

Cooper wondered why he'd starting thinking so much about food. Perhaps it was because he couldn't remember anything he'd eaten during the last couple of months. Had he lost weight, he wondered? Perhaps he could ask Villiers. Or would it make him seem even odder if he revealed that he didn't know?

He left his Toyota in the Barmote Croft car park, where the ticket machine still wasn't working, and climbed into Carol Villiers' VW Golf. It was very tidy inside, no CDs or empty water bottles lying around, as there were in his own car. It even smelled of air freshener. Pine or meadow flowers, something of that kind.

'You're strictly not here,' said Villiers. 'If anyone asks.'

'Of course. I'm just a member of the public getting a ride-along.'

'I don't know whether we're insured for that. Did you sign a disclaimer?'

'As long as you don't crash, we'll be fine.'

Villiers drove out of the car park on to Coldwell Street. 'I'll do my best.'

Even on a wet Friday, the centre of Wirksworth was busy. Liz had discovered the story of this little town from a few minutes at the heritage centre in Crown Yard. History said that it was Henry VIII who'd granted a charter to hold a miners' court in the town, the Bar Moot. The present court building still contained a brass dish for measuring the levy due to the Crown. As recently as the twentieth century, a thief who stole from a lead mine would be punished by having his hand nailed to the winch marking the mineshaft. He then had the option of either ripping the nail through his hand or starving to death. Sessions were still held at the Moot Hall on Chapel Lane. It was the oldest industrial court in the world, with its own terminology, and regulations dating from Saxon times.

As far as Cooper knew, there was no more nailing of thieves' hands to winches. But you never knew in Derbyshire. Anything was possible.

Ingrid Turner's cottage on St John's Street was the first port of call. Cooper loved the house as soon as he saw it. This was exactly the sort of place Liz would have wanted to live. He knew her tastes so well that he could almost see the furniture she would have bought for the sitting room, the colour schemes she would have devised for these walls. He could practically feel the carpet underfoot.

'Someone else has just been here,' said Mrs Turner when they went in. 'The sergeant.'

'DS Fry?' said Villiers.

Cooper looked over his shoulder. There had been no sign of Diane Fry or her car when they arrived. That had been a narrow escape.

'Yes, that's her.'

'Well, we've got several lines of inquiry we're following up,' said Villiers. 'So there are likely to be more questions yet.'

'I know. I suppose it'll never end.'

Cooper turned back to her. 'Oh, I'm sure it will,' he said.

Mrs Turner smiled at him. Then she frowned, as if

puzzled by something that wasn't quite right. He'd become used to that look. He expected it, because he knew himself that something wasn't quite right. He was sure it must show on the outside too. It was why he felt so reluctant to meet people face to face, strangers and familiar acquaintances alike. Being with Villiers made it different, just as he'd hoped it would. In a way, he felt he'd be able to hide behind her, so that people would see her and not him. She was the only one who could have made that work.

Cooper stayed silent while Villiers ran through her questions. He could tell from Mrs Turner's reaction that she'd answered them all before. Had her son mentioned that he was planning to go anywhere or meet anyone on Tuesday evening? Had he been having any problems? Money troubles, a girlfriend? Could she suggest anyone else they might talk to about him?

They were questions that were always worth asking a second time, or even a third. People recollected details that hadn't occurred to them the first time round. Something popped into their head when they weren't thinking about it, and they forgot it again until they were prompted. Sometimes it seemed heartless to be questioning a bereaved relative over and over. But there was no doubt it could achieve results, and that was the objective.

'Thank you, Mrs Turner,' said Villiers finally.

'Anything I can do,' she said.

Back in the centre of Wirksworth, there were uneven stone setts on the narrow footways in front of some of the houses on Green Hill. Today they were acting like drainage channels for the water running downhill, which might have been their original purpose.

'What next, Carol?' asked Cooper.

'Diane wants me to visit Ralph Edge,' said Villiers.

'And who is he?'

'Glen Turner's colleague at Prospectus Assurance. He's the one who told us about the paintballing.'

'Paintballing?' said Cooper.

'Oh, you don't know.'

'Not unless you tell me, Carol.'

Cooper listened quietly while Villiers told him the story of the team building weekend and Glen Turner's paintballing injuries.

'Of course, I only picked this up myself today, since I came back from Chesterfield just this morning.'

'You seem to be on top of things,' said Cooper.

'I try. It's not easy sometimes.'

'Oh, tell me about it.'

'You're feeling out of the loop, I suppose, Ben?'

'Yes.' Cooper hesitated. 'Carol, can I ask you a favour?'

'Of course. Well . . . what?'

'I'd like you to keep me up to date with anything concerning Eliot Wharton and Josh Lane. You know – dates of hearings, pleas, bail conditions.'

'I suppose I could do that,' said Villiers. 'Though there are systems . . .'

'They take forever.'

'All right, then.'

'And any new evidence that might turn up,' said Cooper quickly.

'I don't know, Ben.'

'Just do what you can. Okay?'

She sucked in a breath, and he could see that she was torn. He shouldn't push her loyalty too far.

'And in the meantime can you keep me up to date with this murder inquiry?' he said. 'I'm really interested.'

Villiers let out her breath in relief. 'Well, that's better,' she said.

Ralph Edge lived a few miles outside Wirksworth, in Carsington village. His house was just past the Miners Arms pub. The opening of the reservoir in the 1990s had transformed Carsington. A bypass had been built to take construction traffic, new homes had appeared, and some of the barns were converted to residential use.

There were no farms left in the village now, and of course the post office had closed years ago. Yet some of the older cottages were said to be built right over mineshafts. One was supposed to have tunnels still underneath it.

A tiny Gothic-style church was hidden among yew trees on the lower slopes of Carsington Pasture. It had neither tower nor spire, just a small bellcote on the western gable. Cooper was struck by the sight of a new grave standing ready in the churchyard, the hole covered by a couple of planks, and a heap of soil piled next to it.

The Edges' property was about twenty years old, built from local limestone with dressed stone quoins. Inside, the dining room was set out with a large pine table and eight dining chairs, as if the Edges held regular dinner parties. Garden furniture stood out in the rain, the chairs tilted forward against the table to allow the water to run off. He wondered if the Edges had a dinner party planned this week. If so, it would certainly be held indoors.

'No, it means nothing to me,' said Edge, when Villiers described the stranger seen by Charlie Dean and Sheena Sullivan. 'I mean, that could be absolutely anybody.'

'What sort of car do you drive yourself, sir?' asked Villiers.

'A Mercedes saloon. It's not brand new, by the way. And it's definitely not four-wheel drive. In this weather, I sometimes wish it was.'

'I'm sorry to have to ask you these things.'

'I expect it,' said Edge. 'I've dealt with police officers before.'

Cooper was pleased to see that Villiers was looking round the house, taking in details.

'Do you have family, sir?' she asked.

'I'm not married, but my parents live here with me. They're quite elderly.'

Cooper tilted his head on one side as he looked at the man. Glen Turner had lived in his parents' house, but Edge had brought his parents to live with him. There was a distinct difference.

'Could we speak to them? Just routine. I'm sure you understand.'

'Well, if you must.'

Ralph Edge's parents were actually quite excited about the idea of talking to the police. They were a pair of tiny, bird-like people. Not all that elderly perhaps, but frail looking. Mr Edge senior in particular looked as though a strong wind blowing off Carsington Pasture would carry him away. Glancing from the old couple to their son and back again, Cooper found himself thinking of the cuckoo, which left its egg in the nest of a bird from another species, and a chick hatched which vastly outgrew its surrogate parents.

But the Edges had never even met Glen Turner. From what Villiers had told him in the car, that hardly came

277

as a surprise at this stage in the inquiry. Turner was the proverbial man who kept himself to himself.

Cooper turned back to Ralph again.

'You work at Prospectus Assurance,' he said. 'What is your job?'

Edge had been polite until now, but he looked Cooper up and down with a faint hint of contempt.

'A fraud analyst,' he said tersely. 'Your colleagues know all about me.'

'I doubt it,' said Cooper.

'What is that supposed to mean?'

Villiers almost physically interposed herself between them.

'That will be all for now. Thank you, sir,' she said. 'We'll be in touch if we need anything else from you.'

'Why are you at home?' asked Cooper. 'It's Friday afternoon. Shouldn't you still be at work?'

Edge stared at him with undisguised animosity. 'I don't know what it has to do with you,' he said. 'But we're allowed to work flexitime at Prospectus. It means we can look after our families better. As long as the hours are put in and the job gets done, I can take Friday afternoon off, if I want to.'

Villiers put her hand on Cooper's arm, and he let her steer him towards the door.

'Just one more thing, sir,' said Cooper. 'What do you know about A.J. Morton and Sons?'

Edge opened his mouth as if he was about to answer, then hesitated and frowned.

'A.J. . . ?'

'Morton. They're based near here. A quarry supplies company.'

Ralph Edge shook his head vigorously. 'Never heard of them. What do they have to do with anything?'

'Nothing, sir, I'm sure,' said Villiers hastily. 'Thank you for your time.'

When they were outside, Villiers looked at him oddly. 'Ben,' she said. 'Focus.'

'That's what I'm doing.'

'A.J. Morton and Sons? I don't know who they are, but it's nothing to do with Mr Edge.'

'So he said.'

Cooper felt sure Edge had been lying, but he didn't know why. But then, who knew why people told lies? There could be all kinds of reasons. Sometimes they just wanted to present themselves in a better light, and that was all. Some individuals felt a desperate need to be seen as braver, cleverer or more successful than they really were. And the further they strayed from the truth, the more they had to carry on lying. So dishonesty became a part of their daily camouflage, a central theme in the narrative of their lives. Cooper had met people who hardly seemed to be aware that they were lying. For them, deception took less effort than telling the truth.

'I think I'd better take you back to your car,' said Villiers.

'Just drop me in the Market Place.'

She drove back down into the centre of Wirksworth. Cooper expected her to be angry with him, or demand to know why he'd asked those questions. But she drove in silence for a while.

'So, Ralph Edge and Glen Turner,' said Villiers finally. 'Two loners together there?'

'And that's the trouble,' said Cooper.

'What do you mean?'

'Well, they were both loners. Oh, they might have had a few things in common, but a loner is still a loner. I bet they hardly knew anything about each other. Edge didn't even know exactly where Turner lived. He wasn't really interested, either. That's hardly what you'd call a friend.'

'No, you're right.'

'I usually am,' said Cooper confidently, as he got out of the car. 'About other people, anyway.'

A few yards away, Diane Fry stopped abruptly on the pavement in St John's Street. A figure was moving ahead of her towards the corner by the town hall.

She stared at the figure, her hand in her pocket reaching for her radio and cuffs, even as she was overcome with the feeling of familiarity. For some reason, that feeling churned her stomach with dread. She felt like a ghost hunter finally facing the moment she'd dreamed of, yet afraid to look the phantom in the face. She was terrified of what she'd see. Yet she couldn't hold back from looking.

'Ben?' she said.

The shoulders of the figure stiffened. It might, or might not, be him. Even as she told herself this, she was moving forward in complete certainty, her physical instincts sure of what her mind still doubted. It was that stiffening of the shoulders to the sound of her voice. She'd seen the reaction before, so many times. Too often to mistake it.

'Ben?' she said again. 'It's Diane. Diane Fry.'

At last he answered. 'Oh. Hi.'

He sounded distracted and vague, as if he wasn't quite sure who she was at first. Fry had to repeat her name.

'It's a bit of a surprise seeing you here,' she said.

'Why here?'

'Well . . . anywhere, I suppose.'

Cooper just looked at her. Fry began to feel uncomfortable. She felt like a child, finding herself unexpectedly thrust into a social situation with an adult, and having no idea what she was supposed to say. None of the conventional small talk seemed appropriate.

'You know, we've all been worried about you, Ben,' she said.

He raised an eyebrow, the first sign of animation in his face.

'Have you? All of you?'

Fry bit her lip, tried not to look guilty. 'Everyone in the office has been asking how you are. But we haven't been able to make contact with you. Why do you never answer your phone?'

She realised she was already starting to sound accusatory. Hearing her voice rising an octave towards shrillness, she fought to control it.

'Well, I'm sorry,' he said. 'I just wanted a bit of time on my own, without having to explain myself over and over again. I know everyone means well. But it gets too much. You can't imagine what it's like.'

Having delivered these words, he gave her a kind of curt nod. Fry thought he was about to walk off, and she couldn't help blurting out the first thing that came into her head.

'I do understand, you know,' she said.

'What?'

'I know all about it. Of course I do.'

'Knowing about it and understanding are two totally different things,' said Cooper. 'Did you never grasp that? You have to experience something to understand it properly.'

'Okay, okay. Explain it to me, then.'

'Explain it?'

'Yes.'

'You want me to *explain* it.'

He looked as if she was asking him to do the impossible. Well, perhaps she was. She had no idea, really.

'It's like . . . it's like having a huge build-up of pressure inside you,' said Cooper. 'Talking about it achieves nothing. But you know that one day the dam is going to burst, that the whole massive weight will explode and take you with it. Isn't it better to do something about it before that happens?'

'You can't do that,' said Fry.

'Do what?'

'Whatever it is you're planning, Ben.'

Cooper shrugged. 'I'm not planning anything. I'm just coping day by day, you know.'

Fry was unconvinced. She gazed at him, wishing she could see into his mind. She used to be able to guess his thoughts more or less accurately but now he was too distant, too detached. It was as if he'd severed the connection between them, cut the line and drifted away. He'd got caught up in an unpredictable current that might lead him anywhere. Danger could lurk downstream when you allowed yourself to drift like that.

'Ben, I don't know what's on your mind,' she admitted.

'Well, then. Maybe there really isn't anything on my mind at all.'

But something about the way he spoke made Fry's creeping feeling of unease return. She'd heard a similar tone too often from people she knew were lying but who needed to keep up a facade, an official assertion of innocence for the records. Fry reminded herself that she couldn't know what it was like to be in Cooper's position. She had no inkling of how his mind might be working right now, what emotions would be flooding through him, potent and uncontrollable. Her insights were lacking, just at the moment she needed them most.

Yes, she was ignorant, and incapable of guessing his real intentions. But still she couldn't resist her conviction – that something dark and bad was in his heart.

Cooper broke eye contact and pulled his old waxed coat round his shoulders as he began to move away.

'Ben,' she blurted, 'remember, won't you . . . ?'

'What?'

'Remember – whatever happens, we're still the good guys.'

Cooper stared at her, his mouth twisted oddly as if he was about to break into a laugh.

'No, Diane,' he said. 'You're wrong. I don't think we were ever that.'

'But what are you going to do, Ben? Surely there's nothing you *can* do.'

But Cooper didn't reply. He turned and walked away without another word.

And, in the end, that was what bothered Fry most of all.

*   *   *

284

After the unexpected meeting with Diane Fry, Cooper walked for a while in the rain, until he was so wet that he felt washed clean. It was lucky he knew how to pull himself together and make an effort when he encountered other people. He didn't want anyone thinking he'd gone completely off the rails. He could always make sure he was properly dressed, clean shaven, attentive and capable of making intelligent conversation.

It was important to keep up the facade, though he wasn't sure why. He just knew that if he'd started to doubt the reasons for it he would have given up entirely by now, and that he couldn't do.

So he'd made sure Diane Fry (and Carol Villiers) saw him just as he'd always been, a Ben Cooper no different for the experience he'd gone through, just someone recovering slowly from a physical injury, dealing day by day with grief, the trauma of loss. They had to believe that he was getting over it. He'd be back to normal soon.

When Cooper had gone, Fry looked round and saw Carol Villiers. Fry didn't want to be the one to speak first, so she waited, wondering whether Villiers could bring herself to be disloyal to her old friend and DS. It was a difficult judgement to make, but there could only be one conclusion, even if you didn't admit it out loud.

Finally, Villiers shook her head. 'Poor Ben,' she said. 'He's lost it.'

'I've never seen him like that before,' said Fry, relieved.

'Nor me. What can we do?'

'Perhaps he just needs time.'

'Perhaps.'

'Well, he's had the counselling, the medical attention,' said Fry. 'He's on extended leave. Some people just take longer to get over these things.'

There was a small silence, which stretched out just long enough for Fry to start feeling uncomfortable.

'Perhaps,' said Villiers again.

As she left St John's Street, Fry noticed there was a call on her phone, and saw from the display that it was Becky Hurst. She opened her car door and got in out of the rain before she answered it.

'I went to check out the paintballing centre,' said Hurst. 'They remembered Glen Turner pretty well.'

'Why?' asked Fry. 'Because of his injuries?'

'Well, sort of. His injuries were where it all started. But they remember him most of all because he was planning to sue them.'

23

Becky Hurst had brought back a copy of the solicitor's letter the paintballing centre had received. It carried the heading of a well-known legal practice in Edendale, Richmond Jones. Fry had dealt with them often enough, but only the partners specialising in criminal law. They were a favourite choice for defendants in local magistrates' courts, because they had a reputation for being able to get you off a minor charge, no matter how guilty you were. Many police officers had returned angry and frustrated from court proceedings after listening to a Richmond Jones solicitor arguing the innocence of some notorious lowlife.

But this was a civil case, the threat of private action for personal injury compensation. That would be a different partner. The letter was signed simply with the company name 'Richmond Jones', which surely wasn't actually a signature at all, since it wasn't the identity of an individual. But at the top, under the heading, was a phone number and the information that the partner dealing with the case was Mr K. Chadburn.

Most of the solicitors in Edendale had offices in or around the Market Square. Diane Fry even knew why this was. Ben Cooper had once explained to her that it dated to the time when people from the surrounding area came into town only once a week, on market day. It was a major journey for them, and they wanted to do all their business in one trip – buy their vegetables, go to the butcher's, stock up with paint and nails at the ironmonger's, and visit the solicitor's to sort out their wills.

Whether that was true or not Fry wasn't sure. Cooper had tried to explain lots of things to her during the years she'd been in Edendale, and she was still convinced that he'd made some of them up. They sounded too bizarre, even for Derbyshire.

But it was true that the solicitors' offices were all in old buildings and prominently located, probably some of the most valuable properties in the town.

The premises of Richmond Jones looked as if it might

once have been the home of a wealthy merchant. Through an archway like the entrance to a coaching inn she glimpsed half a dozen expensive cars parked in a cobbled yard. The signs outside were discreet, and the front door was a heavy affair, with a bell that rang when she opened it to step inside.

Kenneth Chadburn was expecting her. He was exactly what she would have expected for a provincial solicitor. Middle aged, grey haired, wearing glasses and a faded pinstriped suit that was getting a little too tight for him. When she walked into his office, he seemed to be sweating. But that might have been because of the enormous radiator on the wall behind his desk. It was an ancient iron affair that would have been more suited to a hospital ward or a cavernous classroom in a Victorian school. She could feel the heat it was throwing out the moment she stepped through the door.

'Yes, yes. Ah, yes.'

Chadburn was nodding agreement before Fry had even asked him a question. He shuffled through a set of files on his desk until he found the right one. It was fastened with a strip of ribbon, an archaic touch that contrasted sharply with the computer monitor displaying a familiar landscape screensaver.

For a moment, Fry wondered why lawyers insisted on retaining these ancient trappings and traditions when they had so much modern technology at their disposal.

But then she remembered she was a police officer. Some of her colleagues flew in helicopters full of high tech equipment but others still wore headgear designed in the 1860s and modelled on Prussian army helmets. Solicitors weren't alone in clinging to tradition.

'Mr Turner. Yes, that's very sad.' Chadburn looked up at her over his glasses. 'Do we know what happened?'

'No, I'm sorry,' said Fry.

'Yes, of course. Confidential information.'

'No, sir. We just don't know what happened.'

'Ah, well. Criminal law isn't my area, I'm afraid.'

'I thought I hadn't seen you in court, sir. But I'm familiar with some of your colleagues.'

Chadburn cleared his throat and wiped his forehead with a handkerchief.

'Of course, confidentiality is our watchword here. And normally I wouldn't be able to share any information with you about our client's affairs. I'm sure you understand that, Detective Sergeant.'

'But since he's dead . . . ?'

'Yes, that does make a difference. And naturally we want to be of help to the police in discovering who perpetrated the crime. I, er . . . take it Mr Turner's death *was* the result of a crime?'

'We're treating it as a murder inquiry,' said Fry.

'That's what I understood. So how can I help?'

'Well, we've been told that Glen Turner was planning to sue the Eden Valley Adventure Centre for injuries he sustained during a recent paintballing session.'

'I thought that might be it. Well, it's true – in a way.'

'He did suffer injuries,' said Fry. 'They were visible on his body.'

'Yes, of course. And, in fact, we have some photographs.'

'Really? May I see them?'

Chadburn passed her a series of fairly low quality pictures, which looked as though they'd been printed on a standard laser printer. They showed Glen Turner with his shirt removed, from the front and from behind, the lesions on his torso clearly visible as painful looking red blotches, though the accuracy of the colour on the printouts was doubtful.

Fry recognised the background in the photographs. The red striped curtains, the computer work station with two monitors. They had been taken in Glen Turner's bedroom at the cottage on St John's Street.

'Who took these?' asked Fry.

'I believe it was my client's mother,' said Chadburn.

Fry put the photos down. As evidence, they were dubious. Any one of Kenneth Chadburn's colleagues on the criminal side of the practice could have demolished their validity in court in a few minutes. It was impossible to tell whether the marks on his body were

291

genuine bruises or had been created using make-up. And they were taken in his bedroom by his mum?

'Of course, they were relatively minor injuries,' said Chadburn. 'Soft tissue damage, causing considerable pain but with complete recovery expected within twelve months. Normally, we'd be looking for a level of compensation at around three or four thousand pounds. That would be in the case of a car accident, say, or if you slip on a spillage and suffer a fall in a supermarket. We deal with a lot of those.'

'That's probably why the price of shopping has been going up so much,' said Fry.

He looked puzzled. 'I'm sorry?'

'Never mind, sir.'

'I see. Well, the big companies like supermarkets have policies for this sort of thing. If a customer reports an injury in one of their stores they offer a small amount of compensation – a discount on the next purchase, a few points on a loyalty card. You see, they rely on members of the public not being aware of the amount of compensation they might get or the right steps to take at the time, such as getting the names of witnesses. Those sort of cases can be a waste of time for us. But smaller companies are a different matter.'

'Why so?'

'They're not used to it. When they get an incident, their staff often don't know what to do. And they tend to get worried about the potential damage to their reputation, which makes them more willing to settle without a court hearing.'

Fry looked at the photos again. She remembered thinking how painful they looked. They'd given her the impression Turner might have been tortured before he died.

'But you said yourself these are minor injuries,' she said. 'And paintballs are just gelatin capsules, surely?'

'Yes, we did a little bit of research when Mr Turner came to us, of course.' He referred to a note in the file. 'It seems paintballs consist of a gelatin shell containing mostly polyethylene glycol and dye. They're designed to break on impact. Even the dye washes out of most clothes. But when fired from a gun – more properly known as a marker, I believe – paintballs may travel at speeds up to three hundred feet per second. As you can imagine, they have the potential to cause considerable damage to a human target, depending on the velocity and angle and the particular part of the body they hit.'

'What exactly happened to Mr Turner, then?'

Chadburn adjusted his glasses. A small trickle of sweat had run down his forehead on to the centre of the frame and he dabbed it from the lens.

'Well, as you may know, these paintballing sessions were part of a team building weekend organised by his employers, Prospectus Assurance. There had been other activities during the weekend, which might not be of any relevance to you.'

'Role playing, blind driving, motivational talks.'

'Just so.' The solicitor gave her a rather sad smile. 'Legal practices like ours never go in for that sort of thing. The older partners would be horrified. But I sometimes think it's rather a pity.'

'I don't think it's all that much fun,' said Fry.

'No?' Chadburn looked disappointed. 'Ah well, on to the paintballing. In his statement to us, Mr Turner described how the staff at the adventure centre split his party from Prospectus Assurance into two teams. They explained that the objective of the game was to capture the other team's flag without getting hit by a paintball. Anyone hit is effectively out of the game, I understand. If you get shot, you're . . . Well, you're . . .'

'Dead,' said Fry.

He cleared his throat. 'Precisely. Dead. Well, then they were given safety goggles and loaded guns. In the first game, a gun misfired and a paintball hit Mr Turner in the, er . . . crotch area.'

'The crotch area?' repeated Fry.

'Yes, erm . . . the crotch area. A largely unprotected part of the body, you understand.'

'And that was an accident?'

'According to my client.'

Fry didn't need to wonder for very long why there was no photograph of that particular injury. Even Glen Turner wouldn't have wanted his mother taking pictures of his genitals. Perhaps he hadn't mentioned that shot to her. It was the sort of thing he could only share with his doctor or his lawyer.

'Go on,' she said.

'Well, Mr Turner told me that this injury was particularly painful. And he admitted that . . . well, he gave expression to the pain rather loudly, I gather.'

'He . . . ? Oh, you mean he screamed.'

'Ah. Yes.'

Fry nodded. She could imagine how that would have gone down with Turner's colleagues. There was nothing like someone else's discomfort for causing hilarity. She hardly had to ask the rest of the story. By screaming like a girl the first time he was hit, Glen Turner had made himself the preferred target for every trigger-happy employee on the paintballing field.

'And it seems in the next game my client took several hits, some of them at point blank range,' said Chadburn. 'One shot hit him on his uncovered neck and others hit him in the side, on his back and on his stomach. At first he thought his neck was actually bleeding, but it was just the oily paint running down his skin. The bruises stung for hours afterwards, he said. But when he complained the other players just laughed at him and said he should think of them as battle wounds.'

'Battle wounds?'

'Yes, that was the phrase.'

'Didn't you say a few moment ago that when you were hit by a paintball, you were out of the game.'

'That seems to be the way it works.'

'So how was it that Mr Turner was hit so many times in one game? Surely he would have been out on the first hit?'

'Indeed.' Chadburn even smiled a little now. 'Many of those shots must have been fired at him after he was officially dead. Very much against the rules of the game, I imagine.'

Fry nodded. 'I assume the adventure centre must have public liability insurance.'

'Of course.' Chadburn looked smug now, as if he'd been saving this nugget of information to himself. 'But perhaps I don't need to give you many guesses who their insurance policy is with?'

'You're joking.'

'Not at all. In fact, because of their existing business relationship with Prospectus Assurance, the adventure centre gave them preferential rates on their team building weekends.'

Fry shook her head in amazement. 'Unbelievable.'

'Deliciously ironic, I think.'

'So do you think Mr Turner would have had a case against them?'

'When he came to me on Monday, I told him he was unlikely to have a case against the adventure centre itself, as the injury wasn't caused by an act of negligence on their part – and I believe he signed a waiver before the game started. I expect the safety briefing mentioned a ban on head shots and so forth. *Volenti non fit injuria.*'

'I'm sorry?'

'It's Latin. *To a willing person, injury is not done.* It's a common law doctrine, meaning that if someone willingly places themselves in a position where harm might result, they can't bring a claim against the other party. But . . .'

'What?'

'Well, the person or persons who directly caused the injuries are a different issue. Consent wasn't given to an actual assault. In my opinion, Mr Turner's injuries might be considered to have resulted from the reckless act of another. I advised him that he could consider reporting the incident to the police as a criminal assault, possibly actual bodily harm. And I suggested that if he decided to pursue that course, he should get photographs taken of his injuries sooner rather than later. In fact, it provides more convincing evidence if the police take the photographs themselves. I'm probably telling you something that you already know, Detective Sergeant.'

'But Mr Turner didn't take your advice, did he? He never got to the point of reporting this incident as a criminal offence.'

'No, I don't believe so. I suspect he was having second thoughts. With all due respect to my client – my late client – he didn't strike me as the most decisive of individuals. All I could do was advise him on his legal position. It wasn't my place to persuade Mr Turner towards one course of action or another.'

'What were his reservations?'

'Oh, the consequences for the people involved. A criminal record, the loss of employment. It's a serious matter.'

'Did he name the individuals he believed caused his injuries?'

'Oh, of course. After all, he knew everyone involved in that team building exercise. It was all in the family, so to speak. The named parties were two of his colleagues at Prospectus Assurance.'

Fry recalled Ralph Edge's account of the staff being divided into teams based on their departments, which meant he'd been on the same team as Glen Turner. So who had they been competing against? Yes, that was it. *Some of those women in Sales are merciless.*

'Are you going to tell me the names?' she said.

'Oh, well . . . I suppose that will be acceptable, in the circumstances.'

Chadburn made a performance of looking for a specific page in the file. He did it so slowly that Fry began to grow irritated. But she didn't dare express her irritation out loud for fear that he might decide this was one detail he should claim confidentiality for.

'Yes, here we are,' he said finally. 'The two gentlemen alleged to be responsible for my client's injuries go by the names of Mr Nathan Baird and Mr Ralph Edge.'

24

Diane Fry never realised it could be so dark during the day. Even when there was a total eclipse, you got a bit of light creeping round the edges to remind you that the sun was still up there, the universe still functioning in the normal way. Today, there was almost no natural light in Edendale. The clouds were so dark that the sky seemed to have decided it could do without the sun.

She had to walk a couple of hundred yards from the offices of Richmond Jones in the Market Square to reach the car park where she'd left her Audi. In the distance, above the roofs of Edendale, she could see clouds lying against the hills on either side of the valley, blocking the skyline and swallowing the horizon.

Fry began to feel suffocated. The air was so humid

and thick it felt as if she was walking through warm soup. She knew she'd have a headache before the day was over. The tension in the air was concentrating behind her eyes, squeezing her head until it buzzed. Was it possible to feel so claustrophobic in a wide open space like the Eden Valley? With weather like this, it was. Natural forces were pressing down with all their might, trying to squash a nest of ants. It would be a relief when it rained again. And rain it surely would, before long. An ocean of moisture was gathering overhead in that sagging grey blanket. It couldn't hold much longer.

Lights had come on in the shops along Clappergate. Cars drove on sidelights as they crossed the junction. People were hurrying along the street, their heads down as if they needed to get home before a curfew. An air of tension was palpable. The whole world was waiting for the moment.

Suddenly the atmosphere changed. A moment of hesitation, a pregnant pause. People stopped and looked up, perhaps sensing the first, solitary plop of rain on the back of a neck, then responded to the warning, quickening their pace in the vain hope of reaching shelter before the deluge. Most wouldn't make it. In the next few seconds they vanished in sheets of water, vertical curtains of rain soaking them in an instant, plastering their hair to their skulls, penetrating their summer clothes, bouncing mud off the pavement on to their shoes.

As she ran for her car, Fry was deafened by the roar of the torrent. Cars swept by on the road, swishing through pools of water, hissing over wet tarmac, throwing up spray like a tidal wave. A Transit van went past and its nearside wheels hit the deepest part of the water, creating a tidal wave that surged across the pavement and swept over Fry's shoes. The force of the water as it withdrew to the road almost pulled her off her feet.

There was still time for her to get to Prospectus Assurance before the end of the afternoon. As Fry arrived in Nathan Baird's office she was conscious of a murmur of speculation from the bank of call handlers she passed. Word had gone round the company. Perhaps some of them were hoping that their manager would be arrested for crimes against humanity.

'Yes, well, the incident itself was just a bit of fun,' said Baird when she challenged him on Glen Turner's paintballing injuries. 'It's part of what team building is all about, letting your hair down and having a laugh with your colleagues. People get to know each other better that way, in an informal setting.'

'It seems Mr Turner didn't think it was a bit of fun,' said Fry. 'He wasn't laughing at the time.'

Baird waved his slender hand in a gesture that Fry

remembered, as if an irritating fly had returned. 'Oh, I know Glen took it a bit too seriously. But he got over it.'

'He had photographs taken of his injuries, and he went to see a solicitor on Monday to discuss legal action. Possibly against you, Mr Baird.'

'No, no, no. That was all a lot of nonsense. Glen was sulking for a while. He didn't come in to work on the Monday, just to make a point. And when he appeared on Tuesday morning, he had this exaggerated limp, as if his leg had been shot off. I suppose he thought people would feel sorry for him. But it didn't wash. We just got on with the job as usual. Water under the bridge and all that.'

'Did you actually talk to Mr Turner about it?'

'Yes, he came in here and we had a chat. As I said to you yesterday, my door is always open. Glen knew perfectly well he could talk to me about things. So that's what we did. He never seriously considered suing me or any of his colleagues. It was just hot air, believe me. He got it all off his chest, we shook hands on it, and he went back to work. Job done.'

'You did tell me yesterday that nothing unusual had happened on Tuesday, sir.'

'Well, it wasn't all that unusual. I'm team leader. Sorting out little issues like that – well, it's all part of my job. Besides . . .'

'What?'

'Well, poor old Glen. It didn't seem fair to spread the story far and wide. You don't want to make your employees' discomfiture public, do you? What happens at Prospectus stays at Prospectus. Do you know what I mean?'

Fry discovered that Ralph Edge wasn't at work, so she phoned him at home. He laughed at her question.

'Yes, poor old Glen,' he said. 'I told you he was sore afterwards, didn't I? I mean, I was the one who told you about the paintballing excitement, Sergeant.'

'You didn't tell me you were one of the individuals responsible for it,' said Fry. 'You let me believe it was the opposing team from Sales.'

'Well, is there actually any proof who did it?' asked Edge in an innocent tone.

'Mr Turner's statement to his solicitor.'

'Would that stand up in court?' He laughed again. 'No, it's a fair cop. But it was all part of the office banter, you know. Someone gets paintballed every time. This time, it was Glen. It could just as easily have been me, or Nathan Baird. Nothing to get upset about. He didn't report it to the police or anything, did he?'

'No, he didn't,' admitted Fry.

'There you are, then. He calmed down, saw the funny side eventually. He probably did something weird to make himself feel better, if I know Glen. Bought himself a little present, maybe. Oh, I'm sorry he's dead and all that, but he was a bit of a funny bugger in some ways.'

'Maybe so.'

'Speaking of funny buggers,' said Edge, as she was about to end the call. 'You've got some among your people too, haven't you? A right weirdo we had here this afternoon.'

When she got back into the office, soaking wet and uncomfortable, Fry found that Luke Irvine had been developing a theory. Suspicious, Fry glanced at Gavin Murfin, who smirked back at her round a cheese pasty. Had he been taking the mentoring role too seriously?

'Go on then, Luke,' she said. 'Let's hear it.'

'Well, first of all, you have to realise there are a lot of angry people around at the moment. I mean home owners who've lost everything in the floods, and not for the first time either. This time round, some of them have been abandoned by the insurance companies.'

'Yes, I've heard that. There was a failure to reach a deal that would let everyone get flood insurance, even if they'd made claims before.'

'Exactly. So imagine how those people are feeling now. Betrayed and upset.'

'What has this got to do with Glen Turner?'

'It was his job,' said Irvine. 'Turning down legitimate claims.'

'Wait a minute,' said Fry. 'Are you suggesting a posse of outraged citizens are roaming the country to hunt down insurance claims adjusters?'

'No, but—'

'What, then?'

'Well, it would only take one or two, wouldn't it? People who had personal dealings with Glen Turner, and were furious at what they saw as an injustice. Angry enough to want revenge. Some form of justice. It's difficult to focus that sort of emotion on an anonymous institution or the people working for it. But if you've got an actual human target for your vengeance right in front of you, that's a different thing.'

'If home owners couldn't get insurance against flooding any more, it surely wasn't the fault of a claims adjuster like Turner,' put in Hurst. 'Isn't it the job of underwriters to assess the risks?'

'Probably. But if you're angry enough, who's going to be thinking logically or asking questions about the structure of the insurance industry? No, I don't think so. A target is a target. It's whatever comes within reach.' Irvine looked pleased with himself now. 'Revenge isn't about a fair distribution of justice, but about making yourself feel better.'

'So whoever carried this out, it might all have been about them, and not about Glen Turner at all?'

'That's it,' said Irvine. 'It's a small flaw in the theory of victimology, I think.'

'You'll be lecturing to Senior Investigating Officers at Bramshill next.'

'It's true, though, isn't it?'

Fry looked at him. It wasn't very compelling as a theory, of course. It had too much of a revenge fantasy about it, and she'd never be able to justify putting resources into following it up. Not unless some concrete evidence presented itself, which seemed unlikely. But at least Irvine was thinking for himself a bit. That fresh view was what she needed. A challenging opinion, even if she didn't agree with it. It was surprising how much that helped to focus her own mind.

'Mr Turner bought his mother a new greenhouse recently,' she said. 'Expensive looking. He had a windfall from somewhere.'

'There's no record of any large amounts of money coming into his bank account,' said Irvine. 'And since he's been paying all the household bills for the property on St John's Street, he hasn't been putting much aside in savings from his salary either.'

'He must have received cash.'

'A pay-off for something?'

'Yes, but I don't know what.'

Photographs of Glen Turner's Renault Mégane were on her desk, including a shot of the fossil and its accompanying receipt from the National Stone Centre. Well, she'd said that she wanted everything.

Fry examined the fossil. It was just a dead sea creature that had been turned to stone over millions of years. She shared Mrs Turner's view on these things. They were dead and gone, rock and dust. So what had interested Mr Turner so much about this object that he'd gone to the stone centre to buy it straight after his consultation with Mr Chadburn at Richmond Jones?

That evening at the Wheatsheaf, Luke Irvine was eager to be the first to buy Carol Villiers a drink when she described the time she'd spent with Ben Cooper earlier that day.

'How did you do it?' asked Irvine in admiration.

'It was actually quite easy,' said Villiers. 'He's still the same old Ben Cooper deep down, you know. Some things he can't resist. An interesting case, for example.'

'You've been giving him information about the murder inquiry?'

'Yes, some.'

Irvine felt uneasy. 'It's up to you. But Diane Fry mustn't find out.'

'No, Diane mustn't know.'

He looked at Murfin and Hurst, checking to see that they shared the need for conspiratorial silence. He could see from their faces that they did.

'So do you think you've distracted him from his obsession, Carol?' asked Irvine.

'Sure.' She hesitated only slightly. 'Well, I think so.'

'You can have my medal,' said Murfin, raising his glass in a toast. 'You deserve it more than me. It's still in my drawer at the office.'

'Your Diamond Jubilee medal? I thought it was your most treasured possession, Gavin. You couldn't wait for it to arrive.'

'I know,' said Murfin. 'It's funny, though. Getting it was the really important thing. Just knowing they hadn't forgotten me completely, the people up there. The thing itself, well . . . it's just a bit of old metal, isn't it?'

Irvine watched them in silence. He wasn't convinced about Ben Cooper. But he didn't feel able to say so. Both Carol Villiers and Gavin Murfin had known Cooper much longer. They ought to be right about these things.

Still, Irvine had an uneasy feeling – one of those feelings you were supposed to keep to yourself. So that was what he'd better do, he supposed.

25

The one thing Ben Cooper couldn't ask Carol Villiers to do was run a PNC check. Unauthorised use of the police national computer system was a serious disciplinary offence. Many officers around the country had been sacked for accessing information from the PNC, or passing it on to members of the public. Some had even been prosecuted for breaches of the Data Protection Act.

At one time, Cooper might have turned to his contacts on the local newspaper for information. There was a journalist called Erin Byrne that he'd dealt with in the past. But the *Eden Valley Times* no longer had an office in Edendale. Its parent company had been swallowed up by one of the big publishing corporations that already owned half of the regional newspapers in the UK. What was left of the editorial staff had been centralised and now worked from a production hub twenty miles away in Sheffield. Like most small towns, Edendale would probably never have its own local paper again.

So who could he talk to? Who would have the same sort of local knowledge that an old-fashioned newspaper reporter used to possess? Who would know the area and its characters well, particularly its villains? He needed someone like his father, the old-style copper. But they didn't exist any more, did they? Well, not still in the service.

The old police station at Lowbridge had been closed in the previous year's cutbacks. It was just one of the county's assets to be offloaded, following cuts in the annual policing budget. Many of the force's properties had been under-used for years – or so the argument went. Money could be saved, and revenue earned, by selling off surplus buildings like this one. Yet here it still stood, empty and abandoned, its doors and windows boarded up and scrawled with obscene graffiti. No one wanted to buy a disused police station in Lowbridge.

And why would they? There were already enough empty properties waiting for a buyer. If you were looking for somewhere to open a shop, you were spoiled for choice on the high street. 'For Sale' and 'To Let' signs sprouted on almost every frontage. If you wanted a property to convert into flats, there was the old primary school, or the Mechanics' Institute, or the magistrates' court. They'd all stood empty for years. Prime residential development opportunities for someone with the money, the vision, and a massive amount of optimism. But a derelict police station? Surely it was best left to the ghosts of old coppers, to the memories of prisoners who'd literally left their mark on the walls of the disused cells, or even to the vandals who'd swarmed to the empty building like locusts. Its symbolism made it a prime target for protest and abuse.

Stanley Walker still had keys to the place, though. He'd been Police Constable Walker in the old days, and could still tell you his collar number. In fact, he would recite it at any opportunity, like a prisoner of war giving his name and rank. He'd completed thirty years' service in uniform, including spells in Public Order, Response and Traffic, but had started and ended his career right here in Lowbridge. Then he'd become Old Stan, a part-time civilian employee standing behind the front counter, a friendly face to greet the public.

'Only, some of the public weren't so friendly,' he said, as he made Cooper a cup of tea in his house in Lowbridge. 'Especially the ones that remembered me from when I was in uniform.'

'I can imagine.'

'So I was glad to go in the end. There comes a point when you want to be out of the firing line.'

Now that Stanley Walker was retired, he lived on his memories. Word on the grapevine had it that he was writing it all down, working on a memoir. Cooper wondered if that might be true. There was supposed to be quite a market these days for first-person accounts by police officers, paramedics, doctors, firefighters – in fact, anyone who'd met the public on a day-to-day basis for a few decades and could write about it with humour. If you could look back to a period like the 1970s, you might be on to a winner. The public loved nostalgia, and the Seventies had been a different world. As a young PC, Walker would have been unencumbered by PACE, or the Scarman Report, or political correctness.

Cooper looked around Walker's house for signs of a manuscript, or at least a laptop or computer. Most police officers weren't known for their literary talent, but even if you couldn't get a publisher, you could upload your work to the internet yourself as an eBook and hope for the best. Your family and friends might buy a few copies, at least.

Walker opened a drawer and rattled a large bunch of keys.

'Want to take a look at the old hellhole, then?' he said. 'I can offer you the fifty pence tour of the cells, or the one quid tour. Ask me the difference.'

'What's the difference, Stan?' asked Cooper.

'For a quid, you get to come out again.'

Walker put his coat on and they walked a couple of streets through Lowbridge to the old police station. Though Lowbridge was called a village, the spread of development along the valley bottom from Edendale meant there were no longer any green fields to separate the two places, only a road sign at the point where one house was in Edendale and the next one in Lowbridge.

A glimpse of the swollen River Eden and the water already lying in surrounding fields reminded Cooper that properties to the east of Edendale were among those most at risk of flooding. He knew that most of Lowbridge sat in the 'purple area' on flood maps, where homes and businesses received warnings when flooding was expected.

A housing development had been built here on what local people insisted had always been a floodplain for the River Eden. They'd said it loudly at the time, when planning permission was given, and they'd said it again when the builders moved in and started work on the foundations. Just because the area hadn't flooded recently, that didn't mean it would never flood again. But nobody took any notice of them. Not until occupants had moved into the houses and the first floods arrived. Now the access road was closed to traffic by deep water and front doors all along the new crescents were protected by sandbags.

But some home owners at Lowbridge were the lucky

ones. At least they had insurance against flooding. All across Derbyshire, there were people whose properties had been affected by flooding in the recent past and who were no longer able to take out insurance policies, being considered too much of a risk.

Cooper thought it must be devastating to lose everything in your house to flood water. Your home should be your refuge, the place you could come back to after everything the world threw at you. It shouldn't be a disaster zone where all that you valued had been taken from you. And, for some of these people, it had happened more than once.

The old police station was still distinctively identified by the blue lamp over its front door. But they entered through a yard at the back, where police vehicles would once have been parked. It was surrounded by a steel palisaded security fence with triple-pointed heads, and there was a hefty padlock on the gate. Walker had the key for the padlock, a key for the back door and a security code to tap in before they could enter.

'You wouldn't think it was empty,' he said. 'Well, almost. If you want my opinion, they'd be better off just demolishing the whole thing.'

The reception area looked sad and dusty. It hadn't been used for a while, even before the station closed. It was part of a general trend in Derbyshire, and everywhere else in the country. In the past year, front desks had been closed at police stations across the county. Heanor, New Mills, Chapel-en-le-Frith, Belper and others. Even some of the larger inquiry offices like Matlock had their opening hours reduced. Members of the public were supposed to stay at home and make a phone call.

Though the desks and chairs were pushed aside, stacked in a corner or lying in broken heaps, some recognisable features remained in the offices behind the front desk, including what Cooper had hoped for – a rogues' gallery on the back wall. Photos of all the villains in Lowbridge were pinned together on a large corkboard. Any new PC coming into the station could have studied the gallery to help him identify the characters he was likely to meet out on the street.

'This is what I remember,' said Cooper.

'Who was it you were looking for?' asked Walker.

'Name of Gibson.'

'Oh, there were two of those buggers. At least.'

'There was one called Ryan.'

'Yes, he's here somewhere.'

But Walker hesitated and looked at him curiously.

'You could just have got him off the PNC or the intelligence system, couldn't you?' he said. 'You have everything on computer these days. At least, that's what the last sergeant here kept on telling me.'

'Not quite everything,' said Cooper. He tapped the side of his head. 'Some things are up here.'

'Damn right. I'm glad to hear there are still a few who think that way. It makes me feel a bit less of a dinosaur.'

'Not you.'

'Oh, yes. Me. A right old brontosaurus. I was never exactly the type to be intelligence led.'

Cooper laughed. For some years now, 'intelligence-led policing' had been one of the buzz phrases echoing around meetings of Senior Management Teams up and down the country. It was said to be one of the most efficient and cost-effective ways of tackling crime. But intelligence-led policing required people sitting in front of computer screens in a back office. Officers like PC Stanley Walker could never have done that job.

'Yes, Ryan Gibson,' he said. 'Here he is.'

The Gibson in the photograph was in his twenties. Short-cropped hair, a sullen expression, the blue ink of a tattoo visible on the side of his neck. He had the look of a young man who'd been in a fight or two and had quite enjoyed it. When he saw that look, it always raised a question in Cooper's mind about the way the young man had been brought up. What had happened to him as a child that made him see violence as acceptable, just a part of normal life?

'Our Ryan did a stint in the army, you know,' said Walker. 'He saw some service overseas, but missed out on all the major conflicts. I don't reckon he had what you'd call a distinguished career exactly.'

'Is there an address for him?'

'It should be on the back of the photo. Yes, here we are.' Walker laughed. 'It's lucky the Data Protection Act doesn't apply to us, eh?'

'Yes, lucky.'

Cooper wrote the address down and studied the photograph again. Gibson would be a good few years older now. Some men changed. They matured, settled down, had families of their own and learned to take their responsibilities seriously. Others never did. Or never could.

'For me, he always had that look,' said Walker. 'Do you know what I mean? The look of a man whose face was bound to appear on the news bulletins one day, after he was arrested for doing something appalling. His neighbours would say he'd "kept himself to himself".'

'And he ended up with his face immortalised in a custody suite photograph.'

'He tried to be too clever. Ryan decided to get involved in a blackmail racket. It wasn't his style. And definitely not his brother's. Too much brain work involved.'

'Oh yes, the brother.'

'Sean. He's on the board too.'

There was a distinct similarity of features. But Sean was younger, still in his teens when the picture was taken. Unlike his brother, he didn't look strong. Despite his youth, his face was becoming gaunt and his eyes shadowed and sunken.

'Drugs,' said Walker. 'Sean started with a bit of glue sniffing when he was about twelve or thirteen, and progressed from there. If you can call it progress.'

'What happened to him?'

'He had a couple of spells inside. Short sentences. Nothing that took him out of circulation for too long, but just enough time for him to make a few contacts among the real criminal fraternity. He never worked for a living that I know of. The army certainly wouldn't have had him.'

'There was a particular inquiry I was remembering,' said Cooper. 'You were a big help at the time.'

Walker laughed. 'Yes, I recall. You were wet behind the ears in CID then. You needed a bloke with experience like me.'

'You're right, I did. Do you remember . . . ?'

'Hicklin,' said Walker promptly. 'Poor old bugger. Chaps like him always come off worst when they encounter the Gibsons of this world.'

'When you knew him, Ryan Gibson had a straight job though, didn't he?' asked Cooper.

'Yes, both Gibson and Roger Hicklin were working

in the stores yard for one of the quarry companies. Gibson drove a forklift truck, as I recall.'

'What was the name of those employers?'

'Wait a bit,' said Walker. 'It'll come to me in a minute.'

Cooper waited patiently. He knew the information he wanted would be there, filed safely away. It was just the retrieval system that had become a bit slow.

'Now, it's funny,' said Walker, 'but I heard that Ryan had gone back working for that same company when he got out last time. You've got to hand it to employers who have loyalty to staff like that. You wouldn't get some folk round here giving you a job if you had a record.'

'Maybe he was just very good with a forklift truck,' said Cooper.

'Yes, that was it,' said Walker. 'I knew it would come back to me. They're called A.J. Morton and Sons.'

When Cooper left Stanley Walker, he called Carol Villiers on her mobile. From the background din, it sounded as though she must be in a pub. He wondered who she was with, for a moment picturing a strapping ex-squaddy with a desert suntan and tattoos. But it was none of his business, was it?

'Ben, what is it?' she said. 'Are you okay?'

'Yes, I'm . . . I'm all right.'

The noise was reduced suddenly, as if she'd stepped

out of the bar and closed a door behind her. Somehow, that made Cooper feel better. It suggested that she was giving him her undivided attention, no matter what else was going on.

'Carol, I need to see the crime scene,' he said.

'The crime scene?'

'The area of Sparrow Wood where Glen Turner's body was found.'

'Oh, that crime scene.'

'Could you take me there this weekend?'

'Ben, I can't just do that. I mean, what would Diane Fry say?'

'Make it Sunday,' said Cooper. 'She won't be around then. There'll just be a scene guard, maybe some forensics staff at most.'

'No, I can't.'

'You're the only one I can rely on, Carol,' he said.

She was silent for a moment. He heard laughter, a few bars of music, the faint chink of glasses. At one time, he would have longed to be there himself in the bar, chatting and drinking with a crowd of friends. Right now, the thought made him nervous. The idea of that sea of curious faces staring at him was intolerable. Sweat broke out on his forehead. He felt the tremor beginning in his hands, the irritation burning at the back of his throat. In another second, he would have to put the phone down and forget the whole thing.

'You'll get me in real bother, you know,' said Villiers.

'It'll be worth it,' he said.

He heard her sigh. 'It had better be, Ben. It had better be.'

That night, Ben Cooper sat above Josh Lane's home at Derwent Park. He was watching the colour of the stone in the quarry change from grey to black as clouds covered the stars. It was as if someone had turned the lights off in the Peak District, plunging the valley into darkness. The air felt chilly. And he could see from the sky in the west that another deluge was on its way.

Cooper settled down under a hawthorn tree to watch. A few cars arrived, people greeted each other, but no one came near Josh Lane. Music played somewhere, a woman laughed, a phone rang. But Lane's curtains remained drawn, and his door closed.

As midnight approached, it began to rain again. Cooper unfolded his waxed coat, pulled it on and drew up the hood, letting the raindrops drum on the fabric. A sheep approached the tree, stared at him with wild eyes, then moved on to the next shelter, bleating its annoyance.

Sitting here, the feeling of freedom was invigorating. Tomorrow, Diane Fry would be up to her neck in prioritisation and resource allocation. But he would still be free. It was only when he went to sleep that reality came crashing into his head, the reek of smoke and the scorch of flames, the images of a roaring inferno.

His nightmares did change sometimes. There were nights when he dreamed he was choking on a tube, unable to breathe normally because of the plastic cylinder thrust down his throat. He would wake up thrashing in his bed, wanting to pull the tube out to get air into his painful, burning lungs.

But of course, that had really happened to him, so perhaps it couldn't be called a nightmare at all. The distinction between a dream world and the quagmire of distorted memories was a difficult one to make. He hadn't yet learned to detect the dividing line, couldn't distinguish one from the other. As a result, he never quite knew which world he was in.

Intubation, they'd called it in the hospital. Necessary because he was showing symptoms of upper airway problems. A tube had to be inserted in his throat to keep his airway from closing due to swelling, the result of heat damage to the tissues of the respiratory tract. It was just one of the major consequences of smoke inhalation. Smoke also blocked the intake of oxygen to the lungs and raised carbon monoxide levels, reducing the ability of the blood to carry oxygen to the body's tissues. Inhalation of smoke particles and chemicals like carbon monoxide and cyanide caused direct irritation of the lung. But at least smoke cooled rapidly once it was inhaled and heat damage was limited to the tissues of the mouth and upper throat.

His latest test results at the hospital showed that there was still a significant decline in his PEF, his peak expiratory flow. Permanent respiratory tract damage would be bad news. It could even see him leaving the police service completely. Those memories weren't something he could put behind him and forget, as many people thought. Because they didn't just belong to the past. They affected his present, and would have an impact on his future too.

No, it wasn't possible to keep those memories out. Far from it. Sometimes he felt as though they were tearing through the walls, trying to get inside his head.

26

Saturday

There was free parking near Ravenscar station. That was hardly ever the case inside the national park. As he headed up the path, Cooper passed a few people walking their dogs back to the car park. The figure ahead of him was moving slowly, so he stopped to look down the slope at the railway line.

Ravenscar station was a grand name for what was basically a platform a few yards long, where a spur stopped at the buffers to let off passengers for the National Stone Centre and the High Peak Trail. This had never served as a station in the days of British Rail or its successors. It had been built in the middle of abandoned quarries by a group of enthusiasts who wanted to run restored steam locomotives up the incline from Wirksworth. There was only a summer service on the Ravenscar line. In winter it would be dead here, apart from the occasional maintenance team perhaps.

A tarmac freight truck stood on rails by the exit from the station, still loaded with stone, though brambles were growing over it now. The hoppers above it would have tipped the stone in from the quarry.

They were moving again. Cooper began to walk up the steep incline, passing waymarks for the Stone Centre. A hum in the trees above reminded him of the industrial centre close by. There was wet limestone dust under his feet, masses of tall buddleia in flower on the slopes, butterflies flitting from blossom to blossom over his head. They would disappear when it rained again.

A bridge crossed the track at a sharp angle, and he passed the remains of a large lime kiln buttressed like the walls of a castle. The entrances to the kiln had been sealed up with breeze block, but of course someone had knocked holes into the bottom sections. A glimpse inside suggested that the alcoves had been used, probably by rough sleepers, certainly for smoking cigarettes and drinking cider.

He slipped in a patch of mud. An off-roader had been through here and churned up the track. When the winter came, and these beeches and sycamores shed their leaves, it would be impossible to use this route past the lime kiln.

Lane had disappeared round a bend at the top of the slope. Cooper put on a bit more speed. He still didn't cope well with hills. His lungs burned whenever his breathing became hard. But it was appropriate, in a way. It was a constant physical reminder of the reasons why he was here.

At the top, he emerged in an old quarry. There were six of them within the site of the National Stone Centre, so he'd probably reached his destination. Limestone quarrying had created an amphitheatre here, with an almost level floor and sheer rock faces on three sides. Dozens of jackdaws circled overhead, or perched in the trees struggling to maintain a foothold on the upper ledges.

Cooper had been here on a school outing not long after the centre opened. Groups were allowed to go gem panning, sifting through buckets of wet sand to find interesting semi-precious stones, which they were allowed to take home. A lot of kids loved that. But the young Ben Cooper couldn't help being disappointed by how obvious it was that the bits of stone had been planted for children to find. He found the genuine bits of geology on the site far more interesting.

There were so many fossils underfoot in the rocks as he walked along the paths that he'd been aware of walking on history here, more than anywhere else he knew. In his imagination, he was moving through exotic sea creatures, touching a coral reef, paddling on the floor of an ancient lagoon. He was just three hundred million years too late for his tropical holiday.

He could see Josh Lane clearly now. He was dressed in a black anorak and blue denims, and his head was bare, showing a gleam of gelled hair. At least his boots must be practical. Cooper noticed that he'd come to a halt by a picnic area. It had been built by young people serving community sentences, part of a system called restorative justice. It was supposed to be based on the the concept of 'closing the circle', a North American Indian belief that a circle was broken when a crime was committed in a community. Restoration could only be achieved when the offender made amends to the community and closed the circle.

Here, the amends to the community consisted of a circle of stone seats, with relief carvings depicting the prehistoric sea creatures which had once lived here. The reef they'd lived on was just behind him, exposed by centuries of quarrying.

Cooper looked round, and stepped behind a stretch of stone wall. In fact, it wasn't just any wall, but the Millennium Wall, a series of dry-stone sections representing a range of styles from all over the UK. Round boulders from Galloway, tight wedges from Caithness, a stone-faced earth wall from Wales that looked like a length snipped from Offa's Dyke.

From Lane's stance, it looked almost as though he was aware of being watched. His interest in the restorative justice project seemed to Cooper to be an act of defiance, a provocative gesture. Lane was symbolically putting two fingers up, just as he had been all these months. Could that really just be in his imagination?

Right in front of Cooper's face as he ducked down was the Derbyshire section, built in two contrasting styles – the irregular fractures of limestone and the regular coursing of gritstone. Even in the construction of its walls, the Peak District was divided: rolling farmland and bleak peat moor, picturesque villages and the empty black wastes. The White Peak and the Dark Peak. Good and evil. Their presence in the landscape had never been so obvious to Cooper as he crouched behind that wall.

The frustration was beginning to get difficult to tolerate.

'Move on, move on,' he muttered to himself.

As if he'd heard from this distance, Lane began to walk up the slope again. Through the trees above, Cooper glimpsed the blue glass of the Discovery Centre. In front of the entrance was a set of wide steps, where he'd once walked up through the different eras of stone, right up to the final step made of Antrim basalt, a mere sixty million years old. He assumed that Josh Lane was going into the café at the Discovery Centre. He would probably sit and have a coffee, maybe a sandwich.

Cooper sat down to wait. The High Peak Trail ran over the bridge just before the car park and he could hear people chatting as they passed overhead. Just beyond a small lime kiln there had once been a small settlement of half a dozen cottages. The Coal Hills hamlet. With that kiln smoking all day and all night, it must have been a nightmarish place to live in. But the hamlet had been abandoned and demolished in the 1930s – not because of the smoke, but when the water supply in this limestone area became unreliable. All that remained now were a few heaps of tumbled stones covered in moss.

Nearer to the road was the Derbyshire Eco Centre, where even the bike shed had solar panels. He saw more and more solar panels these days. Wind turbines too – sometimes just the odd one running a small-scale rural enterprise, but in other locations an entire wind farm, the turbine blades turning slowly, some even stopped.

There was no wind this summer, let alone any sun. Soon there'd be talk of harnessing water power to plug the gap in the country's energy supply. Cooper had heard there was already a water turbine operating down in Alport, a derelict watermill converted to harness the flow of the River Bradford. Surely that was a better idea? It reused an existing site, and a water turbine was always hidden away in a valley. Not like these giant structures on the hillsides, visible for miles. They made him think of Don Quixote, famous for his futile tilting at windmills in the cause of justice. But at least he'd never given up.

A Royal Mail van pulled into the car park and an employee in his orange reflective jacket got out carrying a parcel of fish and chips for his lunch. The smell as he passed reminded Cooper that he was likely to miss lunch himself. But it was good that he was thinking about food with enthusiasm, even if he wasn't actually eating.

'What is it you're after? You must want something?'

Cooper turned at the sound of the voice, and found Josh Lane looking down at him, his hands thrust into the pockets of his anorak. The defiant expression was certainly deliberate now. He stood just out of reach, his boots firmly planted on the limestone, dirt from the path crumbling on to the embedded fossils.

It took Cooper a moment to recover from the shock.

'Perhaps just to talk,' he said.

Lane laughed. 'I don't believe that.'

'It's true.'

'Look, I'm on bail. I've already been charged. So you can't ask me any questions. You shouldn't even be talking to me. My brief says once I've been charged and appeared in court, that's it.'

'You probably have a good defence lawyer.'

'No, he's just some duty solicitor they gave me.'

'He'll be all right,' said Cooper. 'Most of them are. But I've had the training. I know the way it has to be done.'

'There are regulations. The Police and Criminal Evidence Act.'

'That's right, as a rule. But in fact there's a paragraph in Code C of PACE. I don't suppose you read it? It allows an interview after charge, if it's necessary to prevent harm to another person or to clear up ambiguity in a previous statement.'

'That's an anti-terrorism measure, surely.'

Cooper shrugged. 'It's open to interpretation.'

'So where's the caution? What about "You do not have to say anything, but it may harm your defence"? Why aren't you taking me down to the station? Where's the interview room and the tape recorder? And why are you here on your own? Do you think I'm stupid?'

'No, not that,' said Cooper.

'You're going to be in big trouble, my friend. And we both know it.'

'I want to hear from you if you understand what you did.'

Lane looked at him more closely. 'You look like shit. You're sick.'

Cooper nodded. 'I've been better.'

'What is this? Do you want me to say I'm sorry or something? It's not going to happen.'

But there was nothing else to say now, nothing that

332

was worthwhile, nothing that could help him or Liz. His fists clenched inside his waxed coat, Cooper continued to watch Lane, oblivious to the rain that was beginning to fall.

Lane shook his head, exasperated at his silence.

'Come on, come on,' he said. 'Do something. What is it? Do you want to take a swing at me? Do it, then. That would finish your career for good. But maybe you don't care.'

Cooper still said nothing.

'Suit yourself, then. I'm out of here. But if you don't stop following me— Well, if you come near me again, I'll report you for harassment.'

He began to walk away, then turned as Cooper remained standing on the path.

'You know, you're sick,' he said. 'Sick.'

Cooper watched him go. How had he managed to let Josh Lane spot him so easily? Was he so out of practice? Or could it be that he'd deliberately revealed his presence? Had he intended that Lane should see him?

It was confusing, not knowing his own intentions. Right now, his emotions seemed to be leading him, instead of his brains or his professional instincts.

Lane probably thought Cooper would back off and give up after their confrontation at the National Stone

Centre. But that would have defeated the whole object.

Cooper got back in his Toyota and kept Lane's Honda in view as it drove back into Wirksworth. He followed it all the way through the town and into the Market Place, where Lane turned past Crown Yard and the Blacks Head pub and climbed the hill called West End. They passed through the Yokecliffe area and were soon out into the country heading towards Hopton.

By the time they reached the wetlands at the northern end of Carsington Water, Cooper's mind had begun to stray towards the Knockerdown Inn again. Lane certainly had a tendency to be drawn to pubs. But instead he indicated right on the Carsington bypass and drove into the village past the little Gothic-style church, where the open grave had been filled in and marked with a brand new headstone.

Was he heading to the Miners Arms for a pint of Marston's Pedigree? No, he was stopping just past it. Cooper didn't slow down, but drove on towards the gardens of Hopton Hall.

There was no need for Prospectus Assurance flexi-time. It was Saturday morning, and Ralph Edge was at home. Cooper had seen his Mercedes standing on the drive.

27

Sunday

Diane Fry had been expecting to be pushed out of the way at any moment. She knew better than anyone how these things worked. The Major Crime Unit would arrive, DCI Alistair Mackenzie and an entire team to take charge of the inquiry, including whoever had replaced her as a DS at St Ann's in Nottingham. So far it hadn't happened. The MCU had been too busy with ongoing operations, their resources stretched too far. There must have been discussions at a higher level, but no one had bothered to fill her in yet. She'd been quite happy to leave it that way. She'd been enjoying the freedom of action.

But on Sunday morning, all that changed. An email came through, informing her that DCI Mackenzie would be assuming the role of Senior Investigating Officer and setting up an incident room. And that was it – an email. Was that all she was worth now?

Fry felt her determination harden. Before the MCU arrived, she ought to get everything done that she could. It would be perfect if she could make some positive progress on the Glen Turner murder inquiry. She hadn't been back to the scene at Sparrow Wood since Thursday. There was time to put that right today. Already she was putting her coat on when the call came in. There had been an incident at Sparrow Wood. Time to get on the road.

The B5056. It was probably the quietest stretch of road that Ben Cooper had ever driven on in the Peak District. Its route parted from the busy A515 just north of Ashbourne and snaked its way northwards, heading vaguely in the direction of Bakewell some twenty miles away. A substantial length of the B5056 formed the eastern boundary of the national park. But that seemed to be almost its only purpose. The road successfully managed to avoid villages, except for the tiny settlements of Longcliffe and Grangemill, each of them more of a glorified crossroads than a village.

Further north, it nearly reached Winster, but shied away from it at the last minute, as if it had the plague.

The road continued to meander between Harthill and Stanton Moors, more at home among the ancient stone circles and rocky tors than human habitation, until it finally hit a T-junction on the A6 near Haddon Hall and couldn't go any further.

Cooper had driven along this road at night, and during the day, and he could barely remember passing any traffic. Everyone seemed intent on cramming their cars into Dovedale or Ashbourne at one end, and Bakewell at the other. It was the perfect road to drive on, if all you wanted to see was the occasional rabbit or pheasant, and nothing to remind you of other people.

He'd parked in a gateway near Eagle Rocks, one of the outcrops on the high ridge around Brassington, their jagged outlines looked eerie and mysterious in foggy conditions.

A dilapidated complex of barns and farm buildings stood near the junction of Pasture Lane and the B5056. They were a complete hotch-potch of brick, random stone, and corrugated iron roofs, all tumbled into ruins and overgrown with weeds, dank and sodden in the rain. Layers of rotting leaf mould lay in the mud.

Just over the fields at Ballidon an abandoned twelfth-century church stood alone in the middle of a field, its deteriorating structure left in the care of an organisation called the Friends of Friendless Churches. The village of Ballidon had shrunk to a point where its single road was no more than a rat run for the quarry lorries that rumbled backwards and forwards from the limestone works at the end of the dale. In the driest months, grey dust covered walls and doorways, including a Victorian postbox set into the stones of a farm, still carrying the VR initials. Just now, he supposed Ballidon would look better than usual, thanks to the rain washing off the accumulated dust.

Sparrow Wood spread down the slopes of the hill, dank and dark. The trees were heavy with foliage, which dripped water on the ground, creating an irregular pattering sound as if hundreds of small animals were moving invisibly around him.

Cooper had always thought late autumn was the best time to commit a murder. There were so many places like this to conceal a body – lots of secluded little hillsides close enough to the road, but where no one ever went. Later in the year they were knee deep in freshly fallen leaves. You could cover a corpse in a blanket of foliage several inches thick, yet leave no sign of disturbance. The body would decompose with the leaves as winter came on, kept warm under its covering even if the surface frosted over. There would be no visible trace of human remains, until the first heavy rain of spring washed the top layer of debris away, or the first dog came foraging in the woods for rabbits.

A body could lie undiscovered for years, if you were

lucky. Yes, it was during the murder and the disposal of the corpse that you were most likely to be seen. Concealment itself was easy.

But no one had bothered concealing this body, had they? Maybe they'd been in too much of a hurry, or didn't know the area well enough to find the right spot. Or perhaps they'd wanted the body to be found. Yes, there was always that possibility.

He found a deep hole in the rocks above Sparrow Wood. The entrance was equipped with bolts for descending on ropes, but uncovered. Dangerous for the merely inquisitive. The drop from the level of the hillside was perpendicular and he couldn't make out the depth. All kinds of things had been found dumped down shafts like this in the past – human and animal remains, toxic chemicals, discarded weapons.

He felt that shivery anticipation, his senses honed to an unusual sharpness. And there was a smell . . . It was something he couldn't identify, and he wasn't even sure it existed. So he'd better be careful that he didn't mention it to anyone, in case they thought he was mad.

He remembered Claire telling him that she sometimes experienced phantom smells when she was about to have a migraine. But that was Claire. She was the migraine type. As far as he could remember, he'd never suffered a migraine in his life.

'You're looking better, Ben,' said Carol Villiers, when she met him by his car a few minutes later.

'Am I?' said Cooper, surprised.

'Definitely.'

Cooper had to admit that the tremors had gone. He'd hardly coughed this morning. The pain was still there, but subdued and in the background. As long as he kept his mind on other things, it was like an analgesic.

'So it seems Mr Turner's paintballing injuries were caused by his immediate boss at Prospectus Assurance, Nathan Baird, and a colleague, Ralph Edge, who was supposed to be his friend,' said Villiers.

He smiled with a sense of anticipation again. 'Yes, that's right. Prospectus Assurance.'

Villiers shook her head. 'Ben, you're very frustrating to talk to sometimes. You always were, actually.'

'Was I?'

'Absolutely. But you're worse now. You hardly talk at all. And when you do, you don't seem to make any sense.'

Villiers was bringing him up to date on the latest information from the briefing of the previous day. Cooper listened with interest to an account of Luke Irvine's theory about angry insurance policy holders, but then found his attention wandering. Delays in getting forensic results and threats of legal action didn't seem relevant to him.

'Uh-uh,' said Cooper. Then again, when her voice stopped. 'Uh-uh.'

Villiers looked at him. 'You said yesterday you were really interested in this case.'

'Oh, yeah. That's all fascinating,' he said. 'I was just thinking about . . . something else.'

She sighed. 'As usual.'

They'd reached the outer cordon of the crime scene, lengths of tape strung between the trees and guarded by a uniformed officer with a clipboard. SOCOs in scene suits were moving among the trees and a group of officers were picking their way up the slope.

'They had to dam the stream to be able to pump the water out,' said Villiers. 'I think forensics are still working on the immediate site.'

'There seems to be a lot of activity, though,' said Cooper.

'Yes, there is.' Villiers looked round. 'Oh, damn. Keep your head down.'

Diane Fry stepped out of her Audi and looked around the scene at Sparrow Wood. It was seething with activity. As she passed the constable on duty at the cordon, she took a glance at the scene log to see who was already present. There were the usual suspects, the same cast of characters who appeared at the scene of every suspicious death. Forensics, a few uniformed officers to secure the scene, others to conduct a search. Lots of familiar faces. Some of them too familiar.

She stopped, turned back towards the cordon. Yes – much too familiar.

Fry splashed across the verge, the remains of a path already churned to mud. A female officer grasped her arm to support her as she skidded and almost covered the last few yards on her backside.

'Thank you,' she said, keeping her eye on the figure she'd spotted.

She reached the cordon and faced him. He didn't look away, didn't try to hide his face this time.

'What are you doing here, Ben?' she said.

Cooper didn't even blink at her tone.

'I'm outside the cordon,' he said. 'Like any other member of the public.'

'That doesn't answer my question.'

'I don't need to answer your questions. I'm a law-abiding citizen standing on a public highway like anyone else, watching our public servants go about their business.'

She gritted her teeth, fighting a conflict within her. There was only one thing she could do if her suspicions were correct. Loyalties had to be broken. There was no other choice.

'If you get in the way,' she said, 'you realise I might have to arrest you.'

Cooper raised an eyebrow. 'Would that give you some kind of satisfaction, Diane?' he said quietly.

She watched the rain running off his face, the lights of the vehicles reflected in the wet slickness of his coat, water droplets dripping on to his shoulders like jewels, sparkling as they caught the lights. He looked like the picture of someone else she'd been imagining. But he was just Ben Cooper.

'Ben, why won't you give me the opportunity to help you?' she said.

But she turned away before he could reply and began to slither back across the grass verge towards the activity in the woods. She didn't want to look at him any longer. She didn't want to see the answer in Cooper's eyes.

Cooper raised his eyes from the ground and looked up at the series of jagged stones rising above the woods.

'Have you looked in the rocks?' he called.

Fry stopped and followed his gaze. 'Why would we?'

He hesitated, then shrugged. 'No reason.'

Fry immediately regretted her response. Of course there was a reason. He wouldn't have suggested it without one. She was just being too obtuse to see it, and too stubborn to listen to his suggestions. And Cooper had changed. He was no longer in the frame of mind to persist in the face of her stubbornness. That shrug told her quite clearly that he'd given up. He couldn't be bothered trying again, wouldn't make the effort to explain his thoughts. Why should he, when she dismissed them so easily? Fry realised she was treating him as if he was the same old Ben Cooper just because he looked so much like his former self on the surface. But he wasn't the same. Something inside him had been changed.

'Do you know anything about those rocks?' she said.

'No. But they're a good place for somebody to watch from, aren't they?'

'What? Who?'

Fry shook her head in despair. It was always like this when Cooper was around. He made her feel she had no idea what she was doing, because she was lacking the important knowledge that he was privy to.

She wondered why Carol Villiers was here too. Had she been called out to the scene? Well, that was something she could deal with later.

'There are caves as well, you know,' said Cooper.

'What?'

'Caves. It's limestone, so there are always caves. They're hidden by the trees in summer. But there are several caves at the foot of these cliffs. You should get someone to check them out.'

'I will.'

Fry learned that the farmer, Bill Maskrey, had confronted an off-roader in the woods. He'd described a man on a trail bike sliding down the hillside through the trees, spraying mud everywhere. He'd almost been at the stream when he stopped and dismounted.

Maskrey had been carrying his shotgun, and he'd fired a warning shot. All hell had broken loose then, of course. Most of these officers were here because a weapon had been discharged. Maskrey had been detained to explain himself, as was procedure in these cases.

There was no sign of the trail biker except for deep ruts carved into the hill, heading towards the rocks above.

Fry knew that Sparrow Wood wasn't alone in this problem. Protestors had been complaining about several sites in the national park being carved up by off-roaders. Organisations had been lobbying for action at locations like Long Causeway, near Stanage Edge. But off-roaders had staged counter-protests too. There was always the potential for conflict. But Mr Maskrey had stepped over the line on this occasion. That was all there was to it.

She decided to deal with Carol Villiers.

'Carol,' she said quietly. 'Can I have a word?'

'Of course.'

Villiers was waiting expectantly. When they were out of earshot, Fry leaned in closer.

'When did you last speak to Ben?'

'Yesterday.'

'How does he seem to you?'

'Oh . . . okay. Fine.'

'Are you sure?'

'Well, not quite his usual self, obviously. But getting there.'

'What did he talk about?'

'This and that.'

Fry began to lose patience. 'For God's sake, why is this so difficult? It's like interviewing a suspect who's been told to go "no comment". What are you frightened of telling me?'

Villiers grimaced and looked away. Yes, it was just like in the interview room, when your suspect felt a stab of guilt and didn't want to meet your eye. Fry stared at her fixedly until she gave in.

'He was asking me about Eliot Wharton and Josh Lane,' said Villiers.

'Oh, was he indeed?'

'It's perfectly natural. He wanted to know what was happening to them.'

'He was fishing for inside information.'

'I wouldn't say that, Diane.'

'Well, I would. And I know something else. He wouldn't have dared to approach me or DI Hitchens to ask for that sort of information, so he came to you.'

'I didn't tell him anything.'

'You might not have intended to. But I bet he got

something out of you. He made sure you let your guard drop and began to feel sorry for him, didn't he?'

'Well, maybe . . .'

'It's an old trick. I'm surprised you fell for it.'

She had the satisfaction of seeing Villiers' face go faintly pink. At least she'd think twice before she was such a sucker again.

Cooper studied Diane Fry as she stamped about giving orders. It was hard seeing people change in front of your eyes. But it was even harder trying to remember who they used to be. The new person supplanted the old one and displaced their memory.

But Fry still had that look. He'd seen it in her the first time they'd met, years ago on her transfer to Derbyshire. It was a look that suggested the whole world was a terrible place. Everyone must know how awful it was. So, if you smiled too much, you must be an idiot. Too stupid to see how bad everything was. Stupid enough to be happy. She never saw any blue sky, only grey.

When she came back again, he was still standing there, just outside the outer cordon. She hadn't told him to go away, and she didn't seem able to resist drifting towards him again, as if she wanted to ask him something but couldn't find the right opportunity.

'You know,' said Cooper. 'I drive around sometimes,

late at night. I just stay in the car for hours, not really knowing where I am, or where I'm going.'

Fry looked uncomfortable, as if he'd just confessed to some sexual perversion.

'Why?' she said.

'Just for the pleasure of driving, being on empty roads. The feeling that I'm getting right away from all the places I know.' He looked at her. 'Perhaps you don't understand.'

'Can't say I do.'

Cooper decided not to tell her any more. If she didn't grasp that part, she wouldn't be able to understand the rest of it.

'Diane, did it not occur to you to wonder why anyone would choose Sparrow Wood for this murder?' he asked.

'Yes, of course. But without a suspect to ask . . .'

'Yet the answer is obvious, without asking the question,' said Cooper. 'It was convenience. They chose it because it was handy.'

Fry waved at the surrounding landscape. 'Handy for who? No one lives here.'

'Not many,' said Cooper. 'Some do work here, though.'

Fry realised one of the uniformed officers was trying to attract her attention. He had hold of a scruffy man

348

with a dense beard, who wasn't even attempting to struggle against the grip on his arm.

'Who is this?' said Fry.

'We found him dossing in one of the caves, Sarge.'

'They're nice and dry,' said the man. 'You wouldn't expect me to sleep rough in this weather.'

'A cave isn't sleeping rough?'

'It's all relative, isn't it?'

'What do they call you?' asked Fry.

'Spikey.'

'That's your name?'

'You asked what they called me. They call me Spikey.'

'Can you produce any ID?' asked the officer holding his arm.

Spikey laughed at him. 'Do I look as though I'm carrying my driving licence and credit cards?'

'We need your name and address so we can check you out.'

'My name's John Clarke, known as Spikey to my mates. Not that I have many friends. People don't drop in for tea much any more.'

'John Clarke. Is that with an "e"?'

'If you like.' The officer let go of his sleeve, and Clarke watched him write the name down. 'Now put "no fixed abode". I love that word "abode". You only ever get it in police reports, like "proceeding" and "persons unknown".'

349

'Have you been the subject of many police reports?' asked Fry.

Clarke had a mischievous grin behind his beard. She caught a glimpse of yellowed teeth.

'That's for you to find out,' he said. 'I suppose you'll be getting your man here on the radio.'

Fry nodded, and the officer walked away to get a PNC check.

'Of course, we have no proof of what your name really is,' she said.

'Why not?'

'Because you're not carrying any ID, Mr Clarke.'

'Spikey,' he said.

'I thought that was how your mates know you.'

'Aren't you my mate? I thought the police were supposed to be our friends. You know, protecting your community and all that.'

'What do you live on here? What do you eat?'

'Fresh lamb and mutton,' said Clarke. 'There's lots of it about. You just have to catch it.'

'Sheep?'

'Aye. I'm bypassing the grasping farmers and taking animals direct from the wild.'

'I don't think there's such a thing as a wild sheep. Not in Derbyshire, anyway. All the sheep that you see belong to farmers.'

'Not all of them, surely?

'Well, yes.'

'What about the ones wandering loose on the moors? They're wild, aren't they?'

'No, they're just, er . . . shafted.'

Cooper sighed. 'Hefted.'

'They're hefted,' said Fry.

'I don't know what you're on about. They're not even fenced in, they wander where they like. It looks to me as though they're there for the taking. Just like the way you might find a pheasant by the side of the road, or the odd rabbit in the woods.'

Fry's shoulders began to tense, as they did when she was angry. Cooper touched her arm.

'Diane, he's winding you up,' he said.

Just then Fry received a text on her phone. The Crime Scene Manager, Wayne Abbott, had some news for her. She shook Cooper off.

'Look, if you have anything useful to share, tell it to DC Villiers, will you? Or write it down.'

Cooper pulled a notebook from his pocket and tore off a page.

'Gibson,' he said. 'Ryan and Sean. There, I've written it down for you.'

Fry snatched the paper from Cooper's hand and headed towards the stream bed, covering her nose against the stench of the mud now exposed at her crime scene after the water had been drained away. If she stayed here for too long, she'd have to ask Scenes of Crime for a mask.

'So. What is it?' she said.

Wayne Abbott appeared from among the trees and gestured her over to the Scientific Support van, where he had his laptop set up.

'I'm expecting an SIO to arrive—' began Abbott.

'But he's not here yet.'

'True.' He turned over an evidence bag in his hand. 'Well, we found this in the mud.'

'A mobile phone,' said Fry.

'A Nokia 100, to be exact. In a nice leather case.'

'It can't be our victim's. We found that one, and we're still waiting for some results.'

Abbott smiled. 'The leather case is important.'

'Why?'

'Well the phone itself is wrecked. It's been lying in water for four days at least. I doubt even the clever boys at the lab will get anything off the SIM card. But the case protected the casing of the phone well enough for us to lift some prints off it.'

'That's excellent news,' said Fry.

'Even better, since we now have the new Identification Bureau in Nottinghamshire, we've got some real-time forensics at our disposal. We've entered the prints and got a hit from the database already. Take a look.'

Fry stared at Abbott, and back at the display on his laptop, where the identity of the fingerprints' owner was displayed.

'Damn it,' she said. 'Ben Cooper. Where the heck is he again?'

28

Ben Cooper had walked across the field towards the old cottage he could see standing on its own at the end of a muddy track. It really *was* old. Random stone walls, slipped and broken tiles on the roof, an overgrown patch of garden, rank with elder and willowherb. It had probably once been associated with a quarry, or provided accommodation for a farm worker. Its position was too uninviting to be considered suitable for anything else. Well, a holiday cottage, perhaps. Holiday cottages could be situated anywhere these days. But this was no tourist destination. It would never get any AA stars.

Cooper saw a splash of bright red and the outline of a piece of agricultural equipment standing on the edge of a field. A thousand-kilo-sized Portequip bull beef feeder with a rain canopy, positioned close against the stone wall. He passed a long line of individual sheep pens running along the edge of the sweeping pasture below Eagle Rocks, each pen with its own gate and corrugated iron roof, like a sort of sheep motel.

A death wish sheep had hurled itself off the rocks above. Its body lay broken on the track, the flesh on its head and legs already picked clean from the bones. Nothing to do with the floods, or with Spikey Clarke. Sheep were genetically suicidal.

Close up, the cottage barely looked habitable. The dirty curtains in the windows might have been there for decades. But when he knocked on the door, it was answered fairly quickly. An old man looked out at him with weak blue eyes, one skeletal hand clutching the door knob, an old grey cardigan sagging from his emaciated chest.

'Hicklin? Is it Mr Roger Hicklin?' asked Cooper.

'The very same. What can I do for you?'

'I just want to talk to you for a few minutes.'

'Are you selling something?'

'No, sir.'

Hicklin peered at him closely, and seemed to come to a decision.

'Come in out of the rain.'

'Thank you.'

Cooper shook some of the rain off his waxed coat

on to the flags in the hallway. 'It doesn't look as though it's going to stop,' he said.

'Not likely.' Hicklin laughed wheezily. 'I'd like to think it's the Great Flood. You know . . . the Deluge.'

Cooper could hear the capital letters, and guessed Mr Hicklin was referring to the Old Testament story of Noah and his ark. *The rain was upon the earth forty days and forty nights.* It wasn't far off the mark this summer.

'You would, sir?'

'Well, the world needs a good clean-out, don't you think?' said Hicklin. 'We've turned it into a global cesspit over the centuries. It's time that Mother Nature washed it all away and started again. Surely you must agree?'

'No comment,' said Cooper. Even as he said it, he reflected that he must have sat in on too many suspect interviews. '*No comment, no comment*' – he'd heard it so often it had become a mantra, a line he couldn't get out of his head, like the chorus of a cheesy pop song. It was a phrase that solicitors trained their clients to repeat ad nauseam, in order to avoid committing themselves.

So why had he evaded an answer to Hicklin's question? Did the world need a good clean-out? Maybe. But not in this way.

He followed Hicklin through the hallway into a small sitting room. The grubby curtains were matched by the damp wallpaper and a few feet of grimy, rubbish-strewn carpet. The old man offered him one of the two armchairs in the room, and settled himself down in the other. Once he was inside the house, Cooper soon became aware of a steady drip, drip, drip. Not a regular pattern, but an irregular sound like a piece of avant-garde music, imaginatively played on plastic bucket and steel saucepan.

'Aye, the Deluge. Quite a lot of us think that we're living in depraved and degenerate times,' said Hicklin with an enigmatic smile. 'I've been waiting decades for a nice, deadly disease to wipe out a large part of the earth's population. That's the only answer to the situation the human race has got itself into. It's the natural solution, the way that Mother Nature deals with chronic overcrowding in the population of any other species. I'm certain it will happen one day.'

Cooper just nodded in acknowledgement, recognising that he was obliged to listen to Hicklin riding this hobby horse if he was to get the chance to ask him any questions. Some people didn't get many visitors. They stored up things like this, went over and over them in their own minds, and needed to let off steam when they got the opportunity. Cooper guessed he must be the first visitor to this cottage in days, perhaps weeks.

'What will happen one day?' he said.

'Ah, well. These floods and hurricanes and

earthquakes are all very well, but disasters are a drop in the ocean. The only thing that can do the job is an outbreak of a new flu strain, like the one back in 1918 that killed five per cent of the world's population. Do you know it caused more deaths than the Great War did in five years of slaughter? With the enormous increase in air travel and the expansion of global trade, pandemics spread even more quickly now. One of those every month for a while would sort things out nicely.'

'Oh, nicely,' said Cooper.

He found it difficult to tell from Mr Hicklin's enigmatic little smile how far he was joking, and what exactly he was serious about. A lot of Derbyshire people were like that. They could tell you anything with a straight face, and then think you were simple for believing a single word they said.

'People are always predicting the end of the world. The Apocalypse, the Rapture, the last day of the Mayan calendar. But it never happens, more's the pity. We live in a strange world. And people are the strangest things in it.'

'You won't hear me arguing with that, sir.'

'So I suppose that's why we have all these hippies about here,' said Hicklin.

'Hippies?'

'Students, ramblers, campers, motorcyclists. You know.'

Cooper nodded. He'd heard it said, or read it some-where. As far as some of these old farmers and quarry-men were concerned, a hippy was anyone not wearing a tweed cap and wellies.

As he sat in Hicklin's armchair, Cooper began to notice that the sounds around him were changing, their pitch rising and becoming more liquid as the buckets gradually filled with water. Drip, drip . . . ping.

Hicklin noticed his attention straying.

'Lead,' he said. 'You just can't get it these days. Or at least, not without nicking it off someone's roof.'

Cooper produced his identification. Mr Hicklin should have asked for it before he let him into the house, of course. But Cooper had felt reluctant to use it, and it might not have got him in any more easily.

'You probably don't remember me,' he said. 'I'm a police officer.'

'I thought you were,' said Hicklin.

'I dealt with a case some years ago that you were involved in. You were a victim of the Gibson brothers.'

'They bled me dry,' said Hicklin. 'I should have stood up to them, I suppose.'

'Sometimes it's not so easy, sir.'

'Has something happened?'

'I'm following up on a new inquiry.'

It was a vague enough statement, but he would have a hard job justifying it if he was ever challenged on the truth of it. 'They were blackmailing you, weren't they?' he asked.

'Yes. Well, you'll know all about it. Ryan was the one who put the squeeze on me, and enjoyed doing it too. He has a brother, who was just as nasty.'

'Sean.'

'Yes, Sean. Ryan and Sean Gibson. Two signs that we're living in a cesspit, if ever I saw them.'

'What they were blackmailing you for – it wasn't very serious, as I recall,' said Cooper.

'No. I was only siphoning off a few stores – an air filter, a box of washers, some small electrical items. And farmers have all kinds of uses for a length of conveyor belt. I was just trying to make a bit extra to keep us going. It might seem like nothing to some people now. What's a bit of thieving these days? But I felt ashamed of what I was doing. And I knew it would have killed Mary if she'd found out where the money came from. She thought I was working overtime.'

'Mary. Yes, that's your wife.'

Hicklin followed his gaze as he looked round the old cottage, taking in the damp wallpaper, the dirty curtains, the carpet covered with rubbish.

'Yes, Mary died anyway,' said Hicklin quietly. 'A heart attack. And I lost my job. So it was all for nothing.'

Cooper shifted uncomfortably. 'Mr Hicklin, I

remember you, and I think I know the sort of man you are. You believe in justice, don't you?'

'I believe in it,' said Hicklin. 'But I don't expect it. Not any more.'

'But I think you might have kept track of what happened to the Gibson brothers. Their court cases, the length of their sentences, when they were released. Perhaps where they're living now?'

With suddenly astute eyes, Hicklin studied him for a long moment. 'What is this about really?'

'I can't tell you exactly, sir.'

Hicklin seemed to come to a decision, just the way he had when he first saw Cooper standing on his doorstep. He heaved himself out of his chair and shuffled off into another room. Cooper heard him opening a drawer. He came back with an old yellow pocket file, well worn around the edges and repaired with a bit of sellotape.

'This will be what you mean,' he said.

'Can I borrow it, please?'

'Aye,' said Hicklin. 'Just bring it back when you can. If the world hasn't ended by then.'

Cooper stood up and slid the file under his coat, then said, 'Ryan Gibson worked just over there at A.J. Morton and Sons, didn't he?'

'Still does,' said Hicklin. 'I see him occasionally. You can imagine how that feels.'

A few minutes later, Cooper left Mr Hicklin in his old house with its leaky roof. Outside, the downpour was torrential. He might even have said biblical. The landscape had disappeared behind dense curtains of rain, and large pools of water had formed in Hicklin's overgrown garden, almost blocking access to the gate.

'You're not in danger of flooding here, are you, sir?' he asked.

'I hope not,' said Hicklin. 'I can't afford the insurance.'

Ryan Gibson was on his forklift truck in the huge storage yard at A.J. Morton & Sons. The site was well screened from the nearby roads. Even from the entrance, you would never guess the size of it. Everywhere he looked, Cooper saw stacks of crusher and screening spares, conveyor belt sections and rubber skirting, boxes of bearings and filters.

Cooper stood in front of the forklift and waved him down. Gibson stopped in surprise and turned off the engine.

'What do you want? You'll have to go into the office.'

Gibson looked over his shoulder and began to swing the steering wheel to reverse away from him.

'Ryan?' said Cooper.

Gibson turned and stared at him. Recognition was

a long time coming, but it reached his face eventually. 'I don't want to talk to you,' he said. 'I never talk to the coppers. And I'm not supposed to stop work to chat anyway. So you might as well be on your way.'

'How's your brother?' asked Cooper. 'Sean?'

'No idea,' said Gibson. 'I haven't seen him. He's gone abroad.'

'Oh? Where to?'

'I don't know. He doesn't send me postcards.'

Gibson revved up the forklift and headed away across the yard to lift a pallet of rollers.

Cooper watched him working for a moment. He hadn't expected to get any answers here. Not from the likes of Ryan Gibson – he was too old a hand. All he'd wanted to do was see him, and read whatever he could find in Ryan's face. And that had been bad enough.

When he arrived back in Edendale town centre, Cooper thought about Roger Hicklin and his Deluge. *The world needs a good clean-out, don't you think?*

Cooper looked at the water pouring down the main roads and swirling away into the alleys on either side. The water was dirty brown, and its stink was vile. It was filled with mud and debris scoured from the hill-sides or forced up out of the drains and dumped on to the streets of the town. For all the world, it looked and smelled as though nature had developed a nasty case of unstoppable diarrhoea. Clean wasn't the word for it.

By the time Charlie Dean and Sheena Sullivan left the house in Green Hill that Sunday, it was already late afternoon, and it had started to rain again.

They'd stayed much longer than Charlie had intended, and they would both have to work on their excuses before they got home. But the house had been so comfortable compared to other locations they'd used in the past that it was hard for either of them to tear themselves away.

As he waited for Sheena, Charlie looked out of the sitting room window. This property had views to die for over Wirksworth, and beyond the town to the hills on the far side of the Ecclesbourne Valley. It stood at the top of one of the steepest hills in Derbyshire, and on one of the narrowest roads in the county too. He knew exactly what it was like up here – his own house was on the adjacent road, The Dale, which was just as steep and narrow. It curled back and linked into Green Hill at the top, where the sides of the quarries prevented either road from continuing further west.

'Are you ready?' he called. 'We need to be moving.'
'Nearly.'

Charlie cursed quietly. She could be such a nuisance. She didn't seem to take things seriously enough. This was all going to fall apart one day, thanks to her. Either Barbara or Jay would become too suspicious, and that would be the end of it. He could foresee unpleasant scenes sooner or later.

When Sheena finally appeared, they went outside. The BMW had been standing under the car port out of the rain, and out of sight of the neighbours. The owners of the house must have kept cans of petrol here, or some motor oil. He could smell it when they left by the back door and he paused for a moment to unlock the car. He wasn't worried that the car might have developed an oil leak – he was very careful about things like that, and always had the BMW serviced regularly. It paid to look after the possessions you valued. He walked round the car, though, just to make sure.

'Hurry up, Charlie, I'm getting wet,' said Sheena. 'I hate getting wet. You know that.'

'Well, don't stand out in the rain, silly cow,' he said.

'Don't call me a silly cow.'

'For goodness sake—look, the car's open. Get in. And be careful where you're stepping. It smells as though there might have been some oil spilled in here.'

As soon as he pulled out on to Green Hill, Charlie Dean knew there was something wrong. The brake pedal felt spongy when he pressed it to hold the car on the steep hill. He pumped it desperately, got only a slight response, then felt the pedal go flat to the floor.

'What's wrong, Charlie?'

'There's nothing in the brakes,' he said.

'We're going too fast.'

'I know!'

The car just made the first of the tight corners.

The pedal hit the floor.

'Shit.'

'Charlie, do something!'

'I can't. The steering's gone too.'

The car slewed round another corner, scraping the wall of a house and peeling off shards of limestone. Metal screeched in protest all along the side of the car. A flower tub went flying, a recycling bag scattered its contents across the windscreen. Sheena began to scream.

'Shut up, shut up!' yelled Charlie, wrestling the steering wheel in futile fury.

His tyres bumped crazily over the stone setts, the nearside wheel hit a step and a tyre burst. The wing of the BMW dipped and sparks flew into the air as the bodywork scoured itself against the stone, leaving a trail of red paint flakes on the road. The rear end began to slew from side to side, swiping a Fiat Uno parked at the kerb and sending its wing mirror spinning off into the distance.

The car continued to veer from side to side, dented a telegraph pole on one side, and took out a plastic grit bin on the other. An overhanging bough of ivy rattled across the roof like gunshots.

Eyes wide, his hands sweaty, Charlie stared at the hill ahead. The narrowest corner was coming up, where there was an ancient stone house with mullioned windows. He knew it was the last bend before the run down into the Market Place past the bookshop and the hairdresser's. Beyond it, if he couldn't stop the car, he'd be flying out into the traffic on St John's Street.

He'd forgotten the junction with The Dale. Ironic, when it was the street he lived on. When he was within a few yards, a white delivery van nosed out of the junction. The driver saw him coming and stopped, gaping at the vehicle swinging from one side of the road to the other.

Charlie only had one option. He yanked on the handbrake. The rear wheels locked, the back end swung round, the nose caught a stone step and the BMW flipped over, turning twice in the air before it hit the van, crushing its bonnet, then bounced off and slid into St John's Street on its roof. A Sixes bus ploughed into it, pushing it up on to the pavement in front of Ken's Mini Market, where it lay with its engine still running and fragments of glass showering into the gutter.

For a moment, everything was unnaturally silent. Then people began to shout. And Sheena Sullivan continued to scream.

29

Barbara Dean had always known there were moments when your life changed. When a ring on the doorbell might mark the end of *then* and the beginning of *now*. A before and an after, divided by a turn of the latch and the opening of a door. A moment when you found two police officers standing on your step. And you *knew*. It was more than an interruption of normality. It was a closing down of life, as if someone had turned off the power to your world and plunged it into darkness.

As she stood and stared at the two officers, Barbara realised that one of them was speaking. She could see his mouth moving. But the sentences had gone missing in the air somewhere between them. It was as if there was a time lag, his words bouncing off a distant satellite and returning slowly to earth, reaching her ears long after they'd been spoken. But no – not reaching her ears, but her brain. She heard the sounds, but her mind wouldn't process them into anything that made sense. This wasn't what she'd expected to happen.

They came into the hallway and sat in her lounge. Their presence on her leather sofa was so unnatural that they might as well have been wax dummies that had been stolen from Madame Tussaud's. They looked almost like real police officers, but there was something creepily wrong with them.

'They crashed at the bottom of Green Hill,' the first officer was saying.

Barbara could detect from his tone that he'd said it already, perhaps more than once.

'Was he badly injured?' she said.

'I'm afraid so.'

'Is he dead?' she said.

'Yes.'

She sat for a few moments trying to make sense of the answers. The two officers sat forward on the sofa, uncomfortable and anxious to leave.

'They?' she said.

'Your husband had a passenger, Mrs Dean.'

'I'm sorry?'

'There was someone else in the car with him. A woman, we believe. We thought—'

'What?'

'We thought it might have been you.'

So that explained the looks of surprise when she answered the door. They'd expected to find no one home, or a teenage child perhaps. That would have been worse for them, she supposed – having to break the news to a child that their parents had been in an accident. It was foolish that she should feel a surge of relief on their behalf. As if it was some consolation that they only had to inform the grieving widow.

'Could it be a mistake?' she asked. 'Are you sure it was Charlie?'

The other officer consulted a notebook. 'He was driving a red BMW 5 series.' He read out the registration number. 'Does your husband own that vehicle?'

'I can't remember registration numbers,' she said.

'It's registered in his name.'

'Well, then. That's probably right.'

She felt a laugh beginning to rise up in her chest, and stifled it with a cough. They would think she was hysterical. Did they still slap women across the face to cure hysteria? Or was that only in films? She was laughing at herself, though – at her silly inability to make the right responses.

'What am I supposed to say?' she asked, looking at the older of the two. The officer must have dealt with situations like this before, would know what words people normally spoke in these circumstances, how a well-balanced woman responded to the news of her husband's violent and sudden death.

'Is there anyone we can call to be with you?' asked the officer instead. 'A friend or relative? It's best not to be on your own.'

So that was how she was supposed to behave. She should seek a shoulder to cry on, turn to her best friend for support or run to her mother for comfort. She didn't feel like doing any of those things. So what was wrong with her?

'I was cooking supper,' she said. 'He should have been home by now.'

Both officers nodded sympathetically. To Barbara, it looked like approval. So perhaps, after all, she was behaving exactly the way they expected.

'You shouldn't be alone.'

'But I want to be alone.'

'You might want to talk to someone.' The female officer pulled a leaflet out of her pocket. A list of grief counsellors and their phone numbers. In case she wanted to talk to a stranger.

'Thank you.'

She made no effort to take the leaflet, so the officer placed it on the table, then added her card. 'You can reach us here.'

'Thank you,' she said again.

She wondered how she was doing, whether she was repeating meaningless phrases too much. How would these police officers be judging her? Too cold, too unemotional? She knew enough about the police to realise they were always judging the way people acted, how they responded to questions, whether they looked guilty or furtive, or ashamed.

'Will you be all right?' The younger officer sounded genuinely concerned. But it was probably just an act. They did it all the time. But for Barbara, it was a first.

And Barbara Dean had no idea why she'd reacted in this way to the news. It was the last thing she would have expected of herself. If she'd ever thought about it, she would have imagined feeling a huge sense of relief at the news of Charlie's death, the knowledge of a burden lifted from her life, the end of ten years of torment.

But now she was thinking that those ten years could have been worse. After all, he'd never shouted at her, and she had never screamed at him. They'd hated each other, but only in whispers.

At least it was an opportunity to stay away from the office. With news spreading that the team from the Major Crimes Unit were arriving at West Street, Diane Fry was keeping clear. In fact, it was a miracle the MCU had been able to find Edendale so quickly. Normally, officers based in St Ann's were like lost sheep without a sheepdog when they had to venture over the M1 into Derbyshire. The Eden Valley probably wasn't even on their satnavs.

So here she was in Wirksworth, following up the death of the estate agent, Charlie Dean, and feeling like a version of Ben Cooper, chasing some mystery that she couldn't explain, but which was challenging all her instincts.

And that was another thing she had to do. She had to corner Ben Cooper . . . If it took her the whole of the next week, she would have to pin him down and force him to explain how he knew the name of Sean Gibson, the man whose fingerprint was found on the phone lying in the mud of the stream bed at Sparrow Wood, the same man who was now being sought by the MCU from their incident room in Edendale. Cooper couldn't be allowed to get away with being so enigmatic, even if she had forced him into it herself.

Fry turned up The Dale, passing the exact spot where Charlie Dean's BMW had been flattened by the number 6.1 bus from Belper. Parking was difficult enough everywhere in Wirksworth, and there was certainly nowhere to park at the Deans' house – not without completely blocking the road. It was far too narrow to risk her car.

Fry could see the family liaison officer's Vauxhall on the gravel. There might have been enough room for two vehicles, if it wasn't for a heap of sand and a pile of breeze blocks and other building materials occupying the space next to the Vauxhall.

She had to carry on all the way up The Dale and turn round at the top, where the road curved back into Green Hill. She came down again slowly, and had gone past Magnolia Cottage again before she reached some residents' parking spaces under a high retaining wall, where she was able to park the Audi between a flowering cherry tree and a pink Citroën 2CV. It was a fifty-yard walk back up to the house. Much too far, especially in the rain.

'How do people manage for parking here?' she asked the FLO.

'Mrs Dean has a resident's permit to park in Rydes Yard, the council car park a few hundred yards down.'

Fry examined Barbara Dean critically. She was one of those women worn down by life, so drained of energy and emotion that she looked like a washed-out shadow. Mrs Dean seemed slow to respond to anything, reluctant to express an emotion in case it squeezed out the last drops of her spirit and left her empty and crumpled, like an old plastic bag. Her eyes were withdrawn, her face devoid of expression.

Fry had seen this sort of woman before. When others around them smiled or laughed, their mouths barely twitched. In some women, that might suggest too much Botox, their facial muscles frozen from attempts to resist the process of ageing. But not the likes of Barbara Dean. These women were frozen on the inside, their souls crushed by the intolerable strain of being alive. Now and then, Fry was consumed by the fear that she might end up like that herself in a few years' time. It might only take one bad decision to trap her into a situation she was unable to escape, and all the life could be drained from her too.

'What was her name?' asked Barbara. 'The woman. The other officers wouldn't tell me.'

'Sullivan,' said Fry. 'Sheena Sullivan. She's a hairdresser, here in Wirksworth.'

'The girl at . . . ? Oh, I think she did my hair once.'

'She says she met your husband on a speed awareness course.'

'Oh, that,' said Barbara. 'He met too many of the wrong kind of people on that.'

There was a big fireplace, and a heavy beam dividing the living room. Upstairs, a wide landing was in use as a home office, a computer workstation occupying one corner, bookshelves lining the wall.

Fry looked out at the rooftop views over Wirksworth, and the actual magnolia tree in the garden. From here, residents had the best outlook: eastwards across the town, not at the ragged wall of abandoned quarry immediately behind their houses. An area had been dug out behind the house, as if in preparation for foundations.

376

She remembered the pile of breeze blocks and building materials.

'What are you planning, Mrs Dean?' she asked.

'A kitchen extension. Charlie had been promising it to me for years, but he never seemed to have the money. The property market has been so depressed, you know. He was finally getting round to it, when . . .'

Fry nodded. It was strange that someone else had found a source of extra cash, as well as the Turners. Or perhaps not so strange.

'Mrs Dean, do you know of anyone who might want to harm your husband?' she asked.

Barbara gave her a small, humourless smile.

'Well, that's obvious,' she said. 'Me.'

The vehicle examiner had Charlie Dean's wrecked red BMW 5 series up on a ramp when Fry arrived in the police garage. It was a complete write-off, the front end crumpled beyond recognition, the roof peeled back by the fire and rescue crew to free the occupants. Dean himself had been dead on arrival, his body crushed by the bus, but Sheena was in hospital in Derby. Doctors were hoping she'd escaped life-threatening injuries thanks to airbags and her position in the rolled car when the bus hit it.

'Were the brake lines cut?' Fry asked the examiner.

'Looks like it at first glance. It's becoming a bit of an epidemic.'

'Sorry?'

'We've had quite a number of incidents around the county of brake lines being cut in the last few months. They all appear random at first, with no apparent intention of harming any specific victim. A bit of superficial investigation turns up several vehicles damaged in the same street, which suggests mindless vandalism, though of a particularly reckless kind. But usually some of the cars turn out to have had their fuel lines cut instead, which is the real clue.'

'You're talking about fuel theft.'

'Yes. A litre of fuel costs almost one pound forty pence at the pumps now, and thieves are looking for an easy way to steal petrol. Most filler caps have secure locks these days, but it's perfectly possible to drain petrol from a car by cutting through the fuel line, if you have the opportunity and a few simple bits of equipment. Of course, these guys aren't experts, just chancers. On some vehicles, they mistake the brake line for a fuel line and find themselves draining hydraulic fluid instead of petrol. But they're never going to put their hands up and admit their mistake, are they?'

'Unlikely.'

'Fortunately, no one has suffered a serious accident as a result of one of those incidents. Before now, anyway.

But I dare say there are a few motorists driving around Derbyshire testing their brakes at regular intervals, convinced that someone is out to get them.'

'Mr Dean was just unlucky that he was on such a steep hill, then.'

'Maybe so.'

Ursula Hart was one of the partners in estate agents Williamson Hart, Charlie Dean's employers. Though it was Sunday and the office wasn't normally open, she'd agreed to meet Fry in their old fashioned premises just off St John's Street in Wirksworth.

'He was a good estate agent in a lot of ways,' said Hart. 'Great at doing the hard sell without putting off the buyer completely, which is a rare skill these days. But we were going to have to let him go.'

'You were?' asked Diane Fry. 'Why? Are you cutting back? Is the business in trouble?'

'No, no. Well, not since we found out what Charlie was up to, thank goodness.'

'And what was that?'

'Oh, it was a clever scam. After completion on a property, he was maintaining contact with many of our clients – buyers and vendors alike. He got himself into a position of trust by concluding a successful transaction, which can be quite stressful for clients. And then he was using that trust to advise people on financial matters and brokering insurance policies, which of course he wasn't qualified to do. And he certainly wasn't doing it on our behalf. Charlie Dean had quite a nice little earner going there. Well, we couldn't tolerate that. Our company's reputation was at risk.'

'He sounds like a fairly typical con man,' said Fry.

'I suppose you'll say that's what an estate agent is anyway. I've heard it all before.'

'I wasn't going to say that at all. I don't have enough experience with your profession.'

'You don't own a property yourself?'

'Not at the moment.'

'Well, if you're looking for somewhere in the area . . . we have some very nice starter homes. Or perhaps a rental property?'

Her hand hovered a pile of brochures, but Fry stared at her coldly, and she slowly withdrew it.

'Not appropriate, I suppose?' she said.

'No.'

'Well, some time when you're off duty, perhaps.'

Fry didn't respond. She couldn't imagine herself house hunting. And if she ever did, it wouldn't be here. Not in rural Derbyshire at all, in fact. She'd be terrified of turning into the sort of person who felt obliged to have a wood-burning stove and logs neatly stacked up in a wicker basket. A nice, modern loft apartment in the centre of Birmingham would be about the mark. Not that she'd ever be able to afford one.

'So when did you find out about Mr Dean's unauthorised activities?' she said.

Ursula Hart laughed. It was quite a dirty laugh, almost a snigger.

'Did I say something funny?' asked Fry.

'Unauthorised activities,' said Hart. 'It sounds like a euphemism. Particularly apt for Charlie. We found out what he was up to when one of his girlfriends wrote to us and shopped him. It seems he'd dumped her and she wasn't happy about it. So she wanted revenge, and decided to get him into trouble. Hell hath no fury and all that. That was a bit remiss of Charlie, I think. He'd let her into his secrets. I suppose he must have decided to trust her.'

'Always a mistake.'

'Well, not always . . .'

'And when was this exactly, Ms Hart?'

'About two months ago. Obviously, we had to investigate her allegations. But the evidence seemed pretty conclusive. So we'd taken a decision to sack him next week. My partners will be relieved that it isn't necessary now. This sort of thing always creates awkward scenes and recriminations.'

'Were you planning to report him to the police? It sounds as though Mr Dean's activities were illegal.'

She shook her head. 'No. Reputation, you know.'

'That again.'

'It's important in business. We have too many competitors in the property market. If people start to hear bad things about us, they'll go elsewhere with their properties. It was bad enough that Charlie was messing around with these women of his.'

'Women? Ah, you said "one of his girlfriends".'

'Exactly. I gather the latest one was with him when he crashed the car.'

'Sheena Sullivan.'

'I don't know her. But there have certainly been others over the years. He was using our properties for his assignations, you know. Any that had been left standing empty. If he was handling the marketing of the property he had access to the keys for accompanied viewings. We knew about all that, thanks to the woman scorned.'

'We'll need the name of this woman who wrote to you,' said Fry.

'Will you? Isn't that a confidential detail?'

'Not in a murder inquiry, I'm afraid.'

'Ah, well. I suppose there might still be some collateral damage to our reputation, then.'

'It's possible,' said Fry. 'It depends if we can get anyone in court, and how they plead.'

'Meaning?'

'Well, a not guilty plea means a full trial has to take place – witnesses, cross-questioning, all that. Every relevant detail will be explored, and it can go on for weeks. A plea of guilty avoids a lot of that, and the hearing is over more quickly.'

'I see.'

'So it's in all of our interests to get as much evidence together as possible and create a nice watertight case from the start. Then the defence has no room for manoeuvre and is more likely to go with a guilty plea to get a lesser sentence for the accused.'

Hart smiled. 'You've convinced me, Sergeant. You'll have full co-operation from this office. Let's get the bastard who did this thing.'

30

Monday

Sean Gibson was gaunt and bony, with yellow skin that barely covered the network of veins and arteries in his body underneath.

When Fry saw him on Monday morning, she was reminded of Juliana van Doon's description of a waste product in the blood, bilirubin. It caused the yellow colour in bruises, and it was also what turned the skin yellow if there was too much for the liver to get rid of. But Sean Gibson wasn't suffering from jaundice. The colour of his skin was the result of age, and a body abused by alcohol and drugs, not to mention a bad diet.

Sometimes, Fry wondered if the human race was evolving in reverse, gradually regressing to stunted troglodytes with primitive language skills and shorter lifespans. Sean Gibson was well along that evolutionary path.

DCI Mackenzie's team had Gibson in an interview room, sweating it out as he made a world record attempt for the number of times he could say 'no comment'.

'We've pulled his brother in too,' said Mackenzie. 'He had a trail bike hidden in a shed at his address. The tread on the tyres matches the tracks made in the wood.'

The DCI had called in to see Fry while a DS from his team took over the interviewing. He was a big man, over six feet tall and wide across the shoulders, and he had the air of a rich uncle visiting distant cousins. Fry recalled the first time she'd worked with him. He was the only person who could ever have thought she was a farm girl. Everything was relative.

'The theory we're working on is that the Gibson brothers were aware that the Nokia mobile phone had been left behind at the crime scene and were making an attempt to retrieve it when they thought it would be quiet. Lucky your local farmer Mr Maskrey spotted him. Though obviously we can't condone the use of a shotgun.'

He gave each of the local CID officers a shrewd stare, weighing them up in that way an experienced officer did, even with colleagues. His gaze dwelled briefly on Gavin Murfin, then moved on to the younger DCs, who seemed to meet with approval.

'They would have had to watch the forensic teams working at the scene,' said Mackenzie, 'to be able to tell when the water level had fallen sufficiently and there was no one around. I don't know how they did that.'

'From the rocks above,' said Fry automatically.

'Oh? Well, you're probably right, DS Fry. Local knowledge and all that. But we were lucky that your vagrant identified Ryan Gibson.'

'My vagrant? Do you mean the man who calls himself Spikey Clarke?'

Mackenzie looked at her with his head tilted on one side. She'd seen that mannerism in him before, and she'd come to dislike it.

'Didn't you know that Mr Clarke witnessed the incident with the farmer and got a good look at the biker?' he said.

Fry shook her head. Mackenzie reached out a hand, and for a moment she thought he was going to pat her on the arm consolingly.

'Well, don't worry, Diane. It's all dealt with now. And we're getting some useful results from the analysis of Mr Turner's computer too. That's a bonus.'

As soon as his back was turned, Fry cursed under her breath. This wasn't supposed to be the way it went.

'I'm very glad we were able to raise the priority of this inquiry and move against some known suspects,' said DCI Mackenzie before he left. 'Thanks to good intelligence.'

Irvine looked at Fry when he'd gone. 'What intelligence, Diane?'

Fry threw her hands in the air. She didn't know. But she was afraid she might be able to have a good guess.

Later that day, it struck Fry that Nathan Baird was almost as thin and gaunt as Sean Gibson, though perhaps for a different reason. But only perhaps. His sharp cheekbones were a design feature, like the oak finish desk in his office at Prospectus Assurance.

'Insurance fraud?' he said. 'Yes, everyone regards it as a victimless crime. But the fact is, fraudulent claims add about fifty pounds a year to the insurance bill of every honest customer. Undetected claims fraud costs the industry more than two billion pounds a year. And it's rising every year.'

'What type of fraud?' asked Fry.

Baird gestured at her eagerly. 'Home insurance frauds are the most common, though the highest-value claims are in the motor insurance sector – that costs nearly six hundred million pounds a year. We're talking big numbers either way, Sergeant.'

Fry had heard of some common types of fraud. In the more traditional scams, a criminal set himself up as an apparently genuine insurance adviser, complete with a shopfront and a variety of products, though motor insurance was favoured. Unsuspecting customers paid a premium and were provided with false documents giving the impression their car had been insured. In one variation, the illegal adviser simply advertised their services through a newspaper or on the internet, often targeting specific vulnerable communities. In London, the Metropolitan Police had arrested a man on suspicion of conspiracy to defraud and money laundering offences. He was alleged to have made thirty to forty thousand pounds a year by trading as an illegal insurance adviser, targeting members of the Chinese community and students.

Increasingly common were whiplash claims after car accidents, where the extent of injury was difficult for doctors to diagnose. Organised gangs operated 'cash for crash' schemes, staging collisions in which some unsuspecting motorist crashed into the rear of a vehicle that stopped suddenly with its brake lights disabled. Just like the cannabis gardeners, those at the bottom of the food chain in those schemes were often poor and ignorant immigrants, who were paid a few hundred pounds to put themselves physically in harm's way. Any genuine injuries they sustained were collateral damage as far as the gang leaders were concerned.

'Are we talking hard or soft?' asked Baird.

'I'm sorry?'

'Basically, hard fraud is when someone deliberately invents a loss covered by their insurance policy. Criminal gangs get involved in hard fraud schemes, because they can obtain large amounts of money. Soft fraud is far more common. It's more opportunistic. Policyholders exaggerate an otherwise legitimate claim. Almost anyone can be involved in that type of fraud. It's so tempting just to overstate the amount of damage or the value of items lost. And of course, most small frauds go undetected, so it's known as an easy crime to get away with.'

Fry shook her head. 'Not soft fraud. There must be large amounts of money involved.'

He bit his lip. 'I see.'

'Those gangs who stage collisions to collect insurance money. The set-up sometimes involves insurance claims adjusters, doesn't it? They create phoney police reports to process claims.'

'It's possible,' said Baird slowly.

It was an evasive, noncommittal reply, if ever she'd heard one. Fry waited in silence for him to say more.

'The sheer number of claims submitted each day makes it far too expensive for companies like ours to have employees checking each claim for signs of fraud,' he said. 'So we use computer systems and statistical analysis to identify suspicious claims for investigation. There are drawbacks.'

'Such as?'

'The system can only be used to detect types of fraud that have been identified before. Claims adjusters can be trained to identify "red flags" or symptoms that in the past have often been associated with fraudulent claims. Statistical detection doesn't prove that claims are fraudulent. It merely identifies claims that need to be investigated further.

'If a red flag is triggered on a claim, it's passed on to a specialist loss adjuster to investigate. They'll interview the policyholder, carry out background checks. Often the result of our fraud checks and an investigation is that the claim process becomes a bit long-drawn-out. Then some claimants simply withdraw their claim, and we never hear from them again. That's a result too.'

'An unscrupulous staff member could take advantage of that system,' said Fry. 'Meeting claimants and doing background checks – it puts someone in a position of power. Some individuals can't resist abusing that sort of power.'

'We participate in the Insurance Fraud Bureau scheme,' said Baird. 'Any legitimate insurance company would be mad not to. The IFB have recorded tens of thousands of staged collisions and false insurance claims across the UK. In one year, their use of data mining led to seventy-four arrests of individuals involved in insurance fraud networks.'

'Data mining. Would that be in the job description of a fraud analyst?'

'Like Ralph Edge?'

'Yes, that's who I'm thinking of.'

Baird looked suddenly alarmed. He stared out of the window as a defeated-looking Ralph Edge was led past his office by two men, each with a hand on an elbow. Fry jumped up and went to the door to watch them disappear down the corridor.

'Who were *they*?' asked Baird.

'Those,' said Fry, 'were two of my colleagues from the Major Crime Unit. They appear to have arrested Mr Edge.'

'You're not going arrest me too, are you?' said Baird. 'Please tell me you're not. It was just a bit of fun.'

'What was?'

'The paintballing.'

'It has nothing to do with that, sir.'

'Thank goodness.'

Baird wiped his hands on a tissue from a box on his desk.

'Ralph?' he said. 'I can't believe it. Really?'

'He didn't take advantage of your open door to talk to you about it?' asked Fry.

'No.'

'No doubt they'll be taking away his files and computer,' said Fry. 'Of course, Mr Edge isn't the type to do the dirty work himself.'

Baird waved his bony hand nervously. That imaginary irritating fly in his office had become an entire swarm of wasps.

'How am I going to explain this to my managing director?' he said plaintively.

'Perhaps you could send a boy with a message,' said Fry.

Fry knew Ben Cooper had his phone switched on now, so she called him first to make sure he'd be in. She would have spent the rest of the day trying to track him down if necessary, but he answered straight away and agreed to see her.

She parked right outside number eight Welbeck Street this time, just behind Cooper's Toyota. Inside his flat, he offered her a coffee, which she accepted reluctantly, feeling obliged to maintain a veneer of sociability when her instincts urged her to do quite the opposite.

Fry sat on his settee with her mug, exchanged glares with the cat, which stalked out of the room, and decided not to beat about the bush any more.

'Why didn't you just tell me everything you'd worked

out?' she said. 'You could have given me the whole damn case.'

'Would you have appreciated it?' asked Cooper.

Fry hesitated, realised there was no point now in telling anything but the truth.

'No,' she said.

'Well, then.'

'I never really understood this obsession of yours,' said Fry.

'Obsession?'

'All those cuttings on your kitchen wall. I call that the sign of an obsession.'

'How did you know about those?' asked Cooper quietly.

'I . . .'

'You've been in here somehow? Oh, wait a minute – Mrs Shelley mentioned that friends of mine had called looking for me. That would have been you, I suppose? So you made sure I was out of the way, then you talked your way into my flat.'

'It might sound that way.'

'Yes, it does.'

'Let me explain, Ben. We're all—'

He turned away. 'No,' he said. 'I'm finished listening to your explanations, Diane. Just leave me alone, why don't you? Everyone else does.'

'No, wait. That wasn't what I came here for.'

'What, then?'

'I want you to explain it to me, Ben.'

He put down his coffee on a low table. 'I suppose you haven't been following the news stories the way I have over these last few months, Diane. Did you actually look at my cuttings?'

'Of course I did.'

'I mean, did you look properly? The way you would look if you were presented with them as evidence and you were trying to put the clues together, to make connections? Or did you just take one glance and jump to a conclusion?'

Fry didn't answer. Well, she couldn't respond to that without admitting a failure. So she said nothing. It didn't matter. Cooper knew the answer to his own question anyway.

'Some of them aren't really what you'd call cuttings,' he said. 'They're printouts from the internet. Specialist news sites, mostly. You'd be amazed what you can turn up just by creating a few Google alerts. That's how I know about Prospectus Assurance. It was a buyout, you know.'

'Oh, I had a feeling when I went there that it used to be called something different.'

Cooper nodded. 'It used to be owned by a firm called Diamond Finance. They were also the parent company for Diamond Hybrid Securities, based in London. But the insurance division has different owners now. They became Prospectus a few months ago. I read all about the takeover and the rebranding. The details are right there on my wall.'

'So?'

'Before Prospectus Assurance was bought out it was called Derbyshire Reliance Insurance. I know that, because they provided the insurance cover for the Light House pub.'

31

Sitting opposite Diane Fry in his own flat, Ben Cooper began to feel that familiar sensation of unreality. The moment he mentioned the Light House, his head swam and he felt the stirrings of that tremor in his hand, the ache in the back of his throat. But they were fainter now, as if they were fighting a losing battle for control of his body. His mind felt clearer than it had for a long time. Though that wasn't necessarily a good thing.

'Well, despite the takeover,' he said, 'many of the staff are still there in some departments. Call handlers come and go, but experienced people tend to stay on. They're better paid, and they might find it more difficult to get the same level of salary elsewhere. Ralph Edge was working in the side of the business providing financial advice. He's a fraud analyst. He knows what methods of fraud work, and which bring in the largest amount of money with the least risk. In fact, he was in a position to cover up fraud, if he wanted to. A gamekeeper turned poacher.'

'How did he get away with that?' asked Fry.

Cooper smiled. 'How did people get away with losing billions of pounds for the banks? Well, they get put into positions of trust, where they're left to handle huge amounts of other people's money every day. As long as everything seems to be going okay, no one asks any questions. It's only when it all goes wrong that people start saying there ought to be more regulation. And by then it's too late.'

'And poor old Glen Turner? Turner was pretty weird. He lived a strange life. But he was getting money from somewhere.'

'Yes. From Ralph Edge,' said Cooper. 'Turner had been roped into his fraudulent money making schemes somehow.'

Fry nodded. 'He was probably very willing at first. God knows, Turner had little enough excitement in his life. I can just imagine him hugging that secret to himself, knowing he'd broken away from his mother's expectations of him. Then he bought her the greenhouse with the money.'

'He sounds a sly beggar on the quiet.'

'But still weird,' said Fry.

'And then I suppose he must have begun to feel he still wasn't appreciated. He was still getting pushed around and disrespected at work. I bet he resented that even more when he'd just begun to feel he was a cool, edgy sort of guy underneath.'

'After the incident at the paintballing session that Sunday, it all changed, though.'

'That incident would have been the last straw for Mr Turner,' said Cooper. 'The final humiliation. Not only was he the butt of the joke yet again, but his humiliation was orchestrated by Ralph Edge, who he thought was his friend. Perhaps his only friend. But everybody has a limit. Even Glen Turner could only be pushed so far. I think he told Edge exactly that on Tuesday.'

'He stood up for himself,' said Fry. 'Finally, the worm turned. He probably felt in a stronger position after he'd been to the solicitor, and believed he could sue Edge and Baird, even get them prosecuted for assault. I bet Mr Turner came away from that consultation with Mr Chadburn feeling happier and more confident than he had for a while.'

'And he went straight off to confront Edge the next day.'

'No,' said Fry. 'First he went and bought himself a fossil.'

Cooper hadn't known that. 'It takes all sorts,' he said. 'Some people would have gone a for a drink, or a slap-up meal, or bought themselves a box of chocolates, or whatever.'

'Are we saying that it was feeling better about himself suddenly that got Glen Turner killed. Is that it?'

'Pretty much,' said Cooper. 'Yes, pretty much. I imagine he went to see Mr Edge on Tuesday and told him he was going to pull the plug on the insurance fraud scheme.'

'Or he demanded a bigger share of the proceeds,' suggested Fry. 'So he could buy his mother more presents.'

'Possibly. Either way, Edge and his associates must have realised they'd misjudged him. Glen Turner wasn't to be trusted any more.'

'So they decided to kill him, to get rid of the problem? There must have been an awful lot of money at stake to justify that solution.'

'Oh, yes, I think there was,' said Cooper. 'When you follow up all the cases they were involved in, I bet you'll find the total just keeps mounting up and up.'

'It will be the Major Crime Unit who do that,' said Fry. 'In fact, I suppose they're doing it right now.'

She looked at her mug, and realised she'd drunk her coffee without noticing. She put it down empty on the table.

'And the Gibson brothers . . .' she said.

'The strong-arm boys of the operation. I'm not sure how much control Ralph Edge, or anyone else, ever had over the Gibsons.' Cooper shook his head. 'You know, it's been very strange these past few months. I told you once that I'd been driving around at night, didn't I? Often I couldn't remember where I'd been, or what I'd been doing. But I saw that sign one night. *A.J. Morton and Sons.* And I remembered Ryan Gibson. He was one of the first suspects I ever dealt with when I joined CID. PC Stanley Walker was the bobby with the local knowledge back then. He still is – except, of course, they've retired him. That was lucky from my point of view. Old Stan had become just another member of the public. Like me.'

'What's the connection between Ralph Edge and the Gibsons?'

'Josh Lane is the connection.'

'Josh Lane. The barman at the Light House.'

'Yes, Josh Lane. My obsession,' said Cooper.

He waited for Fry to make a sarcastic comment, but it didn't come. He noticed the cat slink back into the room and sit watching them curiously, her whiskers twitching as if trying to detect something in the air.

'According to the intelligence at the time, Lane was involved in the drugs trade on a small scale. He even supplied Ecstasy from behind the bar at the Light

House. Selected customers only, of course. But you have to be very careful when you play that game.'

'You certainly meet some unsavoury characters when you get involved in the drugs business,' said Fry.

He was glad she understood that, at least. 'Yes, it's easy to get yourself in too deep. Those people have no hesitation in putting pressure on you, forcing you to do what they want. You have to go along with them. So you find yourself drawn in deeper and deeper. And then it's too late. It was too late for Josh Lane. The only wonder is that he's still out and free.'

'Obsession,' said Fry, surprisingly gently.

'All right. Well, Lane knew the local drug dealers,' said Cooper. 'He had no choice but to acknowledge them. Sean Gibson introduced him to Ryan. Now, Ryan Gibson was in the army. He always claimed that he'd been a member of special forces. SAS, you know.'

'They all claim that.'

'Ryan either genuinely had been, or he'd mixed with people he learned things from. He was one of those men who was never able to go straight once he was out of the services. He'd learned so much discipline, and taken so many orders. Some men can't adapt to civilian life, you know. They go to pieces without the discipline and structure, without all their mates around them. They can never hold down regular jobs, because they can't tolerate taking orders from people they don't respect, and don't like dealing with members of the public.'

'He drove a forklift truck, though.'

'Yes, out in the yard at the depot, thinking his own thoughts, not having to listen to pointless chatter because of the noise of the truck.'

'Did he crave a bit of excitement?'

'Of course.'

'I suppose Carol Villiers told you all about this sort of thing,' said Fry. 'The effect on individuals who've left the forces?'

Fry's tone of voice was one Cooper was familiar with, a tone that he felt could lead to unpredictable results.

'She understands,' he said cautiously.

'Mmm.'

'So Josh Lane. He met Ralph Edge through the Gibson brothers. They had this little scheme going between them. Well, quite a big scheme, I imagine. Edge identified fraud cases, and the Gibsons put the squeeze on the parties involved, blackmailed them for a share of the money. Insurance fraud attracts big penalties these days. And who's going to admit they're being blackmailed for the proceeds of a crime? The Gibsons thought they'd hit lucky. They had the best inside information they could get. They had Ralph Edge.'

'Until Glen Turner threatened to put a spoke in it.'

'That's it,' said Cooper. 'That's the whole thing. By the way . . .'

'What?'

'Are you looking for anyone in connection with a drugs inquiry at the moment?'

'As it happens, yes.'

'You could try talking to Sean Gibson about it. There's a good reason he was lying low and getting his brother to lie about him.'

Cooper broke off and went into his kitchen to take a long drink of water. His throat was getting sore. He could sense the approaching spasms of pain and dizziness that he always experienced when he was forced to relive his memories.

'What you call my obsession,' he said, when he sat back down again. 'It was all about the fire. The fire that Liz died in—'

'I know,' said Fry.

Cooper nodded, grateful to her for not making him spell it out.

'Well, it always seemed too convenient to me, the arson,' he said. 'I mean, when you think about all those moorland fires they started beforehand. It was obviously part of a bigger plan. I think it was always part of their plan to burn down the Light House.'

'For the insurance money?'

'Yes, Diane. The Whartons were desperate for money.

You remember them living in that grotty little council house on the Devonshire Estate? And Maurice Wharton, dying in his hospice bed?'

'Yes, I remember.'

'Maurice was tormented by the fact that he'd left his wife and children with nothing. But they had that last resort. Stage a fire that would burn down the Light House for the insurance money. It had to be done before the auction or the building would have passed to new owners, and the bank were waiting to take the proceeds from the sale. They had one chance to do it. And we just got in the way, Liz and I. We were in the wrong place at the wrong time. Eliot Wharton was too hot-headed to consider a change of plan. He did it because he was angry. But Josh Lane . . .'

Cooper stopped talking. He was fighting to control a surge of anger that burned through him so fiercely that his voice was reduced to a charred croak. It seemed to be a long time before he found the ability to speak again. Then the words were spat out like hot coals from the fire.

'Josh Lane,' he said. '*He* did it for the money.'

For a moment, he thought he was going to break down in front of Fry. He covered his face with a hand to hide his eyes. But she seemed as stressed as he was, shifting uneasily in her seat, clearing her throat anxiously, finally getting to her feet and pacing the short distance to the window.

'They've brought Ralph Edge in,' she said. 'He's obviously no hardened criminal. He knows what will be found when they start looking into his computer files and emails. The Gibson brothers are already under arrest.'

'So they will be the focus of the MCU's case. But not . . .'

'Not Josh Lane,' said Cooper.

Fry shook her head. 'There's no evidence, Ben. The CPS won't even consider amending the charges against him.'

'So he stays out on bail.'

'Yes. I'm sorry. Really sorry.'

'So am I,' he said.

There was another long silence. Thoughts were going through Cooper's head that he didn't want Diane Fry to know about, that he didn't want to share with anyone. They were too awful. He didn't want these thoughts in his own head, but he knew he'd never get them out now. Securely entrenched, they were dug in like an army of barbarians, wild eyed and with blood in their hearts.

But with an unerring instinct, Fry put her finger right on those innermost thoughts.

'So what are you going to do next?' she said, turning back to him.

'Is that any of *your* concern?' snapped Cooper.

Fry flushed angrily. She strode into the little kitchen and in a sudden burst of rage ripped a handful of cuttings off the wall and threw them to the floor.

'Whatever you do next, it's got to be better than this!'

Cooper looked at the torn paper on the carpet. He leaned forward and picked up a drawing pin, placing it safely on the table, out of the way of the cat. As she watched him, Fry's spasm of rage drained away as suddenly as it had come.

'You know,' she said. 'It won't help Liz if you do something stupid.'

'No,' said Ben quietly. 'But it might help me.'

32

All through Monday, the river levels continued to rise. The rainfall intensity had risen from heavy to violent, meaning a precipitation rate of more than two inches per hour.

At Bridge End Farm, the mud was almost knee deep in places where the drainage was poor and tractors and machinery had been turning. In the fields, the sheep had the benefit of their water-resistant coats, but some of the cattle were starting to look miserable as the mire oozed over their hooves and spattered their legs.

As Ben Cooper splashed down the potholed lane to the farm, he could see that the ground around one of the cattle feeders had become so churned up and waterlogged that it was almost impossible for the cattle to reach it without swimming.

Earlier in the year, arable farmers had been worrying about frosty conditions affecting their early crops. The cold weather had meant a slow start to the season, but crops were now growing on time and would benefit from the rain, but ideally it needed to be a bit warmer. Crops like rapeseed, which grew in the fields to the south and east of the county, were resilient to the wet. It was different for livestock farmers on the higher ground, though. Hill farmers who were lambing sheep would have preferred the weather to be drier. Newborn lambs could get chilled in the rain, sometimes with fatal results.

Farmers complained about the weather all the time, of course. But what they wanted was stability, a predictable weather pattern that would allow them to plan their growing seasons. If they planted winter wheat, they needed to know they'd be able to harvest it at the end of the summer, rather than watching it rot in the field. If they kept livestock, they needed to mow the hay when it was ready and let it dry before bringing it into the barn. Damp, mouldy bales were no good to anyone.

When he'd left hospital, Ben's sister-in-law Kate had tentatively suggested that he might want to move back to the farm again, at least for a while. But it wouldn't have worked. Yes, he'd grown up here, and had remained living at Bridge End well into his twenties, until his mother died. But he'd stayed too long. Much too long. In the end, the urge to get away had been too strong for him just to forget it and go back.

The farm was his brother's territory now anyway. It was where Matt's family were growing up. That made it a different place, where the memories would be someone else's, not his. In that world, he would be an intruder.

As so often happened when Ben called at Bridge End Farm, Matt himself was nowhere to be seen. He'd be lurking in the workshop or the machinery shed, or poking about in a blocked drain to divert that flow of water he could see streaming across the yard, scouring a winding track through the mud.

So he called to say hello to Kate and the girls first. Now that his nieces were growing up he didn't see them quite so often, and he hardly recognised them sometimes. They changed so fast. Worse, they seemed to have no interests in common with him any more, but talked only about their friends and their complicated social lives, or about programmes on TV that he never watched. Yes, they were definitely growing up, or he was getting old. Or possibly both.

At least his sister-in-law hadn't changed much. Kate was a rock, who'd held the family together on more than one occasion. As far as Ben was concerned, marrying her was the best thing his brother had ever done. It was amazing that he'd ever got round to it.

When he came into the kitchen, Kate looked round at him with an expression he recognised. Ben's heart sank.

'What's the matter, Kate?'

'This came,' she said.

'What?'

A parcel lay on the dresser. It was a substantial package, a large postal envelope enclosing a cardboard box. It was addressed to him, but at Bridge End Farm. He thought he knew why that should be the case.

Kate had been a big help after Liz's death. She'd stepped in to sort out all those details of the wedding preparations that Ben had been unable to face. She'd picked up Liz's lists, attached herself to a phone for hours on end, and dealt with everything. She'd cancelled the booking for the venue, the hotel room, the honeymoon flights, the wedding cars. She'd informed everyone who needed to know, accepting their condolences on his behalf, deflecting at least some of the unstoppable tide before it overwhelmed him.

'What is it?' he said.

'I think I must have missed something, Ben.'

'It's not your fault, Kate. You've been brilliant.'

'Do you want me to open it?'

He hesitated. But time had passed since then. Surely he ought to be capable of a simple task like opening a package?

'No, I'll do it. Thanks.'

He tore open the outer paper, but within seconds he knew it was going to be bad. Inside the box, he could feel rectangular shapes, something heavy. When he got through the last of the packaging, he saw pristine white card, and silver lettering. Of all the things it might have been. His wedding invitations had arrived.

'I'm so sorry,' said Kate, looking over his shoulder. 'I couldn't cancel them. They'd already been printed.'

'We ordered them months ago.'

'I asked them just to destroy them,' she said. 'Really I did. I have no idea why they just decided to send them anyway.'

Ben freed one of the invitation cards from the wrapping. 'It doesn't matter,' he said.

'It might be best . . .' said Kate.

'What?'

'Well, perhaps best not to look at them, Ben.'

But it was too late. He'd spent so long over these cards with Liz anyway that they were imprinted on his memory. *Colin and Linda Petty invite you to the wedding of their daughter, Elizabeth Anne.*

He heard Matt come in from outside, clattering noisily in the doorway as he kicked off his boots and thumped down the passage to the bathroom. There was no mistaking his presence in the house. It was like a slow rumble of thunder threatening to break the heavy silence of a humid summer's day.

'You'll be staying for dinner with us, Ben,' said Kate, making it a statement rather than a question. 'I know Matt wants to talk to you about something.'

In the dining room, Matt Cooper waited until Kate had taken the two girls out of the way. Then he took a deep breath. He reached down beside his armchair and laid a gun slip on the table in front of his brother. He put it down gently, almost reverently, like a priest placing an offering on the altar. Then he lowered his head and looked at his hands, as if surprised to find them empty. He turned them palms upwards and back again, absorbed in their appearance.

'What's this?' asked Ben at last.

Matt still didn't look at him. 'It's my Remington.'

'Your Remington?'

'Yes. The new one.'

Matt unfastened the straps and opened the slip. The shotgun lay between them, the stock gleaming. Ben could see that it had been cleaned, lubricated and polished. His brother always looked after his guns well, but this one had been the object of lavish attention

412

quite recently. He could smell the cleaning solvent and the stock oil as soon as the slip was opened.

'Yes, I can see it is.'

'There are plenty of cartridges. Number one shot. I use them for foxes.'

For a long moment, neither of them said anything. The ticking of the old grandfather clock against the far wall became very loud. Ben could hear the voices of his nieces somewhere in the house, asking Kate a question. One of the dogs outside began to bark, probably at a passing hiker.

Matt seemed to take his silence to mean something. He slid a drawer out of the mahogany sideboard and placed a box on the table next to the shotgun. A grey box, full of bright blue cartridge cases. Express Super Game, forty-two grams.

'They lose pattern density if the range is too great,' said Matt. 'But otherwise they do the job fine.'

'You mean . . .'

'If you need them,' said Matt. 'It's up to you. Then you can't say that I never helped you.'

'Helped me?'

'Well, you can't go on like this,' said Matt. 'You've got yourself into a state that's no good for you. So you have to make a decision, Ben, one way or the other. For God's sake, do something about it – or move on.'

Matt got up from the table, heaving himself wearily

upright. His increasing bulk was weighing him down more and more, his heavy shoulders hunched as if he was carrying the whole world.

Ben looked up at his brother. 'Matt . . .'

'I've got a few things to do,' said Matt. 'I'll say goodbye to Kate and girls for you, if you need to get off.'

Ben nodded, and swallowed, struggling to find anything to say. He only managed one word.

'Thanks.'

Half an hour later, after Ben's Toyota had driven out of the yard, Matt Cooper came slowly back into the dining room. The shotgun and the box of cartridges had gone from the table where he'd left them. Matt breathed a long groan of despair.

'Oh God,' he said. 'What have I done?'

33

Fry had been expecting the incident in which Charlie Dean had died to be similar to the spate of botched petrol thefts in the county. Brake lines cut in mistake for the fuel line. Local officers had been despatched to ask questions of the neighbours and check other vehicles on Green Hill and neighbouring properties on The Dale. Given the nature of the roads and their steep inclines, the exercise had been given priority. The results were already in. Nothing. No other reports of brake or fuel lines being tampered with.

'Deliberate, then?' asked Fry when she arrived back at the garage, taking Luke Irvine with her from West Street.

'Certainly,' said the vehicle examiner. 'And one other thing I can tell you – this was a professional job.'

'Professional?'

'Skilled, anyway. Oh, the lines are steel and you can cut right through them easily enough with a wire cutter. If a line is cut, the fluid takes the path of least resistance, which is the hole. It won't leak out of a small hole unless you press on the brake, and then you'll feel it getting mushy. A big hole will leak it all out before the person gets in the car, and the dead brake will be pretty obvious right away.'

'So . . . ?'

'Well, to catch somebody out, you want the brake to appear functional when they get in the car and start moving, but then have all the fluid leak out and the brakes totally non-functional once they get up speed.' He shook his head. 'Personally, I just don't see how that's possible by simply damaging the line. I think the whole cutting of the brake line as a method of murdering is a Hollywood fantasy. If a line is cut through, a driver would have to be pretty clueless not to notice it on the first application of the brakes.'

One of the mechanics emerged from behind a van where he'd been listening, and grinned at her.

'Some mice with a taste for brake fluid gnawed through the brake line on my wife's new RAV4,' he said. 'She backed out of the driveway fine, drove to the end of the road, hit the brakes at the lights, and rolled out into the junction. There was no traffic coming, but if there had been she'd have been hit by a vehicle at thirty-five miles an hour.'

'That was your own fault, Gary,' said the examiner. 'You should have made sure you did it when the traffic was busier.'

Gary laughed and wandered off, pulling on a new pair of latex gloves.

'Anyway,' said the examiner, 'if you're clever, you use a different method. You could add a substance that lowers the boiling point of the fluid. The brakes heat up and the fluid boils. Gas pockets mean no brakes, see. As soon as the brakes get used hard, they'll fail. You have the added bonus that when everything cools off it all looks normal. Unless you do a chemical analysis of the brake fluid, no one would ever know.'

'Was that done here?'

'No. Either way, brake sabotage is a sloppy way to try to harm someone. There are too many ways it could fail. If you're smart, you look for an alternative. Your man was smart. It's even cleverer to interfere with the physical linkage from the pedal to the brake master cylinder. Maybe replace part of the linkage with something that will break on application of the brakes. That's the only sure way to have a one hundred per cent failure that wouldn't be noticed before it happens.'

'Is that what happened here?'

'Yes. The steering linkage has been sabotaged. It can

417

be done pretty easily and there'd be a sudden, unpredictable loss of steering control. Our saboteur went for the double whammy here. Brakes and steering. He wanted to make sure it worked properly.'

'I don't think we're looking too far for this one, do you?' said Irvine as they left.

'Why do you say that, Luke?'

'Well, what does Sheena Sullivan's husband do for a living?'

'He's a garage mechanic.'

'Exactly.'

'Jumping to a conclusion?'

'I suppose so.'

'Me too,' said Fry, grateful that something appeared straightforward at last.

Even when there were no injuries, cutting the brakes on someone's vehicle would result in charges of attempted malicious wounding, causing criminal damage with intent, vehicle tampering, destruction of property. In Jay Sullivan's case, it would be manslaughter at least.

The Sullivans' house was a fairly modern three-bedroom detached on Yokecliffe Avenue, with a pocket handkerchief garden in front – a few feet of unfenced grass surrounding a patch of soil which contained more ornamental rocks than plants.

In Fry's view, the house could only just be described as detached – the neighbouring properties couldn't be any more than four or five feet away. There were no windows in the side walls, because there was nothing to look out at except the brickwork of the house next door. But the property did possess off-street parking – and that seemed to be quite something in Wirksworth.

She entered through a sun room into a large kitchen. There was a wood burning stove in the lounge, but it looked too clean, as if it was only there for show and had never been used for anything so messy as burning wood. The gas central heating was much more convenient.

Fry had noticed this phenomenon often enough around the villages of Derbyshire. House owners seemed to hanker after a rustic look inside their homes, but without the trouble of real country life. Sometimes it wasn't just the stove that had a purely decorative purpose, but the logs too. She'd seen them stacked up by the fire, all perfectly round and symmetrical, cut cleanly and in identical lengths. The giveaway was their unnatural air of permanence, as if they were dusted and sprayed with air freshener once a week. They were more of an art installation than a stock of winter fuel.

Naturally, Fry had come to regard this as one of the symptoms of middle-class bucolic pretensions, like green wellies and an overfed pony in a paddock. She wasn't surprised that Sheena Sullivan had developed those pretensions. Sheena had turned away from the car mechanic husband with a garage full of oily engine parts to the smooth estate agent lover with a red BMW. It was upward mobility of a kind, she supposed. But her upward mobility had ended in a tragic downward plunge as that BMW hurtled uncontrollably down Green Hill. She wondered if Jay Sullivan had worked out the symbolism in it. Probably not, she thought.

Sullivan had been arrested and escorted to the station in Edendale for processing. Fry wasn't sure what she might find in his house. Evidence that he'd been aware of the affair between his wife and Charlie Dean, perhaps.

She could see that Sullivan had been to the local Chinese takeaway for his evening meal last night. Sweet and sour pork with boiled rice, and a special chow mein. The foil containers still lay on the kitchen counter, red streaks of sweet and sour sauce, a blob of uneaten rice, the remains of a side order of prawn crackers in a grease-stained bag. This was a meal for two people, surely. Who had Jay Sullivan been entertaining while his wife was in hospital?

Fry found a fortune cookie, opened but abandoned.

The strip of paper inside it read: *Now is the time to try something new.*

Diane Fry was back at her desk, tapping irritably at her keyboard to input a report when Matt Cooper called. At first, she had no idea who she was talking to, and that made her more irritable.

'Sorry, who are you?' she said.

'Matt Cooper. I'm Ben Cooper's brother. That *is* Detective Sergeant Fry, isn't it? I thought you might remember.'

'Oh. Of course, I do remember you. There was the incident at the farm . . .'

'Yes, the burglars. But I'd rather not think about that too much.'

Fry looked back at her computer screen and tapped a few more keystrokes, mentally dismissing the call as unimportant.

'It all turned out well for you in the end, though, Mr Cooper,' she said.

'Yes, but that isn't why I'm calling you. You left your card when you were here at the time. And I knew . . . well, I knew that you worked with my brother. It's him I'm phoning about.'

She stopped typing. 'I can't discuss colleagues with you, sir. It's not appropriate.'

But Matt seemed not to have heard her. His voice kept on droning in her ear. It was as if he'd wound himself up to say something, and nothing was going to stop him getting it all out now that he'd started.

'I just can't get through to him,' he was saying. 'Not in the state of mind that Ben's got himself into now. And the doctors are no use at all. He's going to them regularly, keeps all his appointments. Physically he's healing, but they can't touch what's going on inside.'

'Mmm,' said Fry. She'd spotted an error on screen. It was lucky that she'd seen it. If she let herself get distracted she'd make more mistakes. She needed to get off this call as soon as she could, without being too rude to a member of the public.

But Matt was still speaking.

'And now I'm getting worried that he might do something really stupid,' he said.

The idea of Ben Cooper doing something stupid wasn't exactly a new one in Fry's experience. She'd first set eyes on him when he was making a fool of himself, and his capacity for doing stupid things hadn't diminished over the years. She could have begun to list them and still be remembering more when it was time to go home for the night. But probably his brother wouldn't want to hear them right now.

'Like what?' asked Fry instead.

'Well, you know how the death of Liz Petty has

affected him. She was his fiancée. It should have been their wedding next week, and it's all such a nightmare . . .'

'Yes, I know about that,' said Fry impatiently.

'The thing is, Ben is all eaten up with the idea that some of the people responsible might get away without being punished properly for what they did. Obviously, he's seen an awful lot of cases – and I'm sure you have too – where the guilty parties are let off by the courts. Not enough evidence, and all that. Reasonable doubt, some technicality in the law, a clever defence lawyer. You know what it's like.'

'Mmm.'

On the other end of the phone, Matt took a deep breath. He finally seemed to be winding down, or getting to the end of his speech. Not that it had been much of a speech so far. Fry remembered him as a sullen, taciturn Derbyshire farmer who didn't say more than a few words if he could avoid it, and then only to complain about the weather and the price of milk. This call must already have used up all his available words for the rest of the year.

'And I think Ben might be going to take things into his own hands and make a mistake that he'll regret. That we'll all regret.'

'Like what?' she said again.

But he didn't spell out what he meant. Perhaps he

couldn't. He was a member of the public, and they were notoriously vague and unable to explain themselves. Her life would be so much simpler if she didn't have to deal with MOPs.

'Well, I'm wondering if we should do something about him,' said Matt. 'Oh, when I say *we* . . . I mean, I've tried and it's all gone wrong. Not that Ben ever listened to me anyway. Not to his older brother. Oh, no. That would be much too sensible. So when I say *we*, I mean I'm wondering if *you* . . .'

Fry rolled her eyes to the ceiling in exasperation and banged her mouse on its mat with an angry little flash of red laser light. So after all, this was just one more person who'd decided she was the perfect choice to sort out Ben Cooper and whatever his damn problems might be. Were they all mad? In what crazy, upside down universe did everyone go rushing to Diane Fry for help in coping with their personal problems? And not even their own problems. Ben Cooper's, for heaven's sake. If there was a league table of people who cared about Cooper's psychological welfare she'd be right at the bottom of it, deep in the relegation zone and in danger of dropping into another division altogether, where she didn't care at all.

'I'm sorry, Mr Cooper, but I think you've called the wrong person,' she said, her fingers already tensing to put down the phone.

'It's just . . .' said Matt hastily, as if sensing correctly that she was about to hang up. 'I thought you ought to know . . . he's got my gun.'

Fry froze, wondering if she'd misheard him. She pressed the receiver closer to her ear.

'Did you say . . . ?'

'Yes, he has my gun. My shotgun. And a box of cartridges.'

'What is he planning to do with it? Where is he going?'

'I don't know for sure,' said Matt. 'But he's been obsessed for weeks with this barman, Josh Lane. You know, he—'

'Yes, I know.'

Fry had a horribly clear recollection of the moment she'd entered Ben Cooper's flat in Welbeck Street with Becky Hurst and set eyes on the collage of cuttings on his kitchen wall. The arson at the Light House, the shocking death of Derbyshire Constabulary civilian scenes of crime officer Elizabeth Petty. The funeral, the tributes the uniformed pall-bearers. *Killed in the line of duty*. And all the photos of Eliot Wharton and Josh Lane. The free space left for the ultimate fate of the owners of those two faces.

She put the phone down, her mind whirling. Around her, the normal activity of the CID room continued. Hurst and Irvine were engaged in calls and were taking no notice of her. Murfin was out of the room, probably gone to the Gents, or to sneak a surreptitious snack.

Only Carol Villiers looked up, sensing that something had happened. Fry refused to meet her eye. She was staring out of the window at the rain, feeling thoughts falling in and out of her mind as fast as the raindrops hitting the pane. She ought to say something at once, report what she'd been told by Matt Cooper. She should raise the alarm. Within minutes, armed response would be mobilised, units would be despatched to locate Cooper, there would be a massive, high-profile operation. Ben Cooper would be arrested at gunpoint. But how could she allow that to happen?

But the longer Fry sat there thinking about it, the more certain she became that she wasn't going to do that. She couldn't set off that kind of commotion, couldn't put Cooper through it.

She remembered their last conversation clearly. The talk about his obsession with Josh Lane and the fire at the Light House in which Liz Petty had died.

'There's no evidence, Ben. The CPS won't even consider amending the charges against him.'

'So he stays out on bail.'

'Yes. I'm sorry. Really sorry.'

'So am I.'

'So what are you going to do next?'

'Is that any of your concern?'

426

But it *was* her concern. She was responsible for this situation. And, when it came down to it, there was the question of loyalty.

In Welbeck Street, Diane Fry was not surprised to find that there was no answer to her knock at Ben Cooper's flat. In no mood for patience or discretion now, she went straight to the landlady's house next door.

'Can I help you?' said the old lady from behind her security chain.

'Mrs Shelley,' said Fry.

'Yes? Who are you?'

Fry realised that the old lady didn't remember her from five days previously, when she'd called here with Becky Hurst.

'I'm a police officer.' Fry showed her warrant card. 'I'm Detective Sergeant Fry.'

Again, Mrs Shelley didn't even look at her ID, but peered at her as she shushed the dog.

'I'm a friend of Ben's,' said Fry, speaking as loudly as she could. 'Do you remember—?'

'He told me he's fine,' said Mrs Shelley. 'Just fine.'

And she slammed the door.

34

Ben Cooper had tuned the radio in his car to the local BBC station in Derby to catch the news bulletins. That morning, the Environment Agency had already issued flood alerts for five rivers in Derbyshire, including the Derwent and the Eden.

Several of the major waterways in the county were prone to flooding. In neighbouring Nottinghamshire, a fifty million pound project had been completed to construct flood barriers on the River Trent to protect the city of Nottingham after disastrous flooding thirteen years ago. But not here in Derbyshire. Not yet.

Today, the Trent was the first river to be affected. Low-lying agricultural land was flooding, and residents were being warned that access to villages could be cut off if water levels continued to rise. Nearby, the River Erewash was presenting a risk, and another alert had been issued for the Amber. But those were the concern of D Division, down there in the south of the county.

More locally, firefighters had been called out to deal with a flood at Buxton Opera House earlier in the day. An underground stream ran beneath the theatre, and heavy rain had led to flood water seeping into the building. About two feet of water had been pumped from the orchestra pit alone. But the opera house remained open, with a performance that night due to go ahead as planned.

Early in the afternoon, as he drove away from Bridge End Farm, the news came in that Cooper had been expecting. After days of heavy rain, the River Derwent was flooding all the way from Rowsley to the point where it met the Trent – a distance of more than thirty miles. A good ten or twelve miles of that was in E Division. Darley Dale, Matlock, Cromford and Whatstandwell were all affected. The B5057 between Darley Bridge and Two Dales was closed. Cooper remembered seeing a pub at Darley Bridge almost overwhelmed by flood water two years ago. He hoped this wasn't going to be a repetition.

The Highways Agency was reporting that the village of Beeley, near Chatsworth, had been hit by flash floods. A steep stretch of the A619 from Chesterfield to Baslow was said to resemble a river as traffic struggled to force its way through the water. As usual, motorists were abandoning their cars, making it difficult for emergency services to get through. Even for anyone who knew the area well, large amounts of water could change the appearance of a road and make it impossible to gauge the depth. Yet some drivers ploughed into floods oblivious to the risk. The air intake on many cars was low down, and it only took a small amount of water to wreck the engine. You could blow a head gasket, break a conrod, or burst the entire cylinder head off.

Cooper worked his way through the back lanes on higher ground near Youlgreave as the news continued to get worse. Within an hour, the status of the emergency had been raised to a severe flood warning – and that meant danger to life. Emergency sandbags had been issued, pumps were being used to clear sections of road. Rail services were cancelled, flood water had closed more routes and landslides had blocked others. In places, high winds had brought down power lines and hundreds of homes were without electricity.

Now the Fire and Rescue Service had boats operating in the worst-affected areas, picking up people who'd decided to stay in their homes in spite of the warnings. More heavy rain was predicted for the rest of the day.

Falling on already saturated ground, it would make the situation even more critical.

A mile further on, Cooper came across a team of council workers in yellow high-vis jackets, desperately trying to pump water off a flooded section of road. A huge amount of water was surging across the roadway, surely more than would be caused by surface flooding or blocked gulleys. It looked more like a burst water mains. He wound down the window and leaned his head out.

'What's happened?' he said.

'An adit has burst.'

Then Cooper heard the noise. A thunderous roaring in the air, as if he was standing close to a giant waterfall. When he looked up he was amazed to see thousands of gallons of brown water gushing from an enormous hole in the hillside, forced out under pressure by the flood that had built up in the old mineshafts behind it. Where it hit the air, the torrent foamed into a creamy head as though the hill had turned itself into a vast spout of Guinness.

He could see that the water was full of debris being scoured out of the mine. Soil, stones and the occasional larger lump of rock plummeted through the deluge and bounced off the hillside further down the slope before crashing into trees near the stream bed.

'It must have got blocked further down for it to burst here. The water's obviously been backing up for days. There's not much we can do about it until the adit has emptied itself.'

'Where is the water going?'

'On to the road, as you can see. And then to wherever is downhill from here. You'll have to find another way round.'

'I'll try Lea Road.'

'I think you'll find Lea Road is already closed, mate.'

Cooper turned the Toyota round but a few minutes later he discovered the council workman was right. He could see across the valley that the road running down from Holloway into Cromford was flooded in two places, at Bow Wood near the car park for High Peak Junction, and again between St Mary's Church and the railway station, where the rugby field was well under water.

Down in the village, the water was three feet deep, and sandbags were piled at every door. People were always shocked by the speed that this could happen. Within twelve hours of heavy rain, you could find the waterline three feet up your walls and stinking brown sludge filling your ground-floor rooms.

No vehicles could get through in these conditions. Driving at any speed into water more than about fifteen centimetres deep could feel like driving into a brick wall. Unexpected patches of deeper water might be hidden by a bend or a dip in the road. Just two feet of standing water could float your car, and just one foot of water if it was moving. As wheels failed to hold their grip, you lost control.

The Toyota had an air intake higher off the ground then most modern cars, so Cooper had an advantage. But even a four-by-four vehicle could get swept away by flood water. It might be four-wheel drive, but it wasn't amphibious. The abandoned cars standing in deep water for hours would need to have their spark plugs or injectors removed and their engines turned over to expel water from the cylinders before anyone tried starting them. But he bet that wouldn't happen in a lot of cases. There would be a surge of claims on motor insurance policies for Glen Turner's colleagues at Prospectus Assurance to deal with in the next few days.

Walking could be just as dangerous. If the flow reached four miles per hour, anyone would be knocked off their feet and never be able to regain their footing.

Cooper left his car, and looked over the wall. These low lying fields would have been constantly waterlogged at one time, a permanent marshland. Derbyshire's answer to the Everglades. But the path through them was an ancient trackway. Centuries ago, stones had been laid to raise it above ground level, so that people were able to walk across the marshy fields. The river that started as a trickle a few miles to the north-west had collected water from the surrounding hills and swollen to a powerful torrent by the time it reached this point. A substantial bridge had been built to cross it. The meadows on either side had been flooded a week earlier, and large pools of surface water had been left behind. It was strange to think that the climate here was classified as a Marine West Coast. Temperate summers, and no dry season, waterlogged soils with poor drainage.

Beyond the river, the trees of Shining Cliff Woods looked dark and eerie. It had started to rain again, not with a gentle transition but a dramatic opening of the sluice gates, a torrent of water instantly cascading through the air. If he was to reach his objective, he would have to drive all the way round via Wirksworth.

Cooper looked north, back towards Carl Wark's stone ramparts, which marked the edge of the Dark Peak. A large part of him felt he belonged up there, among the bleak expanses of peat moor and the twisted gritstone outcrops. He'd felt at home in the darkness, surrounded by hostile reality. It had reflected what was happening inside him.

There was only one place Ben Cooper could be heading for. Diane Fry called into the office and obtained the address of Josh Lane. A mobile home park? She looked at a map and struggled to locate it. She was lost in this area without someone like Cooper or Irvine to give her directions.

Fry put her foot down and drove on through the rain, peering through the water that sluiced across her windscreen to catch a glimpse of a signpost or a familiar landmark. The Peak District looked darker and more dangerous than she'd seen it in all these years.

Cooper could see the rising flood water lapping at the walls of the homes in the lower part of Derwent Park. Some residents had already left, advised to evacuate by the police. Others had stayed, determined not to be forced out of their homes but to see it out, trusting that the flood would subside within a few hours. This was England, after all, not New Orleans or the Indian Ocean. Surely the weather would change soon, and things would be back to normal, except for a major clean-up operation.

A church stood on higher ground in the nearby village, but no one had gone there. Even in the middle of a natural disaster, they didn't think of turning to God, but preferred to rely on a few sandbags. Those who had left were refugees now, with suitcases and carrier bags.

Outside, fence posts dragged out of the earth by the flood bobbed to the surface. A sheep tried to swim, its eyes wild with fear as it was carried along by the current. The river had burst its banks, spilling out over the lower-lying fields, spreading inexorably into the bumps and hollows of the abandoned lead mines, filling the shallow bowls between the old spoil heaps and pouring through holes in the crude concrete caps that covered the shafts.

Josh Lane's home stood on its own shrinking island. Finally, Cooper saw his car, the silver grey Honda. Lane was trying to make a run for it. Had someone tipped him off? Who would do that? Cooper didn't have time to worry about it.

It was obvious that Lane had left it too late. All the other residents of Derwent Park had been evacuated but Lane must have been concerned with packing his belongings into the Honda. By the time he came out and got into his car, the roadway was already submerged, and water was lapping at the base of his mobile home.

But like so many other motorists that week, Lane decided to risk it. He pointed the Honda towards the exit and drove into the water, hoping for the best. Cooper could see that he was driving too fast: his instinct was to put his foot down and get to the safety of the public road as quickly as possible. But it didn't work that way when you were driving in a flood.

Within seconds, the car had stalled. But then it began to move slightly. Not under control, but bobbing in the water as its wheels left the road surface. Its bonnet slewed to the left, in the direction of the current. A moment later, it was floating freely, swept away by a powerful flow of water strong enough to lift a car clean off the road.

A hundred yards downstream was a low stone bridge, a single arch carrying the little back road from Cromford over the stream. Already, the level of the water was almost up to the top of the arch. As Lane's Honda spun in the current, it gathered speed until it was heading rapidly towards the bridge. A few seconds later, a bang and a crash of metal against stone told Cooper that the car had impacted with the bridge.

He ran towards his Toyota and started the engine. Slowly he crept down the road, staying in first gear, trying not to send up too much of a bow wave, slipping the clutch and revving the engine to clear the exhaust and keep the engine running if any water splashed on to the electrics.

In a shallow dip, the Toyota began to aquaplane. He held the steering wheel lightly and lifted his foot off the accelerator until the tyres regained their grip. Like many four-wheel drive vehicles, this one had a high-level air intake, allowing him to drive through water a few feet deep, though he knew he could say goodbye to his carpet. And even a four-by-four could be swept away in flowing water.

Cooper felt his wheels start to lose grip again halfway

through the flooded section. The car was trying to float. He opened the driver's door and allowed some water into the car to weigh it down until the tyres gripped the road surface again. At the same time, he continued revving the engine and slipping the clutch.

Finally, he reached the bridge. He slid the Toyota to a halt and looked down at the trapped car. When he stepped out of the driver's door, he was relieved to feel tarmac beneath an inch or two of water streaming down towards the flood below.

He leaned over the low parapet. Josh Lane's Honda was firmly jammed against the side of the bridge, its roof touching the top of the arch. The immense pressure of the torrent rushing downstream was pinning it against the stone like an insect crushed by a giant hand. The driver's side window was partly wound down, and Cooper saw a struggling figure, arms flailing against the white blanket of an airbag inflated by the impact.

As Cooper watched, Lane managed to get his head and part of his upper body through the window, then became stuck. The electrical wiring was dead, so the window wouldn't wind down any further. And the pressure of the water was too strong for him to push against, even if there had been room to open the door against the stone arch. From here, he looked no more than a bundle of clothes, the material of his anorak billowing out in the water.

Looking down from his vantage point, Cooper realised this was his best opportunity. Josh Lane was at his mercy. It was the moment he'd been dreaming of for months, his chance to take revenge for the death of Liz. On this bridge, he'd been presented with the possibility of achieving justice, at least a kind of justice that would make sense in his own world. All his thoughts and nightmares had been concentrated on the arrival of this moment. What was it Matt had said? *For God's sake, do something about it, or move on.*

He felt as though everything had led him to this point. The system had let him down all the way along the line. It had been made clear to him that Josh Lane would never face real justice. It was as clear as it could possibly be. And yet chance had presented him with this opportunity. If this wasn't fate, he didn't know what was. Destiny had put him on this bridge at this moment, and he knew what he had to do.

With slow deliberation, Cooper opened the boot of his Toyota. Thanks to Matt, he had exactly what he needed.

Diane Fry's Audi ploughed into the water, sending up great tidal waves on either side. The surge hit the stone walls edging the road then was forced back towards her, water swamping her bonnet and lapping right up against the windscreen. Suddenly, the engine coughed and died.

Fry tried her key in the ignition, but could get no spark. She looked down, and saw water creeping under the door sills and trickling from the engine compartment below the dashboard. The carpet behind her accelerator and brake pedals was already glistening with damp. The floor squelched when she moved her foot.

'Damn.'

Ben Cooper stood in the torrential rain. He was without his waxed coat now, had nothing to cover his head, but was apparently oblivious to the water soaking his clothes and plastering his hair to his skull. His shirt darkened, the rain ran down his arms and dripped from his fingers. He raised his hand slowly and looked at his wet palms, stared down at the widening pool at his feet, the stream gushing down the side of the road in front of him.

His face was wet, and he blinked his eyes to clear his vision. But all he could see was water. He was surrounded by a world of it, rain falling all around him and covering the earth. If he stood still long enough, he imagined, it would continue to rise steadily until it was over his head. And he'd be standing in ocean where once the Peak District had been.

He recalled being taught in school that three hundred

million years ago Derbyshire had been covered by a series of shallow tropical lagoons, that the crags of Winnats Pass were formed from coral reefs: fossilised sea creatures could still be dug out of the limestone slopes. It had been impossible to imagine then.

But standing in the centre of the deluge, he knew that everything came full circle, that human existence was no more than a few hours in the history of the earth and the life of one human being over in a second.

His superstitious ancestors had dreaded fire and flood. But they'd been frightened of a lot of things. Every bump in the night was a devil at the door, every stranger a spy, every bird an ill omen. They lived in terror of the natural and the supernatural until finally they faced their greatest fear of all – death itself.

Gradually he became conscious of a voice. Someone was shouting. As his awareness returned, he began to shiver. This was no tropical sea he was standing in. The rain was freezing.

Diane Fry was wading through water that came almost up to her waist. Finally, Cooper saw her and shouted.

'Diane, what are you doing?'

'I came to find you.'

'For God's sake, if you lose your footing, that water will sweep you away. You could be killed.'

441

'Well, help me out, then.'

When he pulled her up to the bridge, she saw a body on the ground, streaming water.

'Josh Lane,' she said.

'Yes.'

'What have you done?'

Fry gripped the edge of the parapet and stared down at the trapped Honda. The flood water was up to its roof now, but she could see the smashed windscreen. She could also make out a sledgehammer wedged through the broken glass.

She turned back and looked at Cooper, noticing now his sodden clothes, the blood trickling from half a dozen cuts on his hands. The body on the ground groaned, coughed out a gush of water, and gasped for breath.

'You pulled him out of the car,' said Fry.

Cooper looked down at the ground, as if baffled by what he saw.

'Of course I did,' he said.

35

Tuesday

Ben Cooper had become a hero. No one quite knew how that had happened, least of all Cooper.

When he came into West Street on Tuesday morning he looked almost the old Cooper, clean shaven and upright, though he was several pounds thinner and the shadow in his eyes was still there, the way that Fry had seen it in Wirksworth a few days ago.

She watched Cooper shaking hands with everyone – Gavin Murfin, Luke Irvine, Becky Hurst. And of course Carol Villiers, though that was hardly necessary. Fry felt sure that none of them needed to be quite so enthusiastic about his reappearance.

No matter what had happened, and what anyone else said, she didn't feel able to treat Cooper like a hero.

She was aware of what had been in his heart, if not in his mind. And she knew how close it had come to ending completely differently.

But with the shotgun safely back in its locked cabinet at Bridge End Farm, there seemed to be no reason to mention it to anyone now. It felt strange to be sharing a secret with Matt Cooper, but there were stranger things in life.

Detective Superintendent Branagh came through the office to greet Cooper. Another handshake there. Branagh stopped at Fry's elbow, and smiled.

'It was good to have DS Cooper's input, wasn't it?' she said. 'If only unofficially.'

Fry swallowed. 'Yes, ma'am.'

No need to ask where that intelligence came from, then.

By the time Fry finally got Cooper on his own she was fighting conflicting emotions. That always made her say the wrong thing.

'Ben, I know you've been talking to members of my team,' she said. 'Trying to get information out of them. Don't do it again. I don't need to remind you – while you're on leave, you're just another member of the public.'

Cooper gazed back at her, unblinking.

'If you mean Carol, she's my friend,' he said simply.

Fry bit her lip. For some reason, that reply hurt her more than anything else he might have said. She didn't understand the sudden welling of pain it had caused, a confusing ache in her stomach as her diaphragm spasmed. She was overwhelmed by a desire to lash out in retaliation, as if she'd been physically attacked.

As Cooper walked away, she remembered Carol Villiers saying that it was the name of Turner's employers Prospectus Assurance that had sparked Cooper's interest in the first place. At the time, she'd thought it was just familiarity, that he'd heard of the firm before. They had offices in Edendale, after all. But then, Ben Cooper had heard of everybody. He was the fount of all local knowledge. The name of one specific Eden Valley firm shouldn't have made a particularly deep impression on him. There was more to it than that. There always was.

Fry shook her head. It ought to have dawned on her before. Why hadn't she figured this out earlier? She'd failed to see that something else might have been going on in Cooper's mind. Something much more devious and worrying. Perhaps an indication of how close he was to tipping over the edge, how dangerously unbalanced he'd become.

Fry sat down with Luke Irvine. The job wasn't done yet. She reminded him about the interviews they'd done with Charlie Dean and Sheena Sullivan when Dean's

BMW was first traced. There was that frightening stranger in the red, hooded rain jacket.

'Luke – in her statement, Sheena Sullivan said something about the stranger breathing heavily.'

'He was helping to push their BMW out of the mud,' said Irvine. 'It's a heavy vehicle. I think anyone would be a bit out of breath—'

'No,' said Fry. 'Before that. When he first got out of his car. And she mentioned his voice. Where are those statements? Can you dig them out?'

'Here.'

Irvine passed across the files, and Fry flicked through them until she found the page she was looking for. It was a small detail, so apparently unimportant that it might have been left out of Sheena's written statement altogether by another interviewing officer. But Becky Hurst had recorded it word for word.

'*And there was something about his voice,*' she read.

Irvine shrugged. 'What does that mean? Nothing.'

He was right, of course. Hurst had done the right thing, recording the comment on the statement form, but she should have followed it up. Perhaps she'd thought it was just a bit of imaginative over-dramatisation on Sheena Sullivan's part, trying to make the stranger sound more menacing in hindsight. But still, Hurst ought to have asked the obvious question. *What was it about his voice?*

'Has Ben Cooper left yet?'

'Yes, I've just seen him driving out of the gate.'

Ben Cooper had barely been in his flat for five minutes, when there was a banging on the door. He opened it and was astonished to find Diane Fry standing on his doorstep again.

'We must stop meeting like this,' he said.

'Right.'

'Do you want to come in?'

'Just for a few minutes.'

'I was going to ask why you didn't phone first this time,' said Cooper. 'But there doesn't seem much point. It's not twenty minutes since I saw you.'

'No, that's right.'

'I suppose you forgot something? Is there . . . ?'

Cooper hesitated. Fry was looking at him oddly, her head cocked slightly to one side as if she was listening hard, waiting for him to speak again. He'd never known her to be so intent on his words, so eager to hear what he had to say. Normally, she treated him like an idiot. She dismissed his ideas instantly and just went her own sweet way no matter what he said.

So what had changed? Was she humouring him because she thought of him as an invalid? He could almost work out her thought processes. *Poor old Ben, still on extended sick leave. You've got to feel sorry for him. Shut up in here, he's probably desperate for someone to talk to. I'd better pretend I'm interested in what he has to say.*

'Diane, was there something you wanted to ask me?' he said.

She shook her head. 'No, it's just good to hear your voice.'

Cooper laughed. And, as so often happened, the laugh caught the rawness in his throat and turned into a cough. It was the dry, irksome hack that made him step into the kitchen for a drink of water to ease the irritation.

'Are you okay?' asked Fry when he returned.

'Fine. It's nothing.'

'So,' she said, 'you're still suffering a few after-effects, I suppose. From the smoke inhalation.'

He nodded. 'Yes, that's what causes the cough now and then.'

Fry tilted her head, waiting for him to speak again, listening for his voice. Sheena had said: *There was something about his voice. It wasn't right. It made me shudder.*

'But it will pass,' he said.

Fry opened her mouth to speak again, but her phone rang. She answered it automatically. She always did during a major inquiry. Nothing reflected more badly on you than being out of touch when you were needed. It was Gavin Murfin.

448

'I thought you'd want to know, Diane. We've got test results.'

'I'm on my way,' she said.

Fry looked out of the door of Cooper's flat. His Toyota stood at the kerb. She'd seen his car often enough. So why had she forgotten that it was red?

'Ben, did you say that you sometimes drive around the area at night?' asked Fry.

'Yes. So?'

'Even in the rain? And you don't really know where you are, or where you've been?'

'When you put it like that, it makes me sound a bit crazy.'

'Yes.'

Fry looked down at the cat as it walked into the room. It gave her a hard stare and turned its back on her. It was time to leave.

'Okay. Well, I suppose that's all.'

Cooper shrugged. 'Whatever it was.'

'I hope we see you back permanently before too long.'

'I think it will be soon now.'

But before she reached the street, Fry stopped in the hallway of the flat. A coat rack was fixed to the wall just inside the door. It was an unusual design, made of polished steel and shaped like the head of an upturned rake. Over the prongs were hooked jackets, a scarf, even a set of keys.

'It was a flat warming present from my uncle when I first moved in,' said Cooper, noticing her interest.

'I think I remember.'

Fry had been here that day herself, briefly. She'd called in at the flat with a gift for Cooper, thinking it was something you were supposed to do, a gesture to a colleague, a minor effort to oil the wheels of social interaction. A nuisance, but not a huge commitment of her time. She'd bought him a plant, she recalled. No idea what species. She almost looked round to see if it was still there in his flat, thriving. But in the next instant it dawned on her that she couldn't remember what she'd bought, and wouldn't recognise it if she saw it.

'It's a bit of a joke, I suppose,' said Cooper. 'The design is called Harvest. I moved here from the farm, you see—'

'Yes, I know.'

Still Fry hesitated, knowing she would have to ask the question that was burning in her mind. Her professional instincts wouldn't let her leave the flat in Welbeck Street without making the inquiry. It was as if her feet were literally nailed to the floor. She couldn't make it to the door without releasing herself with the question. She knew without turning round that Cooper was watching her curiously. She could feel the silence between them growing, becoming more and more uncomfortable until it had to be broken.

Finally, she laid a hand lightly on one of the garments hanging from the rack. She could feel the dampness still in its fabric. Her fingers came away with traces of mud.

'Can I ask you . . . ?' she said.

'What?'

'Where did you get the coat?'

It was Cooper's turn to let the silence develop. Fry had the feeling she sometimes got in an interview room, when a routine question struck a nerve, drew an audible gasp from the suspect, and filled the the room with a sudden charge of nervous static. The times when she'd knew she'd scored a hit.

She forced herself not to meet Cooper's eye, though she could sense him tensing, knew that he was considering his reply, trying to steady his voice before answering.

'It was a present,' he said. 'It was the last thing that Liz ever bought me.'

Fry turned the garment over and opened it. It was just what she thought. Hanging behind Cooper's front door was a dark red rain jacket with a peaked hood and a storm flap. It had the Berghaus logo above the left chest pocket.

When Fry had gone, Cooper took down the coat. It was a Berghaus Hurricane with a two-layer Gore-Tex shell and a roll-away hood, adjustable cuffs and shock cords, with dual zip fastening to allow a fleece layer to be attached. Liz had known that he liked lots of pockets. The coat had two on the front, zipped internal and external pockets on the chest, and an internal map pocket. But best of all was its double-layered storm flap. It was vital in this weather. Especially if you didn't want people to see your face.

Liz had bought him the Berghaus because the old waxed coat he'd worn for years hadn't been smart enough. Perhaps it was too rustic, or too ingrained with dog hairs and the smell of cows. It had lasted him well, and would be perfectly fine for a good few years yet. But he'd put it aside without regret. It was one of the symbols of a life he was leaving behind.

But he hadn't worn the Berghaus for a week, not since last Tuesday. It had been spattered with mud that night, and somehow he'd never got round to wiping it off. Hanging in his hallway, it hadn't even dried properly. It didn't seem right to wear it in that condition, so he'd reverted to the waxed coat for a few days, intending to get the rain jacket properly cleaned.

Why had Fry been so interested in it? What was she looking for? There must be lots of them around, like white vans.

Cooper looked at the cat, feeling bemused.

'What was all that about, do you think?'

452

The cat seemed to shrug, but it was probably just his imagination. Perhaps a flea was bothering her. Yes, that was most likely. It was time to get out the Frontline. Sometimes it was necessary to dispose of the irritating parasites.

When he thought about Liz, he still experienced a stab of fear. It wasn't the usual form of dread any more. It was a fear that he might be remembering her wrong.

Diane Fry had known she would have to wait until this week for test results. It was five days after the body of Glen Turner had been found in the stream. But it seemed to Fry that she'd been talking about him for much longer than that.

When she was back at divisional headquarters in West Street she stared out of the window at the sheets of rain blowing across the west stand of Edendale FC. It had been raining continuously since last Thursday, too.

On her desk were two reports, one from forensics and the other from the pathologist, Juliana van Doon. Even though the case had passed into the hands of the Major Crime Unit, Mrs van Doon had sent her a copy of the final post-mortem report. It was about the first courtesy that Fry could remember receiving from her.

'Luke, what do forensics have to say?' she asked.

'They've been going over that BMW belonging to Charlie Dean,' said Irvine. 'You know they've been investigating the cause of the crash, looking for mechanical defects. But the first thing they found was a hand print on the boot. Sharp eyes, one of those forensic examiners has. He realised there was something iffy about the print, and ran a few appropriate tests. Lucky for us that he did. Whoever that hand print belonged to, it left traces of blood on the paintwork.'

'Really? So someone injured themselves when they interfered with the vehicle?'

'It doesn't seem likely. There was enough blood scraped off the car by the examiners to get a DNA match in the database. That DNA – well, it seems it came from our earlier murder victim. It was Glen Turner's blood.'

36

Sheena Sullivan twisted her hands anxiously on the bed. Watching her, Fry guessed she was probably longing for a cigarette, if only to give herself something to do with her fingers. But there was no smoking in a hospital ward. This was one place the law couldn't be overlooked.

Sheena had one leg in plaster as a result of a compound fracture, and a few broken ribs. She'd been under observation for a possible concussion, but now the bandages had been removed and a series of stitches were visible running through her hair where her scalp had been laccrated by broken glass. Her eyes were blackened, but Fry could see that the bilirubin was already starting to turn the bruises yellow. Mrs Sullivan had been very lucky that her face was otherwise untouched.

'Charlie Dean had a good scam going,' said Fry. 'And Williamson Hart seem to have known about that. They were about to sack him.'

'Were they?'

'What they didn't know is that he was being black-mailed. His activities came to the attention of Ralph Edge at Prospectus Assurance. That would all have come apart when he lost his job, wouldn't it?'

'I don't know what you're talking about.'

'It's so difficult to avoid getting drawn further and further in when someone is able to put pressure on you like that. Before you know it, you're in too deep, and it's too late for you. Charlie was given a role in what happened to Glen Turner, wasn't he?'

Sheena stared at the wall. She was pale, but Fry couldn't be sure whether that was from the pain of her injuries, or the shock. It didn't matter. She was happy to carry on talking for a while, sorting out the facts in her own mind.

'I bet Charlie thought they were just trying to get information,' she said. 'But maybe the Gibsons always intended to kill Turner, or didn't care. How was Charlie involved exactly, Sheena? What was he supposed to do? Whatever it was, the man in the red rain jacket turned up and scared him so much that he cleared off and didn't go back. He was terrified that there was a witness who'd be able to identify him. So he just drove away and prayed.'

Sheena blinked a little. Fry thought she might be getting close to the truth.

'So – Charlie. He sounds like a man who was able to compartmentalise his life pretty well. He had everything separated out, didn't he? His job, his wife, his mistress, his criminal activities. He must have worked out a set of roles for himself, changing into a different Charlie Dean according to the circumstances. Who said men can't multitask, eh?'

Sheena even smiled a little at that.

'The only wonder is that he managed to juggle all those balls for so long,' said Fry. 'His wife was getting nearer and nearer to the point where she would have divorced him, I think. That would have been a shock for Mr Dean. I bet he thought he was the only one who could do that, and his marriage would last for as long as *he* decided it would. And there were his employers at Williamson Hart. Ursula Hart told me they were planning to sack him. That would have brought the whole pack of cards tumbling down too. But your husband Jay got to him first.'

Sheena had listened long enough. Finally, she decided to talk. Perhaps Fry had just driven her to it.

'There were these two men that Charlie met,' said Sheena.

'Yes, the Gibson brothers.'

'That's them. Ryan Gibson was on a driving course that we both did in Chesterfield. I didn't like him at all. And his brother was even worse. I can't remember his name, but he was horrible.'

'The brother is called Sean,' said Fry.

'Well, they were doing the job on this Glen Turner character. Charlie and me, we were supposed to go back and get him after a while. We were only going to scare him, you see. Charlie said what they were doing was only like waterboarding. No worse than that.'

'Waterboarding?'

'The CIA do it with al-Qaeda suspects. Turner would never have gone to the police and reported us. He would have had to explain why it happened. Charlie had all that figured out. He's a clever bloke, Charlie. I mean, he was.'

Fry stared at her. Yes, waterboarding was clever, but simple. Among torture methods, it had a history as old as civilisation itself. She had no idea who invented it, but she knew it had been popular across the world, from the Spanish Inquisition to the Khmer Rouge. The Americans had executed Japanese soldiers on war crimes charges for using it during the Second World War, then decades later had used it themselves. It needed so little equipment. Just a cloth and a bucket of water – and someone to hold your victim down.

Layers of cloth were placed over the face, the head

tilted back and downwards, and a slow cascade of water was poured over the cloth. You would hold your breath for a while, and then you'd have to exhale. The next inhalation brought the damp cloth tight against the nostrils. She imagined it would feel something like a huge, wet paw suddenly clamped over her face. They said you were unable to tell at that point whether you were breathing in or out. You were flooded more by sheer panic than by water. No one lasted long, they said. You would pray for the relief of being hauled upright and having the stifling layers pulled off.

As the prisoner gagged and choked on the water, they said, the terror of imminent death was overwhelming, with all the physical and psychological reactions. An intense stress response, a rapid heartbeat, the gasping for breath. There was supposed to be a real risk of death from actually drowning, or from a heart attack, or from damage to the lungs by the inhalation of water. As a result of physical fatigue or psychological resignation, the victim might simply give up, losing consciousness as water was allowed to fill the airways. Waterboarding could cause the sort of 'severe pain' prohibited by the United Nations Convention against Torture. Long-term effects for survivors included panic attacks, depression and post-traumatic stress disorder. People would panic and gasp for breath whenever it rained, even years afterwards.

There were instructions for waterboarding on the

internet now. You could even watch a video of the journalist Christopher Hitchens going through it himself and managing to last only sixteen seconds before he capitulated – but at least he'd volunteered for the experience. Once you made information like that generally available, people were bound to use it. Not long ago, in another part of the country, burglars had broken into an expensive house and waterboarded an elderly woman to get the combination of her safe.

Like them, Charlie Dean and his associates hadn't felt bound by the United Nations Convention. Who did, these days?

Fry thought about the position of the body, the doubt over whether Glen Turner might have died from drowning. There had been a two-litre Coke bottle, perfect for pouring a controlled flow of water. And the towels. Oh, God the towels. They would have been put over Turner's face and soaked with water. When he was finally forced to breathe in, his body would tell him he was drowning, whether he was or not.

'*Like* waterboarding?' she said. 'It undoubtedly *was* waterboarding.'

'You know what it is?'

'Yes, I know what waterboarding is. But . . . ?'

'What?'

'Glen Turner. He was hardly a terrorist. Did he really deserve what you did to him?'

She turned her face away and stared at the wall. 'We thought so at the time. I suppose things look different when you think about them afterwards.'

'You said you were supposed to go back after a while to rescue him. But you didn't go back, did you?'

'Not then. Not straight away. It was the man in the red rain jacket—'

'He scared you. Yes, you said so. But it turns out *he* should have been more scared of you, doesn't it?'

'I don't know what you mean by that.'

Fry sighed. She could see it was true. The woman really didn't know what she meant. So often, people couldn't see how dangerous they were.

'But you did go back later? Is that what you're telling us?'

'Charlie said he went back.'

'On his own?'

She gave a melodramatic shudder. 'I couldn't have faced it.'

'Oh? You couldn't face the reality of what you'd done?'

Sheena clamped her lips tightly shut and stared back at Fry mulishly. 'Charlie went, anyway. Like I said, we didn't mean him to die. So Charlie went back to the woods when it was safe. But he was too late. He said it was obvious that Turner was, well, already . . .'

'Yes.'

'But he couldn't have drowned? Not in so little water. We made sure it was shallow.'

'You didn't take into account the amount of rain that's fallen in the last few days,' said Fry. 'Haven't you noticed the flooding? That stream started off shallow, but the water became deeper and deeper while you were sitting at home feeling sorry for yourself.'

'That's horrible,' she said. 'Drowning.'

'Yes, it is,' said Fry.

'Oh God,' said Sheena. 'Did we let him drown?'

Fry shook her head. 'As matter of fact, you're right,' she said. 'It wasn't clear, but I got the final post-mortem report only this morning. Glen Turner didn't drown. It turns out he had an undiagnosed heart condition. Mr Turner's heart gave out on him before the water killed him.'

'Oh.'

'Does that make it better?' asked Fry.

Sheena didn't answer. But Fry could see from her face that it did. Somehow the fact that their victim had died from some other cause lifted part of the guilt from her shoulders.

'But here's the bad news,' added Fry. 'It won't make any difference to your sentence. In the eyes of the law, you're still guilty of murder. And that means life.'

'Prison?'

'I'm afraid so.'

Sheena groaned. 'I don't suppose it matters now anyway. I've lost everything.'

Fry stood up to leave.

'One last thing. Where did the blood come from? Who caused that?'

'I think it was Ryan Gibson who hit him a couple of times,' said Sheena, as if it was an everyday occurrence. 'Just a few slaps, that was all. But Turner's nose was bleeding a bit afterwards.'

'When noses bleed, they tend to produce quite a lot of blood.'

'I suppose so.'

It wasn't important. There hadn't been much blood evident at the crime scene. Just those few traces she'd glimpsed on the parts of the body above the waterline. The amount lost in a nosebleed would soon have been washed away by the running water. Charlie Dean had taken some of it away on his hands, though. And one of his hands had transferred that blood to the paintwork of his car when he was trying to push it out of the mud. That was what forensics relied on – the transfer of traces from every contact.

'Charlie did have some blood on his hands,' said Sheena. 'I saw it after the man in the red rain jacket got back in his car. I wondered if the stranger noticed it. I imagined him phoning the police as soon as we'd left, to report what he'd seen.'

'I don't believe he noticed anything,' said Fry. 'And, even if he had, he probably wouldn't have thought to phone the police.'

'Oh? Why not?'

'Well,' said Fry. 'I think he *was* the police.'

After the interview was finished and the tapes had been sealed and signed, Fry went back to her desk in the CID room and phoned Ben Cooper to arrange another meeting. It would be best to do it now, rather than leave it. He would only hear the details from someone else, anyway.

But Fry wondered how she was going to break it to him. How was she going to tell Cooper the truth? She knew what he was like, and she had to explain a fact to him that he'd never be able to live with.

In his own helpful, Good Samaritan way, Ben Cooper had been responsible for the death of Glen Turner.

Ben Cooper was sitting on a bench by the River Eden, where it flowed shallow and fast through the centre of town. This stretch was wide enough to accommodate the extra volume of water that had come down from the hills. There had been some overflow on to the walkways, and the mallard ducks which nested in the undergrowth on the little island had been flooded out.

The rain had stopped hours ago, and the sun was breaking through in a patch of blue sky. The Eden was almost back to its normal levels, and sunlight glittered on its surface. But the mallards were still complaining. They splashed about frantically among the debris of their nests and a tangle of mud-covered rubbish dragged down from upstream.

Cooper felt as though he'd been like those ducks for a while now, splashing about in the wreckage of his life with no real hope or sense of purpose. He'd been in danger of watching everything get washed away downstream for ever.

Of course, you always brought along a lot of baggage as you went through life. Some of it clung so persistently that it could weigh you down for years. But surely there was even more baggage that you left behind, wasn't there? Memories and experiences, and failed relationships, that you shrugged off and left at the roadside when you moved on. Cooper pictured a mass of sagging cardboard suitcases, all sealed with grubby parcel tape and bulging at the corners. He could imagine a long row of them, standing at the edge of a pavement, awaiting collection by the binmen. There was no point in going back and poking open the lids to look at what you'd left behind. The accumulated mould was likely to choke you, the dust would get in your eyes.

But he was over that now. He really was feeling different today. Perhaps it was time to leave the debris behind.

Cooper looked up, and saw Diane Fry coming towards him. When she realised he'd spotted her she seemed to slow down, her feet dragging as if she never wanted to reach him. And he saw straight away that she had *that* look again.

From her expression, he knew without doubt that Fry expected the worst of the world. Even today, she couldn't see any blue sky.

Don't miss the next Cooper and Fry case

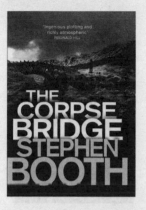

The old Corpse Bridge is the route taken for centuries by mourners from villages on the western fringes of Derbyshire to a burial ground across the River Dove, now absorbed into the landscaped parkland of a stately home. When Earl Manby, the landowner, announces plans to deconsecrate the burial ground to turn it into a car park for his holiday cottages, bodies begin to appear once again on the road to the Corpse Bridge. Is there a connection with the Earl's plans? Or worse, is there a terrifying serial killer at work?

Back in his job after the traumatic events of previous months, Detective Sergeant Ben Cooper knows that he must unravel the mystery of the Corpse Bridge if he's going to be able to move on with his life. As the pressure builds, Ben doesn't know who he can trust and, when the case reaches breaking point, he has to make a call that could put everything – and everyone – at risk . . .

Out now

'One of our best storytellers'
Sunday Telegraph

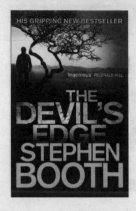

In the heart of summer, in the dead of night, something wakes you. The house is quiet. The children are sleeping. The kitchen is empty.

Except for the body on the floor.

A series of brutal home invasions is terrorizing the Peak District. Until now, the burglars haven't left a clue. This time, they've left a corpse. But as the death toll rises, two intrepid cops begin to suspect that the robberies – and the murders – are not what they seem. Beneath the scorching summer sun, a dangerous game is in play . . . and a merciless killer is hiding in plain sight.

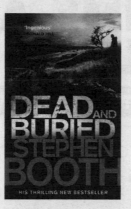

Brutal acts of firestarting have ravaged the Peak District, and now a new wave of moorland infernos sweeps across the national park. For DS Ben Cooper, the blazes are best left to the firefighters, even with the arsonists still at large.

But when an intruder breaks into an abandoned pub, Cooper is on the case – and he swiftly unearths a pair of grim surprises. The first is evidence of a years-old double homicide. And the second is a corpse, newly dead . . .

What links the three deaths? Where are the missing bodies? Who is responsible – and how do the raging fires fit in? For Cooper and his rival DI Diane Fry, it's the most twisted investigation of their lives . . . and with an ingenious killer pulling the strings, it could also be their last.